Albert H. Markham

Life of Sir John Franklin and the North-West Passage

Albert H. Markham

Life of Sir John Franklin and the North-West Passage

ISBN/EAN: 9783337334048

Printed in Europe, USA, Canada, Australia, Japan

Cover: Foto ©Andreas Hilbeck / pixelio.de

More available books at **www.hansebooks.com**

The World's Great Explorers
and Explorations.

Edited by J. Scott Keltie, Librarian, Royal Geographical Society;
H. J. Mackinder, M.A., Reader in Geography at the University
of Oxford; and E. G. Ravenstein, F.R.G.S.

LIFE OF SIR JOHN FRANKLIN.

The World's Great Explorers and Explorations.

The following Volumes are already published, and may now be obtained
in three different bindings:—   Price per vol.

1. Plain neat cloth cover 4/6
2. Cloth gilt cover, specially designed by Lewis F. Day, gilt edges . 5/-
3. Half-bound polished morocco, marbled edges 7/6

1. **JOHN DAVIS, Arctic Explorer and Early India**
   Navigator. By CLEMENTS R. MARKHAM, C.B., F.R.S.
   Crown 8vo. With 24 Illustrations and 4 Coloured Maps.
   [*Second Edition.*]

   "If the succeeding volumes attain the high standard of excellence of this
   'Life of John Davis,' the Series will, when complete, form a biographical
   history of geographical discovery of the utmost value and interest."—
   Academy.

2. **PALESTINE.** By MAJOR C. R. CONDER, R.E., Leader
   of the Palestine Exploring Expeditions. Crown 8vo. With 26
   Illustrations and 7 Coloured Maps. [*Second Edition.*]

   "It is charmingly written, contains much information in a convenient
   form, and is well illustrated by woodcuts and maps."—*Athenæum.*

3. **MUNGO PARK AND THE NIGER.** By JOSEPH
   THOMSON, Author of "Through Masai Land," &c. Crown
   8vo. With 24 Illustrations and 7 Coloured Maps.

   "Mr. Thomson's book is to be strongly recommended to all who wish to
   understand the position in Africa to-day, as an intelligent Englishman
   should do."—*Saturday Review.*

4. **MAGELLAN and the First Circumnavigation of the**
   Globe. By F. H. H. GUILLEMARD, M.A., M.D., Late Lec-
   turer in Geography at the University of Cambridge. Crown 8vo.
   With 17 Illustrations and 13 Coloured and 5 Uncoloured Maps.

   *A few copies may still be obtained of the Large Paper Edition, on hand-
   made paper. Price on application.*

   "This is not only a record of splendid and successful adventure (not the
   less successful because Magellan died, like Wolfe, in the arms of victory)
   but the story of an exquisitely noble life."—*County Gentleman.*

5. **JOHN FRANKLIN AND THE NORTH-WEST**
   PASSAGE. By CAPTAIN ALBERT MARKHAM, R.N. Crown
   8vo. With 20 Illustrations and 4 Coloured Maps.

   To be followed very shortly by

6. **LIVINGSTONE AND THE EXPLORATION OF**
   CENTRAL AFRICA. By H. H. JOHNSTON, C.B., F.R.G.S.,
   F.Z.S., &c., H.M. Commissioner and Consul-General. With
   24 Illustrations from Photographs and from the Author's Drawings, and 3 Coloured Maps.

   *Also a Limited Edition (Large Paper), printed on hand-made paper,
   with additional Illustrations from the Author's Drawings, and an Etched
   Frontispiece. Price 25s. net.*

SIR JOHN FRANKLIN.

(From a lithographed copy of the painting by Negelin.)

LIFE OF
SIR JOHN FRANKLIN

AND

THE NORTH-WEST PASSAGE.

BY

CAPTAIN ALBERT HASTINGS MARKHAM,
R.N., A.D.C.

LONDON:
GEORGE PHILIP & SON, 32 FLEET STREET;
LIVERPOOL: 45 TO 51 SOUTH CASTLE STREET.
1891.

PREFACE.

"To live with fame
The gods allow to many ; but to die
With equal lustre is a blessing Heaven
Selects from all the choicest boons of fate,
And with a sparing hand on few bestows."

—GLOVER.

THERE are few names that have been more prominently brought to the notice of students of geographical research, during the present century, than that of Sir John Franklin. It will occur to them as that of a skilful sailor, an ardent explorer, an able administrator, and above all, as that of a daring and successful Arctic navigator. Not only is his name connected with good and useful service accomplished in those capacities, and more especially with the discovery of those northern regions in the exploration of which he eventually sacrificed his life, but it is also associated at an early period of his professional career, with the survey and exploration of that Greater Britain of the southern hemisphere, Australia. Moreover, it was subsequently connected for many years with Van Diemen's Land, over which colony he ruled with ability, and with a wise forethought for its future prosperity and development.

The history of the life of such a man, one who has

so deservedly **earned for himself a** conspicuous **place** on the list **of** distinguished explorers **in** various **parts of** the globe, should not remain **untold and** practically unknown. It **is therefore not inappropriate that it** should **form the** subject **of a** biographical **sketch,** in a series **the main object of which is to** impart geographical information.

In his exertions to increase our knowledge **of geo**graphy, **especially in those** regions **whose southern** limit is **bounded by the Arctic circle, Sir John** Franklin occupies an almost unique **position among** the numerous gallant and able explorers who **have** both **preceded** and followed him. It is only necessary to glance **in a** superficial way **over** the published records of Franklin's **naval career, to** be satisfied that **he** was **a man of** dauntless **courage,** indomitable energy and perseverance, **brave and resolute in overcoming** difficulties. **He was** a courageous leader, **combining tact and** discretion with **a daring which might almost be considered as** bordering on rashness; **above all, he** possessed **a rare** capacity for encountering, **with** a cheerful and contented spirit, hardships and privations of no ordinary **kind.** He was, in its fullest sense, a born leader, evincing on several occasions a resolute determination and dogged inflexibility of purpose, under circumstances and conditions sufficiently appalling **to test the** courage and the **endurance of the** bravest of men.

To those who have interested themselves **in Arctic** research, the name of **Sir John Franklin is of course** familiar, not only **from** the discoveries he achieved in high latitudes, but also **on** account of that halo of romantic uncertainty which kept his fate, and that of his brave companions, enshrouded in mystery for such a long time. The numerous expeditions that were despatched for the purpose of endeavouring to obtain information regarding the missing **ships,** also absorbed **a** large share of public interest for **many years.**

It is a very safe assertion to **make that if it had not** been for Sir John Franklin, and the exertions that were made to ascertain his fate, **our knowledge of the North Polar regions would be a great deal more limited than it is** at present ; **for the fact must not be lost sight of that the** result of the examination made by the several search expeditions **sent in** quest of Sir John **and** those **under** his command, was the achievement **of** valuable geographical and other scientific results, that would otherwise, in all probability, never have been accomplished. It is therefore only due to the memory of Sir John Franklin **to say that** to him, directly and indirectly, **we owe the discovery and exploration of a** very **large** portion **of the Arctic basin.**

It is earnestly to be hoped that the **work so energetic-**ally and so ably commenced by Sir **John** Franklin, **and** for the accomplishment of which he laid **down his life, may** again be resumed, **and** eventually **brought to a glorious** and successful termination. We **shall then be** able to say, that **the lives of Franklin and his** gallant companions **have not been** sacrificed **in vain, and we** shall be able to reflect with pride **on** the share, and let us hope it will be a large one, that our countrymen have had in **the successful** achievement of this great geographical work.

In the compilation of this volume I have endeavoured **to** introduce, as much **as** possible, in accordance with the expressed wish of my Editors, the personal element, **and to** render it as true and as complete a narrative of the life of Sir John Franklin as the materials at my disposal would permit.

The authorities I have been able to refer to, for reliable information in connection with his life, **have been** very few, and have been confined principally to the logs, journals, and other documents I was permitted to consult in the Public Record Office.

The compilation of the work has, in consequence of the nature of my professional duties, occupied me for some time, but the dove-tailing together of all the information I have succeeded in obtaining, and which has reached me in a somewhat piecemeal fashion, has been a labour of love, and a task in the execution of which I have been deeply interested. Any shortcomings or incoherence in the narrative that may strike the critical reader will, I hope, be ascribed to the difficulties under which I laboured, and to the meagreness of all authentic information that has hitherto been published in connection with the subject of this memoir.

I was fortunately successful at the outset in enlisting the sympathy of Miss Sophia Cracroft, the talented niece of Sir John Franklin, in my undertaking, who most kindly placed at my disposal information that I should otherwise have been unable to obtain.

My thanks are also due to Colonel John Barrow, who, directly he was made acquainted with the nature of my work, most generously afforded me all the assistance in his power, and kindly placed at my disposal his collection of the portraits of Arctic worthies, painted by the eminent artist Mr. Stephen Pearce, some of which have been photographed and reproduced here as illustrations. And last, but not least, my grateful thanks are due to Sir Leopold M'Clintock, who kindly looked over the proofs of my narrative relating to that most successful journey of his which definitely cleared up the mystery attached to the fate of Sir John Franklin, and who also made many valuable suggestions of which I was only too glad to avail myself.   A. H. M.

CONTENTS.

ILLUSTRATIONS IN TEXT.

MAPS (*Printed in Colours*).

MAPS IN TEXT.

LIFE OF SIR JOHN FRANKLIN.

CHAPTER I.

CHILDHOOD—ENTERS THE NAVY—BATTLE OF COPENHAGEN.

1786–1801.

" All my delight on deedes of armes is sett,
   To hunt out perilles and adventures hard,
   By sea, by land, whereso they may be mett,
   Onely for honour and for high regard,
   Without respect of richesse or reward."
                                             —SPENSER.

SITUATED on an eminence of the wolds in Lincolnshire, and overlooking an extensive tract of fen-land to the southward, is the picturesque market-town of Spilsby. Plainly visible above the trees and houses, and standing out in conspicuous relief against the sky, is seen the square tower of its church, surmounted by a pinnacle at each of its angles.

Pretty as is the outside of this little church, the chief interest connected with it is centred in the interior, where are the tombs of departed worthies, who once were powerful in Lincolnshire. On the north side of the chancel is the Willoughby Chapel, containing the

A

tombs of John, second Lord Willoughby of Eresby, who fought at the battle of Cressy; of John, the third Lord, who was at the battle of Poitiers; of the fourth and fifth Lords; of Richard Bertie and his wife, the Duchess of Suffolk (who was Baroness Willoughby in her own right), and many others. At the west end

SPILSBY CHURCH.

of the church, and facing the south, are three marble mural tablets, which are specially interesting to us. One has been erected to the memory of Sir Willingham Franklin, a Judge of the Supreme Court of Judicature in Madras, who died on the 31st May 1824, in the forty-fifth year of his age. Another is to the memory of Major James Franklin, a distinguished officer of the Indian army, and a Fellow of the Royal Society, who died on the 31st August 1834, aged fifty-one years. The third tablet bears the following inscription :—

In Memory of Captain Sir
John Franklin K.C.H.
K.R.G. D.C.L.
Born at Spilsby 16 April 1786.
Erected by his Widow.

These three men, all of whom attained eminence in their several professions, were brothers, sons of Willingham and Hanah Franklin. They were born in the little town of Spilsby, and all were baptized in that same church in which is now briefly recorded the history of their lives.[1]

The time when the Franklin family settled at Spilsby has not been accurately ascertained, but that members of it must have resided there during the greater part of the eighteenth century, engaged probably in mercantile pursuits, is evident from an examination of the parish register. In 1779 Willingham Franklin, the father of the subject of these memoirs, purchased the freehold of a small one-storied house, situated in the main street of Spilsby, nearly in the centre of the town, and not far from the market-cross, which is a plain octagonal shaft

---

[1] A description of the interior of the church would not be complete without allusion to a black board hanging up in the inner porch at the west end, on which, in large white letters, is quaintly announced that on the 31st December 1786 (the year in which Sir John Franklin was born), seven six-bell peals were rung in the church, consisting of 5040 changes, in two hours and forty minutes! The sturdy villagers who accomplished this feat, which has been considered sufficiently worthy of being chronicled, were, we are informed, J. and Jo. Haw, G. and J. Houlden, and T. and Rd. Martin.

with a quadrangular base on five steps. This house, in which John Franklin was ushered into the world, is still in existence, but it is now the property of a coach-maker, who is, however, always ready and willing to show the little room upstairs in which, it is said, the distinguished Arctic Navigator was born. It was sold by William Franklin in 1796. It was bought by Lady Franklin in about 1873, with the object of using it as a museum, in which to exhibit the many articles and curiosities collected by her husband, during his long and adventurous career in different parts of the globe. This laudable intention was, however, frustrated by the death of her Ladyship, which event occurred before her wishes could be accomplished, and the house was then sold to its present occupier.

The town-hall of Spilsby was built in 1765, but calls for no special remark.

At the west end of the town is a fine avenue which leads to the site of Eresby Hall. This charming residence was destroyed by fire in about 1768, and has never been rebuilt; it was the seat of the Duke of Ancaster, who represented the Willoughby family.

John Franklin was the youngest son of a large family, consisting of four boys and six girls. Nine were born at Spilsby, and their births are duly recorded in the parish register.

Thomas Adams, the eldest son of Willingham Franklin, was born in November 1773. In after years he raised a regiment of yeomanry cavalry and was nominated its colonel. He died at Spilsby on Oct. 11, 1807.

Willingham Franklin, the second son, was born in November 1779, and was therefore John's senior by seven years; he was educated at Westminster, where he got head into College when he was fourteen years of age. He was a Scholar of Corpus in 1776; Fellow of Oriel in 1801; M.A. 1803; called to the Bar of the Inner Temple, and was made Puisne Judge in the Supreme Court of Madras in April 1822. He died of cholera at Madras on June 1, 1824.

James Franklin, who was born in May 1783, was also a very distinguished man. Educated at Addiscombe, he entered the East India Company's service in 1805. He served with distinction in the Pindari war, and as major of a cavalry regiment was Assistant-Quarter-master-General of the Bengal army. He was a very accomplished officer, and was employed on important surveys. Among others, he surveyed the whole of Bandalkhand (1815–21), and executed a valuable map of that region, accompanied by a memoir on its geology. His field-books are still preserved at the India Office. He was a Fellow of the Royal Society. He died on the 31st August 1834, aged fifty-one, and was buried in St. John's Chapel, Marylebone.

Isabella, the ninth child, was born on the 12th April 1791, and was married to Thomas Robert Cracroft. They had issue Miss Sophia Cracroft, the niece and devoted friend and companion of Lady Franklin.

Henrietta, the youngest daughter, married Mr. Richard Wright, and died in 1884, at the advanced age of ninety, at Wrangle, near Boston. Her son is the present Canon Arthur Wright, Rector of Coningsby, Lincolnshire.

John, the youngest of the four sons, was born on the 16th April 1786, and was baptized two days afterwards in the parish church. He was first sent to a prepara-tory school at St. Ives, in Huntingdonshire, and subsequently, at the age of twelve, was entered as a scholar at the Louth grammar-school. This educational establishment bore a very high reputation in the county. It was originally founded by Edward VI. in 1552, out of the funds of three suppressed guilds, namely, those of "Our Blessed Lady," the "Holy Trinity," and the "Chantry of St. John of Louth." The

LOUTH GRAMMAR-SCHOOL, 1796.

head-master, when Franklin was admitted, was Dr. Orme, to whose memory a monument is erected at the east end of the parish church of Louth. He was head-master from 1796 to 1814. The boy Franklin must have often regarded with admiration the lofty spire of this magnificent church, with its delicate tracery and exquisite flying buttresses connecting the base of the spire with the pinnacles of the tower on which it stands.

The good people of Louth are deservedly proud of their beautiful church.

The "Lodge," the residence of the head-master, and probably the house in which John Franklin boarded, was built in 1789, and is very prettily situated within a short distance of the school. Although this scholastic establishment was, as already stated, founded so

SEAL OF LOUTH GRAMMAR-SCHOOL.

far back as the middle of the sixteenth century, the building in which Franklin was educated was only erected in 1710. This was pulled down in 1869, when the present school was built.

John Franklin is not the only boy who, receiving the rudiments of education at the old Louth Grammar School, has distinguished himself in after years;

for the institution claims as one of its scholars Alfred Tennyson, the Poet Laureate, who was an inmate of its walls from 1816 to 1818. Augustus Hobart, more generally known as "Hobart Pacha," who made for himself a world-wide reputation as a dashing and resourceful officer while employed in the Turkish naval service, was also at the school from 1831 until he joined the Royal navy in 1834.

Born and brought up within ten miles of the coast, and almost within sound of that murmuring ocean on which he was eventually destined to play such a prominent part, it is not surprising that a thirst for adventure and enterprise took possession of young Franklin. Those were stirring times in which the boy's early days were passed, rendered all the more fascinating to a youth of imaginative temperament, by the exciting events that were being enacted in Europe.

We can well picture to ourselves the feverish excitement with which the dark-haired, well-knit youth would gaze on the ever-heaving billows, and how his bright eyes would kindle with enthusiasm and pride, as he called to mind the many brave and heroic deeds that were being performed by his countrymen on the sea in various parts of the world ; it is not, therefore, surprising to learn that the wish to become a sailor, and to be permitted to share in the glorious triumphs of his countrymen, should take possession of the lad. Naturally quick and impulsive, the desire of becoming a sailor, was only the forerunner of being one. A story is told of the boy—and it has been generally accepted as true —that having employed a holiday in an excursion to the coast, accompanied by a playmate, he beheld the sea for the first time in his life. So impressed was the lad with its sublimity, **and** the prospects it offered as a field for future action, that **he** then and there determined to be a sailor.

Whether it was really **this view** of the sea, that he is supposed to have seen for the first time, or whether it was a dislike to scholastic life at the Louth Grammar-School, whatever the cause, it became very evident to his parents that the boy's mind was fully made up, **and** that a sailor's life with all its fascinations and adventures, was the only one that had any charm for him. Life at school became distasteful; the pleasures of home had no attraction for him; he longed to **be away** on that blue sea whose waves dashed their white foam and spray along the Lincolnshire coast—away **assisting** in those thrilling events in which our countrymen were taking part, and which aroused the enthusiasm of the **loyal** and patriotic burghers of Spilsby, as they received the intelligence of some great and glorious naval victory —triumphs that paved the way to that maritime supremacy which England has since held and maintained.

His ardent longing **was soon to** be gratified, for, hoping to cure him of his cravings for a sea-life, his parents, **who** had other intentions regarding the **boy's** future, being desirous he should become a clergyman, withdrew him from school, and sent him on board a small merchant ship, in which he made a trip to Lisbon and back. The effect, however, of this voyage, the result of which might perhaps be traced to the kindness of the captain of the ship, who, it is said, regaled the boy with oranges and grapes and treated him with much consideration, was the reverse of what his friends had anticipated; for, like other illustrious men, like Cook, Nelson, and Flinders, he returned more than ever charmed with the

novelty of a sailor's life, and more than ever bent **on**
adopting the sea as a profession. Life, however, in the
mercantile marine was not to his liking; it was much
too tame and quiet; nothing would satisfy the boy but
service in one of His Majesty's ships. **In the navy**
alone, he thought, he would be afforded **the** opportunity of sharing in those glorious deeds which formed
the principal topics of conversation in every town and
village throughout the country, and which, **associated**
with the names of such men as Howe, St. Vincent, and
Nelson, were adding honour and renown to the English
nation. This was the height of his boyish ambition; it
was uppermost in his thoughts by day, and present in
his dreams by night.

At length his hopeful anticipations were realised, for
his friends, yielding to his earnest entreaties, succeeded
in obtaining for **him** an appointment as a first-class
volunteer in H.M.S. *Polyphemus*, then fitting out at
Chatham. **He joined** her on the 9th of March 1800.
The *Polyphemus* was a fine two-decked **ship, carrying**
sixty-four guns, and was **commanded by** Captain George
Lumsdaine. On the 1st of May, Rear-Admiral of the
Blue, Robert Kingsmill, hoisted his flag on board, and
on the 13th of June she sailed from the Nore, anchoring
in Yarmouth Roads the following day, in the immediate
vicinity of young Franklin's beloved coast **of Lincolnshire.** We can well imagine the pleasure with which the
Lincolnshire boy entered on his new duties, and how he
paced the quarter-deck in **all the** pomp and pride of a
newly-created naval officer.

On the **1st** of August, Captain John Lawford was
appointed to the *Polyphemus*, and **on the** 4th **his commission was read on the quarter-deck, and he assumed**

command.   In this ship John Franklin was destined **to share** in one of the hardest-fought sea-battles in which the English navy has ever been engaged.

On the 9th of August the squadron **to which the** *Polyphemus* **was** attached, consisting of the *Monarch, Romney, Ardent,* **Isis,** *Glatton,* **and** *Veteran,* with one frigate, two sloops, four bombs, and several gun-vessels, in all twenty-six ships, sailed from Yarmouth Roads, and anchored off Elsinore the 20th of the same month. The visit of the English fleet to this Danish **port was** intended as a demonstration, but no hostile **act was** committed.   **The** ships **remained at** anchor off the picturesque **castle of Kronberg for about three weeks,** and then returned **to** England.   **The remainder of the** year was spent **by** Franklin **on** board the *Polyphemus,* either at the Nore or at Yarmouth.   In the early part **of** 1801, Rear-Admiral of the Blue, Thomas Graves, hoisted his flag on board the *Polyphemus* in succession to Rear-Admiral Kingsmill.

In consequence of the threatening attitude of the Northern Powers, necessitating decisive and **immediate** action on the part of the British Government, **a large** squadron, consisting of eighteen line-of-battle ships, including the *Polyphemus,* **with** several frigates, corvettes, sloops, brigs, bombs, and fire-ships, assembled at Yarmouth under the command of Sir Hyde Parker, whose flag was flying on board **the** ninety-eight-gun ship *London,* with Vice-Admiral Lord Nelson as his second in command in the seventy-four-gun ship *Elephant.* This large force left Yarmouth Roads on the 12th of March 1801, and passing the batteries at Elsinore with but little effective opposition, although a hot fire was opened on the ships as they sailed by, came to an anchor off the island of Hven **on the 30th** March, about six miles from Copenhagen.

On the **1st of April a** division of the fleet under the immediate command of **Lord** Nelson, and to which the *Polyphemus* was attached, got under weigh and moved to an anchorage in seven and a half fathoms, to the southward of a shoal called the Middel Grund, and only about a couple of miles from the main defences **of the capital.**

The navigation among the numerous shoals off Copenhagen is at all times exceedingly difficult and **intricate,** and it was rendered all the more so on this occasion, from the fact that the Danes had caused all the buoys and beacons, that usually marked the channels, to be **removed.**

It is **not** my object, or intention, to give a detailed account **of** the great battle that was fought on the **ensuing** day, and which Nelson himself characterises **as** " the greatest victory he ever gained " [1]—the " most hardfought battle **and the most** complete victory that ever was fought and obtained by the navy of this country ; " [2] suffice it to say that the *Polyphemus* bore **herself** bravely, and took a very prominent part in that day's glorious but sanguinary engagement.

Young Franklin, ever since he left the grammar-school at Louth, had been yearning for active service ; he must have experienced it to his heart's content when the old *Polyphemus,* in charge of brave Captain Lawford, in her appointed station **in the line of** battle, stood in and engaged the Danish block-ships, *Wagner* and *Provesteen,* besides receiving a very fair share of attention **from**

---

[1] *Vide* Lord Nelson's letter to the Crown Prince of Denmark.

[2] See Lord Nelson's letter to the Lord Mayor of London, 21st June 1802.

the guns of the formidable Tre Kroner **battery**. Her loss **on** this occasion **was six** killed and twenty - four wounded, among the former being one **of** Franklin's messmates, Mr. James Bell, midshipman. The **total** loss of the British during this engagement was 255 killed and 688 wounded; but this does not include those who were slightly wounded.[1]   Rear - Admiral **Graves**, whose flag was flying on board the *Polyphemus*, was invested with the Order of **the Bath as a reward for** his services during the battle.

On the 12th of April the English squadron left Copenhagen, and passing through the **tortuous and** shallow channel **in** the **Sound, known as the Drogden**, **entered** the Baltic.   In **order to effect** this passage, the heavy-draft vessels had to be considerably lightened, **the** majority of them had consequently to transfer their guns temporarily into merchant ships, while special

[1] The following is an extract from the official **log of** the *Polyphemus* for the 2nd of April 1801:—

"At 10.30 A.M. the division weighed per signal, the *Edgar* leading, the van consisting **of *Edgar*,** *Elephant, Monarch, Ardent, Glatton, Defiance, Isis, Polyphemus,* **Bellona,** *Russell,* and **Ganges.** At 10.45 the **Danes opened** fire upon our leading ships, **which was** returned **as they lead in. We** lead in at **11.20.** We anchored by the stern abreast of **two** of the enemy's ships moored in **the** channel; the *Isis* next **ahead of us.** The force that engaged **us was** two ships, one of 74, the other 64 guns.   At half-past eleven the action became general, and a continual fire was kept up between us and the enemy's ships and batteries.   At noon a very heavy and constant fire was kept up between us and the enemy, and this was continued without any intermission until 45 minutes past 2, when the 74 abreast of us ceased firing; but not being able to discern she had struck, our fire was kept up 15 minutes longer; **then we** could perceive their people making their escape to the shore in boats.   We ceased firing, and boarded both **ships and took possession of them.**   Several others **also** taken possession of by the **rest** of our ships; one blown up in action, two sunk.   Mustered ship's company, and found we had 6 **men** killed and 24 wounded, and 2 lower-deck guns disabled."

officers were employed in laying down buoys to mark the channel and point out the dangers. This, we may be sure, afforded our young friend valuable experience in the practical work of his profession ; it may reasonably be inferred that it was among the shoals and sandbanks, and rapid irregular currents of the Baltic, that Franklin acquired his first lesson in that art of marine surveying in which he afterwards became so proficient.

On the 13th of April, affairs between Denmark and England having, at any rate for the time, been amicably adjusted, young Franklin was discharged from the *Polyphemus* to the *Isis* for passage to England. After a quick run home we find him, on the 27th April 1801, entered on the books of the *Investigator* as one of six midshipmen appointed to that ship, which had been specially brought forward and commissioned for discovery in the Southern Hemisphere. Her commander was Lieutenant Matthew Flinders, an officer who had already made a name for himself in the scientific world as an energetic explorer and a talented and skilful navigator.

Flinders was appointed as lieutenant in command of the ship on the 26th January 1801, and on the 16th of the following month was promoted to the rank of commander. Being related to Franklin, he had, no doubt, used his influence in getting the boy home and appointed to his ship.

The *Investigator* (late *Xenophon*, an armed ship used for the purpose of convoying merchant vessels in the Channel) was an old vessel of about 330 tons burthen, somewhat of the size and description recommended by that eminent and successful navigator Captain Cook, as best adapted for voyages of exploration. She had been purchased into the Royal Navy some years previously, and having been newly coppered and thoroughly equipped, was considered as the most suitable vessel that could at that time be despatched for the contemplated exploration of Terra Australis and adjacent seas. She carried a complement of eighty-three officers and men.

No better selection for the command of the *Investigator* could have been made, for Captain Flinders, besides being an officer of great experience, had already achieved much valuable and important geographical work in Australian waters. Matthew Flinders, like his young relative Franklin, was a Lincolnshire man, born and educated at the small town of Donington, where his father was in practice as a surgeon. Living in the immediate vicinity of the sea, and constantly associating with seafaring men, it is not to be wondered at that he was soon imbued with the desire to become a sailor. His earnest entreaties were complied with, and at the early age of fourteen he was bound apprentice in the merchant service; joining a ship shortly afterwards, he sailed on a voyage to the South Seas, where he had the rare treat of beholding and visiting the lovely islands of the Sandwich and Society Groups. This trip to the Pacific only served to whet the appetite of young Flinders for the sea, and to arouse in him a desire for further exploration and adventure. On his return to England from this first cruise, so persistent was he in his importunities to become a sailor, and above all a naval officer, that he succeeded, through the influence of Admiral Sir Thomas Pasley, in obtaining, in the early part of 1795, an appointment as midshipman on board the *Reliance*. This ship was at the time fitting out for the purpose of conveying Captain William Hunter to New South Wales, in succession to Captain

Phillip **as** governor **of** the newly-formed colony. **The** Lincolnshire **boy was** delighted with his appointment, believing that the Australian station of all others would offer the best opportunities for the exploration of un-**known regions, and** would, therefore, the **better** enable him to gratify his cravings for the discovery of new countries.

Perhaps it will be as well to give in the next chapter a very brief sketch of the geographical work that had already been accomplished in the Southern Hemisphere, **prior to** the departure from England **of the** *Reliance* in 1795 with young Flinders on board.

CHAPTER II.

EXPLORATION OF AUSTRALIA.

1567-1795.

> " Ye lonely isles ! on ocean's bound
> Ye bloom'd through time's long flight unknown,
> Till *Cook* the untrack'd billow pass'd,
> Till he along the surges cast
> Philanthrop's connecting zone."
> —HELEN M. WILLIAMS.

FROM earliest times there had always been some vague idea of the existence of a large southern continent in the immediate neighbourhood of the South Pole, to balance, as it was believed, the great accumulation of land in the Northern Hemisphere. Imbued with this idea, the Spaniards were the first to attempt a practical realisation of the theory that had been so long held and accepted. With this object in view, namely, the discovery of the supposed great southern continent, an expedition consisting of two ships was despatched from Callao in Peru in 1567. The command of it was intrusted to the nephew of the governor, a young soldier named Don Alvaro Mendaña. After a voyage across the Southern Ocean, extending over a period of three months, the welcome report of " Land ahead " was received from the advanced ship, and in February 1568 the vessels cast anchor in a large and commodious harbour. It was not, however, Australia; **after** discovering and naming many islands **in the Solomon Group, the expedition** returned to Peru.

In 1595, twenty-seven years after his return from the voyage above **alluded** to, Mendaña, still bent on discovery, again sailed from Callao in command **of** a squad-**ron** of four small ships. In this voyage the Marquesas and the Santa Cruz islands were discovered, **but they** failed in finding that great southern continent **which was** the principal object of their search. This expedition terminated disastrously. Mendaña **died, and only one** vessel, on board which **was** his widow and **the** pilot Quiros, succeeded in reaching Manilla in safety.

In 1606 another expedition was despatched from the port of Callao under the command of Pedro Fernandez de Quiros, who was **Mendaña's** pilot during his last voyage; **the second in command was Luis** Vaez de Torres. The expedition consisted of two well-armed vessels and a corvette. On the 30th April 1606, land was sighted, and so extensive did it appear, that the explorers had no doubt it was the great Australian continent of which they were in search. The discovery was hailed with joyous acclamations, and the name of Australia del Espiritu Santo was given to the land. But alas! it was not what they hoped and expected; it was simply the largest island of the New Hebrides group, **which** still retains the name given it by Quiros. After leaving this island, they encountered heavy weather, **during** which the ships separated. Quiros then made sail for South America. Torres, however, continued **the** voyage, and in August sighted the island **of** New Guinea, and discovered the strait between that island and the continent **of** Australia which now bears his name. Although this is the first authentic record of the coast of Australia having been actually sighted, it is quite certain, from old maps that are still in existence, that the continent of Terra Australis, as it was then more generally called, had been sighted by Dutch, and perhaps also by Portuguese, navigators. At the same time that Torres was prosecuting his discoveries, a small Dutch vessel called the *Duyfhen* was, it is reported, sent from Bantam for the purpose of exploring the coast of New Guinea. It is alleged that this vessel sailed along the west coast of an extensive continent (supposed to be in the Gulf of Carpentaria, and which they thought was New Guinea), to as far as 13° 45′ S. latitude. If this be true—and there is no reason to doubt the accuracy of the captain's statement—the credit for the discovery of Australia should be awarded to the commander of the *Duyfhen*, who actually sighted and sailed along the coast, four months before Torres saw the northern part of the continent.

In 1686 a Dutchman named Dirck Hartog of Amsterdam, in a ship called the *Eendragt*, outward bound from Holland to India, sailed along the west coast of Australia from 23° to 26½° S. latitude. A record of his discovery, cut with a knife on a plate of tin, was found in Sharks Bay in 1697, and subsequently in 1801. It bore the following inscription :—" Anno 1616 the 25th October arrived here the ship *Eendragt* of Amsterdam ; the first merchant Gilles Mibais Van Luyck, Dirck Hartog of Amsterdam, captain. They sailed from hence for Bantam the 27th Dec."

One or two other Dutch outward-bound ships sighted the west coast during the next few years ; and in 1622 the Dutch ship *Leeuwin* sighted the south-west point of Australia, which fact has been permanently established

by that headland still bearing the name of Cape Leewin.
In the following year, two ships under command of Jan
Carstens sailed from Amboyna on a voyage of discovery.
At New Guinea, Carstens with eight of his crew were
treacherously murdered by the natives. The vessels, however, proceeded on the voyage, and made some discoveries
to the southward; but the accounts are too vague to
ascertain accurately the exact **track of the vessels. In**
January 1627, the south coast of Australia was discovered by Pieter Nuyts in the Dutch ship *Gulde
Zeepaard*, and was called by him Nuyt's Land.

The most important Dutch voyages made at **about**
this time were those of Abel Janz Tasman, who was
despatched in 1642, and again in 1644, on voyages of exploration by the Dutch governor-general **of Java, Antony**
Van **Diemen, "who** sent us out to make discoveries."
Tasman sailed from Batavia on his first voyage in August
1642, in the yacht *Heemskirk*, accompanied by the fly-
boat *Zeehaan*. **In** October he reached Mauritius, thence
he steered to the south-east, and on the 24th November
sighted land which proved to be the island now **known as**
Tasmania, but to which Tasman gave the name of his em-
ployer, Van Diemen. Sailing round the south end of the
island, they eventually came to an anchor in a sheltered
harbour on the east coast, to which they **gave** the name
of Frederik Hendrik's Bay, a **name** it still retains.
Here they landed to search for water, wood, and refresh-
ments. Although traces of men were found, and human
voices it was supposed were heard, they did not succeed
in establishing communication with, or even seeing, the
natives. On the 4th December **they** weighed anchor and
continued their course to **the eastward, and on the 13th**
sighted the high mountains **on the** west coast of **New**

Zealand, in latitude 42° 10′ S. Tasman anchored his ships in a bay at the entrance of the strait separating the two islands. Here his boat was attacked by the natives, and several of his men were killed : he named the bay, in consequence, "Moordenaars" (Murderer's) Bay ; it is now known as Massacre Bay. Tasman gave the name of Staten Land to this newly-discovered country, after the States-General of the Netherlands, imagining it was part of the great southern continent. Its name was, however, subsequently changed to New Zealand, by which it is now known. Steering to the northward, he sailed up the east coast of Australia, but without sighting it, and returned by the north coast of New Guinea, arriving at Batavia on the 15th of June 1643. Tasman was again despatched the following year on a voyage of discovery, but it is much to be regretted that no accounts of this voyage have ever been made public. It seems, however, clear from his charts that he made a careful exploration of the Gulf of Carpentaria, so named after Carpenter, who was the President of the Dutch East India Company. Tasman was a bold and fortunate navigator, but he was also a careful and a skilful one, as is evidenced by his surveys, which, considering the somewhat rude appliances that were in use in those days for determining and fixing positions, are very fairly accurate.

In 1688, our famous buccaneering navigator, William Dampier, made a voyage round the world, and anchored on the north-west coast of Terra Australis Incognita, as it was then called, in a harbour in the neighbourhood of King Sound, for the purpose of careening and repairing his ship, an operation which occupied the crew about two months. Dampier writes : " New Holland is a very large tract of land. It is not yet determined whether it is an island or a main continent; but I am certain that it joins neither to Asia, Africa, nor America."

In 1696, another Dutch captain, named William de Vlaming, visited the west coast of Australia in the ship *Geelvink*, and discovered and named the Swan River.[1] He brought back two live black swans to Batavia with him, the earliest notice that we have of the existence of these birds. Whilst exploring along the coast to the northward, the tin plate with the inscription commemorating the discovery of Dirck Hartog in 1616 (see page 19, *ante*) was found. This expedition made a thorough examination of the west coast from the mouth of the Swan River to the North-West Cape.

Three years afterwards, namely, in 1699, the west coast was again visited by Captain William Dampier in H.M.S. *Roebuck*, who was sent out on a voyage of discovery by William III. It was, however, barren of important results, as he simply followed in the footsteps of those who had preceded him, verifying their work but making no fresh discoveries.

In spite of the numerous voyages that had been made to the great southern continent, some of which have been here briefly alluded to, our knowledge of the coast of Terra Australis was very incomplete and very limited, when Captain James Cook sailed on his first voyage of discovery in 1768. The western coast of Australia was then known as New Holland; it had been more frequently sighted and visited by navigators than any other part of the continent. The east coast was entirely unknown. New Guinea to the north, and Van Diemen's Land to the south, were believed to be portions of one

---

[1] It was named, by de Vlaming, the Black Swan River.

and the same continent, the latter being supposed to be a prolongation of the land discovered by Pieter Nuyts to the southward.   Even the Australia del Espiritu Santo of Quiros was, if in existence, supposed to belong to the mainland.   **All** was vagueness, uncertainty, and conjecture.   It remained for our great navigator Cook to lift the veil of doubt and uncertainty which still enshrouded the great southern land, and by **his** ability and **energy** to give to his country a **continent that in riches and** importance is now second to no **empire** in the world.

Captain Cook sailed from England in the *Endeavour* on the 26th August 1768 ; the principal object of the expedition which he commanded being a voyage **to the South** Sea for the purpose of **observing** the **transit of Venus.** This being accomplished, the *Endeavour* was ordered to prosecute discoveries in **the Southern** Hemisphere, and make a more accurate examination of the Pacific Ocean. Cook was accompanied by Sir Joseph Banks, afterwards President of the Royal Society, a great scholar and an ardent investigator in the pursuit of **science, and by Dr.** Solander, **an** accomplished botanist and naturalist.

The transit of Venus having been satisfactorily **observed** on the 3rd June 1769 at Otaheite, **the** *Endeavour*, after **a stay of three** months **at** that island, sailed on the 13th of the following month, and after cruising for a short **time** among the islands which **were** named by Cook the Society Group, a course was shaped for New Zealand, which was sighted at daylight on October the 6th.[1] On **the** 8th the ship dropped anchor in a large bay, which received the name **of** Poverty Bay, **on** account

---

[1] The look-out at the masthead, who reported this land, was a boy named Nicholas Young ; it was named, after him, by Captain Cook, Young Nick's Head.

of the inhospitable, **not to** say hostile, reception **the** expedition met with at **the hands of** the natives. Some months were profitably **employed** in the exploration **of the coast of this** little known **land,** during which **New Zealand** was completely circumnavigated, **and found to consist of two** large islands ; after **much** valuable and important geographical work **had** been accomplished, the *Endeavour* sailed **to the westward, bent on** further exploration and **research. On** the morning of the 18th of April **1770, land** was observed by the first lieutenant, and was **named, after him,** Point Hicks. Thence Captain Cook sailed northwards, and rounding the south-east point **of Australia, which he called** Cape Howe, he **anchored in a** safe and capacious **bay** on the 26th, which was subsequently named Botany **Bay,** in consequence **of the great variety** and richness of **the plants collected there by Mr.** Banks and Dr. Solander. **Here they** remained **for ten days,** engaged in scientific pursuits and in endeavouring **to** conciliate the natives, many of whom were **induced** to come down to the ship.

Sailing on the 6th **of** May, they proceeded to the northward, discovering **and naming** Port Jackson, **on** the shores of which is now situated the important city of Sydney, the capital of New South **Wales.** Moreton Bay, at the head of which now stands Brisbane, the capital **of** Queensland, was also discovered and named.

During this voyage **Captain Cook** sailed along **the** entire eastern coast of **Australia,** which he named **New South Wales,** taking possession **of it in the** name of His Majesty **King George the Third.** Hitherto the *En-deavour* **had been safely navigated among** dangerous **shoals** and hidden rocks, **and other** unknown dangers, with a surprising immunity from disaster. This exemp

tion from casualties was, however, not to last; for at
about eleven o'clock on the night of the 10th June 1770,
the ship **struck heavily on a** rock, and remained immovable. **The** situation was certainly not a pleasant
one, for the loss of the ship meant the possible loss of
all on board, as the chances of saving themselves by
their boats alone, so many thousands of miles from any
place where they could hope to obtain relief and succour,
were very small indeed. Everything was, however, done
that skill and experience could suggest in order to extricate the ship from her perilous condition, but **for**
some time without avail, and she continued to beat with
great violence on the rocks upon which she had struck.
By the dim light of the moon that **prevailed, they**
could see portions of the false **keel, and other parts of**
the bottom of their good ship, that had been **torn and**
wrenched off by the sharp, jagged edges of the rocks,
floating around them, and it seemed extremely improbable that she would hold together for another tide.
Fortunately there was but little wind, and as the tide
fell, the ship **settled** down more quietly **in her rocky**
cradle. Every effort was then made to lighten her; six
guns were thrown overboard, as well **as** a quantity of
iron and stone ballast and other stores, and the water
was also started. When daylight broke, they found the
ship was making a considerable amount of water, **which**
the pumps were unable to control. Their great fear
now was that as the tide rose, the ship might float off,
and immediately sink in **deeper water**; but, to their great
surprise, **and no less** gratification, they found, when she
floated, that **not only were their** fears groundless, but
also that the pumps gained considerably on the leak. In
order **to** obtain **this advantage,** however, the men had to

remain unceasingly **at work, a** duty which entailed **hard** and incessant labour. **Being unable to get** at the leak from the inside of the ship, and being naturally desirous of ascertaining its extent, and, if possible, taking such steps to prevent the great inflow of water, which caused such harassing and severe physical exertions on the part **of** the crew, Captain Cook, at the suggestion, he tells us, of Mr. Markhouse, one of the midshipmen of the ship, ordered a sail to be thrummed,[1] and, thus prepared, hauled under the bottom **of the ship.** The suction of the water at the leak dragged the sail into the injured part, and thus materially reduced, to their no small comfort and joy, the amount of water that found its way into the *Endeavour*. The ship was then brought **in** close to the land, and anchored **in** a snug little harbour **at the mouth of a river, which received** the name **of** Endeavour River, **and here** she was thoroughly overhauled and repaired. The point **of** land **in** the immediate vicinity of the **scene of the disaster** was called Point **Tribulation, to** commemorate the unfortunate event. It was during the time the ship was **in** Endeavour River that kangaroos were first seen, **killed,** and eaten. **The** repairs being effected, a start was once more made; and sailing through Torres Strait, though not without experiencing many dangers and no few difficulties, Cook returned to England, passing the Lizard on the 10th June **1771,** thus completing his first voyage of discovery in the South Seas, during which time he circumnavigated New Zealand, sailed along the entire east coast **of** Australia, and performed altogether one of the most remarkable voyages on record.

---

[1] A sail is thrummed by stitching yarns and oakum of the necessary dimensions on to the sail.

It was not likely that so experienced and skilful a
navigator as Captain Cook would be allowed to remain
for any length of time inactive and unemployed. Immediately on his arrival in England he was promoted to
the rank of commander, and in the following year was
appointed to the command of an expedition, that had for
its object the final determination of the existence, or
otherwise, of a southern continent. He was also directed
to circumnavigate the globe in as high a southern latitude
as possible. The expedition consisted of two vessels,
the *Resolution*, under the immediate command of Captain
Cook, and the *Adventure*, commanded by Captain Furneaux.
The ships left Plymouth on the 13th July 1772, and after
touching at the Cape of Good Hope, crossed the Antarctic
Circle, and reached the latitude of 67° 15' S., when their
further progress to the southward was effectually impeded by ice. After vain endeavours to penetrate to a
higher latitude, during which time the ships got separated, Captain Cook sailed for New Zealand, which he
reached on the 25th March 1773, after having been at
sea for 117 consecutive days, during which time he
sailed over 10,000 miles without seeing land. Two
months later the *Adventure* was fallen in with at an
appointed rendezvous, after a separation of fourteen
weeks. During that time Captain Furneaux had succeeded in exploring some portions of Van Diemen's
Land. New Zealand was left on the 7th of June, after
various animals, such as sheep, pigs, goats, cocks and
hens, and even a couple of geese, of each sex, had been
landed, with the view of eventually stocking the country
with these useful domestic animals, whilst potatoes, car-
rots, onions, parsnips, cabbage, beans, turnips and other
edible vegetables were planted. On the 17th of August

the ships arrived at Otaheite, where much-needed rest and refreshment were obtained by the crews. After visiting several islands in the Society and other groups, the expedition again directed its course towards New Zealand, which was sighted on the 21st of October; shortly afterwards they experienced a furious storm, during which the ships were again separated, **never to** meet again during the remainder of the voyage.

Captain Cook sailed from New Zealand on the 26th of November, and proceeded to the southward to renew his search for the great southern continent; but he was again baffled by ice, and after reaching the 71st degree of south latitude, he relinquished all further attempts, and pursued **a northerly course.** Easter Island was **reached on the 11th March 1774,** and the Marquesas **during the early part** of the following month. On April **22nd** the *Resolution* anchored at Otaheite, more for the purpose of determining the rate of the chronometers than for any other reason, although they gladly availed themselves of the opportunity to furnish the ship with a much-needed supply of fresh provisions, which were, it is needless to add, highly appreciated after their long sea-cruise. After a stay of about four weeks, Captain Cook took his departure from Otaheite, and after visiting some of the adjacent islands sailed to the westward, and passing through the New Hebrides Group (so named by him), and visiting and naming several of the islands in it, he discovered and named the large island of New Caledonia, as also Norfolk Island, eventually anchoring **in Queen** Charlotte Sound, New Zealand, on the 18th of October. Leaving **New** Zealand on the 10th of the following month, Captain Cook rounded Cape Horn in December, and after making another attempt **to reach** a high southern latitude, during **which time he dis-**covered and named New Georgia, he sailed for England, **and** finally anchored his ship at Spithead **on the** 30th **July** 1775, after an absence of a little over three years. His consort, the *Adventure*, had reached England **on** the 14th July the previous year.

It is needless to allude here to the great skill, the remarkable energy, and the perseverance that were displayed by our great navigator during this wonderful voyage, for they are matters of history ; immediately on his arrival in England he was advanced to the rank of post-captain and appointed a captain of Greenwich **Hos-**pital ; he was shortly after elected a Fellow of the Royal Society, and presented with the Copley gold medal of **that** institution.

Captain Cook, however, was not permitted to enjoy **his** comfortable appointment at Greenwich for any length of time, for on the 10th February 1776 he was selected for, and appointed to, the command of an expe-dition that had for its primary object the discovery of a north east passage by Bering's Strait, a project the successful execution of which had so long baffled the boldness and skill of many enterprising navigators. The vessels selected for this important service were the *Resolution* and the *Discovery*.   Captain Cook **was** appointed to the command of his old ship, while the command of the *Discovery* **was** intrusted to Captain Charles Clerke.

Captain Cook sailed **from** England on the 12th of **July 1776, and calling** at the Cape of Good Hope in November, proceeded **on** his **voyage** to the south-east, spending two or three days, including Christmas, at Kerguelen Island, where **they** found a record in a bottle, which clearly proved they were not the first people, as they had supposed, who had landed on this sterile and inhospitable island. Van Diemen's Land was reached on the 26th January 1777, and the necessary supplies of wood and water obtained. The next stage **was to** their old anchorage in Queen Charlotte's Sound in New Zealand; thence the expedition proceeded to the Friendly Islands and Otaheite, at all of which places officers and men were regaled with fresh provisions, while a considerable stock was laid in for their forthcoming cruise. The Society Islands were left on the 2nd of December, and three weeks after, the Equator was crossed. **The** Sandwich Islands were reached and named towards the end of January 1778. Continuing **their course** northwards, the ships sighted the coast of **New** Albion **on the 7th of March,** and on the 29th of **the same month anchored off** Vancouver Island, in a large inlet which Cook named King George's Sound, but which they subsequently found was called Nootka by the natives. The ships sailed again on the 26th **of** April, and, in spite of tempestuous weather, slowly but surely worked their way in a northerly direction. **On** May 12th the expedition anchored **in** a large **bay on the** south coast of Alaska, which received the name **of** Prince William Sound. The island of Oonalaska **was** reached on the 27th of June, and, after a stay of a few days, the ships resumed their voyage northwards. **On the 9th of** July, Cape Prince of Wales was named, and on the following day the expedition had the satisfaction of passing through Bering's Strait. Steering first to the east and then due north, the latitude of 70° 33′ was reached on the 17th July, when, after **proceeding** ten miles farther in a northerly direction, their prog-

ress was stopped by a large field **of ice,** so compact as
to defy all efforts at penetration. Captain Cook persevered in his endeavours to penetrate the pack in several
different directions until the 29th July, but always without success, for every day the ice seemed to increase and
offer a more effective obstacle to advancement. Thinking, therefore, that the season was too far advanced, he
relinquished further attempts to explore in a northerly
direction for that year, and returned to the southward,
collecting much valuable geographical information on the
way. On the 30th of November, the island of Owhyhee
(Hawai) was discovered, and seven weeks were spent in
sailing round and exploring its coast. On the **17th of**
January 1779 the two ships came to an anchor in Kara-
kakooa Bay, and here Captain Cook determined to refit
his ships and refresh his men, preparatory to making
another voyage to Bering's Strait. The details of the
lamentable death of our great navigator in this harbour,
on the 14th of the following month, are so well known
that further allusion to it here is rendered unnecessary.

The voyages and discoveries of Captain Cook bear so
intimately on the work of Sir John Franklin in both
hemispheres, that I have touched upon them somewhat
more in detail than I had intended. It is only necessary to add, that after the irreparable loss sustained by
the death **of** their commander, the two ships, under the
command of Captain Clerke, left the Sandwich Islands
in prosecution of the main object of the expedition on the
15th March. On the 28th of the following month the
vessels anchored off Petropaulowski in Kamchatka, where
the officers and men were most cordially received and
hospitably entertained by the Russian authorities, who
provided them with every necessary that the place could

supply, **even** at the **cost of** much inconvenience and privation to themselves.

Leaving Petropaulowski on the 13th June, the expedition sailed through Bering's Strait on the 5th of July, but their further progress was arrested two days afterwards by a solid barrier of ice. They continued to search for a passage until the 27th, but, **in spite of** all efforts, they were unable to penetrate to within ten miles of the latitude reached by them the previous year under Captain Cook. Realising the impracticability, under **the** existing conditions of the ice, of accomplishing **the** much wished-for passage that season, they reluctantly returned **to the southward,** when, after achieving some useful geographical **work in the** Pacific, the ships sailed for England, where **they arrived in** October, after an absence of four years two months and twenty-two days.

Other **navigators,** at different times, visited the coast of Terra Australis, and **even** made the passage through Torres **Strait; but** as the amount of exploration and the work accomplished by them were, for the most part, comparatively unimportant, it is unnecessary to make any further reference to them here. One of the chief and most important results leading from the **discoveries** of Captain Cook, was the formation of a colony in New South Wales. On the 19th of January 1788, nine years after the death **of** the great navigator, **Captain** Arthur Phillip, **of the** Royal Navy, arrived at Botany **Bay in** H.M. **brig** *Supply*, and established the first settlement in **Australia.** He was soon followed by Captain Hunter in the *Syrius*, with six transports and three store-ships. The settlement was shortly afterwards removed to Port Jackson, a much better harbour situated about ten miles to **the** northward, where the present town of Sydney was founded, and Captain Phillip thus became the first Governor of the colony of New South Wales.

In the year 1795, Captain William Hunter was appointed to relieve Captain Phillip in the government of the new colony, and sailed from England in the *Reliance*, taking with him, as was mentioned in the preceding chapter, young Matthew Flinders as one of his midshipmen.

CHAPTER III.

FLINDERS AND BASS—EXAMINATION OF THE SEA-BOARD OF AUSTRALIA.

1795–1803.

> " As when to those who saile
> Beyond the Cape of Hope, and now are past
> Mozambie, off at sea, north-east winds blow
> Sabean odours from the spicie shore of
> Arabie the blest."—*Paradise Lost.*

ON the arrival of the *Reliance* at Sydney Cove, young Flinders found that the existing knowledge of the coast in the vicinity of Port Jackson was exceedingly limited. No detailed survey had been attempted, nor was there even a correct delineation of the coast-line, except in the case of those discoveries that had been published in Captain Cook's general chart. So keen an interest did this young and enthusiastic midshipman take in the work of geographical research that he at once determined to use his utmost exertions in striving to supply the deficiency. Fortunately there was on board the *Reliance* a kindred spirit in the person of Mr. George Bass, the assistant-surgeon, whose enthusiasm for the promotion of geographical discovery was equal to, if not greater than, that of his younger friend. These two officers, although, incredible to relate, they met with no encouragement from their superiors, set to work with resolution and perseverance, fully determined, **to the utmost** of their power and ability, to complete the examination of the coast of New South Wales so far as the limited means at their disposal would admit, and whenever, be it noted, they could be spared **from** their own particular duties on board the *Reliance.*

The success attending the praiseworthy attempts of these young officers to throw light on the darkness that surrounded this hitherto unexplored and almost unknown coast, was commensurate with the energy and resolution displayed. By their own unaided efforts, they equipped **a** small boat only eight feet in length, and not inappropriately named the *Tom Thumb*, and with **a crew** consisting of themselves and one boy, they sailed from Port **Jackson on** their first surveying expedition. Thus the **somewhat** anomalous picture is presented to **us,** of a young midshipman and an assistant-surgeon in the navy, undertaking to execute what must be considered as a very important survey of the hitherto practically **unknown** coast of Australia, entirely on their own resources, unaided and unassisted by those who were better able, and perhaps, from their experience, better qualified to undertake the service and bring it to a successful issue. **The** result of their first attempt was the exploration, **for** a considerable distance, of George's River, which falls into Botany Bay, and an extension of the knowledge of this river to some twenty miles beyond Captain Hunter's **previous survey.** This was a work of some importance, **for** it led to the foundation of a new settlement, which **was** called Bank's Town, after **Sir** Joseph Banks, the companion of Cook in his first voyage, and the learned President of the Royal Society.

Their second venture was of a more extended character

than the first, although their means were just as limited,
for it was carried out, as before, in the little *Tom Thumb*.
Their objective on this occasion was the exploration of
a large river that emptied itself into the sea some miles
to the southward of Botany Bay, but of the existence of
which **there was no** indication on the chart of Captain
Cook. Sailing from Port Jackson on the 5th **March 1795,**
a thorough and careful examination of the coast **was**
effected by these young officers, until a heavy gale of
wind springing up from the southward, not only necessitated **a** temporary discontinuance of their work, but
threatened to overwhelm their tiny boat. **The** dangers
to which our young explorers **were** thus exposed were
materially increased **by the intense** darkness of the
night, the **strong and** irregular currents that prevailed,
and **their ignorance of** any sheltered bay or harbour in
their vicinity. **During** all **this** long, anxious night,
Flinders remained at **the** steer oar, and it was only **by**
his constant watchfulness and skill, that the little craft
did not broach to and capsize. Bass attended the sheet,
an important duty, **on** the vigilant execution of which
their lives depended, whilst the boy was kept fully **em-**
ployed baling out the water that was constantly breaking
into the boat. At length, when their strength was almost
exhausted, breakers were discovered ahead ; the mast and
sail were quickly struck, and bending valiantly to the
oars, they succeeded in carrying their little craft into
smooth water under the **lee of** an extensive reef, **and**
thus reached comparative safety, after being for some
hours in a very perilous and critical position. This was
only one of the numerous dangers and perils, voluntarily
faced in the cause of geographical research by our ardent
and brave explorers. **The bay in which they so miracu-**

lously procured shelter was named by them Providential Cove, in remembrance of their deliverance on this occasion—a name it still bears.

Three years later Dr. Bass, in an open whale-boat with a crew only of six seamen, explored over 600 miles of coast-line to the southward of Port Jackson, 300 miles of which were entirely new. In his small and frail craft, exposed during the greater part of the time to very tempestuous weather, accompanied, as is invariably the case in those latitudes, by a high and raging sea, this energetic officer persevered until he discovered the strait separating Australia from Tasmania, and which now, very properly, bears his name. Although he only carried with him provisions to last for an anticipated absence of six weeks, he was able, with the assistance of petrels, fish, geese, and black swans that he succeeded in obtaining, and also by parsimonious economy and abstinence, to prolong his voyage to eleven weeks! The farthest point on the mainland reached by him was Western Port. This voyage, in a small open boat, was a feat that for fearlessness and determination has scarcely been equalled in the annals of geography or maritime enterprise.

During the period that Dr. Bass was absent on this expedition, his young friend Flinders was not idle; for, having first obtained permission from Governor Hunter, he embarked on board the schooner *Francis*, and sailed in her on the 1st February 1798 to Preservation Island, one of the Furneaux group. This vessel, it should be observed, had been despatched for the purpose of saving the cargo, or some portion of it, of a vessel that had recently been wrecked there, as well as with the object of bringing back the few men who had been left in

charge of the wreckage. During this cruise young
Flinders did excellent **work** in fixing the positions of
various parts of the coast, and in obtaining valuable and
important information on many points relative to the
places **visited,** their inhabitants, natural history, **geo-**
logical formation, &c. He returned to Port Jackson on
the 9th of March. Writing of the Furneaux **Islands,**
and referring **to the** noise made by the **thousands of**
seals that infest the group, **Flinders says :—**

"Those who have seen a farm-yard, **well stocked with** pigs,
calves, sheep, oxen, and with two or three litters **of** puppies
with their mothers in it, and **have heard them** all **in** tumult
together, may form a good **idea of the** confused noise of the
seals at Cone Point. The sailors killed as many of these
harmless and not unamiable creatures, as they were able to
skin during **the time necessary for me to** take the requisite
angles, and **we then left the poor** affrighted multitude to
recover from **the effects of** our inauspicious visit."

At length, after earnest and repeated solicitations, the
zeal and perseverance of **Bass** and Flinders received
some official notice. A small sloop of twenty-five tons,
named the *Norfolk*, was placed by the Governor of New
South Wales at their disposal, for the purpose of completing the survey and exploration of Bass's Strait.
They sailed from Port Jackson on the 7th October
1798, with **a crew** consisting of eight volunteers, and
with provisions to last for a contemplated absence of
twelve **weeks. During** this cruise Twofold Bay was
carefully examined, **and the** northern coast of Tasmania
was thoroughly explored, besides many adjacent islets,
the habitat of seals and albatrosses innumerable. **In-**
deed, on some of the islands on which they landed, **the**
explorers had to fight their **way up the cliffs through**

crowded masses of seals, who indignantly resented the strange, and, to them, unwarrantable intrusion. On reaching the summit, they **were** frequently compelled **to use** their clubs and staves in order to clear a **way** through the albatrosses, which **they** found sitting on their nests in **such** large numbers as to literally cover the surface of the ground. All the different positions of the various prominent head-lands, capes, &c., were accurately fixed by our young explorers by careful astronomical observations, and the fact **of the** insularity of Tasmania, previously reported **by Dr. Bass, was now** actually verified by the *Norfolk* sailing through **Bass's** Strait. This Strait, it may **be noted, was named at the** special request **of young Flinders,** after **his companion** and colleague. **The** *Norfolk* returned **to Port Jackson on the** 11th January 1799.

Flinders was next engaged on an exploring expedition **to** the northward, **when** Moreton and Harvey's Bays, discovered and named by Captain Cook, were thoroughly examined. He returned to England in the *Reliance* in 1800, after an absence of over **five** years, during **which** time he had, by sheer industry and perseverance, **quali-**fied himself as a skilful and expert sailor, and had gained the reputation of being an experienced and accomplished navigator.

On the **arrival of** the **ship in** England, **the** charts containing all **the new surveys** and discoveries were published, **and a** scheme **was** submitted for completing the examination **of the coast of** Australia. This plan met with **the cordial support of Sir Joseph** Banks, the President of **the Royal Society, and** other men interested in the science of geography, **who were** all strongly **im-**pressed with the importance and **necessity of completing**

the work. Backed by such eminent authorities, it is not surprising to find that the scheme was favourably received by, and met with the hearty approval of, Lord Spencer, the First Lord of the Admiralty, who having received the sanction of His Majesty, gave the necessary directions that an expedition, as proposed, should be despatched. Mr. Flinders was, as a matter of course, selected as the most fitting person to command it. The *Investigator*, as already related in a previous chapter, was the ship chosen for this important service, and everything being ready, she sailed from Spithead on the 18th of July 1801. In addition to her complement of eighty-three officers and men, she had on board an astronomer,[1] a naturalist, a landscape painter,[2] as well as a natural history painter, a gardener, and a miner.

The instructions that Captain Flinders received were to make as complete an examination as was possible of the coast of New Holland, as Australia was then called. The south coast was in the first place to be thoroughly explored between King George's Sound and Bass's Strait, and diligent search was to be made for any "creek or opening likely to lead to an inland sea or strait."[3]

Sydney Cove (on the shore of which our first Australian colonists had been established for about thirteen years) was selected as the head-quarters of the expedition, and here they were ordered to refit, and provide

---

[1] Mr. **Crosley,** but this gentleman was subsequently relieved by Mr. Inman, who was the Professor of Mathematics and Nautical Science at the Royal Naval College at Portsmouth for many years.

[2] This was the eminent painter William Westall, who afterwards became an Associate of the Royal Academy.

[3] Extract from the instructions received by Captain Flinders from the Admiralty.

CAPTAIN FLINDERS.

themselves with all the necessary supplies procurable. On the completion of **the survey** of the south coast, Captain Flinders was directed to turn his **attention** to the exploration of the north-west coast of New Holland, where valuable harbours, it was thought probable, might be **discovered.** He was then ordered to **examine the** coast to the Gulf of Carpentaria, and make an exhaustive survey of Torres Strait. This being accomplished, he was instructed to carefully examine the east coast, with permission to visit **the Fiji, and other islands** situated in the South Sea.

It will thus be seen that the work he was required **to** undertake, was **of a** gigantic and elaborate nature, **for** it was, in reality, an examination of the entire sea-board of Australia that he was expected and ordered to carry out; he was, **it may** be observed, significantly enjoined not to return to England until this was satisfactorily accomplished !

With such an enthusiast in the cause **of** geographical science for his captain, **it** is not surprising to find that young Franklin **took** kindly to his new duties, **and** speedily gave practical evidence of his skill as a sailor and his ability as a surveyor. Home associations were undoubtedly a bond of mutual sympathy and connection between the man and the boy, and the friendly intercourse that, **in** consequence, existed between the captain and the midshipman must have been greatly to the advantage **of** the latter, and, doubtless, aided to mould the mind and **guide the** thoughts **of** the younger **to** those scientific pursuits which ultimately so distinguished him. **It is very** reasonable for **us to** infer that it **was,** **in all** probability, **in** exploring **miles of** practically unknown coast-line, and in surveying hitherto undiscovered bays, **reefs,** and **islands in the** Southern Hemisphere, **that John Franklin's** mind **became** imbued with that ardent love of **geographical** research, which formed such a marked and prominent feature in his future professional career. Flinders was the example, and the Australian exploration was the school, that **created one of** our greatest Arctic navigators, and one of the most eminent geographers of his day.

Before the *Investigator* had been many days **at sea,** palpable evidence was afforded **of her** general unseaworthiness, for before even Madeira was reached, she was making as much as three, afterwards increasing to **five, inches of** water per **hour, and** her general unsuitability as an exploring ship, in a part of the world where boisterous weather was sure to be experienced, was only **too plain.** Captain Flinders, ever loyal to his superiors, **endeavours to apologise for** the unseaworthy state and general unfit condition **of his** ship, and **explains as** an excuse for her selection and adoption for the work on which she was to be employed, **that** "*the exigencies of the navy were such, at that time, that he was given to understand that no better ship could be spared from the service ; and his anxiety to complete the investigation of the coasts of Terra Australis did not admit of refusing the one offered.*" It may be here remarked that the distinct **and** appropriate appellation **of** Australia was given to **the great south** land at the suggestion, and on the recommendation, of Captain **Flinders.** Referring to **the** name by which it was then known, namely, Terra Australis, he writes, **in a footnote at** page 3 of the introduction **to his** valuable and interesting work **entitled "A** Voyage to Terra Australis," "*Had I permitted myself any innovation upon the original term, it would have* *been to convert it into Australia, as being more agreeable to the ear, and an assimilation to the names of the other great portions of the earth."*

After touching at the Cape of **Good Hope, the** *Investigator* anchored in King George's Sound, in **Western** Australia, on the 8th of December. Here they remained for four weeks, a period that was profitably employed **in** refitting the rigging and sails and repairing the ship generally, also in examining and surveying the Sound. Thence Flinders sailed along the south shore of Australia, hitherto known as Nuyt's Land, from the Dutch skipper who first discovered it, and carefully examined the **coast** of what is now called **the Great** Australian Bight. **The** running survey that was carried **out** on this occasion was so complete and so accurate, that the coast-line, as delineated by Captain Flinders, **remains** unaltered **on the charts of** the present day. The land along this coast was fringed by a range of high cliffs, estimated at from four to six hundred feet in height, and so uniform was the appearance of the shore in the neighbourhood, that it was found to **be almost** impossible to define, and name, any particular points, or capes, **in** consequence of the similarity of one headland to another. Captain Flinders was under the impression that this bank, or fringe, **of** cliffs, which extends for **a distance of** about 500 miles, was, in all probability, the exterior line of a vast coral reef, which, **from** a gradual subsidence, or perhaps by some sudden convulsion of Nature, had attained its present position and height **above the** surface of the sea. The examination of this interesting coast afforded much new and valuable information.

We may take it for granted that **young Franklin all** this time, was not only rapidly acquiring valuable experience in, and a practical knowledge of his professional duties, but that he was also able to afford substantial assistance in the surveying work that was being carried out. Indeed, we may be assured that this was the case, for we find his name associated with a couple of islands belonging to the St. Francis group, situated **off** the coast of what is now known as South Australia, and which Flinders named the Franklin Isles, after his young protégé. It must have been **a** proud **day for our** Lincolnshire midshipman when he was informed that his name was thus, for the first time, to be immortalised as a discoverer and explorer.

Another island in Spencer **Gulf** was named Spilsby Island, presumably after the home and birthplace of Franklin; whilst a large bight **on** the coast was called Louth Bay, **and two low** islands in the same locality were called Louth **Islands,** after the town in Lincolnshire in which **our** young friend received the rudiments of his education. We may, I think, safely infer, from the nomenclature thus conferred **on** these places, that Franklin was, in some way, instrumental in their discovery, or subsequent examination. **The harbour in** Spencer's Gulf, which formed the most interesting part **of** the discovery, received the appellation of Port Lincoln, in honour of the county from which both Flinders and Franklin hailed.

During this cruise a sad affair occurred through the accidental capsizing of one of the *Investigator's* boats, resulting in the loss of Mr. Thistle (master), Mr. Taylor (midshipman), and six men forming the crew **of the** cutter. This disaster cast a deep gloom over the ship for some days, while it deprived Franklin, and the other members of the midshipmen's berth, of a **mess-**

mate and companion, a young officer of great promise, one of their immediate circle. Mr. Thistle, the master, whose loss they had to mourn, was a most worthy man and deserving officer. He had accompanied Dr. Bass as one of the six men comprising the crew of his whale-boat during his wonderful boat-journey,[1] and he had subsequently formed one of the crew of the *Norfolk*, when that vessel was despatched, under Flinders and Bass, for the exploration of Bass's Strait. For his ex-cellent behaviour, and the ability, intelligence, and zeal displayed by him on those occasions, he was promoted to a midshipman, and was afterwards advanced to the rank of master's-mate. He was subsequently promoted to master, and in that capacity was appointed to the *In-vestigator*, at the earnest request and recommendation of Captain Flinders.

On the afternoon of April 8th, intense excitement was caused on board the *Investigator* by the somewhat unusual, and certainly unexpected, report of a vessel being in sight.

What ship could possibly be sailing about in those unfrequented and hitherto unknown waters? Was she a friend, or could she possibly be a foe? These were questions hurriedly asked, but not easily answered. In anticipation of the latter eventuality, the drum beat to quarters, and the *Investigator* was, as expeditiously as possible, cleared for action, and prepared to meet an enemy. Guns that had been dismounted and struck below, for convenience in carrying out the special and eminently peaceful service on which the ship was em-ployed, were quickly brought on deck; the rust was hurriedly scraped from them, and they were mounted in

---

[1] See page 37.

their proper ports, and made as serviceable and efficient as the short time at their disposal admitted. Fortunately, however, the fighting capacity of the ship and the courage and bellicose propensities of her officers and crew, were not destined to be put to the proof, for the stranger, that had caused all this excitement, turned out to be the French ship *Le Geographe,* employed, like themselves, on a peaceful voyage of discovery. She was commanded by Captain Nicholas Baudin, who, with another ship, *Le Naturaliste,* also under his orders, had been recently engaged in examining the south and east coasts of Van Diemen's Land. Having accidentally separated from his consort, Captain Baudin was then employed in exploring along the south coast of Australia. After friendly visits had been exchanged, and before he had fully realised, or even ascertained, the identity of Captain Flinders, the French commander proceeded to make some adverse criticisms on an English chart of Tasmania published in 1800, that was in his possession. He was overwhelmed with confusion when he found that Captain Flinders, to whom his criticisms were addressed, was the author of the maligned chart, and was therefore responsible for its accuracy or otherwise! The ships parted company on the following day, the *Investigator* resuming her examination of the coast to the south-east, while the Frenchman pursued his investigations in a westerly direction. The place of meeting between the two ships was subsequently called Encounter Bay, to commemorate the event.

The next important piece of work connected with the voyage was the supposed discovery of Port Phillip, which was surveyed and examined with great care. Captain Flinders was so impressed with its admirable situation and the importance of his discovery, that he felt confident it would not be long before it would be selected as a site for a future settlement. His astonishment would indeed be great if he could now see the rich and flourishing city of Melbourne, which has sprung up on the shores of that inlet he was the first to explore. It was only after his arrival at Port Jackson, that he received the somewhat mortifying piece of intelligence, that his discovery had been already anticipated by Lieutenant John Murray, who, ten weeks before, had discovered and named this magnificent harbour.

On the 9th of May 1802, ten months after her departure from England, the *Investigator* anchored in Sydney Cove, Port Jackson. All on board were in the enjoyment of perfect health, and this satisfactory state of affairs in connection with the sanitary condition of the ship, was largely due to the constant and unremitting attention that was paid to cleanliness, a good and nourishing diet, and a free and proper circulation of air between decks. Captain Flinders was one of those officers who had the happy knack of combining strict discipline, with a kindly consideration for the happiness and comfort of those under his command.

There was, of course, much to be done on their arrival at Port Jackson. The ship had to be thoroughly overhauled and refitted ; new spars and sails had to be made, and old ones repaired ; water had to be obtained, and provisions and other stores purchased. While these necessary duties were being performed, the scientific work connected with the expedition was not neglected. An observatory was set up on shore, to which all the chronometers were removed, and where all the necessary satronomical observations were taken. This observatory was placed under the charge of Mr. Samuel Flinders,[1] the second lieutenant, and young Franklin was appointed as his assistant. Here he was kept closely at work, and was probably afforded but few opportunities of rambling about and exploring on his own account, the interesting country in the vicinity of the newly-found colony of Sydney.

In consequence of the particular occupation on which he was employed at this time, Franklin jokingly received from the Governor of New South Wales the appellation of " Tycho Brahe," after the eminent Danish astronomer.

In two and a half months' time, the *Investigator* was again ready to resume her work of exploration along the coast of Terra Australis ; but in order to carry out this important service in a more thorough manner, a brig called the *Lady Nelson*, of light draft, and commanded by Lieutenant John Murray, was, at the express wish of Captain Flinders, attached to his command, with directions to co-operate and assist in the exploration. The two vessels sailed in company from Port Jackson on the 22nd July 1802, and steering in a northerly direction, made an exhaustive examination of the eastern coast, in accordance with the instructions received from the Admiralty. During this trip, Port Bowen was discovered and named. Whilst carrying out this service, officers and men were landed at every convenient opportunity, and as much information of the coast as could be gathered was obtained.

---

[1] Samuel Flinders was a brother of the captain's. He was appointed to the *Investigator* on the 20th November 1800, and appears on her books as having joined as an A.B. from the *Atalante* on 28th February 1801. He was rated midshipman the same day, and was promoted to a lieutenant a week after, namely, on the 6th March 1801.

The *Lady Nelson*, however, instead of being of assistance, as was anticipated, was found to be such an indifferent sailer, and was so leewardly, that she was sent back to Sydney in October, for she proved herself to be, as Captain Flinders reports, " more a burthen than an assistant."

After examining various portions of the Great Barrier Reef, the *Investigator* sailed round the north-east point of Australia and entered the Gulf of Carpentaria. The shores of this extensive gulf were minutely examined, and the whole of its coast-line was delineated on the chart. It was while cruising in this neighbourhood that they had their first, and only, serious conflict with the natives, on which occasion Mr. Whitewood, master's-mate, one of Franklin's messmates, was wounded by spears in four places.

The old *Investigator*, at about this period, exhibiting unmistakable signs of decay, besides making water sometimes at the rate of fourteen inches per hour, Captain Flinders gave orders for a careful survey of her hull to be made, when it was discovered, to their great mortification, that her timbers and planking were in such a terribly rotten condition, that it was not considered likely that the ship would hold together, in ordinary weather, for more than six months, and that in the event of being caught at sea in a heavy gale of wind, she would, in all probability, founder ! This was, it must be acknowledged, a very serious state of affairs. Under the circumstances, Captain Flinders decided that he would complete the survey of the Gulf of Carpentaria, and then make the best of his way to Sydney, by sailing round the west coast of Australia, which he thought would be more easily accomplished than by returning along the east coast. He hoped to be able to procure another ship on his arrival at Sydney, in which to continue, and, if possible, to complete, his interesting work of discovery and exploration.

After a somewhat perilous and anxious voyage, he succeeded in carrying his crippled and sorely stricken ship to Port Jackson, which he reached on the 10th June 1803, after an absence of eleven months. In consequence of the scarcity of fresh provisions, the severity of the work on which they had been engaged, and the privations they had been exposed to, the ship's company was so much debilitated by scurvy and dysentery, that it was with difficulty they succeeded in working the ship into harbour. No less than five of the crew died a few days prior to the ship's arrival, and four succumbed shortly after their admission to the hospital on shore. Flinders was himself attacked with scorbutic affection, and doubtless Franklin was not himself in a more enviable state, and was in all probability suffering from the same terrible wasting disease.

Shortly after their arrival, a careful survey was held on the old and crazy ship by a board of competent officers, specially selected and appointed by the Governor; the result being that she was found to be in such an unseaworthy and rotten state that she was reported to be "not worth repairing in any country,"[1] also, that it was absolutely impossible to "put her in a state for going to sea," with the facilities for repairing ships then existing at Port Jackson. She was found to be incapable of further service, and it was strongly represented by the board to the authorities, that in the event of her being

---

[1] Extract from the report of the board ordered to survey the *Investigator* relative to her sea-worthiness.

caught at sea in a hard gale of wind, she would inevitably go to the bottom.

Under these circumstances, and after numerous consultations, it was eventually arranged that the old *Investigator* should be abandoned, and converted into a storehouse hulk, and that Captain Flinders, with a portion of his officers and crew, should be sent home as passengers in the armed vessel *Porpoise*, in order to report the facts of the case to the Admiralty, and endeavour to obtain another vessel in which to continue the exploration of the coast of Australia.

Twenty-two officers and men, in which number Franklin was included, embarked with Flinders on board the *Porpoise* for passage to England. This was all that remained out of a complement of eighty officers and men that sailed from England in the *Investigator* only two years before. This alarming reduction was not, however, due to deaths alone, for many were invalided, while some few were permitted, at their own request, to remain out and settle in the new colony. Franklin was discharged as a midshipman to the *Porpoise*, and was entered on her books as a master's-mate on 21st July 1803.

CHAPTER IV.

> " I am as a weed
>
> **Flung from** the rock on ocean's foam to sail,
> Where'er the surge may sweep, the tempest breath prevail."
>
> —*Childe Harold.*

THE *Porpoise,* under the command of Mr. Fowler, late
first lieutenant of the *Investigator,* sailed from Sydney
on the 11th of August 1803. Although she was nomi-
nally under the command of Lieutenant Fowler, that
officer was directed to conform to the wishes and orders
of Captain Flinders, who, though a passenger, was really
in absolute charge.

Flinders decided upon returning to England by the
route which, it may be said, he was the first to discover
and to recognise its practicability, namely, by Torres
Strait, for he would then, he thought, be afforded an
opportunity of checking, and perhaps elaborating, a
great deal of the work that he had already accomplished
in those waters whilst in command of the *Investigator.*

On leaving Sydney, the *Porpoise* was accompanied by
the East India Company's ship *Bridgewater,* and by the
ship *Cato* of London, both bound to Batavia, the captains
of those vessels having expressed a wish to be piloted

through Torres Strait by Captain Flinders. All went as "pleasant as a marriage-bell" until the evening of the 17th August, six days after leaving Port Jackson, when the terrible cry of "Breakers ahead!" resounded throughout the ship, and brought everybody on deck. The helm was at once put down, too late, however, to save the ill-fated ship from destruction, for she struck heavily on an unknown reef, the masts went by the board, and falling over on her beam ends, she lay exposed to the fury of the waves, which broke over her mastless hull with irresistible violence. Before any warning of the appalling disaster that had so suddenly, and so unexpectedly, overwhelmed the unfortunate *Porpoise* could be given to her consorts, the *Cato*, following closely at the distance only of a couple of cables, struck on the same reef ; her masts broke short off, she fell over on her broadside, and soon became a total wreck.

The *Bridgewater* escaped, but, incredible as it may appear, made no effort to rescue or to render any assistance whatever to the crews of her unfortunate consorts, although she remained in close promixity to the reef for a period of twenty-four hours, when she heartlessly proceeded on her voyage to Batavia. That those on board must have been fully cognizant of the perilous situation of their unfortunate friends in the wrecked ships is evident, from the fact that on her arrival at Bombay, the captain of the *Bridgewater* reported the total loss of the two ships with all hands ! It may not be out of place to note here that this ship, with the same dastardly captain, sailed from Bombay a few days after her arrival there on her homeward voyage, and was never afterwards heard of. Thus the selfishness and inhumanity of the captain and those on board, met with speedy and retributive justice.

The night that followed the disastrous stranding of the *Porpoise* was one of intense anxiety and suspense to all on board, and was spent in strenuous endeavours to construct a raft, out of the available masts and yards and other spars, capable of **receiving the crew,** in the **not** unimprobable event of **the ship going** to pieces before the morning. This was a new, and by no means pleasant, experience for John Franklin. Although so young in years—for he was only seventeen at the time of the catastrophe—he had braved many dangers and **had** encountered many perils; but this was the first **time** he had been brought face to face with shipwreck, **and in** one of its worst and most dreadful forms.

When, at length, the long-wished-for daylight broke, **and that**

> "Miserable night,
> So full of fearful dreams,"

had passed, they observed **a** dry sandbank about **half** a mile from the wreck. Although its superficial extent was not very great, it was, at any rate, large enough **to** accommodate the crews of the two ships, with as much **of** the provisions and stores **as they hoped** to be able **to save.**

The wretched people **in** the *Cato* were **even in a worse plight** than those on board **the** *Porpoise*, for the forecastle with **the** bowsprit attached, was the **only portion** of the **vessel** that remained above water, and to this the unfortunate crew had clung all that long and weary **night,** until rescued in the morning from their perilous **and** distressing condition **by** a boat from the *Porpoise*.

The only place to which they could secure themselves, and avoid being washed away by the raging surf, was the port fore-chains. In this trying situation, clinging to the wreck and holding on by the chain-plates and dead-eyes, they passed the night, and were found all clustered together in the morning. In consequence of the terrific sea that was breaking over the wreck, it was impossible to take the boat alongside to effect their rescue, and the men were only saved by throwing themselves into the water, trusting to those in the boat to pick them up. Three poor lads were drowned in unsuccessful attempts to reach the boat, and all were more or less bruised and cut by the sharp points and edges of the coral reef in their struggles to get on shore.

In a few hours after the men were landed the *Cato* went to pieces, and not a vestige of her remained visible. Unlike this ship, the *Porpoise* had, luckily, when she struck, heeled over with her upper deck towards the reef, which was to leeward, thus exposing the hull of the ship instead of the deck to the violence of the waves that broke over and against her, and this being stronger and more capable of resistance, she held together. The reef, the direct cause of their disaster, was fortunately nearly dry at low-water, so they had but little difficulty in landing all the available stores and provisions, besides a few sheep and pigs that had escaped drowning. The bank on which they had been wrecked proved to be 900 feet in length by 150 feet broad, and was about three or four feet above high-water; not a very extensive or comfortable place of residence, more especially when it is remembered that the nearest known land was quite 200 miles distant, and that Sydney, the only place from which they could hope to obtain succour or assistance, was about 750 miles off. **They** were, however, for **the** time in comparative safety; they had escaped a great peril, and, like good sailors, they looked forward with hope and trust to the future. It does not even appear that they were at all down-hearted or depressed at the appalling catastrophe that had overtaken them, for **a** great deal of merriment, we are informed, was caused by some of the *Cato's* men, who **had** saved absolutely nothing from their ship, attiring themselves in officers' uniforms that had been saved and landed from the *Porpoise.*

Their first work was to set up a tall spar **on the** highest **part of** the bank, on which a large blue ensign **was** hoisted, with the Union Jack down, as a signal of distress. **This was done in** the hope of attracting the notice of those on board the *Bridgewater,* which, it was still believed, would come to their assistance directly **it was known** that survivors had escaped from the **wrecks** and had reached the bank. They knew very well it was hopeless to expect aid from any other source, for in those unfrequented seas it was not probable **that any** ship would be cruising in the neighbourhood.

Franklin, it may readily **be supposed, experienced his** full share **of all** the dangers **and** privations to which he **and his shipwrecked** companions were exposed, and there **is but little doubt** that **he bore** himself bravely and manfully, **and worked** willingly and zealously in assisting to preserve order, and to maintain cheerfulness and **good** feeling in the small community. With the aid **of** sails and spars saved from **the** wreck, tents were erected on the sandbank, and they succeeded in making themselves as comfortable and **as** happy as, under the

circumstances, could be expected. A reprieved convict,
who formed one of the crew, was alone guilty of mani-
festing a spirit of insubordination, but this was quickly
and effectually suppressed by the culprit being publicly
flogged at the flag-staff. Strict discipline and a due
obedience to orders were almost essential to their ultimate salvation.

By the 23rd of August, everything that could be saved

ENCAMPMENT ON WRECK REEF.

was landed from the wreck; an inventory was then
taken, when it was found that they had sufficient water
and provisions to last, with care and economy, the
ninety-four survivors for a period of three months. All
the books and most important documents, as also the
charts and plans that had been made during the past
two years in the *Investigator*, were fortunately saved,

although somewhat damaged by rough usage and salt water.[1]

Having taken all the necessary steps for the preservation of the stores, &c., a council of officers was called, in order to consider what action should be taken for the purpose of obtaining relief. After much consideration, it was decided that one of the six-oared cutters saved from the *Porpoise*, should be despatched to Sydney with as little delay as possible, to give information relative to their situation and to endeavour to obtain assistance. As an extra precaution, and as they could not conceal from themselves the more than possible contingency of such a small boat failing to accomplish the distance (750 miles) in safety, more especially at that particular season of the year, when strong winds were prevalent, it was resolved to commence, from materials saved from the wrecks, the construction of a couple of decked boats, capable of transporting the remainder of the people. This decision being arrived at, the next question was to decide as to who should be selected to conduct the voyage to Sydney. As it was one of the utmost importance, and also one of no little peril, Captain Flinders determined to proceed on this duty himself. Acting on this resolve, and accompanied by the commander of the *Cato* and twelve men, with his small boat stored with provisions and water to last for three weeks, he sailed on the 26th leaving eighty officers and men on the bank,

---

[1] Some of the original drawings and sketches made by Mr. Westall are still in existence, and are now in the possession of the Royal Colonial Institute in London. They bear evidence of the damage they then sustained from immersion, and some few show slight indentations, caused, it is said, by Franklin and the other midshipmen thoughtlessly driving the sheep saved from the wreck over them, as they were spread out to dry on the sand!

which had so providentially been the means of their salvation after their vessels had been destroyed.

It is hardly possible to conceive the feelings that animated the breasts of those poor fellows who were left behind, and who were well aware that several weeks must necessarily elapse before they could expect, or even hope, to obtain succour. They could not banish from their thoughts the possibility, almost amounting to a probability, of the loss of the small frail boat whose occupants they had just bidden God-speed, as they started on their long and venturesome voyage. In order to prepare for the worst, and also, perhaps, with the object of occupying the minds of the men and thus drown their thoughts in employment, they were set to work to build two boats, which, as a *dernier ressort*, were intended to transport them to the mainland of Australia, in the event of no tidings of the cutter being received in two months; by that time their provisions and water would be nearly expended, for, as has already been stated, they had only saved sufficient from the wreck to eke out a bare subsistence for three months. In spite, however, of their critical situation, the utmost harmony prevailed, and all worked cheerily together, having a common end in view. At length, on the 7th of October, when they were already beginning to despair and to give up all hope of obtaining that help which they so sorely needed, the joyful cry of a " Sail in sight " burst upon the ears of the little community, and aroused its members to a state of enthusiastic excitement, as they rushed out to satisfy themselves of the accuracy or otherwise of the report.

Yes! there was no doubt of its truth, for there, on the horizon, as they strained their eyes to seaward, one, two, three **sails** could be seen making their way, with **a** favourable breeze, towards their island-home.   In a **very short** time they had the extreme satisfaction, **and gratification,** of greeting, **which** they did most sincerely and heartily, their old commander, who had brought his perilous **voyage to** such a successful **and** expeditious **issue,** having returned to their aid and succour **only six** weeks after he had bidden them farewell.

His voyage in the six-oared **cutter,** for a distance **of** 750 miles, had been an extremely hazardous one; but Flinders, by constant care and watchfulness, succeeded in reaching **Port Jackson in safety.**   Doubtless his early experiences in the little *Tom Thumb* stood him in good **stead** during **this voyage.**   Immediately on his arrival **at Sydney, and the tidings of the** disaster **becoming known,** the necessary arrangements for the **relief of the** shipwrecked men were made, three ships being **at once despatched on this service.**   They were the *Rolla,* **bound** to Canton, **and the two** Government schooners *Cumberland* and *Frances.*   The captain of the first-named ship had generously volunteered to accompany Flinders, **who was on** the point of sailing with the two schooners only, **and** he voluntarily agreed to call at the reef on his way to **China, so as to convey** the majority of the shipwrecked **people to Canton, where they would have no** difficulty, it **was thought, in** finding some homeward-bound India-**man, in which they could obtain a** passage to England.

It **is needless to say that but little time was lost in** getting away **from the** scene of their unfortunate adven-**ture.**   Everything **being ready by the** 11th, **and all the stores worth saving having been** embarked, **the three** ships took their **departure from the reef.**   The *Frances* **returned to Sydney** with those officers and men who were desirous of settling in that colony; the *Cumber-land*, with Captain Flinders, two officers, and eight men, sailed direct to England *viâ* Torres Strait, Mauritius, and the Cape of Good Hope; while Lieutenants Fowler and Flinders, with the remainder of the officers and crews of the *Porpoise* and *Cato* (including John **Frank-lin**), embarked on board the *Rolla* for passage to China.

Captain Flinders elected to return to England **in the** *Cumberland*, as he was anxious to get home as soon as possible, in order to report his discoveries, and to pre-pare his notes and charts with a view to publication. On his way home he touched at Mauritius for water and provisions, when **he** was made a prisoner of war **and his** vessel seized by the French Governor. This **act was** a direct infringement of international law, and con-trary to the established and recognised usages of civi-lised nations, for **it** has always been held that marine surveyors, and scientific expeditions of all descrip-**tions,** whose work **is** of importance, not only to the nation that employs them, but **also to** mankind **in** general, are invariably specially exempted from capture, or detention, in time of war. To the discredit of **the** French nation, Captain Flinders, although he was **in** possession of a passport from the First Consul, was **not** only made a prisoner, but he **was** detained on the island for a period of no less than six and a half years!

On his liberation and return to England, he wrote the narrative of his memorable voyage, and, sick at heart and weary at the unjust treatment he had received, died **on** 19th July 1814, on the very day that his **work,** recording the labours of his life, was published.

Under the **command of** such a man as Flinders, an officer who possessed high scientific attainments, combined with the practical knowledge of a skilful seaman, and with whose **professional** pursuits he was closely connected for a period of over two **years,** it is not surprising that Franklin, although **a very** young officer, acquired during **his** service **in the** *Investigator* a thorough knowledge **of** a sailor's work, and was rapidly becoming an experienced surveyor.

The *Rolla,* with Franklin **and his companions on** board, **in** due course of time reached Canton. **Here** they fortunately found **a** large squadron **of** Indiamen on the point of sailing for England, under the command **of Commodore Nathaniel** Dance of the Honourable East India Company's service. No difficulty was experienced **in obtaining a passage home for** the officers and men of the *Investigator,* who were distributed among the different **vessels composing the** squadron ; Franklin, with his late first lieutenant **and commander,** Mr. **Fowler,** being appointed to the *Earl Camden,* which flew the broad pendant of Commodore **Dance.**

The squadron consisted of the following ships :—

Earl Camden.	**Earl of** *Abergavenny.*
Royal George.	**Henry** *Addington.*
Warley.	*Bombay Castle.*
Coutts.	*Cumberland.*
Alfred.	*Hope.*
Wexford.	*Dorsetshire.*
Ganges.	*Warren Hastings.*
Exeter.	*Ocean.*

These vessels were all **over a** thousand tons burthen, and carried from thirty to thirty-six guns, the majority, **however,** being of light calibre. Their hulls were painted in imitation of line-of-battle ships and frigates, the **more easily to** deceive the enemy's cruisers **and** privateers, that were continually on the watch, ready to pounce upon, and snap up, any fat rich Indiaman that might fall into their clutches. Being merchant ships, they were, of course, very much under-manned for fighting purposes, no ship having more than about 140 men in her crew, the greater proportion of which were Lascars and Chinamen. The arrival and subsequent distribution of the shipwrecked **crews** of the *Porpoise* and *Cato*, all stalwart **and** well-disciplined men, must have been a welcome addition to the somewhat weak and inferior crews of the Indiamen.

This **large** squadron, laden with the rich wares and merchandise **of China and** Japan, was accompanied **by** about **twenty other,** though smaller, country ships. They sailed from Canton on the 31st January 1804. No event of importance happened until the 14th of **the** following month, when, as they were entering the Straits of Malacca, near the island of Pulo Aor, some strange vessels were reported in sight from the masthead. These were soon made out to be a French squadron under the command of Admiral Linois, consisting of the line-of-battle ship *Marengo* of seventy-four guns, **two large** frigates, a twenty-two-gun corvette, **and a** sixteen-gun brig. The French admiral having received intimation **of the** sailing **of** the Indiamen, had **put** to sea from Batavia, with the intention of intercepting them, and, as he, hoped, swelling the coffers of France with the rich **spoils** he made sure he was about to capture.

But Admiral Linois had reckoned without **his host,** for, in his calculations, he had not given sturdy Nathaniel Dance **credit for** opposing, much less for defeating, the strong force he had under his command.

Immediately the French sighted the ships they were

in search of, **they** bore down **in** hot pursuit; but instead of seeing the English merchant ships crowd on all sail to escape, as they not unnaturally expected, **they observed** them form in order of battle in perfect **regularity and make the** necessary preparations, **not only for** resisting, but also for acting on the offensive. **The bold front** shown by the English somewhat perplexed the **French** admiral, and as the day was waning, he hauled to the wind, and stood off to some distance, preferring **to wait** for daylight before commencing hostile operations.

The English ships, **all well under command, lay-to** for the night **in** order of battle, **the** brave Commodore scorning to take advantage of **the** darkness to endeavour to effect an escape. Admiral Linois was so deceived by **the confident front shown** by the English, that he felt convinced the squadron was partly composed of men-of-war, and under this impression he hesitated to attack on the following morning. **Observing** the hesitancy **on** the part of the French Admiral, **Commodore Dance** made the signal for his squadron **to continue their course under easy** sail. Seeing his opportunity, Linois also made sail and advanced with the object of endeavouring **to** cut off some of the rear ships of the British squadron. But Dance was fully equal **to the** occasion, and being determined **to keep his squadron intact, he** instantly **ran up the signal, "Tack in** succession, bear down **in line ahead, and** engage the enemy," This plucky signal **was, as may** be imagined, received with ringing cheers by the crews **of** the English ships, and, to the astonishment of the French **admiral, he soon had the** whole British squadron standing towards him in a formidable and resolute line of battle.

It must indeed **have** been **a wonderful** sight **to see a**

DEFEAT OF ADMIRAL LINOIS BY COMMODORE DANCE, 15TH FEBRUARY 1804.

fleet of merchant ships steadily advancing, with a bold undaunted front, to the attack of a hostile squadron composed of smart and efficient men of war, and commanded by one of the most talented and dashing admirals in the French navy. Young Franklin had smelt powder at Copenhagen ; he had subsequently experienced many perils and dangers both by sea and land ; his brief professional career had been an adventurous one, but on this occasion, when he hoisted the signal, by the direction of the brave old Commodore, to "engage the enemy" (for he was doing duty as signal-midshipman on board the *Camden* throughout that eventful day), his bosom must have swelled with pride, and his face flushed with a glow of enthusiasm and triumph when he reflected—if he had time for reflection—that he was fortunate enough to be one of those few destined to play a part in such a gallant affair.

After the action had lasted a little more than three-quarters of an hour, the French ceased firing, having had enough of it, and made sail away. Instantly the gallant Dance threw out the signal for a "general chase;" and then was seen the extraordinary spectacle of a French squadron of men-of-war, commanded by an undoubtedly brave and most distinguished officer, retreating in hot haste, and some confusion, before a fleet of English armed merchant ships ! Having pursued the flying Frenchmen for upwards of two hours, and having fully upheld the honour, dignity and credit of the British flag, and also, doubtless, considering the safety of the valuable merchandise committed to his charge, the Commodore recalled his chasing ships, reformed his squadron, and proceeded on his homeward course, and was not again molested by the valiant Frenchman.

This action fought by Commodore Dance stands out almost unparalleled for skill and daring among the numerous gallant deeds at sea that were constantly being performed in those days.

Admiral Linois candidly acknowledged his defeat, ascribing it to the superiority of the opposing force, little thinking that the squadron with which he had been engaged was composed only of merchant vessels ! He also admitted that he was pursued by the English ships for three hours, during which time, he states, they discharged "several ineffective broadsides" at him.

The promptness and decision of Commodore Dance, combined with his boldness and the gallantry of those who served under him, without doubt, saved from capture the rich and valuable fleet that was intrusted to his care. On the arrival of the ships in England, the Commodore received at the hands of his sovereign the well-merited honour of knighthood, while other rewards and honours, of a more substantial character, were deservedly bestowed on him and his brave companions in arms.

The voyage having terminated, Franklin was discharged from the *Earl Camden* on the 7th of August 1804, and, after an absence of a little more than three years, he had the inexpressible pleasure of returning home, and once more rejoining the family circle, and of visiting his old friends at Spilsby.

CHAPTER V.

APPOINTED TO "BELLEROPHON"—BATTLE OF TRAFALGAR—JOINS THE "BEDFORD"—ATTACK ON NEW ORLEANS—ON HALF-PAY.

1804–1815

> " War, he sung, is toil and trouble,
> Honour but an empty bubble."—DRYDEN.

ON the day following his discharge from the *Earl Camden*, Franklin was appointed to the *Bellerophon*, commanded by Captain Loring; but as she did not arrive from the West Indies until two days after his appointment was dated, and as he does not appear to have joined her until the 20th of the following month, we may assume that he spent the intermediate time with his friends on a well-earned leave.

He first appears on the books of the *Bellerophon*, as an A.B., and then as a midshipman. In those days, it was not an uncommon occurrence for a young officer to be entered on the books of a ship, if there was no vacancy for a midshipman, with the rating of one of the ship's company, with the object of enabling him to continue to count his time in the navy. This was presumably the reason why his name is shown on the ship's books with the rating of A.B. Franklin, it must be acknowledged, had enjoyed but a short leave after his long and adventurous service in Australia before he was appointed to a ship; but in those times the officers of the navy were in constant requisition. England required their services, and there was but little half-pay for her sons, and less leave.

The duty on which the *Bellerophon* was engaged was the blockade of the French fleet in the harbour of Brest, and this was rigidly maintained during the whole winter by the squadron under the command of Lord Collingwood; this service was a new experience to our young friend. On the 24th of April 1805, Captain Loring was relieved in the command of the *Bellerophon* by Captain John Cooke, and on the 29th September, of the same year, Lord Nelson joined the fleet in the *Victory*, and took over the command from Lord Collingwood.

On the ever-memorable 21st of October, Franklin was signal-midshipman of the *Bellerophon*, and was, in all probability, the officer who saw, and perhaps reported to his captain, Nelson's celebrated signal. All who have read the account of the battle of Trafalgar will remember the prominent part that was played in that action by the *Bellerophon*, and how, at the end of that glorious day, she had to mourn the loss of her brave captain, the master, one midshipman, and twenty-five men killed; while her captain of marines, boatswain, one master's-mate, four midshipmen, and 120 men were returned as wounded. No less than six of Franklin's messmates were rendered *hors de combat* during that eventful struggle, but his ship had emerged from it covered with glory, and many of the hostile vessels could vouch for the hard knocks and rough treatment they received, from the stout old seventy-four. Franklin was himself noted for "evincing very conspicuous zeal and activity" during that glorious day. He was stationed during the fight on the poop, and was one, out of only **four or five**, in that particular part of the ship who escaped unhurt. It was well said **of him** that "he was in battle fearless and in danger brave."

The following is an extract from the official **log of** the *Bellerophon* on the day of the battle, which may prove interesting :—

"Ten minutes past noon, the *Royal Sovereign* opened fire on the enemy's centre. At thirteen minutes past **noon**, answered the general signal 16. **At** twenty minutes, the *Royal Sovereign* broke through enemy's **line astern of a Spanish** three-decker. **12.20** opened **fire on** the enemy. **At 12.30** engaging **on both sides** in passing through the enemy's **line** astern of a Spanish two-decker. At thirty-five minutes, while hauling to the wind, fell **on** board **the** French two-decked ship *L'Aigle*, with our starboard bow on her starboard quarter ; **our** fore-yard locking with her main one. Kept up a brisk fire both **on** her and the Spanish ship **on** the larboard bow, **at** the same time receiving the fire of two ships, one astern, the other on the larboard quarter. At one o'clock the main and mizen topmasts fell **over the side. At** 1.5 **the** master fell. **At** 1.11 Captain John **Cooke** fell. Still foul of the *L'Aigle.* The quarter-deck, **poop, and** forecastle being **nearly** cleared by troops on board *L'Aigle.* 1.40 *L'Aigle* dropped to leeward, under a raking fire **from** us as she fell off. At three, took possession of the Spanish ship *El Monarca.* Casualties, twenty-eight killed and 127 wounded."

On **the death of Captain** Cooke, the first lieutenant, **Mr.** William Pryce-Cumby, took command of the ship, and fought her until the end of **the** action. He was relieved on the 4th November by Captain E. Rotheram, who was Lord Collingwood's flag-captain in the *Royal Sovereign.*

The *Bellerophon* anchored in Plymouth Sound on the

3rd December 1805; after making good the injuries sustained in the action, she was employed cruising between Finisterre and Ushant, with occasional visits to Plymouth, during the following eighteen months.

On the 24th of October 1807, Mr. Franklin, with 46 petty officers, 110 A.B.'s, and 92 ordinary seamen, were drafted from the *Bellerophon* to the *Bedford* of seventy-four guns. Franklin was entered on the books as a master's-mate, but was made an acting lieutenant by order of Admiral Sir Sidney Smith on the following 5th of December; he was confirmed in that rank by their Lordships on the 11th February 1808. Prior to joining the *Bedford*, Franklin received intelligence of the death of his eldest brother, Thomas Adams, who died at Spilsby, and was buried on the 11th October 1807, aged thirty-four years.

Leaving Cawsand Bay on the 11th of November 1807, the *Bedford* formed part of a large squadron that was employed cruising for some weeks off Lisbon; she was afterwards engaged, in company with a squadron of Portuguese ships, in escorting the royal family of Portugal from Lisbon to Brazil, whither they fled for safety on the occasion of the invasion of Portugal by Marshal Junot. They reached Rio de Janeiro on the 7th of March 1808. For the next two years the *Bedford* was stationed on the east coast of South America, but she returned to England in August 1810. From the latter end of that year until February 1813, she was employed with the fleet engaged in the unfortunate Walcheren expedition and in the blockade of Flushing and the Texel.

To a man of Franklin's energetic disposition, accustomed as he had been to service of a more exciting nature, this wearisome blockading, cruising in the North

Sea, or at anchor on the seventeen-fathom bank in sight of the West Capel Church, with nothing to relieve the dull monotony, must have indeed been depressing. It was, however, excellent training for both officers and men; the constant sea-work in a latitude where gales of wind and heavy squalls are not unfrequent, was a valuable experience that could not be otherwise than beneficial. It was during the time he was engaged on this service, that he received the melancholy news of the loss of his mother. She died and was buried at Spilsby on the 27th November 1810, aged fifty-nine years.

Early in 1813, to the inexpressible relief and gratification of those on board, orders were received for the *Bedford* to convoy a fleet of merchant vessels to the West Indies, and she left Plymouth on this service on the 3rd April. Barbados was reached on the 23rd May, and after a short cruise among the beautiful islands of the West Indian group, she returned to England, arriving in the Downs on the 6th September 1813. For the succeeding nine months the *Bedford* was stationed on her old cruising-ground off the Texel and Scheveningen, but in September 1814 she was again sent with a convoy across the Atlantic to the West Indies. Thence she proceeded to New Orleans, which was reached on the 13th December, having been despatched in order to assist in the operations about to be undertaken against the Americans.

An attack on New Orleans having been decided upon, it was deemed advisable to land the attacking force at the head of Lake Borgne; but in order to do so, it was necessary to clear the lake of the enemy's gunboats that had assembled there in some force. This service Vice-Admiral Cochrane undertook to carry out with the naval force at his disposal. Accordingly a division of boats, containing about 1000 officers and men, belonging to the British ships that were stationed off New Orleans, left on the night of the 12th of December 1814, under the command of Captain Nicholas Lockyer. Franklin was present on this occasion, and was probably in command of a division, or subdivision, of the boats employed. On the forenoon of the following day, after a long and toilsome pull of thirty-six miles against a strong current, the enemy's gunboats were sighted, and a desperate attack was made on them, resulting in a complete victory for the British; but it was dearly purchased, for so desperate was the resistance, that a loss was sustained on our side of three midshipmen and fourteen men killed, while Captain Lockyer, four lieutenants (including Franklin), one lieutenant of marines, three master's-mates, seven midshipmen (two mortally), and sixty-one men were wounded. The loss sustained by the Americans was slight in comparison. For this action Franklin received a medal, and was honourably mentioned in despatches.

During the subsequent attack on New Orleans, Franklin, having partially recovered from his wound, assisted in conducting the indescribably arduous operation of cutting a canal across the neck of land between the Bayou Calatan and the Mississippi. For his conduct and gallant exertions on the morning of the 8th of January 1815, on which occasion he commanded a division of seamen under Captain Rowland Money,[1] when a large body of Americans strongly en-

---

[1] Captain Rowland Money was desperately wounded at this engagement, having both bones of his right leg shattered by a musket shot as he stormed the battery. For his conspicuous bravery on this,

trenched on the right bank of the river was defeated, he was officially and very warmly recommended for promotion. The *Bedford* sailed on her homeward voyage in March, and reached Spithead on the 30th May 1815. She was paid off on the 5th of July following. In spite of his long and uninterrupted service in the old seventy-four, extending over a period of nearly eight years in that ship, we find him two days after paying off the *Bedford*, appointed as first lieutenant of the *Forth*, commanded by Captain Sir William Bolton. He joined her on the 9th July, and remained as first lieutenant until she was paid off on the following 2nd of September.

During the short time that Franklin was in this ship, she was employed in conveying the Duchesse D'Angouleme to Dieppe, having been specially prepared for the reception of Her Royal Highness. After paying off the *Forth*, Franklin was doomed for the succeeding three years to pass a period of professional inactivity. The peace of 1815 necessitated a serious reduction in the navy, and several officers were consequently thrown out of employment. Franklin was, therefore, like many others, compelled to rusticate on half-pay, waiting for something to turn up. He was not, however, a man to lead a life of idleness; he therefore turned his attention to scientific pursuits, for which he had always evinced an inclination, and which, he thought, would afford fuller scope for his talents.

and other occasions, he was strongly recommended for promotion by Sir Alexander Cochrane. He was sent home with despatches, was posted, and made a C.B.

CHAPTER VI.

RETROSPECT OF GEOGRAPHICAL EXPLORATION IN THE ARCTIC REGIONS.

1607–1773.

> "Oh, who can tell, save he whose heart hath tried,
> And danced in triumph o'er the waters wide,
> The exulting sense, the pulse's maddening play,
> That thrills the wanderer of that trackless way?"
> —*The Corsair.*

ENGLAND in the year 1818 being at **peace** with all the world, had time to turn her thoughts to eminently peaceful pursuits, and to employ her men and money on equally glorious, and perhaps more important, matters than war.

Among other subjects, that of geographical **discovery** was discussed, and the encouragement **of** Arctic exploration which had been allowed to slumber since the unsuccessful attempt of Captain Phipps **to reach** the North Pole in 1773, was again revived.

Foremost among **the** promoters of geographical research in high latitudes **at** this time was Sir John Barrow, the **Secretary of the** Admiralty. This ardent and **zealous** geographer **had very** carefully, **and** with masterly skill and ability, after much tedious research, collected **all the** reports that had been received **during the** early part **of the century,** bearing on the condition and the **locality of the ice** in high northern

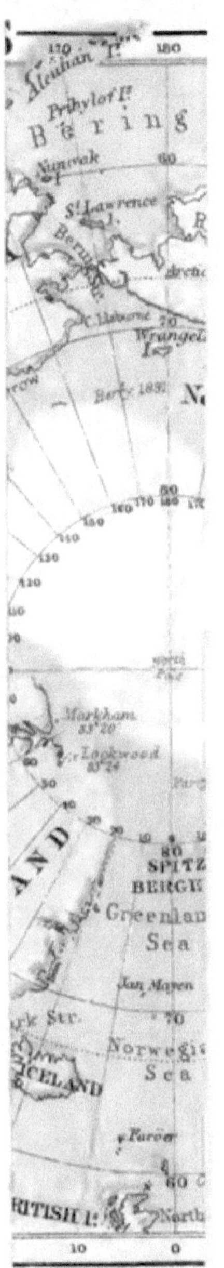
170
180
Aleutian I.
Prybilof I.
BERING
Nunivak I.
St. Lawrence I.
Bering Str.
Arctic
C. Lisburne
Wrangel I.
Barrow
Berg 1897
N
80
160 170 180 170
150
140
130
120
110
100
90
North Pole
Markham 83°20'
Lockwood 83°24'
80
70
60
50
40
30
20
10
0
SPITZ BERGEN
Greenland Sea
AND
Jan Mayen
70
Denmark Str.
Norwegian Sea
ICELAND
Faroe
60
BRITISH I.
North
10
0

latitudes. With this information as a basis, he drew out an elaborate and well-prepared scheme for the exploration of the northern regions. His plan being warmly supported by the President and Council of the Royal Society, also met with the approval of the Board of Admiralty. So well was the idea received by the public, that it was finally entertained and approved by the Government, who resolved, forthwith, to despatch two expeditions, one with the object of endeavouring to discover a north-west passage round the northern continent of America; the other for the purpose of attempting to reach the North Pole.

One of the principal reasons that led to the organisation and despatch of these expeditions, was the very favourable reports brought home by the whalers in 1817, regarding the state and quantity of the ice in the Spitzbergen and Greenland seas; and also perhaps to the writings of, and arguments advanced by, the two Scoresbys, father and son, two of the most experienced, skilful, and talented whaling captains that our country has ever produced. It was also reported that during the preceding three years, large quantities of heavy polar ice had drifted down from the north to unusually low latitudes; and in 1817, the hitherto almost inaccessible eastern coast of Greenland, it was stated, had been actually visited by whale-ships between the 70th and 80th parallels of latitude, while the intermediate sea between Greenland and Spitzbergen had been reported as comparatively free of ice. It was, therefore, considered to be a particularly favourable time to undertake exploration in those waters.

It may be of interest here to note, that in 1745 an Act of Parliament was passed, offering a reward of

£20,000 "to such person or persons who shall discover a north-west passage through Hudson's Strait to the western and southern oceans of America." In the year 1776 a sum of £5000 was offered by the English Government to the first person who should reach the 89th parallel of latitude. In 1818, when it was decided to despatch the two expeditions just alluded to, proportionate rewards were offered by Act of Parliament for the different degrees of latitude reached. Thus, any vessel that first succeeded in reaching the 83rd parallel would be entitled to a reward of £1000; double **that** sum would be granted for crossing the 85th parallel; £3000 to any vessel, or person, that should reach 87° N.; **£4000 for** the 88th parallel; **and** £5000 for the **Pole.** £5000 was also offered to the first ship that should **cross the** 110th west meridian of longitude, north of America.[1]

These large rewards were **offered as** incentives to whaling captains and others, who might be tempted, by the chance of gaining them, to push northwards through the ice, and so increase the limited knowledge we then possessed of the northern portion of our globe.

The command of the expedition that **was** to be sent in quest of a north-west passage was conferred on Lieutenant John Ross, who was ably seconded by that prince of Arctic navigators, Lieutenant, afterwards Sir Edward Parry. The doings of this expedition will not, however, **occupy** any part of this history.

The command of the expedition that it was decided to **send to** the North Pole, was intrusted to Commander

---

[1] **This** reward was actually claimed by, and paid to, Lieutenants Parry and Liddon, who succeeded in crossing the 110th meridian in the discovery-ships *Hecla* and *Griper* in 1819.

David Buchan, and Lieutenant John Franklin was **the**
officer selected as his second in command.

Perhaps it will be as well here to give a brief retro-
spect of the geographical work that had already been
accomplished in the direction towards which one of **the**
new expeditions—and the one in which we are more
particularly interested—was ordered to proceed. Setting
aside **all** the mythical and unauthenticated stories of
voyages, that are reported to have been made with the
object of discovering a short route to China and Japan
in a high northern latitude, we start with the voyage
of Henry Hudson, which, for skill and daring, stands
out conspicuously among the many brilliant and fearless
maritime achievements, for which the sixteenth and seventeenth centuries are so pre-eminently distinguished.

This bold navigator sailed from Gravesend on the 1st
of May 1607, in what in those days was called a " cock-
boat," named the *Hopewell*, with a crew consisting of
ten men and a boy. This was the scale on which Arctic
expeditions in the early part of the seventeenth century
were equipped ! **Hudson's** orders **were** to proceed **to**
India by sailing across the North Pole ; and, with his
mind fully made up to act in accordance with the letter
of his instructions, he confidently started. Stretching
across towards Greenland, and sighting that mysterious
continent, he steered along its eastern coast in a northerly
direction, with, apparently, **but** little hindrance from
ice. Having reached the latitude of 73° N., he named
the land then in sight " Hold with Hope," as he was
then hopeful **of** success ; but being prevented from
making any further **progress** northwards by the heavy
masses of ice he encountered along the coast, he shaped
a course to the north-east, and stood **over** towards

Spitzbergen,[1] which he sighted on the 27th June in latitude 77°, apparently in the neighbourhood of the Vogel Sang Hoek of Barents ; but the sea was much encompassed by ice, and he experienced great difficulty in pushing on.   Subsequently he sighted and named Hakluyt Headland, the north-west point of Spitzbergen, a name it still bears.

The highest latitude reached by Hudson during this enterprising voyage, was about 80° 30′ N. on the 16th of July, probably off that portion of the coast of Spitzbergen, which is separated from North-East Island by Hinlopen Strait.   After again examining the sea between Spitzbergen and Greenland, and finding it impassable to the north, in consequence of a barrier of heavy ice stretching across in every direction in which he sought to penetrate it, Hudson determined upon returning to England.   He reached the Thames in safety on the 15th of September, after a voyage which, for fearlessness and audacity, has no equal on record.   The results of this expedition were, from a geographical point of view, eminently satisfactory, for Hudson had succeeded, in his frail and poorly equipped little craft, in not only discovering portions of the coasts of Greenland and Spitzbergen hitherto unknown, but he had also navigated his little vessel to a position in a higher northern latitude than had ever before been reached. This high position was not surpassed, or even equalled, for more than 160 years, when Captain Phipps in 1773 succeeded in reaching the latitude of 80° 48′ to the north of Spitzbergen.

From a commercial point of view, Hudson's voyage

---

[1] Spitzbergen was discovered by the celebrated Dutch Arctic navigator William Barents in 1596.

must always be regarded as a **great success, for the**
report that he made of the numerous whales and walruses he had seen, led to the establishment of that lucra-
tive and prosperous fishery which has, with varying
success, been prosecuted to the present day. The east
coast of Greenland, discovered by Hudson, was not again
visited by any known navigator for the space of 200
years, when Scoresby, an energetic and enterprising
whaling captain, taking advantage of an unusual opening
in the ice, sailed his ship through the pack, and thus
succeeded in rediscovering that coast which had, **for so**
long, been as a **sealed** book to navigators.

Three years after the return of Hudson, Captain
Jonas Poole was despatched by the Muscovy Company,
in a vessel called the *Amitie*, of seventy tons burthen,
with directions to proceed to Spitzbergen, and to search
for " the likelihood of a trade or passage that way." The
crew of his ship consisted of fourteen men and boys.
Poole **was** much hindered by ice and bad weather, but,
in spite of these obstacles to navigation, he succeeded in
making a fairly good survey of the west coast of Spitzbergen, giving names to the most prominent capes,
headlands, and bays. Failing in his efforts to penetrate to a high latitude, he returned to England in the
end of August. **He was** again **sent up** the following
year, with instructions to explore to the north of Spitzbergen, and **to** report on the existence, or otherwise, of
an open and navigable **sea in that** direction. **This**
voyage was not purely geographical, but had also commercial interests **in** view, the capture **of whales and**
seals being **one of its chief** objects. **It returned** to
England, however, without achieving any great success,
either geographically or pecuniarily.

From this time the west and south coasts of Spitzbergen were frequently, indeed almost annually, visited by ships of different nations, principally English and Dutch, in quest of whales, seals, and walruses; and although there was not, of course, any accurate survey, the coast-line was fairly well delineated on the charts of the day. The reports of these voyages, that are still extant, deal principally with matters relating to the valuable fishing industry that had then been established, and contain but little geographical information of importance, either in connection with discovery, or with the state and locality of the ice.

It was not until the year 1773 that the English Government, at the instigation of Mr. Daines Barrington,[1] decided upon sending an expedition for the purpose of ascertaining how far navigation was practicable in the direction of the North Pole. In this decision they received the warm support of the President and Council of the Royal Society.

The ships selected for this expedition were the *Racehorse* and *Carcass*. They were what were then termed bomb-vessels, and being strongly constructed, were considered the most suitable for the special service on which they were to be employed. The command of the expedition was intrusted to Captain the Hon. Constantine Phipps (afterwards Lord Mulgrave), who hoisted his pendant in the *Racehorse*. Commander Lutwidge was appointed to the command of the *Carcass*, in which ship Horatio Nelson also served as a midshipman; it was thus among the ice floes of the Arctic Seas that our great

---

[1] Mr. Barrington was a son of Lord Barrington, and was brother of Admiral Samuel Barrington, who was a very distinguished naval officer.

naval hero received his first real training in a ship of war, and learnt how to combat with difficulties, and how successfully to overcome them.

The two **ships were thoroughly** overhauled and prepared for the service on which they were to be engaged, and although of strong construction, they were additionally strengthened by a stout doubling of hard wood on the outside, to assist in resisting the pressure of the ice. The complement of each ship was twenty-two officers and seventy men. Captains Phipps and Lutwidge were officers of great experience, **and** of known scientific attainments. The remainder of the officers were also **specially** selected, and a civilian, **Mr.** Israel Lyon, a gentleman of great mathematical reputation, was appointed, on the recommendation of the Board of Longitude, to the *Racehorse* in the capacity of astronomer. Stores and provisions of the very best quality were liberally supplied to the two ships, and they were each fitted with an apparatus for distilling **fresh** water, the invention of Mr. Irving, the surgeon of the *Racehorse*. This was probably the first time that water was procured in the Royal Navy by the condensation of steam.

On the 23rd of May, the First Lord of the Admiralty,[1] accompanied by the French Ambassador, paid the ships a visit, and on the 4th of **the** following month the expedition sailed from Sheerness.

The orders received by Captain Phipps were to the **effect** that he **was**, with the two ships under his command, **to proceed to the** North Pole, or as close to it as ice and other obstructions would permit, as nearly as possible **on** the meridian **of** Greenwich. **If** successful in reaching the **Pole, he** was to return immediately and

---

[1] The Earl of Sandwich.

report himself, and he was specially directed to be careful to make all necessary observations that would assist in improving navigation and promoting general knowledge.

On the 19th of June the Arctic Circle was crossed, and on the 28th the coast of Spitzbergen was sighted, which Captain Phipps describes as being formed of high barren black rocks, in many places bare and pointed, and in others covered with snow. No signs of vegetation were visible. Continuing their course to the northward, the expedition skirted along the west coast of Spitzbergen, until, on the 4th of July, they cast anchor in Hamburg Cove, about three miles south of Magdalena Bay. The weather, however, was exceedingly tempestuous, necessitating an immediate departure, without giving the officers an opportunity of exploring the coast in the vicinity, or of taking any magnetic or other observations. They were not even afforded time to replenish their tanks with water, which, in spite of the distilling apparatus, they were desirous of accomplishing. Proceeding northwards, they encountered an almost impenetrable ice pack in the neighbourhood of Hakluyt Headland. They made many futile efforts to push through this pack, but always without success, although they skirted along it for many miles, running into every indentation, going round every point, and forcing the ships, by carrying a heavy press of sail, through the ice wherever it appeared to be loosely packed. The outlook was as cheerless and unpromising as could be well imagined, for to the northward, as far as they could see, appeared an unbroken frozen ocean, without water or any opening in the pack being visible.

On the 10th of July, after great toil and incessant

labour, and not without severe buffetings from the ice, the latitude 80° 36′ N. was reached on the 2nd meridian east of Greenwich. Four days after, the ships were compelled to seek shelter from a westerly gale in Fair Haven, where they remained until the evening of the 18th. The officers, profiting by their stay, took a series of pendulum observations, and made a rough survey of the harbour and adjacent country. On the 25th, Moffin Island was visited. Thence the ships plied in a north-easterly direction, and on the 27th were in latitude, by dead reckoning, 80° 48′, and longitude 15° E., about due north of the central part of the Spitzbergen group. This was the most northern position reached by the expedition. Here their endeavours to prosecute further researches in a northerly direction were completely frustrated by a large solid pack, which not only defied their efforts to penetrate, but compelled them to retreat to the southward, so as to avoid being beset in the broken-up ice that is invariably encountered on the out-skirts of a large pack.

On the 30th of July the ships were imprisoned in a pool of water, so surrounded by ice that it was impossible to escape out of it. The dimensions of this water-hole gradually diminished, until the vessels were completely beset by the ice, nor was any indication of water seen in any direction. The prospect of releasing the ships from their icy bondage being exceedingly problematical, preparations were made for abandoning them, and the boats were ordered to be equipped with this object in view. Provisions and stores were hoisted up from below and apportioned to each boat, and the studding sails were cut up in order to make belts for the men to facili-tate the dragging of the boats over the ice.

In the midst of all these preparations, the *Carcass*, driven by the erratic movements of the pack, was forced alongside the *Racehorse*, and it required no small amount of exertion and labour, on the part of the officers and men of the two ships, to separate and subsequently secure the vessels in safety. The hazardous expedient of abandoning their ships was, happily, not resorted to, for on the 10th August the ice suddenly loosened, and by noon on that day they had the indescribable gratification and relief of feeling, and knowing, that the peril was past. Captain Phipps being fully convinced that nothing further could be achieved that year in the way of exploration, wisely decided upon returning to England. Spitzbergen was left on the 19th August, and after sailing along the edge of the ice for a few days, the ships bore up for England, arriving at Orfordness on the 25th September, after a most tempestuous passage, during which they lost several boats, and had to throw two of their guns overboard. They were both paid out of commission at Sheerness on the 13th of the following month.

The results of this expedition were, geographically, unimportant; its failure was generally attributed to the fact that the year was an extremely unfavourable one for exploration in high latitudes. The Admiralty, however, to mark their appreciation of the way in which the work had been carried out by the expedition, promoted Commander Lutwidge of the *Carcass* to the rank of captain, and raised the first lieutenant of the *Racehorse* to the rank of Commander.

CHAPTER VII.

EXPEDITION *OF BUCHAN AND* FRANKLIN *TOWARDS* THE NORTH POLE.

1818.

> " High on **the** northern silence, speechless things
> Own the bare ice, and reign the Ocean's kings."
>
> —*Paradise of Birds.*

DAVID BUCHAN, **who was** selected **to** command the expedition **to be despatched** in quest **of the** North Pole, was promoted **to the rank** of lieutenant **on the** 29th of January 1806 ; consequently **he was only** two **years** senior, as a lieutenant, to Franklin. He had, however, prior to his appointment to the expedition, been raised to the rank of commander. He was an accomplished surveying officer, and had done good work in mapping out the coast in the neighbourhood of Newfoundland.

In 1810, whilst in command of the schooner *Adonis*, he had been selected by Sir John Duckworth to conduct an exploring expedition into the interior of Newfoundland, a country in those days regarded as a complete *terra incognita.* This service was satisfactorily accomplished, in spite of the hostile attitude of the natives, who treacherously murdered two of his men. Whilst so employed he penetrated a distance of about 130 miles into the interior. His report of this journey is exceedingly interesting.

The selection of Franklin, who was then a lieutenant

of ten years' seniority, to command the second ship was, in all probability, due to the zeal and ability he had displayed as a young officer when serving under a navigator of such repute as Captain Flinders. The very fact that he had served his apprenticeship in the navy under so renowned and distinguished an officer, was almost, in itself, sufficient justification for his selection to such an important appointment, irrespective of his own personal qualifications, and the extraordinary aptitude for marine surveying and other scientific pursuits, that he had evinced as a young officer. Neither Buchan or Franklin, however, were experienced in ice navigation, although the former must have been able to form some idea of the difficulties of navigating a ship in the pack from his long service in Newfoundland waters.

The vessels selected were the *Dorothea*, a ship of 370 tons, and the *Trent*, a brig of 250 tons. Buchan was given the command of the *Dorothea*, and Franklin was appointed, on the 14th January 1818, as lieutenant in command of the *Trent*. The two ships had been specially built for the whale-fishery, in which they were engaged when chartered by the Government, but they were additionally strengthened and made as strong and durable as wood and iron could make them. The complement of the senior officer's ship was twelve officers and forty-three seamen and marines, while that of the *Trent* was only ten officers and twenty-eight men. A master and mate, experienced in the Greenland fishery, were appointed to each ship to act as pilots when in the ice. The ships were supplied with stores and provisions to last for an anticipated absence of two years, and both were carefully and thoroughly equipped for the important service on which they were to be engaged.

It is much to be regretted that neither Commander Buchan or Lieutenant Franklin published any account of this expedition in which they took such leading and prominent parts; the former omitted to do so, because he was of opinion that the voyage was not of sufficient importance to attract the notice and arouse the interest of the general public, and the latter had no leisure on his return to undertake the work. The only narrative of the expedition that appeared, was the one written by Captain Beechey (who was first lieutenant of the *Trent* with Franklin), and published in 1843, twenty-five years after the return of the expedition. It is mainly from this work that the following account has been compiled.

Captain Buchan's instructions directed him to make the best of his way into the Spitzbergen seas, and then to endeavour to force his ships northward between Spitzbergen and Greenland, without stopping to visit the coast of either of those countries. The authorities at the Admiralty, advised most probably by the leading men of science of the day, were evidently impressed by the vague and unauthenticated reports that, from time to time, had cropped up relative to the marvellously high latitudes attained by the whalers, and other vessels engaged in the slaughter of oil-producing animals, in those regions; for in their official instructions they informed Captain Buchan that the sea, to the northward of Spitzbergen, had been generally found free from ice as far north as 83° 30′ or 84°! Therefore, they said, there is reason to expect that the sea may continue open still further to the northward, in which case Captain Buchan was directed to steer due north, and use his utmost efforts to reach the North Pole.

If successful in doing so, he was ordered, if the weather was favourable, to remain for a few days in the vicinity of the Pole for the purpose of making observations, which, it was remarked, his interesting and unexampled situation might furnish him. After leaving the North Pole, he was directed to shape a course for Bering's Strait, or, if this was impracticable, he was to sail round the north end of Greenland and return home by Baffin's Bay and Davis's Strait. If unable to get to the Pole, he was told to direct his efforts solely to reaching Bering's Strait, and thus accomplish the long-sought-for, and frequently attempted, north-west passage. In the event of this being easily achieved, it was left to Captain Buchan's discretion to return by the same way, or to sail for England *viâ* Kamchatka and the Sandwich Islands. He was also told to arrange with Captain John Ross, who was in command of the expedition that was being despatched by Baffin's Bay in search of a north-west passage, to fix upon a preconcerted rendezvous, at which they should both meet in the Pacific.

The advancement of science, other than geographical research, was one of the chief aims of the expedition, and valuable instruments were therefore supplied to both ships for ascertaining the variation and inclination of the magnetic needle, the intensity of the magnetic force, and how far the needle would be affected by the presence of atmospherical electricity. Various astronomical and meteorological instruments were also provided, as well as those for determining the direction and velocity of the tides and currents, deep-sea soundings, &c. Among the instruments supplied was a timepiece and pendulum, by the vibrations of which latter, in a given time, the form and figure of the earth was to be determined. No care or expense was spared in the equipment of the vessels, and nothing that the commander asked for, which it was thought might promote the efficiency of the expedition, was refused.

On the recommendation of the President and Council of the Royal Society, Mr. Fisher, a member of Cambridge University, and a gentleman well versed in mathematics and in other branches of natural science, was appointed to the *Dorothea* in the capacity of astronomer and naturalist.

The ships sailed out of the Thames on the 25th April 1818, and arrived at Lerwick, in the Shetland Islands, on the 1st May. Here, in consequence of a serious leak that had developed itself on the passage, the *Trent* was beached at high-water, and subjected to a thorough examination. Several rents in the planks were discovered in various parts of the ship, and these were repaired as well as the means at their disposal would permit, but the principal leak, unfortunately, remained undiscovered, in spite of the strenuous exertions that were made to find it. This was naturally very mortifying to Franklin and his officers. The service on which they were about to engage was of such a nature as to preclude all but stout, well-built, and, above all, tight ships being engaged in it. It was therefore a serious matter to them that they should at the outset embark in a leaky vessel, more especially when the leak was of such magnitude as to necessitate the employment of the men during half their watches at the pumps to keep her free. This was, it must be acknowledged, a very distressing state of affairs, and it was rendered all the more so in a ship employed on Arctic service, where the men are kept, night and day, constantly at work, and **where** a vessel is so severely handled by the ice, and subjected to such great pressures **as to** make even those that are strongly built **leak.**

Having done their utmost to remedy the defect, the expedition **sailed from** Lerwick on **the 10th May, and** crossing the Arctic Circle a few days afterwards, they experienced the novelty of beholding the midnight sun, and of enjoying the hitherto unknown experience of **continual** daylight. **On** the 24th, Cherie **or Bear** Island, ·as it is more frequently called, was sighted, and shortly afterwards the ships were separated in consequence **of** thick weather and a violent south-west gale. They met again, however, **in a few** days, a short distance from **their** previously **arranged** rendezvous, **in** Magdalena Bay.

Prior **to this** temporary separation they were, for the first time, made acquainted with the difficulties and the novelty of navigating their ships through a **loose pack.** Indeed, some of the streams of ice through **which they** had to thread their way, were of such a nature, **that** combined with the thickness of the weather, necessitated their laying-to until the latter should moderate. Their position at this time is thus referred to by the first lieutenant of the *Trent :—*

"The weather was **now very** severe ; the snow fell in heavy **showers,** and several tons' weight **of ice accumulated** about the sides of the brig, and formed a complete casing to the planks, which received an additional layer at each plunge of the vessel. So great indeed was **the** accumulation about the bows, that we were obliged **to cut it** away repeatedly with axes, to relieve the bowsprit **from** the enormous weight that was attached to it ; and the ropes were **so** thickly covered with ice, that it was necessary to beat them with large sticks to keep them in a state of readiness for any evolution that might be rendered necessary, either by the appearance of ice to leeward, or by a change of wind."

Encountering what they had every reason to believe was the main body of the ice, extending in one vast unbroken plain along the northern horizon, and finding it absolutely impenetrable, it was determined to wait patiently for a few days in Magdalena Bay, so as to give the pack time to break up and disperse. A wise resolution, considering the early season of the year, namely June 3rd, at which they found themselves in such a comparatively high latitude.

During the stay of the ships at this anchorage, the officers were very actively, and profitably, engaged in surveying the harbour, taking observations in various branches of science, shooting excursions, and, we may rest assured, in keeping a constant and vigilant watch on the movements of the pack, from some convenient look-out station. Here, on the iron-bound shores of Spitzbergen, with its icy peaks and snow-clad valleys, Franklin was first made acquainted with the uninviting aspect of Arctic scenery. The grim and inhospitable appearance of the surrounding country fascinated the tyro in Polar exploration, and made him all the more eager to further explore the hidden mysteries of the sealed North Land. It was, in all probability, the result of this, his first voyage to the Arctic regions, that made Franklin, the already skilful sailor and talented surveyor, one of the greatest Arctic travellers that the world has ever known. How different, he must have thought, was the appearance of the anchorage at Magdalena Bay, with its dreary barren shores fringed by long snow-covered valleys and rugged sterile mountains, between which lay huge milk-white glaciers, their opaque surfaces glistening in the rays of the midnight sun, to the luxuriant vegetation and tropical scenery of the land he had been accustomed to gaze on, while serving under Flinders in the Southern Hemisphere. It was indeed a marvellous change of scenery. In spite, however, of the bleakness and sterility of their surroundings, the anchorage at Magdalena Bay was rendered cheerful by the song of countless birds peculiar to those regions; myriads of little auks, or rotges flew, in long and never-ending processions to their breeding-places on the sides of the cliffs, whilst guillemots, cormorants, gulls, and other aquatic birds enlivened the bay by their presence. Groups of walruses were also seen basking in the sun as they stretched their huge, ungainly forms on loose pieces of ice, while the presence of numerous seals doubtless afforded pastime to the sportsmen, as well as fresh food for the officers' mess.

During their detention in Magdalena Bay, the members of the expedition witnessed, at various times, the breaking-off of immense fragments of ice from the parent glacier. On one occasion this disruption was attended with some little risk and danger, for one of their boats, with its crew, was carried by the wave engendered by the fall of ice into the water, a distance of nearly a hundred feet, when it was washed up on the beach and badly stove. On another occasion, Buchan and Franklin were together in a boat examining the terminal face of one of these glaciers, when they suddenly heard a deafening report, somewhat similar to the simultaneous discharge of many heavy pieces of artillery; on looking up, they perceived to their horror an enormous piece of the glacier sliding down into the sea from a height of at least two hundred feet. This was accompanied by a loud grinding noise and the overflow of a large volume of water, which having previously formed and lodged in the fissures of the glacier, now made its escape in numerous cascades. The boat in which the two commanders were seated was kept with her head to seaward, and by this precaution they succeeded in averting a disaster which would probably have ensued in consequence of the violent agitation of the water, and the succession of heavy rollers that swept across the bay, the roaring of which was heard at a distance of four miles. The fragment that had been detached, and whose plunge into the water had caused all this commotion, disappeared entirely for the space of some minutes, during which time nothing was to be seen but the surface of the water, violently agitated and covered with foam and clouds of spray. Suddenly it appeared, shooting up rapidly to the height of a hundred feet above the sea, with torrents of water pouring down its sides; then, after rocking about for some moments, it rolled over, eventually becoming quiescent, and drifting out to sea under the influence of wind and tide as a newly-formed iceberg. It was ascertained to be a quarter of a mile in circumference, and its height sixty feet above the water. Its weight was computed at about 421,640 tons.

On the 7th June the ships sailed out of Magdalena Bay and steered a northward course, in order to resume the examination of the pack. It was found in much the same state and condition as they had left it, namely, impenetrable. At this time, owing to the wind suddenly failing, the ships were left helplessly becalmed and quite unmanageable in close proximity to the pack, which, in consequence of a heavy swell that prevailed, was in a violent state of agitation. In spite of every effort to prevent it, the ships were driven into the ice, where they experienced some rough treatment from the heaving pack. Towards morning a light breeze sprang up, which enabled them to effect their escape from a somewhat critical and perilous position, after a night of great anxiety and incessant toil.

Having unsuccessfully attempted to find an opening in the ice to the westward, Captain Buchan came to the conclusion that the best chance for the successful accomplishment of the enterprise, was by keeping close to Spitzbergen, so with this object in view the course of the ships was once more shaped to the eastward. On June 10th they sighted Prince Charles's Foreland, and on the following morning were off Cloven Cliff, where they were extremely gratified to find a navigable lane of water existing between the land and the main body of the pack. Thinking that this channel would possibly lead to an open and navigable sea, the ships boldly entered it, but had barely passed Red Bay before the ice closed in, the channel was blocked, and the ships were helplessly caught and beset. In this position, without being able to extricate themselves, the vessels remained for a period of thirteen days, when, under the influence of a fresh north-east breeze, the ice loosened, and they succeeded in getting into open water. The place where the ships were beset, was in about the same locality in which Hudson, Baffin, Poole, Phipps, and other navigators had invariably been stopped.

Their late besetment had, at any rate, one very beneficial effect, for by its means they were led to the dis-

covery of the cause of the leak in the *Trent*, which had
given them so much trouble and anxiety ever since
they left **England.**[1] It appears that one night when
they were lying quietly in the ice, the surgeon's assistant thought he detected the noise of water rushing
into the ship below where he slept. On this being reported, the spirit-room was at once cleared, and on cutting through the inside lining of the ship, the water
poured through in a stream fully four feet in height. **It**
was then found that a bolt, through the culpable neglect
of some dockyard shipwright, had been left out, and the
hole being covered with pitch, its omission was not at the
time detected. The defect was at once rectified, and they
had the happiness to find henceforth that the Trent was
as tight and safe as any ship afloat; but the wretched
shipwright, whose negligence had caused them so much
wearisome labour and fatigue, was not easily or quickly
forgotten, or forgiven, by the men, who up to this time
had been constantly employed at the pumps during more
than half their watches; the discovery and subsequent
stoppage of the leak was therefore **a matter** of great joy
and relief to all concerned.

On June the 28th the ships **anchored in Fair Haven,**
in order to await a more favourable opportunity of
pushing northwards; they hoped **that by** the display
of a little patience the pack would in a short time
loosen and enable them to proceed. The anchorage at
Fair Haven is free from hidden dangers of any kind, and
is tolerably well sheltered from south and westerly winds,
but is exposed **to** the north. Here they were fortunate
enough to obtain some fresh meat in the shape of **rein-**
deer, about forty of these animals falling victims to the

[1] See page 93.

prowess of the sportsmen of the expedition. Four were driven into the water, captured, and taken alive **to the** ships, but the unfortunate beasts were so wild, that they broke their limbs **in** their frantic efforts to escape, and **had to be shot.** Large numbers of eider ducks were also procured, **and** afforded a **very** welcome change to **the** ship's provisions on which they **had for so** long been subsisting.

On the 6th July the ships again put to sea, and **sailed** as far north as 80° **15′,** but here again they were stopped by the same impenetrable barrier of ice that had already, on more than one occasion, so successfully impeded their **advance.** In their endeavours to extricate themselves from the loose fragments by which they were surrounded, the ships received **some** rather severe blows from the larger **pieces. On the** following day they had the intense pleasure **of seeing the** pack loosen, exhibiting lanes of **water** radiating **in all** directions through **it.** All was now bustle **and** activity, and **the wind** being favourable, the ships crowded **on all** possible sail, and pushed onwards with joyful anticipations **of success.**

But changes occur **very** quickly **and very suddenly** in ice-encumbered waters, **and bitter** and **keen** disappointment soon followed their **short-lived joyous** aspirations, **for** in a few short **hours** the channels of water, which they thought might lead **them even** to the Pole itself, gradually diminished in size, until they disappeared altogether, and the ice, with **its** accustomed and erratic rapidity of motion, encircled the two **ships** so closely that they were soon completely beset.

For the succeeding three weeks they remained in **a** perfectly helpless state, although strenuous efforts were made **to** free themselves, by boring through **the ice** whenever the pack loosened, and **by dragging and warp-ing** the ships whenever opportunities presented **them-selves**; in this way they succeeded in **making some** slight progress in a northerly direction, until, however, they discovered, to their great mortification, that a strong current was setting them to the southward, at a greater rate than they were advancing in the opposite direction.

The following extract **from Captain** Beechey's narrative will give some faint idea regarding the dangers **and** difficulties they were at this **time exposed to :—**

"On the evening of the 10th the *Trent* sustained a squeeze which made her rise four feet and **heel over five** streaks ; and on the 15th and 16th both **vessels suffered damage,** especially the *Dorothea*, from her being larger and more wall-sided than the *Trent*. On that occasion we observed a field fifteen **feet in thickness break up, and the** pieces pile upon each other to a great height, until they upset when they rolled over with a **tremendous crash.** The ice near the ships was piled up above their bulwarks, to the great danger of the bowsprit and upper works. Fortunately the vessels rose to the pressure, or they must have had their sides forced in ; the *Trent* received her greatest damage upon the quarter, and was so twisted that the doors of all the cabins flew open, and the panels of some started in the frames, while her false stern-post moved three inches, and her timbers cracked to a most serious extent. The *Dorothea* suffered still more : some of her beams were sprung, and two planks on the lower deck, were split fore and aft and doubled up, and she otherwise sustained serious injury in her hull. It was in vain that we attempted any relief, our puny efforts were not even felt, though continued for eight hours with unabated zeal ; and it was not until the tide changed that the smallest effect was produced. When, however, that occurred, the vessels arighted and settled in the water to their proper draft."

It was during this besetment in the pack that the

ships reached their most northerly position, but, **in con-**sequence of the thick state of the weather, it was only ascertained by dead reckoning; **and** as there was an unfortunate difference in the calculations of the two vessels, the *Dorothea* computing the latitude to be 80° 31′, and the *Trent* making it 80° 37′, the **mean** of the two results, viz., 80° 34′, was the highest position claimed.

Captain Buchan now resolved **to** examine the **edge** of the ice to the westward, having so signally, **and so repeatedly,** failed in all his efforts to advance either in a northerly or easterly direction. **No** sooner **had this** determination been made known, **and** the necessary orders for **acting** upon **it been** issued, than the two **ships were caught in** a furious gale of wind, which necessitated **their resorting to the** desperate expedient of taking **shelter in** the pack, a **step** that can only be justified as an **extreme** measure, **and** as offering the **sole** chance of escaping destruction. In order to protect his ship from the heavy ice floes that skirted the pack, and through which he must necessarily pass, Franklin, fully alive to **the** perilous nature of **his** contemplated action, gave orders to cut up one **of the** largest hemp cables, in lengths of about thirty feet; these pieces, with some walrus hides and iron plates, were then **placed** round the outside of **the ship to act as** fenders so as to **protect the** hull **from the huge** fragments of **ice with which** it would have to come into contact. He also gave orders **for the** masts and other spars to be secured with additional tackles, and **all** hatchways **to** be battened down. Everything being in readiness, Franklin, in a loud **clear** voice, ordered **the** helm **to be** put up, and the brig in obedience to the action flew round and dashed before the gale towards the pack, which presented "**one un-**

broken line of furious breakers, in which immense pieces
of ice were heaving and subsiding with the waves, and
dashing together with a violence, which nothing apparently but a solid body could withstand," occasioning
such an uproar and noisy confusion, that it was with
difficulty that Franklin could make his orders heard
by the men, though given in his customary cool, bold,
and decisive manner. As the brig dashed into that
awful seething mass of ice, Captain Beechey tells us
that—

"Each person instinctively secured his own hold, and,
with his eyes fixed upon the masts, awaited in breathless
anxiety the moment of concussion. It soon arrived—the
brig, cutting her way through the light ice, came in violent
contact with the main body. In an instant we all lost our
footing, the masts bent with the impetus, and the cracking
timbers from below bespoke a pressure which was calculated
to awaken our serious apprehensions. The vessel staggered
under the shock, and for a moment seemed to recoil ; but the
next wave curling up under her counter, drove her about her
own length within the margin of the ice, where she gave one
roll, and was immediately thrown broadside to the wind by
the succeeding wave, which beat furiously against her stern,
and brought her lee side in contact with the main body, leaving her weather side exposed at the same time to a piece of ice
about twice her own dimensions. . . .

"Literally tossed from piece to piece, we had nothing left
but patiently to abide the issue, for we could scarcely keep
our feet, much less render any assistance to the vessel. The
motion was so great that the ship's bell, which in the heaviest
gale of wind had never struck by itself, now tolled so continually, that it was ordered to be muffled, for the purpose
of escaping the unpleasant association it was calculated to
produce."

By making more sail, Franklin succeeded in pushing

his vessel farther into the pack, and this greatly improved their situation.   In about four hours the gale moderated, the swell subsided, and the weather clearing, those on board the *Trent* were much relieved by seeing their consort not far from them, for great apprehensions had been felt during the gale concerning her safety.   They soon ascertained by signal that she had also suffered very severely in her encounter with the ice, and was in a somewhat crippled condition.   On the following morning open water was reached, and the two battered ships, in a leaky, disabled, and almost sinking state, sought refuge in Fair Haven, in order to ascertain the extent of their injuries, and, if possible, repair their damages.   The *Trent* though seriously damaged had sustained less injury than the *Dorothea*, which latter ship had the greater part of her timbers broken, besides several of her beams sprung.   The larboard side of the ship, it was found, had been forced in by constant collisions with the ice; the spirit-room, which was in the centre of the ship, was crushed in; while the casks stowed in the hold were actually stove!   It is hardly possible to imagine how the ship, after sustaining such serious injuries, was capable of remaining afloat.

As it was quite out of the question that the *Dorothea* in her present condition could again risk an encounter with the ice, but must either return to England or be abandoned, Franklin tried very hard to be allowed to proceed alone, in the *Trent*, in the execution of the service on which they were engaged; but as his vessel was in nearly as unseaworthy a condition as her consort, Captain Buchan wisely declined to entertain the request, giving as his reason that the *Dorothea* was not in a fit state to undertake the voyage to England unless accompanied by another vessel. In consequence of the unserviceable condition of the two ships, it was reluctantly, but prudently, decided, to abandon all further attempts at discovery, and to return to England as soon as the vessels could be repaired and made seaworthy. Indeed, any other course would have been as unwise as it would be hazardous. During their stay at Fair Haven, Franklin was busily occupied, not only in superintending the repairs of the *Trent*, but also in surveying and projecting a plan of the anchorage and adjacent islands, and also in assisting Mr. Fisher to determine the geographical position of the place. The ships put to sea on the 30th August, and after making a cursory examination of the ice to the northward and westward, steered homewards; after a somewhat long and anxious passage, they reached Deptford on October 22nd, and were paid out of commission on the 14th of the following month.

The results of this voyage were of a negative kind; the expedition examined about the same extent of the pack edge as did Phipps in 1773, and found the ice equally as impenetrable as he did. It was, however, the first expedition sent to the Arctic regions during the present century, and it was the forerunner of those subsequently despatched by England in search of the north-west passage.

Thus ended this plucky attempt to reach the North Pole, in which everything was achieved that human skill, perseverance, and courage could, under the peculiar circumstances, have effected. Dangers and difficulties of a novel and a terrible description, were successfully grappled with, and hardships and privations of no ordinary kind, were uncomplainingly endured by that small but heroic band **that sailed** under the leadership **of Buchan and** Franklin. The failure to reach a high latitude was due to that vast barrier of ice, **which has** always proved an insuperable obstacle to advance in a northerly direction in the neighbourhood of Spitzbergen. **This great** belt **of** impenetrable ice, has been invariably **met with by all, in a greater** or less degree, who have endeavoured to push northwards, and it has so far successfully defied penetration. **One** most important result of this expedition, was the experience gained by Franklin in Arctic exploration, for it was during this voyage that he won his spurs as a Polar explorer, and gained that insight **into ice** navigation which subsequently proved of inestimable value to his country and to the science of geography.

CHAPTER VIII.

FRANKLIN'S FIRST LAND JOURNEY.

1819-1822.

> " How shall I admire your heroicke courage
> Ye marine worthies, beyond names of worthinesse ? "
> —PURCHAS.

THE return of the two expeditions in 1818, although they had been unsuccessful in accomplishing the main objects for which they had been despatched, viz., the discovery of the North Pole, and the achievement of the long-sought-for north-west passage, so far from throwing cold water on the prosecution of further research in high latitudes, appeared to stimulate the Government into renewed action in the same direction. The reports of the leaders of the two expeditions were well considered and discussed, and with such a satisfactory result as to induce the Government to decide upon sending out another expedition to continue the work of exploration to the westward by Baffin's Bay, while a party was to be sent to explore by land along the northern shore of Arctic America.

The command of the first-named expedition was intrusted to Lieutenant Parry, who had recently been employed in command of the second ship in the late expedition under Captain Ross. The vessels appointed to carry out this service were the *Hecla* and *Griper*,

Lieutenant Liddon being placed in command of the last-named ship. They sailed on the 11th of May 1819, with instructions to proceed up Baffin's Bay, and so endeavour to reach the Pacific, through any channel or opening that might be discovered to the westward.

The other expedition, although it was in a measure intended to act in conjunction with Lieutenant Parry, was of a totally different character, for it was organised with the object of penetrating by land to the Arctic Sea, at or about the mouth of the Coppermine River; thence it was to trace the shore of the north coast of America in an easterly direction, and, if circumstances should admit, to act in concert with Commander Parry, in the event of falling in with that officer.

In the choice of leaders for these two expeditions, it is not surprising to find that Franklin should be the one selected for the conduct of that which must, of necessity, be of a particularly arduous and perilous nature. He had now made a name in the scientific world, and he had also established a reputation for himself in the navy as an accomplished, skilful, and energetic officer. That such a man was not permitted to remain long inactive is not to be wondered at, especially when work of such a congenial nature as geographical exploration was to be undertaken. The man who had braved the elements in their fiercest moods, and who had faced death in many forms in all parts of the world and under various conditions, was not likely to remain unemployed when such interesting and hazardous service as exploration in high latitudes was required to be carried out. Who so fit to undertake the conduct of such an expedition as John Franklin? and who so competent to conduct an enterprise requiring courage, energy, and ability **as the late talented commander of the** *Trent?* It was, therefore, **almost a foregone** conclusion, when the expedition was decided on, that it should be intrusted to the guidance of Lieutenant Franklin. **The** only wonder is, that he was not promoted to the rank of commander in order to lead such an important enterprise ; for, in spite of his excellent services in the junior branches of the navy, he had, **at the** time of his appointment to the command of the proposed expedition, served no less than eleven years in the grade of a lieutenant, eight **of** which **had** been actual service **in a ship at sea.**

With Franklin was associated **Dr. John Richardson, a** surgeon in **the** royal navy and a gentleman of considerable scientific attainments; also Messrs. George Back and Robert Hood, Admiralty midshipmen, both of whom were accomplished artists. Mr. Back had already seen service in the Arctic regions, having served with Franklin in the *Trent*, in which ship he had displayed so much zeal and ability, that his old commander had no hesitation **in** selecting him to take part in an enterprise which, he was well aware, would prove both trying and hazardous. They were accompanied by John Hepburn, an old man-of-war's man, as their sole attendant. It was to the exertions of this gallant fellow that some of the members of the expedition, during the latter part of their journey, under Divine Providence, owed the preservation of their lives. He was a splendid specimen of a British sailor, steady, faithful, willing, always cheerful, and possessing bulldog tenacity of purpose.

It must not be forgotten that, at this time, the northern coast of North America, from Icy Cape north of Bering's Strait, as far as Hudson's Bay to the east, was practically unknown. In two places only had the veil been lifted along the northern shore of Arctic America; these geographical feats were accomplished by two officials of the Hudson's Bay Company, Messrs. Hearne and Mackenzie, who, at different times, had successfully worked their way to the coast, and who were the only white men who had ever beheld the Arctic Sea from the north coast of America. With the exception of the two positions gained by these travellers, a line of coast, extending over eighty degrees of longitude, was an absolute blank on our maps and charts. One of these explorers, Samuel Hearne, had been despatched from Fort Churchill, a post belonging to the Company in Hudson's Bay, in December 1770, in consequence of vague reports that had, from time to time, been received from the Indians, relative to the existence of an extensive sea to the northward. He was ordered to proceed to the coast, directing his route as far as practicable along the banks of a large river which was known to flow to the northward, and which had been named the Coppermine, on account of the reports that had been brought in by the Indians of the discovery of that metal in its neighbourhood. He was also directed to express his opinion on the possibility of using this sea, if he succeeded in reaching it, as a practicable route for the Company's ships, and to report further on the territory through which he journeyed, relative to its capabilities and value as a fur-producing country. He was accompanied on this expedition by several Indians, who acted as guides; he was the only white man in the party, and he appears to have been, more or less, in the hands of the natives, being entirely dependent on them both for guidance and sustenance.

Hearne returned to Fort Churchill after an adventurous journey of nineteen months' duration, during which time he succeeded in reaching the sea at the mouth of the Coppermine River. This position he fixed with a fair amount of accuracy, considering the means at his disposal. Near the mouth of the river they discovered a party of Eskimos, encamped in their summer tents, and peacefully engaged in hunting seals and fishing. Under cover of darkness these poor people were all brutally massacred by the Indians in their tents, in spite of Hearne's earnest pleadings and remonstrances. It appears that a bitter feud had existed, from time immemorial, between the Indians of the plains and the Eskimos of the coast, and that no lapse of time had ever been sufficient to heal the breach. A rapid near the spot where this outrage occurred was called by Hearne Bloody Fall. The hardships and privations experienced by Hearne during this long and remarkable journey were very severe.

Mackenzie made a somewhat similar journey in 1789 to the shores of the Polar Sea, during which he successfully traced the river that now bears his name to its embouchure. These were the only white men who had traversed the barren lands of North America northward to the sea; Captain Cook, it will be remembered, had only succeeded in advancing in his ship a very short distance to the northward of Bering's Strait in 1776.

The instructions that were issued to Lieutenant Franklin were, briefly, as follows :—He was to proceed to Hudson's Bay; thence he was to travel northward with the object of determining astronomically the positions of all capes, headlands, bays, harbours, and rivers, and also to sketch in the trend of the coast-line of

North America, between the eastern extremity of that continent and the mouth of the Coppermine River.   He was left at liberty to select, according to circumstances, the best route that would enable him to reach the shores of the Arctic Sea in the shortest possible time.

In the adoption of the route to be followed, he was in a great measure to be governed by the advice and information he might obtain from the officers of the Hudson's Bay Company that he should meet during the course of his wanderings.   These officials had been requested to afford Lieutenant Franklin all the assistance in their power towards promoting generally the success of the enterprise, and especially in the way of providing him with necessaries for the journey, and in procuring an escort of Indians to accompany him as guides, hunters, and as a means of protection against the Eskimos, or any predatory hostile bands of Indians that might be fallen in with.   Franklin was further directed to deposit any information he might consider of importance in conspicuous places along the coast, for the guidance of Lieutenant Parry, in the event of that officer being successful in reaching the Arctic shores of North America with his two ships.   He was liberally supplied with instruments for determining the dip and variation of the magnetic needle and intensity of the magnetic force, also others for registering the temperature, and other important meteorological observations. On reaching the mouth of the Coppermine River, he was ordered to institute inquiries relative to the presence of native copper, which, it had been alleged, had been discovered in the locality, several specimens having been brought by the Indians to the Hudson's Bay posts. He was to endeavour, if practicable, to visit and explore those places, so as to obtain specimens *in situ*, and so afford Dr. Richardson an opportunity of making "such observations as might be useful in a commercial point of view or interesting to the science of mineralogy."

It will thus be seen that geographical exploration was not the sole object of the expedition, but the interest of science in other branches was also to be carefully studied. The task that Franklin undertook to accomplish was not only difficult, but it was an extremely hazardous one, for it entailed a journey through an unknown and barren country, of the resources of which he was totally ignorant; and yet he was well aware that he would be entirely dependent, not only for the bare necessaries of life, but for the existence of himself and that of his party, on the products of the chase. He was also not ignorant of the fact that he and his companions would be exposed to the merciless rigours and attendant hardships of more than one Arctic winter. The magnitude and novelty of the enterprise, and the possible dangers and privations that would be experienced, rendered it, however, all the more acceptable and fascinating to the gallant little band that set forth full of resolution, determined to carry to a successful issue, and to the best of their ability, the work intrusted to them.

Everything being in readiness, the expedition embarked at Gravesend on board the Hudson's Bay Company's ship *Prince of Wales*, the master of which had been directed to convey Lieutenant Franklin and his party as far as York Factory in Hudson's Bay. She dropped down the Thames on the 23rd May 1819, but, in consequence of bad weather and head winds, did not reach Stromness in the Orkney Islands until June 3rd. Here Franklin engaged the services of four men to accompany him in the capacity of boatmen whilst ascending the rivers in the Hudson's Bay Territory. **More were** required, but there **was a general** unwillingness evinced on the part of the men to join the expedition, on account of the supposed dangerous service on which they would be employed.

On the afternoon of the 16th the *Prince of Wales* put to sea, and commenced her voyage across the Atlantic to Hudson's Bay. The passage was a somewhat protracted one, for it was not until the 7th of August that Resolution Island, situated off the north extreme of the entrance to Hudson's Strait, was sighted. The wind dying away, left the ship drifting about helplessly at the mercy of the strong and variable currents that usually exist in that locality, and they had a very narrow escape from shipwreck. The circumstance is thus alluded to by Franklin :—

"**At** half-past twelve **we had** the alarming view of a barren rugged shore within a few yards, towering over the mastheads. Almost immediately afterwards the ship struck violently on a point of rocks projecting from the island ; **and the ship's side was** brought so near to the shore, that poles were prepared to push her off. This blow displaced the rudder and raised it several inches. . . . A gentle swell freed the ship **from this** perilous situation, but the current hurried us along **in contact** with the **rocky shore, and the** prospect was most alarming. On the outward bow **was perceived a** rugged and precipitous cliff, **whose summit was hid in the fog, and the** vessel's head **was pointed towards the bottom of a small bay** into which **we were rapidly driving. There now seemed to be** no probability **of escaping shipwreck, being without wind** and having **the rudder in its present useless state.**"

At **this** moment, **however, the ship again struck** in passing over a ledge **of rocks, and** by a **curious and** lucky coincidence, the second shock had **the effect of** replacing the rudder, and rendering it again service-able. A light breeze springing **up at the** same time, filled the sails, and they were thus enabled to draw gradually, but surely, away from the danger. **The ship** had, however, made but little progress before the current forced **her** in the direction of a large grounded iceberg, against the steep and rugged sides of which she was driven with such amazing rapidity and force, that they expected every moment to see the masts go by the board.

Fortunately this particular danger was also averted, and the ship again escaped destruction, but **she was** left in **such a** crippled and leaky condition that the crew were unable **to keep her** free of water by the pumps alone, and the officers and passengers were obliged, in order to keep **her** afloat, to bale the water out with buckets. On the morning **of** the 8th, the water had gained to such an extent, that upwards of five feet was reported in **the** hold. Luckily the carpenters were **able** to get at **some** of **the** damaged parts; these were temporarily patched up, and a sail being drawn underneath that portion of the injured part which could not **be** repaired, the influx of water was materially diminished, and the leaks eventually mastered.

On the evening of the 10th, the ship entered Hudson's **Strait,** and without **any** hindrance from ice—indeed without even seeing any—reached the Savage Islands the following day, where they remained for a few hours **for** the **purpose** of **bartering** with the Eskimos, **who came down with their sledges** and kayaks laden with **skins and other** products **of the country. In conse-quence of the entire** absence **of ice** in **the** strait, they **were compelled to stretch over to the** Labrador coast in order to replenish **the ship with** water. On the 19th

Digges Islands were passed, and **on** the 30th the *Prince of Wales* anchored off York Factory, where the mem**bers of** the expedition landed.   Here they obtained from the Hudson's Bay Company the use of one of their large transport boats, in order to enable them to continue their journey, for with the amount of stores, &c., they were compelled to take, the ordinary mode of travelling in canoes was quite out of the question.   They were also fortunate enough to secure the services of an experienced steersman ; the remainder of the crew was composed of the men hired for the purpose at Stromness.

The boats in use by the Hudson's Bay Company for the transport of their goods on the rivers and lakes in their Territory, **are** called York boats.   They were (and even are, for the same description **of** boat is in use in the present day) constructed as lightly as possible, with a view to navigating shallow rivers, and were consequently of exceptionally light draft, barely drawing, when loaded with a heavy cargo **of** furs, more than about **twelve** inches of water.   They were, and continue to be, extensively used in conveying the peltries and necessary stores from one trading post to another.   They are about forty feet in length, sharp at both ends and very full amidships, requiring about nine or twelve men as a **crew**. When the rapids are not too fierce, these boats when unloaded, can be dragged and pushed along with poles ; but where the rapids are, from their velocity, impassable, the cargoes have to be landed, and, with the boats, " portaged " round the falls.   This, **with** such unwieldy craft, is oftentimes excessively laborious.   Going down stream, and also when on the lakes, they are propelled by oars ; but when pursuing their course against the current, they are invariably tracked by **the crew, who,** walking along one bank of the stream, drag the boat after them. Although fitted with rudders, they are usually guided **by a large** steer-oar.   I have been thus minute in describing these boats, for it was in one of them, that Franklin **and** his companions accomplished the greater part **of** their journey towards the Arctic Ocean.

It is almost needless to say that the members of the expedition were received with kindness and courtesy **by** the Hudson's Bay officials stationed at York Factory, who did all in their power, by communicating with their brother officers stationed at the various posts in that **portion** of the country through which Franklin must necessarily **travel,** to facilitate the despatch of the party, and to promote **the** success of the enterprise, besides assisting them with all the available means at their disposal.

The route selected by Franklin, after due consultation with the acknowledged authorities on the subject, was the one by **the** Great Slave **Lake.**   By the adoption of this particular route, the expedition would pass several **of** the Hudson's **Bay** stations that had been established for the collection of skins, &c., and they would thus be able to **keep** their communication **open with** the outer world, **for a** longer **period than would** otherwise be the case.

The necessary preparations for the journey having been completed, the expedition started from York Factory on the 9th of September 1819, **and** after a toilsome journey of **nearly 700 miles,** reached Cumberland House, **on the Saskatchewan River, on the 23rd of the** following month.[1]

---

[1] For about 400 miles of this distance, namely, from York Factory to Norway House, situated in the immediate neighbourhood of the shores of **Lake** Winnipeg, the writer of these pages has, quite

The voyage thus far was not altogether devoid of exciting incident or danger, for on the 2nd of October Franklin had a narrow escape of losing his life by drowning, having accidentally lost his footing whilst standing on a rock endeavouring to force the boat up a rapid; falling into the river, he was rapidly swept away in the swirling torrent. In consequence of the rocks being worn smooth by attrition, the result of the action of the water, his efforts to regain the bank were ineffectual, and he was carried down the stream for a considerable distance. Fortunately he succeeded, after a time, in arresting his progress by grasping the branch of a willow, and he was eventually rescued from his perilous and critical position by some of the Hudson's Bay people, who hurried to his assistance.

On arrival at Cumberland House, he found, to his great mortification, that the guides, hunters, interpreters,

recently, followed along the same road that was traversed by Franklin and his companions; tracking up the same rivers, paddling over the same lakes, breasting the same rapids, and transporting his light birch-bark canoe and necessary impedimenta, along the same portages over which they transported their more cumbersome boat and heavier cargo. He can testify to the excellence of the sketches that were taken by some of the members of the expedition (one of which, Trout Falls, is here reproduced) of various parts of the route, and of the faithful accuracy of the description of the country through which they travelled. This description, written seventy years ago, is now so applicable to the country recently visited by the writer, that it might have been written yesterday! The running survey of the rivers ascended by the expedition was carried out by Lieutenant Franklin and his assistants, and remains unaltered and unchallenged on the maps of the present day.

It may be interesting to remark that at Norway House, the writer found a sundial in the exact position that Lieutenant Franklin had placed it in the garden of the Chief Factor at that post in 1819. On the leaden dial plate is engraved the initials J. H. F., which, it is asserted, was the work of Sir John Franklin's own hands, and there is no reason to doubt the accuracy of the assertion.

&c., whose services he hoped to obtain, were not to be
had for any consideration. He, therefore, resolved to
proceed at once to Fort Chipewyan, another Hudson's
Bay post, situated on the shore of Lake Athabasca,
where, he was informed, there would be no difficulty in
obtaining the services of men who were intimately

THE EXPEDITION MAKING A PORTAGE ROUND TROUT FALLS.

acquainted with the nature and resources of the country
lying to the northward of the Great Slave Lake.

In accordance with this resolution, leaving Dr.
Richardson and Mr. Hood to pass the winter at Cumberland House, Franklin, accompanied by Mr. Back and
Hepburn, started on the 18th January 1820, with a
couple of dog-sledges, and with only fifteen days' provisions. Before leaving, Franklin had made the necessary arrangements for the Stromness men, who did

not evince any inclination to accompany the expedition further, to return *viâ* York Factory to England.

This trip to Fort Chipewyan was a bold undertaking on Franklin's part, for the time selected for making the journey was in the very depth of winter. The cold was intense, for we read **that** the mercury in their thermo**meters remained** frozen during the entire **journey!** The privations endured may **be** imagined, **when we** read in the official narrative such sentences as the following :— "Provisions becoming scanty; dogs without food, except a little burnt leather."—"**Night** miserably **cold**; **tea froze in** the tin pots before **we could** drink it."

On the 1st February Carlton House was reached, and **here they** remained for the space of a week, to recruit their strength and **to** recover from the severities of the journey. They left **again on** the 8th, and after visiting a few Hudson's Bay **posts that lay** on their line of route, they eventually **reached Fort** Chipewyan, **on** Lake Athabasca, on the 26th March, having traversed a distance of 857 miles since parting from their companions at Cumberland House. Here they busily occupied them**selves** during the remainder of the winter and spring **in** making the **necessary preparations for the** continuance **of** the voyage.

Having been **joined by Dr. Richardson and Mr. Hood,** who had been left behind at Cumberland House for the purpose of bringing **on the** stores and provisions directly they could be transported after the rivers and lakes were open **to** navigation, the expedition took its **de**parture from Fort Chipewyan on the 18th July, and proceeding down the Slave River, reached the waters of **the Great** Slave Lake; on the 29th they arrived at Fort Providence, a post situated at the north end of the lake.

Their journey thus far had been chiefly remarkable for the number of rapids they encountered, and the numerous portages that had consequently to be made; **and also,** it should be recorded, for the sufferings they endured from the pertinacious attacks to which they were exposed from myriads of mosquitoes and sand-flies. These pestilential insects were, during the journey, a source of **very** serious annoyance to **the** travellers.

At Fort Providence their **party was supplemented** by the addition of a clerk belonging to the **North-West** Company, a Mr. Wentzel, who had placed his services at the disposal of Lieutenant Franklin; he **was also** accompanied **by an interpreter and a** hunter. The expedition **now** consisted of Franklin and his five European companions, twenty-six men, principally Canadian half-breed voyageurs, three women and as many children. The women were specially engaged for the purpose of making clothes and shoes for the men whilst in winter quarters.

On the 2nd August they left Fort Providence in **four** canoes, and steering to the northward, entered **a country** that had never previously been visited by Europeans. On the following day they reached the Yellow Knife River, where they were joined, as had been arranged, by a flotilla of seventeen canoes, containing Indians who had agreed to accompany them some distance to the northward, **and hunt** for them during the time they were together. Leaving the Yellow Knife River, they proceeded by a chain of lakes, necessitating innumerable long and tedious portages, until Winter Lake, situated in latitude 64° 30′, was reached on August 20th. The season being well **advanced,** it was determined to construct a house on the south-west side of this lake, to be called Fort Enterprise, in which to pass the winter. The distance travelled from Fort Chipewyan to this position was 553 miles.

It may be interesting to know that the united length of all the portages crossed by the expedition since leaving Fort Providence was twenty-one statute miles; over this distance everything, including canoes, had to be carried; and as each portage had to be traversed no less than seven times in order to transport their goods across, a distance of 150 miles had necessarily to be walked. Up to the period when the expedition went into winter quarters at Fort Enterprise, they had travelled a distance of over 1500 miles.

While some of the party were engaged in building the houses in which to pass the winter, others were employed on hunting-parties in order to procure game for their subsistence during the winter, and also for their requirements during the spring travelling. There was, fortunately, no lack of fresh meat, as large herds of reindeer were frequently found grazing along the shores of the lake. The officers during this time were, of course, well occupied, chiefly in the general superintendence of the work and in organising the hunting-parties, and also in the examination of the adjacent country, with a view of ascertaining the direction that would afford the best facilities for making good progress when the travelling season began. During one of these expeditions the Coppermine River was reached.

By the 15th September all parties had returned to Fort Enterprise, and the necessary preparations for passing the winter were made. On the 6th of the following month they moved into their houses. The

one erected for the officers was a log building fifty feet
long by twenty-four wide, divided into a large hall,
three bedrooms, and a kitchen; this was occupied by
Franklin and his companions. There was also another
house constructed for the men, besides a storehouse in
which the provisions were kept.

The winter was a long and cheerless one, and the
privations they endured, cut off as they were from all,
save their little community, were of no ordinary nature;
extreme cold and a scarcity of provisions being the principal enemies they had to contend with, the reindeer
having entirely deserted their neighbourhood shortly
after the occupation of their winter quarters. Before
the winter had actually set in, their store of provisions
was so reduced that it became absolutely necessary to
communicate with Fort Chipewyan in order to replenish
their exhausted stock. For this purpose Mr. Back,
always ready to proffer his services when any undertaking of a particularly arduous or dangerous character
had to be performed, was despatched during the month
of November. He returned on the 15th of March, having
most satisfactorily executed the duty entrusted to him.

During the period of his absence, this intrepid young
officer travelled a distance of more than 1100 miles
on snowshoes, with the temperature frequently down
to -40°, and on one occasion as low as -57°. All
this time he had no covering at night but a single
blanket and a deerskin, and he was sometimes without
food of any description for two or three consecutive
days. This will perhaps give some idea of the hardships and sufferings endured by this gallant young midshipman during his long and arduous journey.

CHAPTER IX.

FRANKLIN'S FIRST LAND *JOURNEY*—(*continued*).

1819–1822.

> "Oh, the long and dreary winter !
> Oh, the cold and cruel winter !
> Ever thicker, thicker, thicker,
> Froze the ice on lake and river ;
> Ever deeper, deeper, deeper,
> Fell the snow o'er all the landscape,
> Fell the covering snow and drifted
> Through the forest, round the village.
> Hardly from the buried wigwam
> Could the hunter force a passage ;
> With his mittens and his snowshoes
> Vainly walked he through the forest,
> Sought for bird and beast, and found none,
> Saw no track of deer or rabbit,
> In the snow beheld no foot-prints
> In the ghastly gleaming forest."
>
> —Longfellow.

At length, after endless troubles with the Indians and the half-breed voyageurs, the party, having been augmented by the addition of a couple of Eskimo interpreters, took its departure from Fort Enterprise on 14th June 1821, with two large canoes and several sledges. The rate of progress, however, was not at first very rapid, for each man had to carry, or drag, a weight of 180 pounds, **a** serious obstacle to quick travelling.[1]

Crossing various lakes that lay in their route, transporting their canoes and stores over long stretches of barren land, and even sometimes over high and rugged hills, launching their canoes again into the rivers, and shooting dangerous rapids, the expedition pushed onwards until it was fairly embarked on the turbid waters of **the** Coppermine River.

That their task was a difficult and a perilous one goes without saying, and we are not surprised **to hear of** the sufferings they endured from swollen **knee and** ankle joints, the result of continuous marching through soft snow, combined with a predisposition to scorbutic attacks; their shoes also were much torn by the ice and sharp-pointed stones over which they had to travel, causing their feet to be painfully lacerated, and they were also subjected to the almost unbearable and never-ceasing persecutions of their relentless enemies, the mosquitoes. Still they pushed on uncomplainingly, regarding these torments as a necessary part **of** their daily routine, and determined, so far as in them lay, to carry out to the letter the particular object of the enterprise, namely, geographical research.

Fortunately, although the country through which they journeyed was barren and sterile in appearance, they saw, and succeeded in killing, many reindeer and musk-oxen, and were thus able to eke out the somewhat scanty

[1] Prior to their departure, arrangements had been made with one of the Indian chiefs, named Akaitcho, for depositing a large supply of provisions at Fort Enterprise during their absence, so that on their return they would find a good store prepared for them, in the event of their having to pass another winter at the station.

stock of dried provisions with **which** they were furnished on leaving Fort Enterprise. **The** scenery along **the** banks of the Coppermine **River** was bold and rugged. Ranges of lofty hills were visible on either side, while broad valleys stretching between them, afforded excellent shelter and pasturage for the **herds of** reindeer **that** were constantly seen. On the 14th **June a** high hill **was** ascended, and their hearts beat with joyful **expectation of** future success, **as** they obtained their first view of the Arctic Ocean. Four days subsequently they **had the** extreme gratification of making their camp on the shore **of** the Hyperborean Sea, **and** had **the** satisfaction **of** feeling that they had almost reached the " Ultima **Thule" of their** journey.

They found the geographical position **of** the mouth of **the Coppermine River to** be somewhat different to that assigned **to it by Hearne,** but everything else agreed well **with the** account given by **that** traveller. The **most** conspicuous headland seen to the northward was **named by** Franklin Cape Hearne, as a just and deserving tribute to the memory of that persevering and energetic Hudson's Bay official. Ever mindful of old friends and patrons, a group of islands was named the Lawford Islands after the commander under whose auspices, in **the old** *Polyphemus,* **Franklin** had gained his first experience **in the navy. Nor were** Flinders and Buchan **forgotten by their** old friend, when **considering** the **nomenclature of** the newly-discovered **land.**

On June 21st the canoes were launched on the Arctic Ocean, and their voyage **to** the eastward commenced. The coast along which they sailed **in** their small and frail barks was a sterile and inhospitable one ; cliff succeeded cliff in tiresome and monotonous uniformity ;

the valleys that intervened being covered with the débris that fell from the cliffs, to the exclusion of any kind of herbage. Occasionally their progress was temporarily impeded by ice, whilst a strong ice-blink was invariably seen to seaward.

It must not be forgotten that the expedition was navigating a rock-bound coast, fringed with heavy masses of solid ice, that rose and fell with every motion of a rough and tempestuous sea, threatening momentarily to crush the light frail canoes, fit only for river or lake navigation, in which Franklin and his party were embarked. This voyage along the shores of the Arctic Sea, must always take rank as one of the most daring and hazardous exploits that has ever been accomplished in the interest of geographical research. Following all the tortuous sinuosities of the coast-line, and accurately delineating the northern shore of North America as they pushed onwards in an easterly direction, naming all the principal headlands, sounds, bays and islands [1] that were discovered, the expedition reached a point on the 18th August in latitude 68° 19′ N. and longitude 110° 5′ W. on the coast of North America, whence Franklin reluctantly came to the conclusion that they had reached the end of their journey, and must return from the interesting work on which they were engaged,

---

[1] It is somewhat significant that a small group of islands discovered by Franklin at this period in the Arctic Sea received the name of the Porden Islands. Miss Eleanor Anne Porden was the daughter of an eminent architect. As a young girl she developed a talent for poetry, and on the despatch of the expedition commanded by Captain Buchan in 1818 she wrote a short sonnet on it. This was the means of an introduction to Franklin, who must have been so impressed by the charms of the young poetess, that he not only named these islands after her, but on his return to England he made her his wife.

and for the following reasons. In the first place, they had only three days' pemmican left, and the Canadian voyageurs had, consequently, manifested a very decided reluctance to continue the work of exploration, believing, and not unnaturally, that great difficulty would be experienced at that late season of the year in replenishing their fast diminishing store of provisions. In the second place, the gales of wind which were so prevalent were, they thought, sure indications of the break-up of the travelling season, and therefore that in itself appeared sufficient reason for them to be thinking of wending their way in a southerly direction. The absence of all traces of Eskimos, from whom they had calculated upon obtaining supplies of food, was also discouraging, while the amount of time that had already been occupied in exploring the various bays and sounds that lay in their route was so great, that it entirely precluded all hope of reaching Repulse Bay before the arrival of winter, a hope they had always cherished might be realised.

Although on the chart the position reached by the expedition, which was very appropriately named Point Turnagain, was only six and a half degrees of longitude to the eastward of the mouth of the Coppermine River, so tortuous and winding was the contour of the newly-discovered coast, that they were actually obliged to sail and paddle in their canoes a distance of 555 geographical miles in order to accomplish the journey; this would be about equal to the direct distance between the Coppermine River and Repulse Bay. It was therefore obvious that the only prudent course that could be pursued, was to return as soon as possible in order to reach the Indians, who had been directed to procure a supply of provisions for the expedition, before the next winter should set in.

From their researches, up to this point, Franklin had arrived at the conclusion (subsequently proved to be a well-founded one) that a navigable passage for ships along the coast by which they had travelled was practicable; and although he was disappointed in not meeting his friend Captain Parry and his vessels, he felt convinced that they stood an excellent chance of satisfactorily clearing up the long unsolved problem of a north-west passage.

It is not in the scope of this work to enter into all the details connected with Franklin's remarkable journey, but the story could only be considered as half told, if an allusion to the return voyage was omitted. The determination to return was, it may well be imagined, hailed with delight by the voyageurs, who for some days had manifested a growing spirit of insubordination, due in a measure to the serious apprehensions they felt for their safety if the voyage was continued. Instead of returning by the way they came, namely by the Copper-mine River, Franklin determined to push up Arctic Sound, and thence proceed by way of a large river (which he named, after his young companion, Hood River), to Fort Enterprise, for he thought by so doing he would pass through a country in which the chances of obtaining game would be greater than by adhering to the outward route.

In accordance with this resolve, the expedition left Point Turnagain on the 22nd of August. At this time the ground was covered with snow and the pools of water were frozen, while other indications of the approach of winter were only too evident. Their provisions at this time were so reduced that they had to content themselves with one meal a day, and this consisted of a small amount of dry and mouldy pemmican. On the 24th they succeeded in killing three very lean and scraggy deer; but beggars cannot afford to be choosers, and this addition to their larder was both welcome and acceptable, more especially as they had already consumed their last remaining meal of pemmican. On the following day, after an exciting run before a gale of wind, in which both canoes nearly foundered, they left the sea, and entering the mouth of Hood's River, encamped that night as high as the first rapid.

Thus terminated their voyage on the Arctic Ocean, on which they had sailed over 650 geographical miles; but their troubles and their sufferings did not cease when they turned their backs upon the sea; indeed, they can barely be said to have commenced. Finding the canoes too heavy and unwieldy for their mode of travelling, especially as the rapids were numerous and the portages long, two smaller boats were constructed out of the materials of the larger ones; having thus reduced their weights and discarded all unnecessary stores, books, &c., which were carefully deposited in a *cache*, they succeeded in making better progress. Ascertaining that Hood's River trended too much in a westerly direction, and being also somewhat difficult of navigation, they quitted its banks on the 3rd of September, and travelled as nearly as they could in a straight line towards their wished-for goal and haven, Fort Enterprise.

Henceforth the journey had to be performed almost entirely on foot over a stony and barren country, but they carried their canoes with them in the event of having to cross any lakes or rivers that might lie in their route, or that flowed in the right direction. On

the evening of the 4th their stock of provisions was
exhausted.   On the two following days a violent gale of
wind was experienced, which necessitated a confinement
to camp; as they had absolutely nothing to eat, and
were even destitute of the means of making a fire, they
remained in bed the whole time.   The temperature at
this time was as low as 20°, and they found their blankets
quite insufficient to protect them against the cold.   On
the morning of the 7th, the wind having moderated
slightly, and anything being preferable to inactivity, the
tents were struck and the march resumed.   So violent,
however, was the wind, that the men carrying the canoes
were frequently blown down by its force; and on one of
these occasions the largest of the two canoes was so
injured as to be rendered utterly unserviceable.   It was
thought at the time that it had been purposely thrown
down and damaged by those who had to carry it.

For some days all they had to subsist on was a lichen,
called by the Canadians *tripe de roche*,[1] with perhaps an
occasional partridge shot by the hunters.   Their sufferings were great, for the temperature was very low,
always below freezing-point, and they were frequently
wet to their waists from having to ford the numerous
rivers and swamps that lay in their path; their remaining
canoe was in such a leaky condition as to be practically
useless.   On the 10th they sighted a herd of musk-oxen,
and were so fortunate as to succeed in killing one of
these animals.

[1] Called by botanists *Gyrophora*, on account of its circular form,
and the surface of the leaf being marked with curved lines. Dr.
Richardson says—"We used it as an article of food, but not having
the means of extracting the bitter principle from it, it proved
nauseous to all, and noxious to several of the party, producing
severe bowel complaints."

The event is thus alluded to in **Franklin's narrative**
of the journey :—

" **About noon the weather** cleared, and to our great joy we
saw a herd of musk-oxen grazing in a valley below us. The
party instantly **halted, and the** best **hunters were sent** out.
They approached the animals with the utmost caution, no
less than two hours being consumed before they got within
gunshot. In the meantime we beheld their proceedings with
extreme anxiety, **and many secret** prayers were, **doubtless,**
offered up for their success. At length **they opened their fire,**
and we had the satisfaction of seeing **one of the largest** cows
fall ; another was wounded, but escaped. This success infused
spirit in our starving party. To skin **and cut up** the animal
was the work of a **few minutes. The contents of** its stomach
was **devoured upon the spot, and the raw** intestines, which
were most **attacked, were pronounced by the most** delicate
amongst **us to be excellent. This was the sixth day** since we
had **had a good meal. The *tripe de roche*, even where** we got
enough, only serving to allay the pangs of hunger for a short
time."

This providential supply **of food** revived their **droop-**
ing spirits, but death stared them **in the face in more**
ways than one, and Franklin himself had a narrow
escape of his life, being capsized whilst **attempting to**
cross a rapid in their crazy canoe ; his escape indeed
was almost miraculous. By this accident he had the
misfortune **to lose** his journal, and the numerous and
valuable scientific observations he had made since the
departure of the expedition from Fort Enterprise.

In order to lighten their burdens, everything but the
clothes that were actually on their backs, their guns and
ammunition, and the instruments necessary for determining their position, **were** abandoned, and rewards **in**
money were **offered** to those who were successful in

shooting game.   On the 17th the **pangs of** hunger, we are told, were somewhat allayed by eating pieces **of singed** hide mixed with **a** little *tripe de roche!* On **the** following day they supped off *tripe de roche,* **and on** the next day had nothing at all!

On the 21st the remaining canoe was irreparably damaged, and was therefore abandoned as useless lumber. On the same day they picked up the horns and bones of a deer that had been devoured by wolves **the** previous year. These were made friable by burning, **and with** some old shoes was the only food they had **that** day. On the 25th they fortunately succeeded in shooting five **small deer out of a** herd; **and,** two days after, they were lucky enough to find the putrid carcase of a deer that had fallen into the cleft of **a** rock the previous spring. We **are** informed that the intestines of this animal, which had been scattered over the rock, were carefully scraped together by the more than half-famished men, **and** added to their meal. **On** the 29th September Dr. Richardson **nearly lost his life** whilst gallantly attempting **to swim across the** almost **frozen Copper-** mine River, **with the** object of establishing communi- cation with the opposite bank, in order that the **re-** mainder of the party might cross. He was hauled **on** shore **in** an almost lifeless condition, and being **rolled** up in blankets, was placed before a fire **that** had been kindled for the purpose. He gradually recovered con- sciousness, but his anxious attendants were horrified to find that his entire left side was **deprived of feeling;** this was due to the fact that, in **their** anxiety, **they had** exposed him too suddenly to the heat. Perfect sensation did not return until the following spring.

On the 1st of October the antlers and backbone **of a**

deer killed the preceding year were found, and **although** they had **been** picked clean by the **wolves** and **birds,** the spinal marrow still **remained,** and this, though **in a** partially decomposed state, was regarded as a valuable **prize** by the starving party. The marrow was **so** acrid as to excoriate their lips **and** mouths. On the 4th of October affairs were so serious **that Mr. Back, the most** active and vigorous **of** the party, volunteered **to** make his way as speedily as possible to Fort Enterprise, in order to give information regarding the helpless condition of his companions, and to send the chief Akaitcho and his Indians, whom he hoped and expected to find at the fort, **back to** their succour and assistance. With this humane object in view he started off at once, accompanied by three of the most robust of the voyageurs. The remainder **of** the party plodded wearily after.

Mr. Hood at this time **was** excessively feeble, consequent on the severe bowel complaints which the *tripe de roche* never failed to give him. This diet was occasionally varied by old shoes and whatever scraps of leather **could** be obtained. Some of the men being even, if possible, in a worse state, and so weak as to **be** almost unable to proceed, it was decided that **Dr.** Richardson and Mr. Hood should remain behind to look after them, while Franklin, with the remainder of the party, should **push on to** Fort Enterprise, twenty-four miles distant, and endeavour to obtain relief. This was considered as the wisest disposition of the party that could be suggested, and was accordingly acted upon. The seaman Hepburn, with four Canadians, namely Michel, Belanger, Credit, **and** Vaillant, **were** left with Dr. Richardson, and they were soon after joined by another voyageur named

Perrault, who, starting with Franklin, found himself too weak to proceed, and therefore returned.

On the 11th October, Franklin, with his more than half-starved companions, after a long and painful journey of five days' duration, during which time the only food that passed their lips was some old shoe-leather and a little *tripe de roche* (for even the latter form of diet was scarce and not easily obtainable), reached Fort Enterprise, where they fully expected that their sufferings would end, and that they would be able to despatch relief to their more helpless comrades. Their feelings may be better imagined than described when, on their arrival, they found a perfectly deserted habitation—no traces of Akaitcho and the Indians they expected to find, and with whom they had arranged for supplies, and not a scrap of food to be found, not even a letter to inform them of the whereabouts of the Indians. There was, however, a short, hurriedly written note left by Mr. Back, who had reached the house two days previously, informing them that he had started in search of the Indians, and in the event of his failing to find them, it was his intention to walk on to Fort Providence, whence, at any rate, he hoped he would be able to send help and succour to the remainder of the expedition; but a significant clause in the note added, that he much questioned whether he and his party, in their weak and debilitated state, would be able to accomplish the journey.

This was a terrible blow to Franklin and those with him, for they well knew that assistance, if it was to be obtained from Fort Providence, would be long in reaching them, and they were fully aware that immediate aid was absolutely necessary for their salvation. They were,

however, somewhat relieved by finding some **old deer-**
skins, which had been thrown away by them during the
preceding **winter, and which,** with some old bones that
were raked **up from the** dirt-heap, and the addition of
a little *tripe de roche*, would serve to prolong existence
for **a few days.** At this time the temperature **was**
ranging from 15° **to** 20° below zero.

The **condition of these poor fellows was now** truly
distressing. They were **so weak and emaciated** as **to**
be unable to move except for a **few yards at a time;**
they were afflicted with swellings in their joints, limbs,
and other parts of **their** bodies; **their** eyeballs were
dilated; they spoke with hollow sepulchral voices; and
their mouths were raw and excoriated, the result of the
fare on which they had subsisted. The story of the
sufferings endured **by this** party is one of the most
harrowing on record. **It is** impossible to imagine, much
less describe, the terrible hardships and privations they
experienced, borne as they were **with manly** fortitude
and Christian resignation.

On the 20th, as there were no signs of the approach
of the Indians, from whom alone relief could be obtained,
Franklin started with the intention of looking for them,
taking with him two men. The other three were quite
unable to move. **On the** following day he had the misfortune **to** break **his** snow-shoes, which necessitated his
return to Fort Enterprise. The two men, however,
went on by themselves in search **of the** Indians. **The**
state of those left behind was **now** very deplorable.
The little strength remaining to them was declining day
by day; when once seated it was **only by exerting the**
greatest effort they could rise; and then **only with the**
assistance of one of their equally helpless companions.

Whilst in this wretched condition a **herd of reindeer**
was suddenly seen one evening close to the **house—**

> "The crescent moon, and crimson **eve,**
> Shone with a mingling light ;
> The deer upon the grassy mead
> Were feeding full in sight ; "

but, alas ! they were too weak, poor fellows, **even to at-**
tempt to shoot at them, and the animals were permitted
to graze and pass on unmolested. The sufferings of Tan-
talus could not have been worse than those experienced
by these starving men when they beheld plenty, which
to them meant existence and life, **at** their **door within**
gunshot range, without being able **to avail themselves**
of the supply which had apparently **been so providen-**
tially sent to them.

On the 29th Dr. Richardson **and** Hepburn suddenly
and unexpectedly made their appearance, bringing with
them a sad tale of woe and horror. Of the eight men
who were left behind at the last encampment, these two
were the sole survivors. Poor Hood had been foully
murdered by the man Michel, who, **a few** days later, was
shot in self-defence by Dr. Richardson. The remainder
had died of cold and starvation. It was a terrible and
a ghastly tale they had to narrate—a story of murder
and cannibalism, combined with almost unheard-of suffer-
ings. Although it was never properly proved, it is more
than certain that the man Michel had taken the lives of
two of his companions (Belanger and Perrault), and had
satisfied his unnatural appetite by feasting on the bodies
of his victims. He had then murdered poor Hood by
shooting him through the **head, while Dr. Richardson**
and Hepburn **were absent from the** camp gathering
tripe de roche. He subsequently conducted himself in

such a threatening and domineering manner, that, under the circumstances, the Doctor felt fully justified in **de**priving this monster in human form of life.

This was the dreadful and mournful story they had to **tell, and it was** one that naturally produced a melancholy feeling **of** despondency in the minds of Franklin and his party. They were all much shocked at beholding the emaciated and haggard appearance of the Doctor and his companion, who were, however, in **no** worse condition, if so bad, than they were themselves. Hepburn having had the good luck to shoot a partridge before reaching the post, it was held before the fire a few minutes, then divided into six equal portions and ravenously devoured. **It was the first** morsel of flesh that had passed their **lips for thirty-one days!** Although herds of reindeer were frequently seen in close proximity to their quarters, and were even fired **at on** several occasions, they never succeeded in killing one, and they were far too weak to go in pursuit.

On the evening of November 1st, one of their party, Peltier, succumbed to starvation, and he was followed the next evening by Semandré, another of the voyageurs. The united strength of the party was unequal **to in**terring, or even removing, the corpses of their two companions, and the bodies had therefore to remain in the house, and in the same position in which the poor fellows had breathed their last. The party was now reduced to four, **viz.,** Lieutenant Franklin, Dr. Richardson, Hepburn, and a Canadian, named Adam, all in a state of great extremity. As their strength declined, so their minds exhibited symptoms of weakness and decay, and they feared their intellects were going. But their deliverance was at hand. On the 7th November, when they had almost made up their minds that death must speedily release them from their terrible sufferings, three Indians unexpectedly made their appearance, having been despatched by Mr. Back, with all possible speed, to their succour. They brought with them some dried deer's meat and a few tongues, which being placed before the famished party, it is needless to say, was eagerly and greedily devoured; but the feeling that they were saved, that deliverance from a long and painful death had actually arrived, acted with even more beneficial effects than the food that was thus providentially provided for them. It undoubtedly saved the life of Adam, whose death, prior to the arrival of relief, was momentarily expected. From this date their sufferings may be said to have terminated. The Indians not only procured game and fish, but watched over them with tender care, and ministered to their wants and comfort.

On the 16th November, their health and strength having been sufficiently resuscitated, they took their departure from Fort Enterprise. Their feelings on quitting this place, where they had experienced a degree of misery scarcely to be paralleled in history, must have been indescribable. Nothing could exceed the kindness of their attendant Indians, who prepared the encampments, obtained food, cooked it, and even fed them, while treating them at all times with the greatest tenderness and solicitude. At length, on the 11th December, the poor wayworn and suffering travellers reached Fort Providence, where they once again experienced the agreeable sensation of being in a comfortable dwelling and in the enjoyment of comparative luxury, so different to the miseries and hardships they had so

recently undergone.   Four days only were spent at Fort
Providence, and on the 18th they reached Moose Deer
Island, where they had **the** happiness of meeting their
companion **Mr.** Back, without whose energy and perseverance they must inevitably **have perished.**

The sufferings **endured by this gallant** young officer,
during his long and arduous journey in **search of** assist-
ance, were quite equal to those of the party he had left
behind; they may perhaps be better imagined when it
is stated that for many days he and his three **men sub-**
sisted on an old pair of leather trousers, a gun-cover,
and a pair of old shoes, with a little *tripe de roche* that
they succeeded in scraping off the rocks!   On the 16th
October, twelve days after he had left Franklin and the
remainder of the party, **one** of his three men died from
starvation **and** exhaustion.   **This loss,** very naturally,
created a feeling **of depression** in the hearts of the sur-
vivors, but still they persevered, resolutely determined
to push onwards, knowing that **the lives of the party**
they had left behind, depended entirely on their exertions.   On the 4th November they, fortunately, fell in with
a party of Indians, and were thus able to send help and
succour to Franklin and his companions, as has already
been stated, at a most critical moment.   Having made
the necessary arrangements for the despatch of further
supplies, Back pushed on **to Fort** Providence, which he
safely reached **on the 21st of** November.   Here letters
for the expedition were received, and among them was
the welcome announcement **of** the promotion of their
gallant leader to **the** well-earned rank of commander, and
the advancement of Back and poor Hood to the equally
well-deserved rank of lieutenant.   Franklin's commis-
sion to a commander bears date January 1, 1821.

The winter was passed by the members of the expedition at Moose Deer Island, and, under the circumstances, a very pleasant and happy one it was. Nothing could exceed the kindness and hospitality of the Hudson's Bay officials stationed at that post, and under their care Franklin and his companions gradually recovered their usual health and strength. On the 26th May they left their hospitable quarters at Moose Deer Island, and visiting Fort Chipewyan on their way, reached Norway House on the 4th July. Ten days later they arrived at York Factory, thus bringing to a conclusion their "long, fatiguing, and disastrous" wanderings in North America, in accomplishing which they had journeyed, by land and by water, a distance of 5550 geographical miles.

On their arrival in England Commander Franklin was immediately promoted by the Admiralty to the rank of captain, in recognition of his extraordinary and eventful journey, in the accomplishment of which he had displayed so much ability, courage, and energy. His captain's commission was dated November 20, 1822. He was, at about the same time, unanimously elected a Fellow of the Royal Society, for his great and invaluable exertions in the cause of geographical science, whilst conducting one of the most remarkable journeys that had ever been achieved. The history of it is of such thrilling interest that it is almost unnecessary to offer any apology for having referred to it at such length—at greater length, perhaps, than is warranted in a work professing to treat more of geography than of the personal incidents connected with the lives of those who, by their dogged perseverance and undaunted courage, have materially added to the greatness and prosperity of our country. The detailed and official narrative, written by the leader of the expedition after his return, should be read by all who appreciate a truly heroic story, told in a modest and unassuming form. **It** cannot but fail to impress those who read it, with that strong and marked feeling of Christian reliance **in** an all-merciful Providence, that self-abnegation and devotion to those entrusted to his charge, and above **all,** that cheerful and reliant disposition which was so conspicuous in Franklin, and which stamped him as **a born** leader of men.

His companion and fellow-sufferer, Dr. Richardson, **who** was intimately acquainted with him, writes of his chief in the following **terms :—**

"**Franklin had a cheerful** buoyancy of mind, which, sustained by a religious principle of a depth known only to his most intimate friends, **was** not depressed in the most gloomy times."

Sir John **Barrow also, in reference to this marvellous** journey, writes :—

"It adds another to the many splendid records **of enterprise, zeal, and** energy of our seamen—of **that cool and intrepid** conduct which **never forsakes** them **on** occasions the most trying—that **unshaken** constancy and perseverance in **situations** the most arduous, **the most** distressing, and sometimes **the** most hopeless, that can befall human beings ; and it furnishes a beautiful example of the triumph of mental and moral energy **over** mere brute strength, in the simple fact that out of fifteen individuals, inured from their birth to cold, fatigue, and hunger, no **less** than ten (native landsmen) were so subdued by the aggravation of those evils to which they had been habituated, as to give themselves **up** to indifference, insubordination, and despair, and finally **to sink** down and die ; whilst of five British seamen unaccustomed to the severity of the climate, and the hardships attending it, only one fell, and that one by the hands of an assassin."

In such a well-merited **eulogy**, every Englishman **must heartily and** cordially concur.

Immediately on his **return to** England, Franklin set **to work** to write an account of the expedition, which was published the following year. This narrative, supplemented as it was by a valuable appendix **from the** pen of Dr. Richardson, assisted very **materially in** increasing the slight knowledge possessed at **that time** of the geography, geology, and natural history of the northern portion of North America, and especially with regard to that **great** extent of coast-line, hitherto **practically** unknown, **that is** washed **by the** waters of the Polar Sea.

Franklin's **personal** appearance at this period is thus described by one of his relatives :—"His features and **expression** were grave and mild, and very benignant ; **his build thoroughly** that of a sailor ; his stature rather **below the middle** height ; his look very kind, and his manner very quiet, **though not** without a certain dignity, as of **one** accustomed **to** command others."

During the period he was employed in compiling the narrative **of his adventurous** journey, he was not, apparently, prevented from finding some little time to devote **to** his private affairs, and especially to cultivating and developing the friendship which **he** had formed with the young poetess (**see note, page 127** *ante*), whose acquaintance he **had** made prior **to his departure in** 1818 in the *Trent.* So well did **he** press his suit that he succeeded in winning the young lady's affections, and on the 19th

of August 1823 Captain Franklin was married to Miss
Eleanor Anne Porden. This lady, as has already been
observed, possessed great poetic talent, and had published an epic poem in two volumes entitled "Cœur de
Lion." She had also written a clever scientific poem

MRS. FRANKLIN,
(From a painting in the possession of Rev. John Philip Gell.)

called "The Veils," for which she received the unusual
distinction (at least for an English lady) of being elected
a member of the somewhat exclusive "Institut" of
Paris.

Shortly after her acquaintance with Captain Franklin
had ripened into friendship, she wrote a little poem,

which was published over the *nom de plume* of " Green-
stockings," in which, assuming the character of an
Eskimo maiden, she implores the return of Franklin to
the wild north-land she loves, where she has—

> " Gathered thee dainties most rare—
> The wild birds that soar, and the fish of the sea,
> The moose and the reindeer, the fox and the bear,
> In a snow-mantled grotto, I guard them for thee."

It is credibly reported that, prior to their marriage,
a mutual agreement was made that, under no circumstances, was their union to preclude him from accepting
any service, no matter how dangerous or perilous it might
prove, that might be required of him. His country
was to be his first love, and his wife must be prepared
to allow him to go wherever duty and his country
demanded. It is well known how well and faithfully
the compact then entered upon was, in so short a time,
to be put to the test and scrupulously adhered to.

On the 3rd June 1824 their only child, a daughter,
was born, and was named after her mother. Mrs.
Franklin's health from this time gradually declined,
and when Franklin started on his next expedition, it
was only too apparent he would never meet his accomplished wife in this world again.[1]

---

[1] The parents of Mrs. Franklin died before they were married. She
had an only sister married to Mr. Kay, whose daughter was Franklin's
favourite niece. Her brother, his nephew, entered the navy, and subsequently served with Franklin in the *Rainbow.*

CHAPTER X.

FRANKLIN'S SECOND OVERLAND JOURNEY.

1825–1828.

> " Ours the wild life in tumult still
> To range."   —*The Corsair.*

WE will now turn to the expedition, under the command
of Lieutenant Parry. He was despatched, it will be
remembered, for the express purpose of attempting the
accomplishment of the north-west passage, by sailing
through Baffin's Bay and Lancaster Sound, Franklin
having been directed to co-operate with him in the
event of their meeting in the Arctic Seas. The ships
selected for this service were the *Hecla* of 375 tons, and
the *Griper* of 180 tons, the latter being commanded by
Lieutenant Liddon. They were equipped and prepared
under the direct supervision of Lieutenant Parry, who
spared no trouble, or pains, in order to render them
thoroughly efficient for the important service on which
they were to be employed.

The expedition left England on the 11th of May 1819.
On the 15th of June Cape Farewell, the southern extremity of Greenland, was sighted. The ships then sailed
up Davis Strait, and entered Baffin's Bay, where they
encountered much ice, and experienced great difficulty
in forcing a passage through. At length, after much

incessant labour, requiring constant **and** unceasing vigilance on the part of the officers, the ships entered Lancaster Sound on the 4th of August, sailing **over** the so-called Croker Mountains, which Captain Ross **had,** the **previous** year, hypothetically placed across the entrance.[1]　Propelled by a fresh and favourable breeze, the ships, sailing in a westerly direction without meeting with ice either of sufficient magnitude or quantity to impede their progress, entered **a large** strait, **which was** deservedly named after **Sir** John **Barrow,** the **Secretary** **of** the Admiralty, the indefatigable **promoter and supporter of Arctic research.** Hopes ran **high as they proceeded,** and some even flattered themselves **that the** north-west passage was almost an accomplished fact, but their joyful aspirations were **soon to be** abruptly and rudely shattered, **for on** reaching **the** neighbourhood of Leopold Island their progress was arrested by **a** large barrier of ice which stretched in a solid mass across the strait, and appeared to defy penetration.　Being unable, therefore, to proceed any further in a westerly direction, Parry turned to the southward, and sailed **up a large** inlet which he named Prince Regent **Inlet, when was** observed for the first time "the curious phenomenon of the directive power of the needle becoming so weak **as** to be completely overcome by the attraction **of the ship,** so that the needle might **now be** said to point to the **north pole of the** ship." The fact being that they were

---

[1] When the truth connected with this discovery was made known in England, it gave rise to the following epigrammatic lines—

> "Old Sinbad tells us, he a whale had seen,
> So like the land, it seemed an island green ;
> But Ross has told the converse of this tale,
> The land *he* saw was—*very like a whale !* "

approaching the Magnetic Pole, and its influence on the needle was felt to such an extent, as to render the compasses so sluggish as to be comparatively useless. It may be of interest here to remark that Sir James Ross, who subsequently discovered the North Magnetic Pole, was at that time serving as a midshipman on board the *Hecla.*

Being again stopped by the ice, the ships returned to the northward to find, to their intense surprise and delight, that the barrier of ice in Barrow's Strait which had shortly before checked their progress had altogether disappeared, leaving a broad channel of open water to the westward, in the direction of which the ships were steered. Light and adverse winds and fogs, however, rendered their progress slow. On the 22nd of August they passed the mouth of what appeared to be a broad and extensive inlet to the northward, to which the name of Wellington Channel was given, and on the 3rd of September they had the extreme satisfaction of crossing the 110th meridian of west longitude, thus becoming entitled to the reward of £5000, granted by Parliament to any person, or ship, who should succeed in penetrating so far to the westward inside the Arctic circle (see page 80). A headland off Melville Island, off which they were at the time, was named Cape Bounty to commemorate the event.

Although they had thus succeeded with comparative ease in crossing the 110th meridian of longitude, they found the ice beyond of such a nature as to entirely preclude all possibility of further advance, and as the navigable season had come to an end, Parry secured the ships in a snug harbour on the south coast of Melville Island, which he named Winter Harbour. Before, however, the vessels could be placed in a position of

absolute security, it was found necessary to cut a channel
in the ice more than two miles in length, through which
the ships were dragged into their winter quarters, an
occupation that occupied the crews the greater part of
three days.

Owing to the care and ingenuity of Lieutenant Parry,
the winter passed pleasantly and happily. Theatrical
entertainments were instituted, plays were written and
acted, and a newspaper, *The North Georgian Gazette
and Winter Chronicle*, was periodically published. In
the spring, and before the ships were released from their
icy bondage, Parry explored the country in the vicinity
of their winter quarters, taking with him a light cart
dragged by men, in which the provisions, tent, &c., were
carried. He had not then commenced the system of
sledging which he subsequently introduced, and which
was afterwards brought to great perfection by Sir Leopold M'Clintock. Parry returned on the 15th of June,
having travelled about 180 miles, at an average daily
progress of about twelve miles. It is a curious fact that
more than thirty years after, the marks of the wheels of
his cart were found by Lieutenant M'Clintock, as plain
and distinct as if they had only then recently been made.

On the 1st of August the ice cleared away sufficiently to enable the ships to make a start, and every
effort was made to push to the westward, but without success, their progress being effectively stopped
by an interminable barrier of " thick-ribb'd ice." As
the season was greatly advanced, and as the ships were
not provisioned or prepared in any way for a second
winter, Parry determined to relinquish further attempts
at discovery, and announced his intention of returning
to England, being satisfied with having accomplished

more than half the distance to Bering's Strait. In arriving at this conclusion, Parry acted with that judgment and prudence which, combined with daring and energy at the right moment, were the conspicuous characteristics of this accomplished and successful navigator. On the return of the expedition to England, Parry received his well-earned promotion to the rank of commander, and in the following February was unanimously elected a Fellow of the Royal Society.

Commander Parry was not the man to remain idle, or content with what had been achieved, when there was yet so much to be done, in the way of geographical exploration, so, immediately on his return, he advocated very strongly the desirability of prosecuting further search for a north-west passage, but, he contended, that the greatest chance of success would in his opinion be obtained by the despatch of an expedition through Hudson's Strait and Bay, and thence to skirt along the northern shore of the continent of America. So much confidence did the Admiralty repose, and very deservedly, in his opinion, and in his capacity as the leader of an expedition, that although his two ships, the *Hecla* and *Griper*, were only paid off on the 21st of December 1820, Commander Parry was appointed on the 30th of the same month, to the command of an expedition consisting of the *Fury* and *Hecla*, with directions to carry out the search for a north-west passage through Hudson's Strait and by Repulse Bay. Lieutenant Lyon was appointed to the command of the *Griper*.

Franklin, it must be remembered, had not yet returned from his wonderful land journey towards the shores of the Arctic Sea, and Parry hoped that he might possibly be afforded the opportunity of meeting his old friend, as **he sailed along** the northern coast **of the** American continent.

It is needless to enter into the details **relative to this** second expedition of Parry's. **It was carried out with all the** energy and ability for which that distinguished **officer** was so famed, but he **had** many difficulties **to** contend with, **and** although **the** expedition **did not** return to England **until** the autumn of 1823, the chief geographical result **was the** discovery of the Hecla and Fury Strait. Beyond **this, the** ships **were** unable **to** proceed, and Parry was reluctantly compelled **to** abandon all further attempts for the discovery **of** a navigable passage in that direction.

Immediately **after** his return **to England he was** attacked by a serious illness, and was **for some time in a very precarious** and critical condition. On his **re-**covery, one of the first letters he wrote was to his old friend Franklin, in reply **to a** letter from that officer congratulating him on his safe return. It is inserted here to **show** how much he admired and appreciated **the** work accomplished by Franklin. It was as follows :—

Stamford Hill, October 23, 1823.

" My dear Franklin,—I can sincerely assure you, **that it** was with no ordinary feeling of gratification, that I read **your** kind letter of congratulation on my **return. Of** the splendid achievements **of** yourself, and your **brave** companions in enterprise, I **can** hardly trust **myself to** speak, **for** I am apprehensive of not **conveying what,** indeed, **can never be conveyed** adequately in **words, my** unbounded admiration of **what** you have, **under the** blessing of God, been **enabled to** perform, **and the manner in** which you have **performed it.** To **place you in** the rank of travellers, above Park, and Hearne, **and others,** would, in my estimation, be nothing in comparison of your merits. But in you and your party, my dear friend, we see so sublime an instance of Christian confidence in the Almighty, of the superiority of moral and religious energy over mere brute strength of body, that it is impossible to contemplate your sufferings and preservation, without a sensation of reverential awe! I have not yet seen your book, and have only read the *Quarterly Review*. Your letter was put into my hand at Shetland, and I need not be ashamed to say that I cried over it like a child. The tears I shed, however, were those of pride and pleasure—pride at being your fellow-countryman, brother officer, and friend; pleasure in seeing the virtues of the Christian adding their first and highest charm to the unconquerable perseverance and splendid talents of the officer and the man. I have a promise of your book this day from my brother-in-law, Mr. Martineau, with whom (surrounded by all my family) I am staying for a week at Stamford Hill. I cannot, at present, enter into any *shop* business—I mean geographical details; but I long very much to see the connection between our discoveries. Ours are small, for our success has been small on this occasion. Briefly (for the doctors insist upon it), the north-eastern portion of America consists of a singular peninsula, extending from Repulse Bay in $66\frac{1}{2}°$ latitude to $69\frac{3}{4}°$, and resembling a bastion at the corner of a fort, the gorge of the bastion being three days of Esquimaux journey, across from Repulse Bay to Akköolee, one of their settlements, or stations, on the opposite or Polar Sea side.

"This great southern indentation corresponds, I imagine, with your route, which led you into $66\frac{1}{2}°$, I think, in proceeding eastward; but I have really so vague an idea of your proceedings, geographically, that I can, at present, say very little to gratify curiosity concerning the connection of our discoveries.

"I shall have volumes to say, or write, to you hereafter, but do not be alarmed at the supposition of my expecting volumes from you in return.

"I shall only add that I am, my dear Franklin, your ever faithful and most sincerely admiring friend,

"W. E. PARRY."

Parry was, for his service while in command of this expedition, promoted to the rank of post-captain, his commission being ante-dated to the completion of his one year's service as a commander.

Although Captain **Parry** had failed on two occasions in his attempts to discover the long sought for passage, he was still fully persuaded not only of its existence, but of the feasibility of its discovery by way of Lancaster Sound, and thence, either by Prince Regent Inlet to the southward, or by **Barrow's** Strait to the west. These views were fully laid before the Government, the members of which had such confidence in the judgment and ability of this distinguished officer, that they resolved, and without loss of time, to despatch another expedition, on the lines indicated by him, in quest of the north-west passage, and the entire conduct of it was, very properly, entrusted to Captain **Parry.** It would surely be a valuable aid and assistance to our existing geographical knowledge of the unexplored and unknown regions of the world, if the Government of the present day shared the same liberal and enlightened views, regarding research in high latitudes, as influenced those that procured the despatch of Parry's third expedition in 1824.

In order that the search for the passage should be complete, and also to guard against failure as much as possible, it was resolved to send a second expedition to carry out exploration by land, along the northern shore of the North American coast. This was in accordance with a scheme submitted by Captain Franklin, who proposed that an expedition, on somewhat similar lines to his last one, should be sent to the mouth of the Mackenzie River; there the party were to divide, and while one portion of it was to proceed by sea along the coast to the westward, the remainder would be detached and sent to the eastward, with directions to survey the coast as far as the Coppermine River, and so connect previous discoveries.

Nothing daunted by the terrible sufferings he had so recently experienced, Franklin sought for, and obtained, the supreme command of this expedition ; while his old friend and companion, Dr. Richardson, who had volunteered to accompany him, was selected to take charge of the exploration of that portion of the coast alluded to above, situated between the Mackenzie and Coppermine Rivers. Not content with the despatch of these two expeditions, orders were sent to Captain Beechey to proceed with H.M.S. *Blossom* [1] under his command to Kotzebue Inlet in Bering's Strait, with the object of meeting Captain Franklin, in the event of a successful termination to his journey, and to convey him and his party to Canton, or the Sandwich Islands, as might seem most advisable ; or to carry out any other instructions that Captain Franklin might think proper to issue. Lieutenant Back was again associated with his old chief ; and Mr. Kendall, Admiralty mate, who had recently served under Captain Lyon, in Parry's last expedition, formed one of the party. [2]   Mr. Drummond, on the special recommendation of Professor Hooker, was also appointed in the capacity of assistant naturalist. All the details connected with the fitting out of the expedition, and even the particular route to be followed,

---

[1] The *Blossom* was at that time stationed in the Pacific, under the command of Captain Beechey, who served as first lieutenant under Franklin when that officer was in command of the *Trent* in 1818.

[2] Mr. Kendall subsequently married the favourite niece of Sir John Franklin, the daughter of Mrs. Franklin's only sister.

SIR EDWARD PARRY AND SIR GEORGE BACK.

(From an engraving of Stephen Pearce's picture of the Arctic Council in the possession of Col. John Barrow, by permission of Henry Graves & Co.)

were left entirely to Captain Franklin, who personally superintended the equipment, and made the necessary arrangements with the Hudson's Bay Company's officials for the conveyance of his people, stores, and provisions to the Great Bear Lake. In accordance with his wishes three boats were specially constructed, combining lightness and portability with seaworthiness and stability, with a view of their easy transport over the numerous portages and various rapids that would be met with before reaching the Arctic Sea, on which it was intended they should be used. The largest of these boats was twenty-six feet long, and was capable of carrying eight people; the other two were each twenty-four feet in length, and would hold seven men.

These boats, with all the men and stores required for the expedition, were sent out by the annual Hudson's Bay ship sailing to York Factory in 1824, whence they were immediately despatched to the Great Bear Lake. The officers of the expedition did not leave England until February 16, 1825. They went out by way of New York, and travelling through the States and Canada, reached Fort Cumberland, on the Saskatchewan, on the 15th June. Before, however, this stage in their journey had been accomplished, Franklin, to his inexpressible sorrow, received the mournful intelligence of the death of his beloved wife, who had breathed her last, six short days only after her husband had bidden her farewell. This was a great blow to Captain Franklin, although he was not altogether unprepared for the distressing intelligence, for he was well aware of the delicate, not to say critical, state of Mrs. Franklin's health prior to his departure from England. She was only twenty-nine years of age when she passed away.

Fort Cumberland was left the day after their arrival. Pushing rapidly on they overtook the boats and the remainder of the party that had travelled *viâ* York Factory, on June 29th, in the Methye River, arriving at Fort Chipewyan on the 15th of the following month. This post was left on the 25th, and four days afterwards the expedition reached Fort Resolution, the only establishment of any kind situated on Slave Lake. Here they remained for six days making the necessary arrangements with the Indians for the supply of provisions, &c., to last them during the forthcoming winter. Embarking in their canoes on the 31st July, they crossed the lake and steered for the Mackenzie River. Hitherto they had been travelling along the same route that Franklin had adopted when journeying to Fort Enterprise in 1820, but after leaving Fort Resolution they inclined more to the westward, entering the Mackenzie River on the 2nd August. In a couple of days, they made such good progress that they arrived at Fort Simpson, the principal depôt of the Hudson's Bay Company in that locality. They left the next day and pushing onwards, obtained their first view of the Rocky Mountains, the general appearance of which much resembled, in Franklin's opinion, the east end of the island of Jamaica. The river was, in many places, over two miles in breadth, flowing smoothly, though swiftly, towards the sea. They were not troubled or inconvenienced by either rapids or their attendant portages—indeed, one is, as a rule, the corollary of the other—and they were therefore enabled to proceed with such rapidity that they reached the Hudson's Bay post at Fort Norman on August 7th.

As there yet remained a few weeks of the travelling

season in which exploration could be carried out before the winter set in, Franklin determined to lose no time in prosecuting the work entrusted to him. He therefore, with this object in view, made the following arrangements, which were duly carried out by the parties concerned. Lieutenant Back, accompanied by Mr. Dease,[1] was ordered to proceed at once to Great Bear Lake (a distance that would take him about four days to accomplish), on the banks of which he was to select the site for a house, and immediately to set the men to work on its construction. He was also directed to make all the necessary arrangements for passing as comfortable a winter as, under the circumstances, it was possible to do. Dr. Richardson was despatched, at his own special request, to explore the northern shore of Bear Lake; whilst Franklin himself, with Mr. Kendall as his companion, started in one of the boats, with a crew of six Englishmen, a native guide, and an Eskimo interpreter,[2] for the mouth of the Mackenzie, in order to endeavour to obtain information regarding the state and condition of the ice on the Arctic Sea, and their prospects of pushing on the following year. He was also desirous of ascertaining the general trend of the coast, east and west of the mouth of the Mackenzie River, and of satisfying himself as to the chance of their being able to obtain a supply of provisions along the coast.

The different parties separated to carry out their respective instructions on the 8th of August. Two days

---

[1] Mr. Dease was an officer of the Hudson's Bay Company who had volunteered for, and been attached to, the expedition at the special request of Captain Franklin.

[2] This was Augustus, who was with Franklin in his previous expedition to the Arctic Sea.

subsequently Franklin reached Fort Good Hope, the
most northern Hudson's Bay station in the territory,
much pleased with the speed and general handiness of
his English built boat, in which he had accomplished a
distance of no less than 312 miles in about sixty hours ;
but this rapid travelling was in a great measure due to
a fair wind and a swift current. Fort Good Hope was
left the following day, and the sea was eventually reached
on the 14th. Captain Franklin bears testimony to the
general accuracy of Mackenzie's survey. Some of this
traveller's positions were, it is true, found to be somewhat at variance with those determined by Franklin,
but the differences in latitude and longitude were ascribed
to the possibility of their having been laid down by
magnetic bearings, and not by astronomical observations. Franklin pays a just and generous tribute to
the energy, courage, and skill shown by Mackenzie
during his arduous and trying journey. During their
voyage down the river they met several parties of
Indians, with all of whom they had friendly intercourse,
and from whom they received small supplies of fresh
provisions, although at first they were somewhat shy
and suspicious at the unexpected approach and appearance of the white men.

The sea, to their great joy, was found to be entirely
free of ice, while " seals and black and white whales were
sporting on its waves." Altogether it was a sight that
gladdened their hearts, as it gave rise to hopeful anticipations of ultimate success.

On reaching the coast a silk Union Jack, worked
by the weak and feeble fingers of his sick wife, was
unfurled. This flag was given to her husband, as he
was on the point of leaving England, with strict injunc-

tions that it was not to be displayed until the expedition had reached the Polar Sea. When Franklin bade her farewell it was with the conviction that the hand of death was upon her, and that he should see her no more in this world; but obedient to the call of his country, and exhorted by her own earnest pleadings that he should proceed on the important, though dangerous, service for which he had been selected, with his heart overflowing with feelings of sorrow and despondency, he accepted the gift, assuring his wife that he should not fail to think of her when he planted it, as he felt sure he would, on the wild and inhospitable shores of the Arctic Sea. It must therefore have been with mingled feelings of joy and sorrow, that he saw this last souvenir of his dearly loved wife fluttering out bravely in the wind, in full view of the Polar Ocean, in fulfilment of his promise. In a letter to his sister-in-law, written shortly after his return to their winter quarters, Franklin, in alluding to his having reached the sea on the 16th of August, writes—" Here was first displayed the flag which my lamented Eleanor made, and you can imagine it was with heartfelt emotion I first saw it unfurled; but in a short time I derived great pleasure in looking at it."

The position of the mouth of the Mackenzie River was found to be in latitude 69° 29′ N., and 135° 41′ W. longitude. Depositing a record of the progress of the expedition thus far for the information of Captain Parry, in the event of that officer reaching the neighbourhood, and making it as conspicuous as possible by the erection of a long pole, to the top of which was hoisted a blue and red flag, and having thoroughly explored the country in the vicinity of the mouth of the river, they commenced the return journey, and without any event worthy of special record reached their winter quarters on the Great Bear Lake on the evening of the 5th of September. They found that Dr. Richardson had returned a few days before them, having made a successful survey of the lake to its north-east termination, where it is nearest to the Coppermine River.

Here at Fort Franklin, for so the post had been named in compliment to their leader during his temporary absence, the members of the expedition were for the first time united. They found the houses that had been erected for their accommodation by their comrade Mr. Back, both commodious and comfortable, and all that, under the circumstances, could be desired. The establishment consisted of three buildings, which were so constructed as to form the three sides of a square. The centre one was appropriated to the officers, one was allotted to the men as their quarters, and the other was used as a store and provision house. The number of persons to be accommodated in this establishment was no less than fifty, viz.—five officers (including Mr. Dease), nineteen seamen and marines, nine Canadians, and two Eskimos, the remainder being made up of Indians, men, women, and children, whose services were required for the purposes of hunting, fishing, and for the general supply of game and other provisions. The position of Fort Franklin was ascertained to be latitude $65°$ $11'$ $56''$, and longitude $123°$ $12'$ $44''$.

The winter passed pleasantly enough, and although the cold was great it was not insufferably so, the lowest recorded temperature being $49°$ below zero (Fahr.). The Indian hunters succeeded in procuring a fair amount of game and fish during the winter, although in February, in consequence of a temporary failure in obtaining supplies, they were necessarily reduced to a very short allowance of provisions. The officers occupied their spare time in taking thermometrical, magnetic and atmospheric observations, besides others of a scientific nature. They likewise superintended the school that Franklin established during the winter months, as well as the strict observance of the regular routine that was wisely instituted. As another boat was considered desirable, the carpenters were busily employed on the construction of one on somewhat similar lines to the *Lion*, the boat they had brought out from England with them. This boat, when completed, was called the *Reliance*.

The arrangements for the summer campaign were briefly as follows :—Captain Franklin, accompanied by Lieutenant Back, was to explore by boat along the north coast of North America to the westward of the mouth of the Mackenzie River, if possible to Icy Cape. Dr. Richardson, with Mr. Kendall as his colleague and companion, was to undertake the eastern line of exploration, including the examination of the coast from the mouth of the Mackenzie to the Coppermine River, returning to Fort Franklin before the winter set in. Mr. Dease would remain at Fort Franklin with directions to keep the establishment well stored with provisions for use during the ensuing winter, in the event of Franklin failing in his attempt to communicate with the *Blossom* (see page 154 *ante*). It was, therefore, necessary to make provision on the chance of the entire party having to pass another winter at the post. Fourteen men, including two Canadians, with Augustus the Eskimo interpreter, under Captain Franklin and Lieutenant Back, with the two boats *Lion* and *Reliance*, formed the western party ; while ten men, with the two smaller boats, the *Dolphin* and *Union*, under the command of Dr. Richardson and **Mr. Kendall**, were entrusted with the eastern line of exploration.

Everything being **in readiness, a start** was made on the 24th June. **The** two parties travelled in company down the Mackenzie **River** until **the** 3rd July, **when they reached** that part **of the river where it** bifurcated to the east and **to the west, Franklin** pursuing his course **along the** latter route, while Richardson **proceeded by the former.** They were all supplied **with provisions to** last an anticipated **absence of one hundred days.**

Franklin reached **the coast on the** 7th **of** July, **and on the same day met a tribe of** Eskimos numbering **about three hundred.** At first their intercourse was **friendly enough ;** but the cupidity of these savages being **excited by the articles of, to them,** priceless value that they **saw, an attempt was made to pillage** the boats, **but this outrage was frustrated by** the coolness and forbearance **of Franklin and his men.** It afterwards transpired **that a** massacre of the **whole** expedition **had** been arranged, and was only prevented by the vigilance **and** preparedness of the party. On arrival at the sea they were intensely mortified **to find that** their progress to the **westward was checked by heavy** masses of ice. **These, however, in the course of four or five days,** during **which time the** expedition **was compelled** to remain **inactive, cleared away** sufficiently to **leave a** passage **along the coast, and so** enabled them to push on. Gales **of** wind and **fogs were** unfortunately very prevalent, **and** sadly interfered **with** their progress. The boats **were also very** roughly handled, and were frequently **in danger** of **being** crushed by the large fragments of **ice** with **which they were** constantly **coming into con-**

tact, and which had the effect of causing them to leak considerably.   In spite of all these drawbacks, they steadily persevered, using oars and sail according to circumstances, watching and taking advantage of every opportunity for pushing onwards, battling against all difficulties, and striving to their utmost each day to beat the record of the last in the distance accomplished. Their general course was as nearly as possible in a westerly direction, along a low flat shelving coast, in water so shallow as to compel them to keep at a distance of from two to three miles from the shore.   As accurate a survey of the coast as was practicable was made as they proceeded; it was, however, found to be devoid of all bays or harbours in which a ship could obtain shelter, or remain securely at anchor.

They were not infrequently detained by bad weather, fogs, and impenetrable ice, and on one occasion the detention was for no less a period than eight consecutive days. During these unavoidable stoppages the members of the expedition were not inactive, for they would seize on these opportunities to take astronomical observations, as well as those to determine the magnetic inclination, variation, and intensity, besides observations on the rise, fall, and direction of the tides.   The geology of the country along which they travelled was also carefully studied, and many valuable specimens of natural history were added to their collection.

During all this time the torments they endured from the pertinacious attacks of countless swarms of musquitoes were indescribable; they were regarded as quite the greatest of the sufferings they were called upon to endure! It is a somewhat significant fact that a point of land on the north coast of America was, during the journey, named Point Griffin by Captain Franklin, presumably after the lady who subsequently became his wife.

At length, on the 18th of August, having traced the coast westward, from the mouth of the Mackenzie River, for 374 miles, Captain Franklin very reluctantly came to the conclusion that further advance would be imprudent, taking into consideration the lateness of the season, and the self-evident fact that he had only traversed half the distance between the Mackenzie River and Icy Cape. Before he could hope to accomplish the remainder of the distance that intervened, winter would have set in, and the *Blossom* would, in consequence, have sailed to the southward. He therefore wisely decided to return. To the most extreme point seen to the westward he gave the name of Cape Beechey.

It is interesting to note here that the *Blossom* had successfully carried out her part of the programme, and was off Icy Cape during the middle of August. Thence Captain Beechey despatched one of his boats to the eastward, in the hope of meeting Franklin. This boat actually arrived on the 25th of August within 160 miles of the position reached by Franklin when he resolved to turn back a week before. It would not, however, have been possible for Franklin to have accomplished the distance that lay between them, before the *Blossom's* boat returned to the westward, so that had he persevered in hopes of meeting it, he and his party would in all probability have perished during the winter. It was therefore a wise and discreet resolve on Franklin's part to return. The extreme position reached was latitude 70° 26′ N., and 148° 52′ W. longitude. The return journey was very similar to the outward one, except that they suffered more from cold and less from musquitoes! Through the friendly warning of the Eskimos, they were able to frustrate a plot to assassinate the whole party that had been laid by a tribe of hostile Indians near the mouth of the Mackenzie. This diabolical scheme was prevented by their taking a different route on their return to the one along which they had travelled on their outward journey. The Mackenzie was reached on the 30th August, and the expedition arrived, intact and in good health, at Fort Franklin on the 21st September. The total number of geographical miles travelled by the party since leaving Fort Franklin until their return was 2048, a third of which distance was through a perfectly unknown country.

They were much elated to find that the travellers to the eastward had also made a very successful journey, having succeeded in tracing no less than 863 miles of undiscovered coast-line situated between the Mackenzie and Coppermine Rivers; they returned to Fort Franklin by way of the Coppermine River, reaching that post on the 1st September. Like the western party they reported having experienced strong gales of wind, and their progress was much hampered by ice, in which their boats were often seriously injured, being frequently exposed to the risk of being crushed altogether. They met several parties of Eskimos, all of whom afforded convincing proofs of their dexterity in the art of pilfering, and it was only by the exercise of great tact and forbearance, on the part of Dr. Richardson and his people, that an open rupture was avoided. An accurate survey of the coast was made by Lieutenant Kendall, while Dr. Richardson made many valuable observations in connection with the geology and natural history of the country.

A large bay, discovered on the 22nd of July, was

named Franklin Bay; in conferring this name upon it, the
Doctor, in his **narrative,** indulges in the following eulo-
gistic remarks regarding **his** able and talented leader :—

"In bestowing the **name** of **Franklin** on this remarkable
bay, I **paid** an appropriate compliment **to the** officer under
whose orders and by whose arrangements **the** delineation of
all **that is** known of the **northern coast of the** American
continent has been effected; with the **exception of the parts**
in the vicinity **of Icy Cape** discovered **by Captain Beechey.**

"It **would** not be proper, nor is it my intention, **to descant**
on the professional merits of my superior officer; **but after**
having served under Captain Franklin **for nearly seven years**
in two **successive voyages of discovery, I trust I may be
allowed to say, that however high his brother** officers may
rate his courage and talents, either in the ordinary line of his
professional duty, or in the field of discovery, the hold he
acquires upon the affections of those under his command, by a
continued **series of the most conciliatory** attentions to their
feelings, **and an uniform and unremitting** regard to their best
interests, **is not** less **conspicuous. I feel that** the sentiments
of my friends and companions, Captain **Back and** Lieutenant
Kendall, are in unison **with my own, when I** affirm, that
gratitude and attachment **to our** late commanding officer will
animate our breasts to the latest periods of **our** lives."

On August 4th, Wollaston **Land was discovered to
the northward, and the** channel **between it and the
mainland** was called Dolphin **and Union Strait, after
the two** little **boats in which they were embarked. On
the** 7th they had the extreme satisfaction **of entering**
George 4th Coronation Gulf, and **so** connected **their**
discoveries **with** those of **Captain** Franklin **during his**
voyage in 1820—

"Thus," as Dr. Richardson writes, "completing **a portion of**
the north-west passage **for** which **the** reward of £5000 **was**

established by His Majesty's Order in Council; but as it was not contemplated in framing the order that the discovery should be made from west to east, and in vessels so small as the *Dolphin* and *Union*, we could not lay claim to the pecuniary reward."

The successful issue of their voyage enabled them to return by a shorter and a better route than that adopted for the outward journey. On the following day the mouth of the Coppermine River was reached, and after proceeding up it for some miles, the boats and everything that was not absolutely necessary to be transported, were abandoned, and the journey commenced on those same barren lands, over which Franklin and his party had toiled and endured such sufferings during the previous expedition, but this time under more favourable conditions; the load carried by each man was 72 lbs. Without any further event worth recording, the party reached Great Bear Lake on the 18th of August, and on the 1st of September arrived at Fort Franklin, having accomplished a wonderfully successful journey, during which they traversed a distance, by land and by boat, of 1980 geographical miles, of which 1015 were new discoveries. Immediately on his return to Fort Franklin, Dr. Richardson started off to prosecute his geological and natural history researches in the neighbourhood of the Great Slave Lake, where he passed the following winter.

Franklin and his people were, of course, compelled to spend another winter at Fort Franklin; but having a plentiful supply of provisions and other necessaries, and also plenty of work to do in the way of plotting the charts connected with their discoveries, and arranging their scientific observations, it passed quickly and pleasantly enough, in spite of the temperature falling during the month of February to 58° below zero, the lowest that any of the party had hitherto experienced. By a packet of letters which was conveyed to them by an Indian messenger during the winter, they were all much pleased and gratified to find that their popular companion, Lieutenant Back, had been promoted to the rank of commander.

On the 20th February 1827, Captain Franklin being desirous of reaching England as speedily as possible, left the Fort, in company with five men, leaving instructions for Captain Back to proceed to York Factory with the remainder of the party as soon as the ice should break up; thence they were to sail for England in the Hudson's Bay Company's ship, which it was anticipated would be leaving in the autumn. Franklin reached Fort Simpson on the 8th of March; here he remained a few days in order to rest and recruit the health of his dogs, and arrived at Fort Resolution, on the Great Slave Lake, on the 26th. The return to this neighbourhood must have brought vividly to Franklin's mind the terrible sufferings and privations he had endured in that same locality only a few years previously. Fort Chipewyan was reached on the 12th of April, and here a stoppage of six weeks was made. This place was left on the 31st May, and on the 18th June, Franklin and his small party arrived at Cumberland House, where he had the inexpressible happiness of meeting with Dr. Richardson after a separation of eleven months. From him he learned that Mr. Drummond, the assistant naturalist, had been most indefatigable in collecting natural history specimens. He had travelled, with that object in view, as far as the Rocky Mountains, having been exposed

JANE LADY FRANKLIN.
(At the age of 24.)

during his wanderings to very great hardships and privations.

From Cumberland House, Franklin and Richardson travelled together to Montreal and New York, and arrived in England on the 26th September 1827, after an absence of two years and seven and a half months. Commander Back, with the remainder of the party, reached Portsmouth fourteen days later.

The geographical result of this expedition was the discovery and accurate delineation of over a thousand miles of the north coast of the American continent, hitherto absolutely unknown. The geological, magnetical, meteorological, topographical, and other scientific observations, made by the different members of the expedition, were of the greatest value and interest, more especially those relating to the Aurora Borealis. The important work performed by the members of the expedition was fully appreciated on their return to England, both by the Admiralty and the learned societies, who were unanimous in their acknowledgment of the value of the services rendered, and their appreciation of the skill and ability that had been displayed by officers and men in carrying them out.

France also, not to be behindhand in her admiration at the way in which the leader of the expedition had achieved such a signal geographical success, presented Captain Franklin, shortly after his return to England, with the Paris Geographical Society's gold medal, valued at 1200 francs, for having made "the most important acquisition to geographical knowledge" during the year. On the 29th April 1829 Captain Franklin received the honour of knighthood; and on the following 1st of July the honorary degree of D.C.L. of Oxford was conferred upon him, at the same time that a similar honour was bestowed on Sir Edward Parry.

These events are thus alluded to in the prize poem recited in the theatre at the Commemoration, on the occasion, by T. Legh Claughton—

> " But fairer England greets the wanderer now,
>   Unfading laurels shade her Parry's brow ;
>   And on the proud memorials of her fame
>   Lives, linked with deathless glory, Franklin's name."

On the 5th November 1828 Franklin married Jane, second daughter of John Griffin, Esq., of Bedford Place, a lady of great culture and rare intellectual powers, and one who was in every way qualified to be the friend, adviser, and helpmate of a man of Sir John Franklin's energy and disposition. Her life and character as a woman and a wife are written on the pages of the history of our country.

CHAPTER XI.

PARRY'S THIRD EXPEDITION — HIS ATTEMPT TO REACH THE POLE — SIR JOHN ROSS — DISCOVERY OF MAGNETIC POLE — FRANKLIN IN THE MEDITERRANEAN — GOVERNMENT OF VAN DIEMEN'S LAND.

1824–1844.

> " Where's the coward that would not dare
> To fight for such a land ?"—*Marmion.*

ALTHOUGH Captain **Franklin** had failed, through no want of energy or fault of his own, in the actual accomplishment of the north-west passage, he was fully impressed with its practicability, and openly maintained on his return his own views regarding the feasibility of its achievement in ships. But from his recent observations, especially those relative to the general drift of the ice in the Polar Sea and the prevailing winds that were experienced by his party during their sojourn in that locality, he was of opinion—an opinion that was not, however, shared by his distinguished brother officer, Captain Parry—that the attempt should be made from the westward through Bering's Strait, instead of from the East. Recent experience has proved that he was not far wrong in his conclusions, and the remarkable voyage made in 1850, and two following years, by Captain Collinson in the *Enterprise* proves in a great measure that his opinions were formed on sound and well-considered principles, and, as such, were worthy of due consideration.

Parry's **third** expedition,[1] which had been, as will be remembered, directed to act in concert with Franklin, in the event of falling in with any of his party on their line of exploration, also unhappily ended in failure.

Sailing from England in the *Hecla* and *Fury* on the 19th May 1824, Parry, in consequence of unavoidable detentions in Baffin's Bay, caused by the unusual amount of ice that was collected there during that particular season, did not reach Lancaster Sound until the 10th of September. The season was then far advanced, and he found to his intense mortification that the young ice which was rapidly forming proved such an impediment to his advance, that he was reluctantly compelled to relinquish further attempts to push on, and was, therefore, obliged to seek winter quarters ; he eventually secured his two ships on the 27th September in a small harbour named Port Bowen, on the east side of Prince Regent Inlet. Here the winter was passed, and in the spring of 1825 sledging parties were despatched, which added largely to our geographical knowledge of those parts. On the 20th July the ships succeeded in breaking out of their winter quarters, and standing across to the west side of the inlet, pursued a southerly course. They were, however, almost immediately beset by the ice, in which they were drifted rapidly up the inlet. Being powerless to direct their course, the unfortunate *Fury* was after a time driven on shore, and completely wrecked. Her stores and provisions were landed at the scene of her disaster, which was named Fury Beach, while her officers and crew were received on board the

---

[1] See p. 153, *ante*.

Hecla, for conveyance to England. They arrived at Sheerness in October, and the *Hecla* was shortly afterwards paid out of commission.

Parry was much disappointed at the unfortunate result of a voyage from which he had expected so much; but although it was not in his power to command success, yet no man ever deserved it more than Sir Edward Parry, especially in Arctic enterprise. In concluding his account of the narrative of this voyage he writes—

" May it still fall to England's lot to accomplish this undertaking,[1] and may she ever continue to take the lead in enterprises intended to contribute to the advancement of science, and to promote, with her own, the welfare of mankind at large. Such enterprises, so disinterested as well as useful in their object, do honour to the country which undertakes them, even when they fail; they cannot but excite the admiration and respect of every liberal and cultivated mind, and the page of future history will undoubtedly record them, as in every way worthy of a powerful, virtuous, and enlightened nation."

In less than two years after his return from this unsuccessful attempt to achieve the north-west passage by Prince Regent Inlet, the energetic Parry was again employed on Polar exploration, being entrusted with the command of an expedition that had for its object the discovery of the northern terrestrial pole of the earth.

This enterprise was in accordance with a scheme of his own, plans of which he had previously submitted for the consideration of the Admiralty. His idea was to proceed in a ship as far as Spitzbergen, whence, leaving the vessel securely established in some snug anchorage, a party with boats and sledges were to be despatched for the purpose of reaching the Pole. The *Hecla*, Parry's old ship, was selected for this service, and he was accom-

---

[1] The north-west passage.

panied by many old shipmates who had served with him
on previous expeditions. They sailed from England on
the 3rd of April 1827, and after touching at Hammer-
fest, arrived off the coast of Spitzbergen about the
middle of May; but it was not until nearly a month
later, that they succeeded in finding a harbour in which
the ship could be safely secured. All the necessary
arrangements being completed, the exploring party,
consisting of the two boats *Enterprise* and *Endeavour*,
under the command respectively of Captain Parry and
Lieutenant James C. Ross, with a crew in each of two
officers and twelve men, left the *Hecla*, and proceeded
northwards. So long as the sea remained fairly open
good progress was made, but when the ice was closely
packed, and the boats, with all the necessary impedimenta, had to be dragged across the floes, the toilsome
and irksome nature of the work began to tell upon
the men. The roughness of the ice added materially
to the arduous nature of their work, and their difficulties culminated when it was discovered that a
strong current was carrying them to the southward
at a greater rate than they were advancing to the northward. Under these mortifying circumstances Parry,
convinced of the futility of further perseverance, decided to return, having reached the latitude of 82° 45',
a higher northern position than had been attained by
any previous navigator. The ship was reached in
Treurenberg Bay on the 21st of August, the party having
been absent sixty-one days. On the 28th the *Hecla*
sailed for England, and, by a strange coincidence, Franklin arrived at Liverpool from his journey along the Arctic
coast of America at the same time that Parry reached
Inverness. These two gallant explorers arrived at the

Admiralty within ten minutes of each other, and great was the mutual surprise and joy of the two friends at such an unexpected meeting after so long a separation.

With the return of these two officers from their adventurous voyages in 1827, public interest in Arctic exploration appears generally to have languished. Probably the supposed risk, combined with the cost connected with the equipment of these Arctic expeditions, were considered too great and serious to justify any further attempts being made, at the public expense, with the view of discovering either the Pole or the north-west passage. But although the Government of the day evinced a strong disinclination to prosecute further research in high northern latitudes, private enterprise, as will, we hope, always be the case, stepped in to attempt that which previous Government expeditions had failed to accomplish. In 1829, a small vessel, named the *Victory*,[1] fitted out at the expense of Sir Felix Booth, sailed from England, under the command of Sir John Ross, with the object of discovering the north-west passage. With Captain Ross was associated his nephew, the gallant James Ross, who was the companion and colleague of Parry in his eventful voyage towards the North Pole in 1827.

Sailing up Lancaster Sound and Prince Regent Inlet without experiencing much difficulty from ice, the *Victory* was secured in winter quarters on the east coast of Felix Boothia. In the following spring, a sledge party, under the command of James Ross, succeeded in discovering

---

[1] The *Victory* was fitted with a small auxiliary engine, and with paddle-wheels, eight feet in diameter, so arranged that they could be lifted out of the water when under sail or in ice-encumbered seas. Steam, therefore, would only be of use in calm weather, and when the sea was free of ice.

and reaching the position of the North Magnetic Pole, in latitude 70° 5′ 17″, and longitude 95° 46′ 45″ W., on the western coast of Boothia. For three long years the unfortunate *Victory* was inextricably frozen up in her first winter quarters, although every attempt was made to release her. She was at length abandoned in 1832, and the party proceeded northwards down Prince Regent Inlet, in the hope of falling in with some stray whaler. Unsuccessful in their search for relief, they were compelled to pass a fourth winter at Fury Beach, where the stores and provisions saved from the *Fury* when she was wrecked in 1825 [1] materially aided in their support and sustenance. In the following year they were providentially rescued by a whaler in Lancaster Sound, which was reached by them in their boats ; they were eventually brought to England, where they were regarded as men risen from their graves, for hopes of their safety had almost been abandoned. It is a curious coincidence that the whaler that rescued Captain Ross and his men was the *Isabella*, the same ship that he commanded in 1818 when he made his first voyage to the Arctic regions.

Sir John Franklin, having enjoyed a well-deserved repose after his long and almost continuous service in the furtherance of Arctic exploration, was engaged all this time on duties, if not of the same arduous and perilous nature, of at any rate, great importance and responsibility. On the 23rd of August 1830 he was appointed to the command of the twenty-six gun frigate *Rainbow*, then fitting out at Portsmouth for service in the Mediterranean. This vessel had been paid off the previous year after a four years' commission on the East Indian and China station, under the command of Captain

1 See p. 174, *ante.*

the Hon. H. J. Rous, who subsequently made a reputation
for himself by the skilful and masterly way in which he
succeeded in navigating the frigate *Pique* safely across
the Atlantic, without a rudder and in an otherwise helpless condition.   He is, however, perhaps better known
from his long connection with the Jockey Club, where
his good influence was felt for many years.

The *Rainbow*, being ready for sea, sailed out of Portsmouth Harbour under double-reefed topsails on the 11th
November 1830, and after touching at Plymouth, pro
ceeded to her station.   Mr. Kay, a nephew of Sir John
Franklin, served in her as a lieutenant, and Owen
Stanley, who became a skilful and accomplished surveyor, was a mate in the ship.   Two days after leaving
Plymouth, a little excitement was caused by sighting
the wreck of a brig with only the stumps of her lower
masts standing, rolling heavily in the long Atlantic
swell.   Franklin at once bore down to her relief, with
the object of succouring the crew, in the event of any of
the unfortunate people being still in her.   On approaching the wreck, they hailed to know if any one was on
board, but as no reply was given, Franklin determined
to satisfy himself by a nearer inspection, and took
his ship so close that they actually came into collision,
when the *Rainbow* received some slight injuries to her
mizen chains and quarter gallery.   They remained by
the wreck for a couple of hours, repairing their own
damages, and endeavouring to attract the attention of
any one who might be on board, the state of the sea
and weather rendering communication by boat impossible.   Having satisfied themselves that the wreck
had been abandoned, and that there was no possibility
of saving life, the *Rainbow* proceeded on her course.

For a long time Franklin carried out the onerous duties of senior naval officer in Greece, and especially at Patras, during the disturbances in that country. During those troublous times he was frequently called upon to land his men for the purpose of preserving order and for the protection of the inhabitants; he had also to organise a defence against the rebellious irregular soldiery, whom he prevented, on more than one occasion, from pillaging and destroying the town. He likewise did good service in embarking refugees, and conveying them to places of safety. For his successful exertions in maintaining law and order, and generally for his efficient and important services during the War of Liberation, he was created by King Otho a Knight of the Redeemer of Greece.

On his return to Malta the *Rainbow* flew the flag, temporarily, of Rear-Admiral Briggs, who succeeded to the command of the Mediterranean station on the death of Admiral Hotham. The log of the *Rainbow* during her commission is replete with useful sailing directions, and other interesting hydrographical information.

That Sir John had the comfort and welfare of his men at heart is evident, for the name of his ship was proverbial on the station for the happiness and good feeling that prevailed on board. She was called the *Celestial Rainbow*, and the sailors used to allude to her as *Franklin's Paradise!* She returned to England in December 1833, and was paid out of commission at Portsmouth on the 8th of January following. In recognition of his services off Patras, Sir John Franklin, on his return to England, was made a Knight Commander of the Guelphic order of Hanover.

Before leaving the Mediterranean, he received the following letter from the Commander-in-Chief, Admiral

Sir H. Hotham, written a short time only before his death. It is dated on board the *Royal Alfred* at Malta, March 29, 1833. After acknowledging the receipt of Sir John Franklin's letter reporting proceedings, he writes—

"In the concluding operations of the service you have so long and so ably conducted in the Gulf of Patras and Lepanto, I have great satisfaction in repeating the approbation which I have already at different times expressed of your measures in the interests of Greece, and in the maintenance of the honour and character of the English nation and of H.M.'s Navy on that station; wherein you have entirely fulfilled my instructions and anticipated my wishes. I also take this opportunity of commending the judgment and forbearance which you have exhibited under circumstances of repeated opposition and provocation; and to your calm and steady conduct may be attributed the preservation of the town and inhabitants of Patras; the protection of commerce; and the advancement of the benevolent intentions of the Allied Sovereigns in favour of the Greek nation."

These were high encomiums from his Commander-in-Chief, and plainly show the great estimation in which Franklin was held by his superiors. A copy of this communication was forwarded to the Admiralty by Sir John, in an official letter dated June 18, 1834, written from 21 Bedford Place, in which he made an earnest appeal to be employed on futher active service.

Prior to leaving Patras, Sir John Franklin received the following letter from Mr. G. W. Crowe, the English Consul at that place :—

"BRITISH CONSULATE, PATRAS,
24th March 1833.

"MY DEAR SIR JOHN,—While I beg leave to offer you my congratulations upon being at length released from the anxious and wearisome duty that has detained you before this town for the last twelve months, I cannot refrain, at the same time, from expressing the regret I feel upon my own account in losing your society and that of your officers, which has so agreeably relieved a period that would otherwise have been of unmitigated annoyance and vexation.

"The humane object of your mission is now completely fulfilled. You have the satisfaction to witness the termination of the miseries of the inhabitants of this city, and of the misrule and violence that so long and heavily oppressed them—violence restrained from the worst and grossest excesses only by your presence, being awed into respect by the dignified calm which you ever preserved under circumstances of great irritation.

"But for your forbearance the city, just rising from its ruins, had ceased to exist. You now see tranquillity and order restored to their homes, and a few days have been sufficient to reanimate the activity of commerce.

"Patras owes you a deep debt of gratitude, and I trust feels the obligation. For myself, I hope I need not assure you that I can never forget your unvarying kindness, and that I am sensible of the high value of the friendly and cordial regard with which you have continued to know me. For weeks together your ship afforded a home—a kind home—to my family, and the *Rainbow* will ever be remembered by them with the feelings which home excites."

These letters plainly show the high appreciation in which the services of Sir John Franklin, whilst in command of the *Rainbow*, were held by those who were perhaps the best qualified to judge.

It was, in all probability, in consequence of the aptitude displayed by Sir John Franklin in carrying out the delicate services, more or less of a diplomatic nature, that he was called upon to render on the coast of Greece, that induced the Government to offer him, shortly after his return from the Mediterranean, the Lieutenant-Governorship of Van Diemen's Land, in succession to Colonel Arthur. This he accepted, but it was on the express understanding that he might be allowed to resign his appointment in the event of war breaking out, and his being selected for a command.

Taking passage on board the ship *Fairlie*, and accompanied by Lady Franklin, his daughter, and niece,[1] the new Governor landed at Hobart Town in January 1837, when he immediately assumed the reins of Government, relieving Colonel Kenneth Snodgrass, who had been acting temporarily until his arrival. Ever mindful of the value and importance of hydrography, one of the first acts of the Lieutenant-Governor was to make a requisition to the Imperial Government for means to enable him to carry out a more perfect survey of the channels leading towards the anchorage at Hobart Town. This application was viewed with favour by the home authorities, and Lieutenant Burnett was appointed by the Admiralty to carry out this service under the directions of Sir John Franklin. The new Governor's attention was, for some time, much occupied by the presentation of various memorials from the settlers claiming grants of land, which, they averred, had been allotted to them without title-deeds or other documents by which their claims could be substantiated. All these had to be thoroughly sifted in order that justice should be impartially administered.

One of the most popular measures introduced by Sir John was the admission of the public to the debates of the Legislative Council. While interesting himself in the general well-being of the community at large, he also devoted much time and reflection to the welfare and discipline of the convicts on the island, for at that period

---

[1] Miss Sophia Cracroft, the constant companion and devoted friend of Lady Franklin.

a very large penal establishment existed in the neighbourhood of Hobart Town.

Shortly after he assumed office, Sir John Franklin, realising the want of sufficient means for educating the rising generation in the colony, made strenuous exertions to obtain from the Home Government a charter for the formation of a college on a large and liberal scale. In this he was supported by his Legislative Council, who voted the substantial sum of £2500 towards the institution. On the recommendation of the late Dr. Arnold, head-master of Rugby, who warmly espoused the cause, the Rev. J. P. Gell was sent out from England for the purpose of organising such an establishment as should meet the requirements of the colonists, and on the 7th of November 1840, with imposing ceremony, the foundation-stone of the proposed building was laid at New Norfolk by Sir John Franklin, in the presence of all the local officials and a large assemblage of the inhabitants. In consequence, however, of dissensions and disputes with the various religious denominations, and the selfish opposition of those who wished the college to be built in Hobart Town, instead of at New Norfolk, the Imperial Government withdrew its support, and the scheme fell through. Mr. Gell,[1] however, proceeded to establish a superior school in Hobart Town, on such a scale and system, that it would, he hoped, if properly supported, eventually develop into a college, and so be the means of giving a liberal education to the sons of colonists, and thus prepare them for entering the learned professions.

[1] Mr. Gell married Sir John Franklin's daughter by his first wife. She died in 1860. Mr. Gell was Vicar of St. John's, Notting Hill, from 1854 to 1878, when he was given the Rectory of Buxted in Sussex.

So impressed was Sir John Franklin with the necessity of an institution of this description, that, **before leaving the** island, he presented a donation of £500 **towards it, while** Lady Franklin made the munificent gift of 400 acres of land which she had purchased, with a museum, which, under her direct auspices, had been established on it, in trust for the benefit of any collegiate institution that might be established with the approbation and sanction of the Bishop of the diocese. On an increase to the Lieutenant-Governor's salary being voted by the Colonial Legislature, **Sir John,** in fitting terms, declined to accept it during his tenure of office, but took **pains** to ensure the augmentation of **it** being secured for **his** successor. Shortly after his arrival in the colony, **he** founded **a** scientific society at Hobart Town, which **is** now called the Royal Society of Tasmania. The meetings were **held** at Government House, where the papers **(which** were afterwards printed at **Sir** John's expense) were read and discussed.

It was during Sir John's term of government that the island was visited by the ships of the Antarctic expedition under Sir James **Ross, to** which **it** will be desirable to make a brief allusion.

In 1838, at a meeting of the British Association **in** England, a resolution was passed **to** the effect that a representation should be made to the Government regarding the importance of despatching an expedition to the Antarctic **Seas, for the** purpose of carrying out synchronal magnetic observations **in connection** with other stations established in various parts **of the world; also to endeavour** to obtain observations in terrestrial magnetism in a high southern latitude, **of** which **there had** hitherto been a great deficiency—in fact, none at **all of** any value.

This representation, having **received** the approval **and support of** the learned societies, as well as that of the leading scientific authorities of the day, **was** favourably **received by Her Majesty's** Government, who seemed to be fully imbued with the opinion that practical navigation would undoubtedly derive important benefits from the results that would assuredly accrue. An expedition was, in consequence, ordered to be fitted out, and **the** command of it was entrusted to Captain **James Ross.** It consisted of the *Erebus*, an old bomb ship of 370 tons, and the *Terror*, **of 340 tons.**[1] The command **of the** latter vessel **was given to Captain Crozier.**

The *Terror*, **it may be observed, had** only the **previous year, under the command of Captain** Back, returned from **an** unsuccessful **attempt to** reach Repulse **Bay.** Her narrow **escape** from destruction by the ice **in** Hudson's Bay, and **her subsequent** marvellous passage across the Atlantic **in an almost sinking** condition, although of **thrilling interest, need not here be repeated.** The injuries **she** sustained were repaired, and when **selected** to form one of the ships in Ross's expedition she was in every way fitted for the hazardous **service** on which it **was** decided to employ her.

Captain Ross, in his sailing directions, was ordered to **place** himself in communication with Sir John Franklin **on his** arrival **in Van Diemen's** Land, while Sir John **was, at the** same time, **instructed to render all** the **assistance in** his power to Captain Ross, to select the most advantageous position **for the** erection of a magnetic observatory, **and to prepare the** necessary **instruments.**

---

[1] These two ships, it **should** be remarked, were the identical vessels that, subsequently, under **the** command of Sir John Franklin, comprised **the** ill-fated expedition that left England for **the discovery of** the north-west passage.

One of the principal objects of the expedition was to endeavour to determine, if possible, the position of the South Magnetic Pole.

The ships sailed from England in 1839, and were absent for a period of four years. It is not my object to record the doings of this most important expedition, the only one on a large scale that has ever been despatched from any country for exploration in the Antarctic Seas. It is simply alluded to here because of its connection with Sir John Franklin, who was Lieutenant-Governor of Van Diemen's Land, during the time that the vessels were engaged on this particular service, when they spent two winters at Hobart Town. It may be safely inferred that Sir John took the keenest interest in the ships, and did all in his power, not only to promote the scientific work of the expedition, but also exerted himself to the utmost in endeavouring to make the time pass pleasantly for the officers and men during their stay in Tasmania. The magnetic observatory was erected under the personal superintendence of Sir John, and many of the observations were actually taken by him, assisted by his son-in-law, the **Rev. J. P. Gell.** When the expedition sailed, after the first winter spent at Hobart Town, Franklin's nephew, Lieutenant **Kay,** was left behind in charge of this observatory.

Captain Ross, in his exceedingly interesting narrative of the expedition, thus alludes to the great assistance he received at the hands of the Governor :—

"If the deep-felt gratitude of thankful hearts be any gratification to our excellent friend Sir John Franklin, who not only evinced the most anxious desire, but sought every opportunity of promoting the objects of our enterprise, and contributing to the comfort and happiness of all embarked in it,

I am sure there is not an individual in either of our ships, who would not most heartily wish to express those sentiments towards him, and also to every member of his family, for their great kindness to us during our prolonged stay at Hobart Town."

Alluding to the excellent administrative qualities of Sir John Franklin, Captain Ross, in the same work, writes :—

"Under the wise and judicious government of Sir John Franklin, the revenue of the colony had so greatly increased, that although involved deeply in debt when he arrived in the country, by prudent and well-arranged measures the debt had been liquidated, and a superabundant income produced."

But it was in all probability due to the undoubted success he achieved whilst administering the government of Van Diemen's Land, that a bitter and vindictive feeling was raised against him in the hearts of some few of the colonial officials, who regarded with jealousy the increasing popularity of the Governor. This feeling found expression in attempts to place difficulties in his way while carrying out the duties that devolved on him in the proper administration of the government, and commenced as early as 1841, when the Director of Public Works was dismissed from his office for the unsatisfactory way in which his duties were performed, combined with "an obstinacy of temper and a disposition to enter into long and unnecessary correspondence." In 1843 the police magistrate was suspended from his duties for incautious and partial administration of justice, for want of temper, and for various other complaints with which he was charged. This was done with and by the advice of the Executive Council.

These acts led to the appearance in the local press, of some very hostile criticisms of his government, and also of himself personally, in which Sir John was openly accused of resorting to all sorts of unscrupulous means in order to attain his own ends. These scurrilous attacks were believed to be inspired by the Colonial Secretary, who was accordingly called upon by Sir John for an explanation, which was of so unsatisfactory a character that Sir John suspended him from his official duties.

This was, of course, a very strong measure to take, especially with an official holding such a high position as the Colonial Secretary, and could only be justified by extreme provocation. The charges brought against the Colonial Secretary by the Lieutenant-Governor were—

1. Assumption of undue influence.

2. His having threatened, and subsequently put in practice, a species of passive resistance, by not giving proper assistance in the transaction of official business.

3. Having neglected to take any notice of articles in a local newspaper (said to be established under his patronage) reflecting on Sir John and the members of his family.

4. The tone of his communication when charged by Sir John with these offences.

A long, and somewhat acrimonious, correspondence with the Home Government ensued with regard to this unfortunate affair, resulting eventually in the removal of the Colonial Secretary to a similar post at the Cape of Good Hope. Sir John's action in this matter was not supported by the Secretary of State for the Colonies (Lord Stanley), who informed the Governor in an official despatch that he "was not justified, on his own showing, in dismissing " his Colonial Secretary. He was further informed that this officer " retires from the situation he has so long filled with his public and personal character unimpaired, and with his hold on the respect and confidence of Her Majesty's Government undiminished."

This despatch was, practically, a censure on the Lieutenant-Governor, and it was a rebuke all the more keenly felt in consequence of its having been published without authority in the local press. On the 20th January 1843, Sir John wrote a masterly vindication of his conduct in reply to this despatch, concluding with a request that as he did not possess the confidence of Her Majesty's Government, so indispensable for his own honour and the due discharge of his functions, he hoped Lord Stanley would relieve him from his government as early as possible. Sir John also addressed a confidential letter to his lordship on the 26th July 1843, urging his reconsideration of the case, and hoping that he would give it his serious attention ; at the same time expostulating against the system of persecution to which he had been subjected in consequence of Lord Stanley's despatch, and the machinations of the late Colonial Secretary and his adherents in the colony.

In the following month he was suddenly relieved of his office as Lieutenant-Governor of Van Diemen's Land by Sir Eardley Wilmot, who arrived, unexpectedly, on the same day, indeed in the same ship, that brought the announcement acquainting Sir John of his successor's nomination. He was therefore placed in an extremely embarrassing situation by the sudden advent of the new Governor, being in actual possession of Government House at the time ; he was also naturally much annoyed at the want of courtesy that was thus shown him, as well as the great injustice that was done, in placing him in such a painful and humiliating position. He left Hobart Town in the same ship that took him out, the *Fairlie*, and reached England in May 1844, having been Governor of Van Diemen's Land for a period of over six and a half years.

That the views of the Secretary of State for the Colonies were not shared by the people of Hobart Town, is evident from the demonstrations of regret that were made by all classes at his departure, and from the numerous addresses, both public and private, expressing satisfaction at the way in which he had administered the government of the colony, and regret at his departure, that poured in upon him from all sections of the community. The feelings expressed by the colonists at that time were subsequently emphasised in a more practical manner some ten years later, by the substantial assistance sent to Lady Franklin, in the shape of a sum of £1700, to aid her efforts in endeavouring to discover the fate of her husband, and also by the fact of the erection, at the public expense, of a statue in his honour at Hobart Town.

Sir John Franklin, on his return to England, wrote a complete vindication of the way in which he had carried out the high and important duties that devolved upon him as Lieutenant-Governor of Van Diemen's Land, but this publication did not appear until after he had sailed on what proved to be his last voyage. In this article he severely criticises the action of Lord Stanley, whom he stigmatises as " haughty and imperious."

In alluding to this painful incident in the career of Sir John Franklin, Sherard Osborn writes :—" His sensitive and generous spirit chafed under the unmerited

treatment he had experienced from the Secretary of
State for the Colonies; and sick of civil employment,
he naturally turned again to his profession as a better
field for the ability and devotion he had wasted on a
thankless office."

CHAPTER XII.

FRANKLIN'S LAST VOYAGE.

1845.

> " We are well persuaded
> We carry not a heart with us from hence
> That grows not in fair consent with ours ;
> Nor leave not one behind, that doth not wish
> Success and conquest to attend on us."
>
> *—Henry V.*

THE subject of Arctic exploration, more especially with regard to its relation to the discovery of a north-west passage, had been permitted to remain in abeyance by the Government for some years—in fact since the return of Sir **Edward Parry** from his unsuccessful attempt to reach the North Pole in 1827.

It is very true that the interest of the public in the far north was, for a short time, revived by the prolonged absence of the two Rosses, to which a brief allusion has been made in the preceding chapter, and a land expedition was despatched by Government, under the command of Captain Back, in 1833, for the purpose of seeking for them. This officer was ordered to proceed by the Great Fish River to the northern shore of Arctic America, whence he was to endeavour to reach the neighbourhood of Cape Garry, where, it was anticipated, intelligence of the missing expedition might be obtained, for it was well known that Captain Ross in some measure relied for support, in case of undue absence, on the stores that were landed from the *Fury* when that vessel was unfortunately wrecked in 1823. The Rosses, as has already been narrated, were picked up and brought home by a whaler in 1833;[1] and this intelligence was communicated to Captain Back in a despatch that was forwarded by the Hudson's Bay Company, and which was handed to him before he was altogether out of reach of letters. The main object of the expedition having therefore been otherwise happily accomplished, Captain Back proceeded, in accordance with his instructions, to explore the Great Fish River to its mouth. This was successfully achieved, the expedition reaching, on the 16th August 1834, its most northern point in King William Island. It returned to England the following year, when Captain Back's efforts in the furtherance of geographical and scientific research were acknowledged and appreciated in a fitting manner.

On the return of Captain Back, the Royal Geographical Society urged the Government to undertake the exploration of the North American coast between the Point Turnagain of Franklin and the position reached by Back to the eastward, maintaining that the successful performance of this exploration would, doubtless, result in the completion of the north-west passage.

The Government, fully endorsing these views, gave directions for the fitting out of the *Terror*, and selected Captain Back, who had but recently returned from his land journey, to the command. His orders were to proceed through Hudson's Strait to the Wager River or to Repulse Bay; thence he was to endeavour to pene-

---

[1] See page 178.

trate into **Prince Regent Inlet, and make a thorough**
examination **to the east** and to the west, with the object
of **connecting** his own discoveries with those of Ross
and **Franklin.** The *Terror* sailed from England on the
24th of June 1836; she was beset by the ice in Hudson's
Strait in the following September, in which she drifted
helplessly, daily expecting destruction, for the ensuing ten
months. When released, the ship was found to have received such injuries as to necessitate her immediate return
to England, but she was in such a crippled state that **she**
had, after a perilous and eventful voyage, **to be run on
shore on the** west coast of Ireland to prevent her sinking.

The return of the Antarctic expedition **in** 1843 **once**
more aroused public interest in matters connected with exploration in high latitudes, and this interest was kept alive
by the writings and efforts of English men of science and
naval officers, who urged the necessity of the continuance
of further exploration. In the words of worthy old
Master Purchas, who wrote 250 years ago, the discovery
of the north-west passage was the only "thing yet un-
done wherebye a notable mind might be made famous."

This long sought for passage was at **last to be dis-**
covered, and the "notable mind" that was to achieve
the distinction which the solution of the problem would,
according to Master Purchas, entitle him to, was no less
a person than Sir John Franklin, who had already succeeded in mapping out, by actual personal exploration,
a very large portion of **the** passage. He had, as we
have endeavoured to trace, by patient perseverance, by
great ability, energy, and indomitable pluck, in spite
of unparalleled difficulties and unprecedented sufferings,
in a rigorous climate and in an inhospitable and barren
country, succeeded in showing to the world at large,

that there was **no service** which Englishmen **were not** capable of undertaking, and **no hardships** or privations that would make them waver **or flinch** in the performance of their duties and **in carrying them** out to a successful issue.

In fact, Sir John Franklin **had,** as **we have** already shown, written his name with no light **or feeble** hand in large and unmistakable characters along the **entire face** of our North Polar map, and he was, even at **that** time, the actual discoverer of all, but a very small portion that yet remained to be explored, of the long talked of, but yet undiscovered, north-west passage.

Our geographical **knowledge of the hitherto** almost mythical regions that centred at the northern apex of **our** globe **was, in** 1845, considering our ignorance at **the beginning of the** century, considerable. Parry had **succeeded in pushing to the westward with** his ships **in a** high latitude, through **Lancaster Sound** and Barrow's **Strait, as far as the** 114th **meridian of west** longitude, **while the northern coast of North America had** been thoroughly explored from Bering's **Strait** to **the** 94th meridian of **west** longitude. **The discoveries** therefore, eastward and westward, overlapped each other by twenty degrees of longitude.

To Franklin, it will **be** remembered, **was due the** exploration of the north coast of America from Cape Turnagain westward to Cape Beechey, a survey extending **over forty** degrees of longitude. Captain Beechey, it will also be remembered, **explored from** Bering's Strait to the eastward **as far** as Point Barrow, leaving only 160 miles undiscovered between **his** furthest eastward position and the most western one of Franklin's.

These two positions were, however, connected in 1837

THOMAS SIMPSON.

by Messrs. Dease and Simpson, two officers of the Hudson's Bay Company, who had been specially despatched for the purpose of completing this portion of the unsurveyed coast-line. In the two following years they turned their attention to the eastward, and connected the coast-line between Cape Turnagain and Back's Great Fish River. They also explored the south coast of Wollaston or Victoria Land, as well as the southern shore of King William Island, from Cape Herschel to Point Booth. The extreme eastern position reached by these able and indefatigable explorers was the Castor and Pollux River. The entire North American coast line had thus been delineated. All therefore that remained to be discovered, in order to make the north-west passage *un fait accompli*, was the finding of a channel running in a north and south direction for a distance of a little under 300 miles, or about half the distance between John o' Groat's and the south coast of England. That such a channel existed there was but little doubt, but whether it would be, when found, practicable for ship navigation, was a question yet to be solved. It is therefore not surprising that an attempt should be made to complete the discovery of the passage.

Sir John Barrow, who was at the time Secretary of the Admiralty, and who has so happily been termed the "father of modern Arctic discovery," we may be sure, was not idle. He was fully sensible of the necessity for a renewal of Arctic research, and he was as keen as ever in his advocacy regarding the importance of exploration in high latitudes. When a man like Sir John Barrow, who was prepared with a plan for the prosecution of the search for a north-west passage, and who was supported in his views by such authorities on Arctic matters as Sir

Francis Beaufort, Sir Roderick Murchison, Sir Edward
Parry, Sir James Ross, Captain Sabine, and even Sir
John Franklin himself (who had just returned from his
administration of the government of Van Diemen's Land),
advocated the resumption by England of Polar exploration, it is not to be wondered at that the earnest and
logical pleadings of these great and eminent geographers
met with a favourable response. An expedition was in
consequence decided upon, and it was resolved that its
main object was to be the forging of the last link that
would connect the chain of previous discoveries, and so
achieve the actual accomplishment of the north-west
passage.

The decision was a popular one, not only in the country,
but also in the naval service. The announcement was
no sooner promulgated than hundreds of gallant hearts
sent in their names as volunteers to accompany the
expedition, and to serve in any capacity in the event
of their services not being required in the particular
rank they held in the navy. Candidates also for the
post of leader were not wanting, but this post Sir John
Franklin claimed as his special right, as being the senior
Arctic officer alive in a position to assume it. "No
service," he said, "is nearer to my heart, than the
completion of the survey of the north coast of America,
and the accomplishment of a north-west passage."
Lord Haddington, the First Lord of the Admiralty,
on being informed that Sir John was desirous of being
appointed to the command, at once sent for him, and
gladdened his heart by complying with his wishes; but
thinking that Sir John might have become somewhat
rusty in matters connected with his profession after his
long sojourn on shore, and also perhaps wishing to afford

him the opportunity of declining the command, in the
event of his only having proffered his services from a
keen sense of honour and duty, suggested that after the
good and useful geographical work he had already performed, he might now deservedly rest on his well-earned
laurels, and intimated that perhaps his age might be a
bar to his being selected, as he was informed that he was
sixty years of age.   "No, my lord," was Franklin's ready
but earnest response; "you have been misinformed—I
am only fifty-nine!" This decided the question, and
Franklin was accordingly appointed to the command.
The selection of the leader having been satisfactorily
arranged, Sir John drove home, and on his arrival,
suddenly announced to his wife and niece that he had
been offered, and had accepted, the command of the expedition.   He was wild with delight at the honour thus
conferred upon him, and could hardly conceal his enthusiastic impatience to get away as speedily as possible.

The ships selected for the service were the *Erebus* and
Terror. They had only recently returned from the service on which they had been engaged under Sir James
Ross in the Antarctic, but they had been completely overhauled and thoroughly repaired after the hard buffetings
they had received from the southern ice, and were, in consequence, prepared in every way that human skill and
ingenuity could devise, to undergo similar or even worse
treatment from the ice floes of the north. Captain
Crozier, who was second in command in the Antarctic
expedition, was selected to act in a like capacity to
Sir John, and was appointed to the command of his
old ship the *Terror*, while Sir John flew his pendant
in the *Erebus*. Commander James Fitzjames, an able,
popular, and accomplished officer, was appointed to the

Erebus as second in command under Franklin.   As the principal object of the expedition was the advancement of science, the remainder of the officers were selected as being specially suited by their scientific acquirements,

CAPTAIN FITZJAMES.

professional knowledge, and robust and vigorous constitutions, for the service on which they were to be employed. Among those appointed was Dr. Goodsir, an eminent naturalist. The complement of each ship was sixty-seven officers and men, making a total of twenty-three officers and 111 men—in all, 134 souls. Stores and **provisions were put** on board the ships for an anticipated absence **of three years.** The vessels were also fitted with screws **and** auxiliary engines, capable of working up to about **twenty horse-power.** This was the first time that the **screw, as a means of** propulsion in ships, was ever used in the Arctic Seas, but it was, as may be imagined from the power provided, only to a very limited degree.

Sir John Franklin's orders were to the effect that he was to make the best of his way up Lancaster Sound to the neighbourhood of Cape Walker, in about 74° N. latitude, and 98° **W.** longitude. Thence he was to use his utmost **endeavours, by working to** the southward and westward, to push on in as direct a line as possible towards Bering's Strait; but much **was left to his own** discretion, **and** he was **to be** guided by any circumstances **that** might incidentally arise. **That these orders were in** accordance with Franklin's own **views and wishes is quite** certain. Sherard Osborn, **writing in 1859, makes the following** remarks—

"That this southern course was that of Franklin's predilection, founded on his judgment and experience. There are many in England who can recollect him pointing on his chart to the western entrance of Simpson Strait, and the adjoining coast of **North America,** and saying, **'If** I can but get down there, my work is done; thence it's plain sailing to the westward.'"

All the **arrangements being completed,** the expedition sailed **from** England **on the 19th of** May 1845, officers and men in the very best of spirits, and all fully resolved to do their utmost to bring **the** voyage to a successful issue, and so **set at** rest, and for ever, the **long** vexed question of the existence of a north-west passage. Sir John Franklin was specially careful to promote this proper and commendable spirit evinced by those under his command.   Shortly after their departure from England, he called all his officers together, and carefully explained to them the objects of the expedition, and his views as to the course that should be pursued in order to obtain the most successful results.   He read out to them a portion of the instructions he had issued to the officers of the *Trent*, on his first Polar expedition, and pointed out to them the necessity of noting everything that occurred, no matter how trivial it might at the moment be considered, for future reference and study.   He also informed them that their journals, remark books, sketches, &c., would be required of them on their return to England, for transmission to the Admiralty.   As Captain Fitzjames, in a letter to his friend Mr. John Barrow [1] writes—

"He spoke delightfully of the zealous co-operation he expected from all, and his desire to do full justice to the exertions of each."

With such a pleasant and happy feeling, and such a perfect understanding, pervading the minds of Sir John and those under his command, it is not surprising that all were cheerful and enthusiastic regarding the ultimate success of the expedition.

We obtain a little insight into the friendly and harmonious feeling that existed among those on board the *Erebus*, and the manner in which their time was passed on the voyage to Greenland, from some charmingly written letters sent home by Fitzjames, which have been kindly placed at my disposal by his friend Mr. John Barrow.   As these epistles contain many allu-

---

[1] The son of Sir John Barrow.

sions to the esteem and respect in which Sir John Franklin was held by all on board, no apology is necessary for the insertion here of a few extracts from them, illustrative of the private character of **Sir John** and the happy feeling that reigned on board his ship.

So confident were they of accomplishing the north-west passage, that Fitzjames gave explicit directions for his letters to be sent to Petro-Paulowski in Kamchatka, *viâ* St. Petersburg, in the event of no tidings of the expedition being received before the ensuing June. He also tells his friend, Mr. Barrow, to

" Write on speck to Panama and the Sandwich Islands every six months." "Have a letter waiting for me at Panama on speck next January." "Mind, I say we shall get through the north-west passage *this year*, and I shall land at Petro-Paulowski and shake you by the hand on the 22nd February 1846."

On the day they left Stromness, he says—

" We drank Lady Franklin's health at the old gentleman's table, and it being his daughter's birthday, hers too."

Alluding to Sir John, he writes :—

" I like a man who is in earnest. Sir John Franklin read the church service to-day and a sermon so very beautifully, that I defy any man not to feel the force of what he would convey. The first Sunday he read was a day or two before we sailed, when Lady Franklin, his daughter, and niece attended. Every one was struck with his extreme earnestness of manner, evidently proceeding from real conviction."

Again :—

" Sir John is delightful, active, and energetic, and evidently, even now, persevering. What he *has been*, we all know. I think it will turn out that he is in no ways altered. He is full of conversation and interesting anecdotes of his former voyages. I would not lose him for the command of the expedition, for I have a real regard, I might say affection, for him, and believe this is felt by all of us. In our mess we are very happy; we have a most agreeable set of men, and I could suggest no change, except that I wish you were with us."

In a subsequent letter he tells us :—

"Sir John is full of life and energy, with good judgment and a capital memory—one of the best I know. His conversation is delightful and most instructive, and of all men he is the most fitted for the command of an enterprise requiring sound sense and great perseverance. I have learnt much from him, and consider myself most fortunate in being with such a man, and he is full of benevolence and kindness withal."

Again he writes, in much the same strain :—

"We are very happy and very fond of Sir John Franklin, who improves very much as we come to know more of him. He is anything but nervous or fidgety—in fact, I should say remarkable for energetic decision in sudden emergencies ; but I should think he might be easily persuaded, when he has not already formed a strong opinion."

That his nerve was as good as ever is apparent from the following extract from one of Fitzjames's letters—

"I can scarcely manage to get Sir John to shorten sail at all"

—so anxious was he to push on, and take advantage of every available day of the short navigable season.

Of course the main object of the expedition, viz., the discovery of the north-west passage, was ever uppermost in their thoughts, and frequently formed the principal topic of conversation at the dinner-table, and in the officers' mess. We obtain a glimpse into Sir John's views on this important subject from the following sentence in another of Fitzjames's letters :—

"At dinner to-day, Sir John gave us a pleasant account of his expectations of being able to get through the ice on the coast of America, and his disbelief in the idea that there is open sea to the northward. He also said he believed it to be possible to reach the Pole over the ice, by wintering at Spitzbergen, and going in the spring before the ice broke up and drifted to the south as it did with Parry on it."

Lieutenant Fairholme also, in a private letter, thus alludes to their leader :—

"Sir John is in much better health than when we left England, and really looks ten years younger. He takes an active part in everything that goes on, and his long experience in such services makes him a most valuable adviser. We are very much crowded—in fact, not an inch of stowage has been lost, and the decks are still covered with casks. Our supply of coals has encroached seriously on the ship's stowage ; but as we consume both fuel and provisions as we go, the evil will be continually lessening."

Stromness, in the Orkney Islands, was reached on June 1st, and left two days after. Boisterous weather and head winds were encountered during their passage across the Atlantic. On the 24th June, Cape Farewell was rounded, and on the following day they saw their first ice, consisting of numerous large icebergs, through which they had to thread their way, "some of them falling with an awful roar and rising of the sea ;" but the scenery, especially to those inexperienced in Arctic navigation, was grand and majestic.

On the 4th July the expedition came to an anchor off the Whale Fish Islands, near the island of Disco, on the west coast of Greenland. Here they completed with stores and provisions from a transport, the *Barretto Junior*, which had accompanied them out from England

for that purpose, and to which they discharged five of
their men who had been invalided and sent to her for
passage to England.   As the transport just alluded to
was the last vessel that communicated with the ill-fated
discovery ships, it will be interesting to insert a few
extracts from a letter written by Lieutenant Griffiths,
who was in command of her, to Mr. John Barrow, on
his arrival in England.   He writes :—

"The two ships were perfectly crammed, and were very
deep, drawing seventeen feet. I felt quite low-spirited on
leaving Sir John and his officers—better fellows never
breathed. They were all in the highest possible spirits, and
determined on succeeding if success were possible. I have
very great hopes, knowing their capabilities, having witnessed
their arrangements, and the spirit by which they are actuated
—a set of more undaunted fellows never were got together, or
officers better selected. Never were ships more appropriately
fitted or better adapted for the arduous service they have to
perform. Yes, indeed, certain I am if there be a passage, and
that icy barriers will be only sufficiently propitious to give
them but half the length of their ship, force themselves
through they will at all risks and hazard. God speed them
and send them back by Bering's Strait to their native England, covered with imperishable fame."

Lieutenant Griffiths also reports that

"He left them with every species of provisions for three
entire years, independently of five bullocks. They had also
stores for the same time, and fuel in abundance."

Sir John, in his last despatch to the Admiralty, written
at this time, says—

"The ships are now complete with supplies of every kind
for three years. They are therefore very deep, but happily
we have no reason to expect much sea as we proceed further."

J. FRANKLIN'S TRACK.

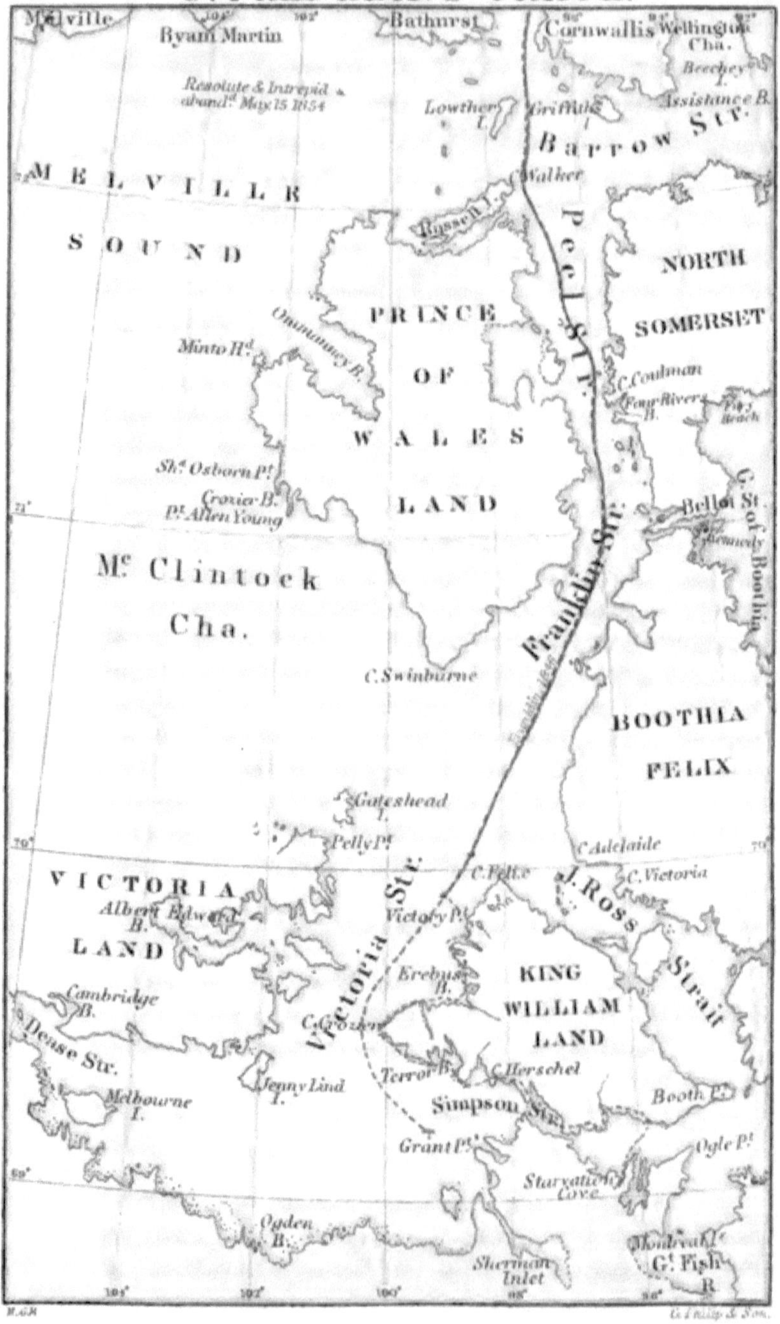

",

On the 10th of July, they parted company with the transport, and sailed from the Whale Fish Islands ; on the 26th of July the two ships were seen made fast to the ice in Melville Bay, in about 74° 48′ N. latitude, and 66° 13′ W. longitude, by Captain Dannet, of the *Prince of Wales*, a whaler from Hull, who received a visit from some of the officers of the expedition ; this was, so far as is known, the last time the unfortunate vessels were seen, at any rate by Europeans. After this date, although traces of the missing ships were discovered many years after, all is conjecture, all must be left to the imagination, to complete one of the saddest stories that has ever been told in connection with Arctic enterprise.

We will, however, endeavour to dovetail together the various scraps of information that have subsequently come to our knowledge, and so trace the proceedings of the expedition from the time when it was last seen by the whaler *Prince of Wales* until the sad and bitter end came, but it must be clearly understood that the greater part of what is here set forth must, of necessity, be purely conjectural.

The ships, we know, pursued their solitary way through Baffin's Bay towards Lancaster Sound. Entering this broad channel, they sailed along the coast of North Devon, continuing their course to the westward ; but ice, that unconquerable foe with which the Arctic explorer has to battle, effectually barred the passage, and prevented further advance in that direction. Wellington Channel, however, to the northward, appeared to be open, and up this they sail, hoping that it may eventually lead in a westerly direction, and carry them into the eagerly sought for passage. But they are doomed to disappointment, for after sailing up this channel for a distance of about 150 miles, they are again stopped by their relentless and implacable enemy the ice, and are compelled to turn to the southward; but their return is made by a different channel to that up which they sailed, a newly-discovered one, which they found to exist, separating Cornwallis and Bathurst Islands, and which ultimately brought them again into Barrow's Strait, about one hundred miles to the westward of the entrance to Wellington Channel, up which they had previously sailed.

Unmistakable signs of the closing in of the navigable season were now apparent; the hills and valleys were already covered with their snowy mantle, and the young ice was beginning to form on the surface of the water to such a thickness as to materially impede the progress of the ships. Taking all these circumstances into consideration, and finding that there was no prospect of advancing further to the westward that season, the ships retraced their steps a short distance to the eastward, and were ultimately secured in snug winter quarters in a partially protected harbour on the north-east side of Beechey Island, the adaptability of which as winter quarters had, in all probability, been remarked and noted by Franklin as he passed up Wellington Channel.

The ensuing winter probably passed as most Arctic winters do, in a pleasant and cheerful manner. The officers busily occupied themselves in their various scientific pursuits, looking after the health and welfare of their men, and earnestly discussing among themselves their future plan of operations, and their prospects of ultimate success; the men in the meantime being actively engaged in those multifarious duties that are incidental to a winter in the Arctic regions, such as banking the snow

against the sides of the ships, building snow-houses
for various purposes, keeping the fire-hole clear in the
ice,[1] and other minor details connected with the routine
and ordinary duties of a man-of-war. We may safely
infer that everybody was profitably employed, and that
they were also happy and cheerful. As the rays of the

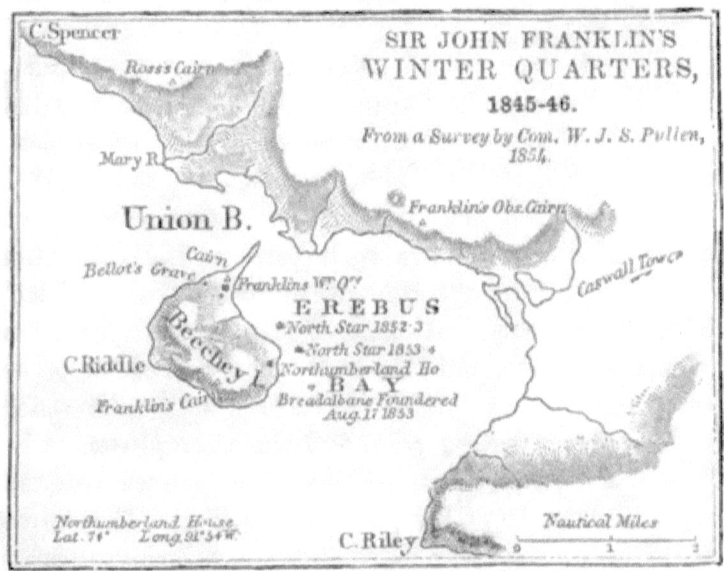

FRANKLIN'S WINTER QUARTERS, BEECHEY ISLAND.

returning sun shed their beams on the distant hills,
sporting parties were doubtless organised for the purpose

---

[1] The "fire-hole" is a large hole that is made in the ice, in the
immediate vicinity of the ship, from which to obtain water in the
event of fire breaking out. This fire-hole has frequently, day and
night, to be kept clear of the ice which forms on its surface. This
is the only way by which a constant supply of water can be kept
ready in the event of fire breaking out, for the pumps of a ship are,
of course, rendered useless in winter from the pipes all being choked
by the water becoming frozen in them.

of scouring the adjacent country in search of game, for
fresh animal food, they were well aware, was essential to
the perfect preservation of health.   A man like Sir John
Franklin, with the experience of several Arctic winters
to look back upon, knew well that in order to preserve
his men in health he must keep them cheerful and in
good spirits, with their minds and their bodies fully
occupied.

Although perhaps the ardent and enthusiastic Fitzjames was somewhat disappointed at the failure of the
expedition to reach a more advanced position before seeking winter quarters, still, on the whole, they could regard
with satisfaction the result of their work during the
preceding autumn, for in their passage up Wellington
Channel and down the New Strait to the west of Cornwallis Island, they had explored and mapped 300 miles
of new coast-line, and they were keenly sensible of the
fact, that only 250 miles of the unknown, intervened
between their furthest point and the accomplishment of
the north-west passage, namely, the distance between
Cape Walker to King William Island.   They were
therefore, presumably, elated with the cheering prospect
that was before them, of satisfactorily solving the great
problem that had so long puzzled and vanquished the
many bold navigators who had preceded them, and they
all looked forward with eager excitement to the termination of winter, when they would be able to continue,
what they felt assured would prove, a most successful
voyage.

CHAPTER XIII.

THE LAST DAYS.

> " O world ! so few the years we live,
> Would that the life that thou dost give,
>   Were life indeed !
> Alas ! thy sorrows fall so fast,
> Our happiest hour is when at last
>   The soul is freed."

THE long Polar night, with all its monotony and cheerlessness, at length came to an end, and in the month of February they hailed with joyful delight the return of the sun which had been absent for so many weeks, and which they knew heralded the approach of summer, and was the harbinger of that navigable season during which they hoped, and expected, to carry to a successful issue the ardent aspirations that animated the breast of each individual member of the expedition.   Death, however, had not been idle in the little community during its sojourn at Beechey Island, for they had to mourn the loss of three of their number—two seamen who died in January, and a marine who died in April.   They were buried on the island, and the finding of these solitary graves, with their simple head-boards and appropriate epitaphs, were among the first indications, discovered five years afterwards, of the expedition having wintered there.

On the release of the ships from their winter quarters, which event, in all probability, did not occur until July or August, a course was shaped to the westward towards Cape Walker, the furthest point reached by them in a westerly direction the previous year. We may assume that the usual difficulties inseparable from ice navigation were experienced by Franklin and his gallant followers; we may also rest assured that these obstacles were resolutely grappled with and manfully overcome. Their chief was not a man to shrink from either difficulty or danger, and he well knew he could safely rely upon the support of his officers and men in the hour of trial. Yet the difficulties in pushing on in the required direction must have been very great in his heavy, slow-sailing, bluff-bowed ships, for the steam-power at his disposal was so limited as to be only of use in perfectly calm weather, and in a smooth sea free of ice.

We know well from the records of previous navigators, and also from subsequent experience, that the ice to the westward of Barrow's Strait, and in the neighbourhood of Cape Walker, is of an exceedingly formidable description. In spite, however, of the ponderous nature of the ice, Franklin persevered in his endeavours to get through, and seeing a channel open to the southward he pushes into it, for surely, he thinks, it will eventually lead in the right direction. He knew, if this channel did not end in a *cul de sac*, and if the ice permitted him to force his ships through, that the last link in the chain would be forged, and the north-west passage would be triumphantly achieved. This channel, separating North Somerset from Prince of Wales's Land, is now called Peel Strait.

All went merrily! everything pointed to a speedy and

successful termination to their voyage. Sailing past
the west coast of North Somerset, they fight their way
bravely mile by mile, and almost inch by inch, along the
coast of Boothia Felix, until they perhaps get a glimpse
of King William Island, and almost feel that success
is actually within their grasp. But alas! although the
distance that intervenes between their ships and absolute
success is, perchance, only a little over one hundred
miles, their further progress is suddenly arrested, their
vessels are caught and held fast in the rigid embrace of
the ice, and thus, fast frozen in a solid and impenetrable
pack, they are doomed to pass their second winter.
Little did the poor fellows then imagine, when they were
busily engaged in making the necessary arrangements for
passing that winter, that their ships were inextricably
frozen in—never again to cleave the blue water of the
ocean, never to rise and fall on its heaving billows,
never to be released from their icy fetters, until their
poor battered hulls are rent and riven by their victorious
enemy, the ice.

To winter in the pack is known, happily, only to a
few—to pass two successive winters in the ice is an
experience that has, fortunately, been vouchsafed to
fewer still; yet the brave survivors of the *Erebus* and
Terror were destined not only to pass one, but two long,
weary, successive winters, helplessly beset, and firmly
frozen up in their icy bondage.[1]

Who can describe the sufferings, the dangers, the
monotony, the eager hopes, to be succeeded by bitter
disappointments, experienced by those unfortunate men
during those two fearful winters? They are known

---

[1] The position in which the ships wintered was latitude 70° 5′ N.,
and longitude 98° 23′ W.

only to Him, the Supreme **Ruler** of the Universe, and will never be revealed **to mortal** man.   How keen must have **been** the **suspense,** and how intense the disappointment, felt by all when the following summer, that of 1847, dragged out its weary length, and still the ships remained irrevocably frozen **in** their icy cradles, without any symptoms being apparent of **the** disruption of the pack.   This feeling must have been all the **more** quickened, when they remembered that only a few short miles lay between them and the successful accomplishment of that grand achievement, " the only thing whereby a notable mind might be made famous," which they had undertaken to risk, and if necessary lay down their lives, in order to bring to a successful issue. Once clear **of the ice,** and, they thought, all further difficulties would **be overcome and** every obstacle removed from their path.

As day succeeded day during that long summer and equally long and weary autumn, so did hope animate their hearts, but at length the days began to shorten and despondency succeeded hope as the sun sank below **the** southern horizon, to be, alas ! seen no more by many on board the two ill-fated ships, its last rays flickering intermittently in the heavens with bright prismatic **colours** as it disappeared, **not to** return for long weary months, ominously symbolical of the fate that **was so soon** to overtake them.

The winter, we may be sure, was not one of ease, comfort, or enjoyment.   There was little now to cheer the drooping spirits of this still undaunted band.   Their provisions were getting low, their ships were helpless logs firmly fixed in **a relentless** grip, and they whispered **among** themselves that help, to be of any avail, must be forthcoming before a third winter seized them in its dread and inhospitable grasp. During those long dreary winter months, the ships were exposed to all the dangers inseparable from a winter in the pack, subjected to severe ice-pressures which, for all we know to the contrary, so strained and damaged the hulls of the already sorely stricken vessels as to render them almost, if not wholly, unseaworthy.

And so the second winter came and went, and the summer sun once more shone forth and gladdened the hearts of those on board with joyful anticipations of release, and the hope that they might yet live to see their efforts crowned with success. As the daylight returns, King William Island, covered in its white garb of winter, was occasionally seen to the southward. Once past that sterile and dreary-looking coast, and the north-west passage would be accomplished, for they would then, they well knew, connect with Simpson's, Ross's, and Back's discoveries; but alas! an ice-encumbered sea intervened, choked with thick-ribbed ice, through which it was impossible to force their heavy and perhaps seriously damaged ships.

The summer was not allowed to pass, however, without some attempt at exploration, for in the month of May, a travelling party was organised and despatched with the object of exploring the shores of King William Island. It consisted of two officers and six men, and was commanded by Lieutenant Graham Gore, the first lieutenant of the *Erebus*. The officer that accompanied him was Mr. Charles F. Des Vœux, mate, belonging to the same ship. Of these two officers, Fitzjames, in one of his letters, written to Mr. Barrow on the passage to Greenland, writes :—

"Graham Gore is a man of great stability of character, a very good officer, and the **sweetest of** tempers. He plays the flute dreadfully well, draws **sometimes** very well, sometimes very badly, **but is** altogether **a capital fellow."**

He died on board the *Erebus* **during the succeeding** winter.

Of Des Vœux he says :—

"**He is** a most unexceptionable, clever, agreeable, light-hearted, obliging young fellow."

The party left the **ships on** Monday, **24th** May, and succeeded **in reaching Point Victory** [1] on King William Island **; thence pushing on towards Cape** Herschel they, perhaps, **saw in the distance the** continent of North **America, and realised that the long** sought for passage **had been discovered, and could be** actually **accomplished if they were but able to force their ships** through the **short icy channel that intervened.** Depositing a record,[2] **containing a brief** account **of their visit, they hurried back to their ships to impart the joyful tidings to their comrades, in order that they also might share in the exultation that they could not but help feeling** at **having ascertained the successful result of the voyage. The record was simply a few lines written on** a printed **form supplied to ships for the purpose of** being corked **up in a bottle and thrown overboard, with the** object **of** ascertaining **the set of tides and currents.**

The lines written by Graham Gore on this printed

---

[1] This point of land was named by Captain James Ross in 1830 after his ship; it was the furthest point to the westward reached by that distinguished navigator on King William Island.

[2] This record was discovered by Lieutenant Hobson in 1859, while **serving in the** *Fox* **under Sir** Leopold M'Clintock.

form were to the effect that the *Erebus* and *Terror*
wintered in the ice in latitude 70° 5′ N., and longitude
98° 23′ W., having wintered in 1846–7[1] at Beechey
Island in latitude 74° 43′ 28″ N., longitude 91° 39′ 15″
W., after having ascended Wellington Channel to latitude 77°, and returned by the west side of Cornwallis
Island. It adds, somewhat significantly, that Sir John
Franklin was still in command of the expedition, but
that all were well. This paper is dated the 28th of May
1847, and is signed by both Gore and Des Vœux.[2]

On their return to the *Erebus* they found a scene of
sorrow and mourning which, perhaps judging from the
somewhat ominous wording of their record, was not
wholly unexpected. They found their beloved chief, he
who had before, so often and in so many shapes, been
face to face with death, stricken down, fighting his last
battle with that unconquerable foe to whom the bravest
must eventually strike their colours and yield. Sir John
Franklin, after a long, honourable, and distinguished
career, after a life more eventful and adventurous than
usually falls to the lot of man, lay on his death-bed.
Silently were their hands pressed by their sorrowing
shipmates as they crossed the gangway, and sorrowfully
was the sad news whispered in their ears, in response
to the anxious inquiries as to the health of their leader,
who they knew would have been the first to welcome
them on board, had not the hand of sickness been upon
him. The end, however, had not yet come, and Sir
John Franklin was permitted, before he passed away,
to receive from the lips of Graham Gore the announcement that the north-west passage, for the successful

---

[1] This is evidently an error, and should be **1845–6.**

[2] See page 270.

achievement of which he had sailed **from** England **two years** ago, and for which **he was** now willingly and cheerfully laying down his life, **had** been discovered, and that he was the **man** who, by its discovery, had, according to old Purchas, made himself famous.

He fell asleep peacefully on the 11th of **June** 1847, with **the news of** the successful result of **the enterprise** ringing in his ears.

> " His soul to Him who gave it rose,
>   God led it to its **long repose**,
>   Its glorious **rest**."

We could not wish a more glorious or a more noble termination **to a life of fame than was his;** to die on the scene of **his discoveries, surrounded** and beset by the ice with which **he had so long been** battling, and with the shout **of triumph, the cheer of** victory, lighting up those **dim eyes with a bright** and lustrous radiance before **they closed to be opened no more.**

Spenser's lines in the *Fairie Queene* **are very applicable to the** death-bed of **Sir John Franklin :—**

> "Is not short payne well borne, that bringes **long ease**,
> And layes the soule to sleepe in quiet graine?
> Sleepe after toyle, port after stormie **seas**,
> Ease after warre, death after life **does greatly please**."

Sherard Osborn, in his brief but graphic description **of the Franklin** expedition, in alluding to the death of the leader, **writes—"Oh,** mourn him not ! unless you can point to a **more** honourable end or a nobler grave. Like another **Moses,** he fell when his work was accomplished, with the long object of his life in view. Franklin, the discoverer **of the** north-west passage, had his **Pisgah, and so long as** his countrymen shall hold dear disinterested devotion and gallant perseverance in a good cause, so long shall they point to the career and fate of this gallant sailor."

Thus died Sir John Franklin—a man of great force of character; one of indomitable energy and courage; an ardent geographer; an enthusiastic devotee of science; a good officer and seaman; and above all, a sincere and true Christian—one who placed a steadfast reliance and implicit faith in an all-wise and beneficent Providence.

We can picture, in our imagination, that last sad and solemn scene on the ice floe; that hushed assemblage of wan and famine-stricken men, whose pinched features and attenuated forms, clad in strange garments, tell of hardships and privations nobly and resolutely borne. They stand with hushed lips and bated breath, with their heads bent in silent sorrow and prayer, round a grave that has been dug out of the solid ice, into which the mortal remains of their beloved chief are quietly and reverently laid. The funeral service for the dead is read by Captain Crozier (who has succeeded to the command of the expedition), or, perhaps, by his more intimate friend Fitzjames, who was now in command of the *Erebus*, whilst that flag, the glorious flag of England, under which he had served so long and so faithfully in all parts of the world, and against many foes, fluttered half-mast from the mizen peaks of the two ships.

It must indeed have been a sad gathering of sorrowful men that assembled in that wilderness of ice and snow on that June day, in 1847, to pay their last mark of respect, love, and devotion to their deceased leader. They were not only lamenting the loss of a revered chief who had endeared himself to them by his many acts of kindness and forethought, one who had instilled into the hearts of those under him his own enthusiastic desire for the welfare and success of the expedition, but, regarding their bereavement **from a** more selfish point of view, they **could** not help feeling that with his death their own chances of being saved were rendered all the more remote and precarious. **They knew** that if necessity, **as** seemed very probable, compelled them to abandon their ships, and seek for aid and **relief at** some of the Hudson's Bay Company's posts on **the continent** of America, they had lost one whose experience **of, and** intimate acquaintance with, those regions would have been invaluable, and who alone would, in **all** probability, have **been able to guide them** to where the assistance and the succour that was so essential to their salvation could **be** obtained. **They** were also well aware, **poor fellows, that** famine, rendered ten times more terrible by disease and the rigorous nature of the climate, would have to be endured, **if** a third winter was to be passed in their present situation ; and as they gazed around on the sad and sorrowful faces of their comrades, the painful reflection was unconsciously forced upon them, **as to** who would **be** alive, if not relieved, in another **year ?** Who would there be left **to** tell of the death of their great and good **leader,** and of the terrible sufferings and privations they had all endured ?

But time **did not permit them to indulge at length in** these or similar **reflections, for the** navigable **season had** arrived, and their utmost exertions must be put forth **with** the view of releasing their ships **from** the icy **thraldom** in which they were imprisoned. The freedom of their vessels must **be** their first thought, for it really was **their** only prospect of salvation. We may be sure that

everything was done with this end in view **that could**
possibly be accomplished.   Ice saws, we may reasonably
infer, were in constant use; **powder was doubtless employed** in futile endeavours to break the frozen **bonds
that** held their **ships** so securely, and every expedient,
we may be certain, was resorted to that **science or**
human ingenuity could devise; but all were fruitless—
the ships remained fixed and immovable.   But although
their vessels remained stationary, the ice in which they
were held captive was not so, and they soon discovered
that they were drifting slowly with the whole body of
the pack in a southerly direction.   **This, at any rate,
was** promising, and served in a measure to revive their
drooping spirits, for they thought they might perhaps
drift down to the American continent, when their chances
of rescue and succour would be materially enhanced.

But as the autumn advanced they had the mortifica-
tion of finding that their daily drift to the southward was
gradually decreasing, until **alas!** it ceased altogether.
They were then **only fifteen** short miles from Point
Victory, and not more than about sixty from the American coast.   God's will be done! for they **know that—**

> " Winter with his naked arms
>   And chilling breath is here;
> The rills that all the autumn time
>   Went singing to the sea,
> Are waiting in their icy chains
>   For spring to set them free."

They **are indeed now in dire** extremities.   It is too
late in the season to think of abandoning the ships in
order to seek for succour by attempting **to** reach the
American coast, and thence to **travel by the Great Fish**
River to some of the Hudson's Bay establishments in

that neighbourhood. They knew, from Franklin's former terrible experiences, that **game** was not to be obtained during the winter **months on** the barren lands of the continent, so that **they were well** aware, in the event of being unable to reach the Hudson's Bay posts, starvation **must be the** inevitable result. Only one course was open to them—namely, to pass another long and dreary **winter in** their ships, and then abandon **them in the** following spring, and this of necessity was the **one** decided on and adopted.

It is unnecessary to attempt **to picture** the miseries of that third winter. Suffice it **to** say that cold, want, and disease did **their cruel** work, and the sun of 1848 rose upon **an** emaciated, **weak, and** alas ! **a** diminished party, for **we know that no** less than nine officers and twelve **men passed away during** those two terrible winters besides the three **who died** during the first winter, and were buried at Beechey **Island.** Among those who died was the first lieutenant **of the** *Erebus,* **"the** sweet-tempered " Graham Gore, who was the **first to discover and** report the existence of the north-west passage, and who had been promoted to the rank of commander in the vacancy caused by the death of Sir John Franklin. **Poor** fellow, he did not live long **to enjoy** his well-earned **step. The** number **of officers who perished up to this time** seems to bear **a remarkable and** unusual proportion to the number **of men who died** during **the** same period, and **can** only **be accounted for by** the supposition that the former exposed themselves more than the latter, in their **endeavours** to alleviate the sufferings of those committed to their **charge.**

The survivors now number 105, **but** we may safely infer that **the** greater part of these poor fellows were sadly reduced by weakness and disease, and some, we may also be assured, were in **a** perfectly helpless condition. Nevertheless, having made the best arrangements that were, under the circumstances, possible, these brave men, in response to the decision to abandon the ships, cheerfully manned the drag-ropes of the sledges that had been previously prepared and packed, and under the leadership of Crozier and Fitzjames, bade farewell to the *Erebus* and *Terror* on the morning of April 22nd, and started on their long journey towards the Great Fish River, where they hoped, at **any rate,** to meet with Indians, who might possibly supply them with food.

Had they but known that Sir James Ross, with **a** couple of ships, would, in four short months, be within three hundred miles of the position of **the** *Erebus* and *Terror* when they were abandoned, and that relief parties from his ships would actually approach more than one hundred miles nearer to them, how different might the result have been!

The necessity for abandoning the ships **so** early in the season seems somewhat unaccountable; it may have been due to the fact that they were running short of provisions on board, or, which is quite possible, to their anxiety to make an early start. **It** is estimated that they were not able to carry away with them on their sledges provisions for more than about forty days, so that even had they succeeded in reaching the continent of America, they would have been without food **for some** considerable time, as their provisions would have been expended before they could possibly hope to find game in sufficient quantity to supply their party with food, for, as a rule, the animals do not begin to frequent the barren lands of the continent before the latter end

of the summer. It would therefore, it seems, have been
better for them to have deferred the abandonment of
their ships until the month **of** May, when they would
have had warmer weather for travelling, provided, of
course, they had **on** board **the** vessels the wherewithal
to sustain **life** for that duration of time; **of this,** however, we have **no** knowledge, **nor will the** information
now ever be forthcoming.

In addition to the provisions and stores with **which**
their sledges **were** loaded, they also carried **a** couple **of**
whale-boats, which were each secured on a separate sledge.
That these sledges must have been heavily weighted, as
seems **more than probable,** or that the physical capabilities of **the** men were much reduced, is evident from
the fact that it took them three days to reach Point
Victory, a distance of only fifteen miles. This painful fact **appears to** have been realised by them on
reaching **the land, for at** this point they seem to have
lightened their sledges by abandoning everything that
could possibly **be** spared, or that might be considered
superfluous, carrying with them nothing but those
articles that were absolutely and essentially necessary
for their sustenance. This was ascertained **in after**
years [1] by finding this particular spot strewn **with an**
accumulation of articles of all sorts, such as clothing
in great quantities, stores of various descriptions, blocks,
shovels, pick-axes, red, white, and blue ensigns, and even
the brass ornaments of a marine's shako, the fragment of
a copper lightning-conductor and a brass curtain-rod !
It is a matter of surprise that so many useless articles
should have been carried away from the ships—articles
that could not possibly be required (unless they were

[1] In 1859, by Sir Leopold M'Clintock and Lieutenant Hobson.

specially taken for the **purpose of barter with the** natives), **and** which could be nothing **else than lumber on their already** heavily laden sledges.

On their arrival at Point Victory, Lieutenant Irving of the *Terror* found the record that had been left **the** previous year by Graham Gore. Unrolling it, Crozier and Fitzjames wrote the following words round the margin, which tells **us** briefly all **we** shall ever **know** of the proceedings of the expedition **to that date** : [1]—

"*April* 25, 1848.—H.M. ships *Terror* and *Erebus* were deserted on the **22nd** of April, **five** leagues **N.N.W. of this,** having been **beset since** 12th September 1846. The officers and crews, **consisting of 105** souls, under **the command of** Captain **F. R. M. Crozier,** landed here in latitude 69° 37′ 42″ N., longitude 98° 41′ W. A paper was found by Lieutenant Irving under the cairn supposed to have been built by Sir James Ross in 1831, 4 miles to the northward, where it had been deposited by the late Commander Gore in June 1847. Sir James Ross's pillar has not, however, been found, and the paper has been transferred to this position, which is that in which **Sir James Ross's pillar** was erected. **Sir John Franklin** died on the 11th **June 1847, and** the total loss **by deaths in the** expedition has **been to this** date 9 officers **and 15 men.** Start on to-morrow, 26th, **for Back's** Fish River."

The document is signed by F. R. M. Crozier, captain and senior officer, **and** James Fitzjames, captain H.M.S. *Erebus.* Regarding the allusion in this record **to** the paper deposited by the sledge party under Graham Gore the previous year, it should be observed that the month **May was originally written, and then** subsequently scratched out and June substituted. This is evidently an error—it **should have** remained May, for Sir John Franklin died on the 11th of June, and we know he was

<hr>

[1] See page 270.

alive when the **travelling party left the** *Erebus* on **the**
24th of May; the paper was written and deposited **in**
the cairn **four** days afterwards.

Having **relieved** their sledges **of** all superfluous
weights, **the retreating** party left Point Victory on

MAP OF KING WILLIAM ISLAND, SHOWING FRANKLIN'S LINE OF
RETREAT.

the 26th April, and pushed on in a southerly direction,
adhering to the coast-line of King William Island. We
will not say that with their lightened loads they were
able **to** make rapid progress, but we may, at **any** rate,

assume that their advance was less slow than when they left their ships ; but what a cheerless and a dismal route was theirs—

> "All waste ! no sign of life
> But the track of the wolf and the bear !
> No sound but the wild wild wind,
> And the snow crunching under their feet."

Poor fellows ! their march was indeed a hopeless one, and as such they must, one and all, have regarded it ; but, at the same time, they knew it was their last and only chance for life, and who will not fight bravely and gallantly when his existence is the stake for which he is contending ? Day by day did the strength of these sorely-stricken men diminish, and day by day were their hardships and privations increased by want and disease. Can we, or shall we ever be able to realise the sufferings, both mental and physical, endured by that half-famished band, as they bravely struggled onward ? It is certainly impossible to pen a description of them that would in any way convey an idea of the reality.

Before they had proceeded many miles, it became only too palpable that in order to afford a chance of salvation to even a portion of the party, a division must be made—their rate of progression, hampered as they were with the sick and helpless, was so slow, that it was evident all must perish unless some such arrangement was made. It is therefore conjectured that the party separated into two bands, the fittest and the strongest being selected to push on with the object of procuring assistance, if indeed aid was forthcoming, whilst the remainder, comprising the weak and the sick, should return to the ships—better, it was thought, to linger in their vessels, where, at any rate, shelter from the inclemency and rigour of **the climate could be** obtained, than to die of cold and **starvation on the barren** snow-covered shores of King William Island. One boat, it is assumed, **was left with the party** that remained ; the **other** was taken **on to** the southward.

All the knowledge we **have been able to gain of** those **poor** fellows who, unable to proceed, had been left behind, **was** the discovery of their boat, **with her bow** pointed **to** the northward in the direction **of the** ships, **and** containing two human skeletons. **It is not difficult to** guess the terrible fate **of** this party, **for although the** boat contained **a** large assortment **of** clothing and stores of all kinds, there was *an entire* **absence** *of provisions*, unless a very **small quantity of tea** and sugar could be considered as **such.** **At any rate,** there was nothing in her **that was** capable **of** supporting life. **The boat** was found about fifty miles from **Point** Victory, **and** about sixty-five from the position **the** ships occupied **when** abandoned. It **is** surmised **that the men com**-posing this party, finding their strength unequal **to** drag the boat any further, pushed on to the ships, and **that the** two poor fellows whose skeletons **were found in** the boat, being too weak or ill to accompany **them, were** left behind until relief could be sent to their **aid.** **That** succour, alas ! never came.

The southern detachment pushed onwards. They were but a small party, and probably did not number more than fifty. **After** struggling painfully onward, knowing **that on** their exertions the safety of their more helpless companions depended, Cape Herschel was reached, and here, it is supposed, they must have passed close to the **cairn erected by Simpson in** 1839. This cairn was

in after years examined by Sir Leopold M'Clintock, but
in spite of all his efforts to discover some record concealed within it, no paper or document of any description
was found.   Had any been deposited, it must have been
destroyed or thrown away by the Eskimos, who would, of
course, be ignorant of its value.   All that was discovered
was a human skeleton, whose bones were found bleach-
ing about ten miles to the eastward of Cape Herschel.
These human remains told with silent eloquence a sad
and mournful tale, for its position—it was lying face
downwards—fully bore out the words of an old Eskimo
woman who had seen, so it was reported, the party retreating to the southward, and who said "they fell
down and died as they walked along."   From Cape
Herschel the remnants of this wretched band of poor
wayworn, starved, and scurvy-stricken Englishmen
crossed over to Adelaide Peninsula, where it is supposed they all perished on their way to the Great Fish
River, where they hoped to obtain assistance and relief.
At any rate, with the exception of a few relics found
at Montreal Island, which may have been carried thither
by the Eskimos, no further traces of the party were
ever found to the southward—all is wrapped in darkness
and mystery.

A faint gleam of light is thrown over the last days
of these unfortunate men by information collected from
the Eskimos by Dr. Rae in 1854, Sir Leopold M'Clintock
in 1859, Captain Hall in 1869, and Lieutenant Schwatka
in 1880.   From what could be learnt from the members
of these nomadic tribes, a party of about forty white
men were seen during the spring of the year (supposed
to be 1848) travelling southwards dragging sledges and
a boat.   They were very thin, and appeared to be in

want of provisions. None could speak the Eskimo language, but by signs they gave the natives to understand that their ship, or ships, had been destroyed by the ice, and they were journeying to where they hoped to get deer or other food.

All this information it must be remembered was obtained at second hand from the natives, who had received the intelligence from others. They affirmed that "several years ago a ship was crushed by the ice off the north shore of King William Island, but all her people landed safely, and went away to the Great Fish River, where they died." A second ship also, we are told, "had been seen off King William Island, and that she drifted on shore at the fall of the same year." When the ship was seen by the natives she was apparently intact—one boat was on deck, and four others were hoisted up outside. Subsequently she was crushed by the ice and destroyed. It was further reported that in one of the ships was the body of a man, "a tall man, with long teeth and large bones." The remains thus found might have been those of some poor fellow who had perhaps breathed his last as the ships were being abandoned, or he may have formed one of that forlorn hope that, as has already been surmised, separated from the remainder of their shipmates, and attempted to return when they were midway between Point Victory and Cape Herschel, only to reach the shelter of his ship in time to die. In spite of the most diligent search that was made, no vestige of either ship was found by M'Clintock or subsequent explorers, so it may reasonably be inferred that they had been destroyed and completely swept away by the ice, as stated by the Eskimos. From the west extreme of King William

Island to **Cape Felix**, the **low barren shore**, destitute of vegetation, **was** strewn **with traces of** the disastrous retreat of our helpless countrymen.

In 1869 Captain Hall was informed, by the natives he **met in** King William Island, that the graves of two white **men** were found **in** the vicinity of the Pfeiffer River, and that there was another white man's grave on a long low point jutting out into the sea, some five or **six** miles further to the eastward. **The remains of five** white men **were also discovered on a small islet, called Todd** Islet, **about two or three** miles **off** this point. Hall **was** further **informed that** in a bay **to** the **west of Point** Richardson, which has subsequently been named Starvation **Cove, a boat covered** with an awning **and** containing the remains of thirty **or thirty-five men was found.** It was also reported **that a tent had been seen in the** vicinity of Terror **Bay, "the floor** of which **was** completely **covered** with the **bodies of white** men." **In** fact, the line of retreat **of these** unfortunate **men** was clearly defined by the skeletons **of** those **poor** fellows who had dropped **down and died as they walked** along.

Thus perished that gallant band **of heroes who, so** full of hope and enthusiasm, left England in 1845 under the leadership **of Sir John** Franklin, resolved to do **all** that lay in **their power to deserve,** even if they could not command, **success.**

How well and nobly, in the face of unparalleled hardships and difficulties, they **carried out that resolution,** has been abundantly **proved. Glorious as is the story** of this ill-fated expedition, **it is a sad and harrowing one.** But it does us good **to think of it, for** it excites our admiration and kindles our **respect for those brave** men, "the World's Great Explorers," who have cheerfully and willingly borne great sufferings and privations—aye, and have unhesitatingly laid down their lives—in the interesting, useful, and great cause of exploration and geographical science.

CHAPTER XIV.

ANXIETY RESPECTING SAFETY OF FRANKLIN—
*EXPEDITIONS **DESPATCHED IN** SEARCH.*

1847–1859.

> "In battle fearless, and in danger brave,
>   Bearing his country's red-cross flag aloft,
>   Triumphant **over** foes and elements,
>   No peril **stopped him.**"

As the year 1847 **arrived, and** brought with it no intelligence of, **or from, Sir** John Franklin, and those
serving under his command, considerable anxiety was
naturally felt in England regarding their safety, **for**
the fact that they were only supplied with stores and
provisions to last until the early **part of** 1848 was **well**
known.   There were not wanting those who already took
a gloomy view of affairs, and predicted disaster ; **while**
others, in responsible positions, looked upon the matter
in a more practical light, and judging that **the time**
for energetic action had arrived, brought pressure to
bear **on the** Government to induce it to consider the
necessity **of** not only sending relief **in** the shape **of**
supplies to various **parts of** the North American
continent, but also urged the desirability **of at once**
instituting an organised search on an **extended** scale
for the absent expedition.   So impressed **were the**
Admiralty **with the views** thus set forth, and **with**

the necessity of adopting some measures of immediate
relief, that in the summer of 1847 they made arrangements with the Hudson's Bay Company for the despatch
of a large supply of provisions[1] to their most northern
stations in North America, in readiness for the crews
of Franklin's ships, should they have abandoned their
vessels and be retreating in that direction.

Instructions were also sent to the various Hudson's
Bay Company's posts to warn the Indians to look out for,
and assist the survivors, if fallen in with.   Large rewards
were likewise offered by the Government to the masters
and crews of all ships employed in the whale fishery in
Baffin's Bay, should they perchance "succeed in obtaining any information or record of the progress of the
Erebus and *Terror* through Lancaster Sound and to
the westward." This was supplemented by a reward
of £2000 offered by Lady Franklin, to anybody who
should obtain reliable information regarding the fate,
or otherwise, of the missing expedition.

When the year 1847 passed without bringing any
tidings of the absent ships, the Government lost no
time in adopting what they considered to be the best
means for ascertaining the whereabouts, or the fate, of
the missing expedition.   In the first place, it was decided
to institute a search by following, very wisely, as much
as possible, in the footsteps of Franklin.   With this
object in view, two vessels, the *Enterprise* of 471 tons,
and the *Investigator* of 420 tons burthen, were selected
and commissioned, and the charge of them entrusted to
Captain Sir James Clarke Ross.   With him was associated Captain Edward Bird, who was appointed to the
command of the second ship.   These officers were ex-

[1] The amount sent was seventy-five days' provisions for 120 men.

perienced ice navigators, and had taken part with Parry during his memorable attempt to reach the North Pole in 1827. The latter served also as first lieutenant of the *Erebus* in Ross's Antarctic voyage.

A second expedition, under the command of Franklin's old friend and travelling companion, Sir John Richardson, with Mr. John Rae (an official belonging to the Hudson's Bay Company), was sent with orders to descend the Mackenzie River, and examine the coast thence to the Coppermine River, as also the southern and western shores of Wollaston Land. In order to render the search as complete as possible, another expedition, consisting of the *Herald*, under Captain Kellett, and the *Plover*, under Commander Moore, was sent to Bering's Strait, with instructions to proceed along the American coast as far as possible to the eastward, and to endeavour to communicate with the party under the command of Sir John Richardson.

Thus it appears that everything was done that could possibly be accomplished, in order to afford relief and succour to the absent explorers, or to obtain intelligence of their fate in the event of any untoward catastrophe having befallen them.

The first-named expedition, that under the command of Sir James Clarke Ross, sailed from England on the 12th June 1848. Proceeding without much difficulty up Baffin's Bay and Lancaster Sound, it was ultimately stopped by an ice barrier across Barrow's Strait, and they were compelled to seek winter quarters in Port Leopold, on the north-east coast of North Somerset. During the ensuing spring, travelling parties from the ships reached Cape Hurd, on the north shore of Barrow's Strait, while the eastern and the western coasts of Prince

Regent Inlet as far south as Fury beach were carefully searched.

Had the survivors from the *Erebus* and *Terror* made for Fury beach instead of attempting to reach the Great Fish River, the probabilities are they would have been saved, for they would there have found all the stores and provisions that had been landed from the *Fury* when that vessel was wrecked in 1825. These would have been more than sufficient to sustain the party until the following spring (that of 1849), when they would have been found and relieved by the search parties sent out by Sir James Ross from Port Leopold. Captain Crozier must have been well aware of the existence of this large depôt of provisions, for he was serving in the *Fury* at the time of her loss. It is, however, assumed that he did not feel justified in conducting his unfortunate men some seventy or eighty miles out of their course, when there was the possibility of the provisions having been discovered and appropriated by the Eskimos. He was not ignorant of the fact that Sir John Ross, with his small party, wintered at Fury beach in 1832–3, and that when he left, there was an ample supply of provisions remaining.[1]

During this spring of 1849, Sir James Ross, accompanied by Lieutenant M'Clintock, travelled as far as Cape Coulman in Peel Strait, in latitude 72° 38′ N. They were then, although they were ignorant of the fact, in the direct track of Franklin's ships. Had it

---

[1] Sir L. M'Clintock visited Fury beach in 1859, and found everything intact.

The Editor also of this work paid Fury beach a visit in 1873, when he found the remaining stores and provisions in a perfect state of preservation.

been possible for them to continue their **journey they** would, in all probability, have seen **the** deserted vessels, but their provisions being nearly expended necessitated their return from this point to Port Leopold. **On the** arrival **of the** *Enterprise* and *Investigator* at Port Leopold in the autumn of 1848, those ships were actually within 300 miles of the position of the *Erebus* and *Terror, four months* **after** those unfortunate vessels had been abandoned !

Ross returned to **England somewhat unexpectedly in** the autumn of 1849, having been beset **by the ice** off **Leopold** Island, in which he had drifted **out of Lancaster** Sound into Baffin's Bay. He missed a store ship, **the** *North Star*, that had been despatched in May to **meet** him, laden with provisions **for his use. She wintered in** Wolstenholme Sound, **on the west coast of Greenland.**

Sir John Richardson **also** returned in 1849, having been unsuccessful in his efforts to discover **any** traces of the missing expedition, although he had made a thorough examination of the Arctic shores of America between the Mackenzie and Coppermine Rivers. His attempts to cross over to Wollaston Land were frustrated by heavy ice being packed in the channel. This accomplished and indefatigable officer subsequently assisted **in the** preparation of the pemmican for nearly all the searching expeditions, **and** personally superintended the supply of the other provisions and stores required by them.

At this time **the** Government offered a reward of £20,000, **to** which Lady Franklin offered a further sum of £3000, **to** any " exploring party or parties as may, in the judgment of the Admiralty, have rendered efficient assistance to Sir John Franklin, his ships, or their crews."

On **the** return **of** Sir James **Ross,** the Government, with commendable promptitude, resolved **upon** the immediate examination of those places in the Polar basin where it was thought most likely that traces of the missing expedition **might be discovered.** With this object **in** view, the *Enterprise* and *Investigator* were at once re-equipped and re-commissioned, but this time for the purpose of entering the unknown **area** from the **westward** through Bering's Strait. The command **of** this expedition was given to Captain Richard Collinson, C.B., an accomplished surveyor and a distinguished officer, who hoisted his pendant in the *Enterprise*, while Commander Robert **J. Le Mesurier** M'Clure, who had served as a mate in the *Terror* with Captain Back in 1836, and was first lieutenant **of** the *Enterprise* in Ross's late expedition, was appointed to the command of the *Investigator*. These vessels left England in January 1850, with orders to pass through Bering's Strait during the following navigable season, and thence proceed with the utmost expedition to **the** eastward, and examine Melville Island, Banks Land, Wollaston and Victoria Land, or otherwise according to the discretion and judgment of Captain Collinson. The *Plover* was **also ordered** to winter in Kotzebue Sound in order to act **as a depôt,** whence assistance could be obtained in the unfortunate event of any serious calamity befalling the two ships.

Four months after the departure of the *Enterprise* and *Investigator*, a **goodly** squadron, consisting of the ships **Resolute,** *Assistance,* **and the steam** tenders *Intrepid* and **Pioneer,**[1] sailed **under** the command **of**

---

[1] This was practically the first occasion on which full-powered steamers were employed in ice navigation. The result was so favourable that steam-whalers were gradually introduced in the Baffin's Bay **whale fishery to the total exclusion of sailing ships.**

HENRY GRINNELL, ESQ.

[From a Photograph by Alex. Bassano.]

Q

Captain Horatio Austin, C.B., with Captain **Erasmus** Ommaney as his second, with the object of carrying out an exhaustive search through **Lancaster Sound** in the direction of Melville and **the Parry** Islands.

In addition to these vessels, a couple of whaling brigs, under the command of Captains Penny and Stewart, two successful and experienced whaling skippers, were also despatched by the Government, with orders to undertake the examination of Jones Sound and Wellington Channel; whilst an American expedition, fitted out **at** the expense of that munificent and philanthropic citizen of New York, **Mr.** Henry Grinnell, and manned by officers and **seamen of** the United States Navy, was sent out to Lancaster Sound in order to assist in the search, and **to co-operate** with their English brethren in the humane and important work entrusted to them. This expedition was commanded by Lieutenant De Haven of the United States navy. Lady Franklin also, at her own expense, equipped the *Prince Albert*, a schooner of ninety tons, which sailed under the command of Commander Forsyth, R.N., with instructions to explore the shores of Prince Regent Inlet. And finally that gallant and intrepid old veteran Sir John Ross, who was then in his seventy-fourth year, and had reached the rank of admiral, **went** up **in a** small schooner called the *Felix*, accompanied by a little yacht of twelve tons named the *Mary*. This latter expedition was equipped and fitted out partly at the cost of the Hudson's Bay Company, and partly by private subscription. It passed the winter of 1850–1 off the coast of Cornwallis Island.

Thus, in the autumn of 1850, there were no less than

fifteen vessels, directly and indirectly, engaged in the search for Sir John Franklin and his missing ships. To these various expeditions must be added a boat journey made by Lieutenant Pullen, who was sent by Captain Kellett from Point Barrow to the eastward along the north coast of America to the Mackenzie River, which he ascended as far as the Great Slave Lake; while Dr. Rae was also employed in exploring the neighbourhood of the Coppermine River and the shores of Wollaston and Victoria Land. It will thus be seen that the entire continental coast-line between Bering's Strait to a position in latitude 70° on the east coast of Victoria Land, was to be thoroughly examined.

Everything was conducted on a most liberal and generous scale, and in such a way as to satisfy the country that no stone would be left unturned in order to find some trace, if any existed, of the missing ships and their gallant crews. The Polar area explored by these several expeditions was very extensive, and great and important geographical work was necessarily effected; but they failed in the accomplishment of the main object for which they were despatched, namely, the relief of Franklin and his companions, and their fate, unhappily, continued to be wrapped in dark and profound mystery.

The ships under the command of Captain Austin wintered at Griffith Island in Barrow's Strait; but before seeking winter quarters, great joy and no little excitement was caused by the discovery that the missing expedition under Sir John Franklin had passed their first winter (1845-6) at Beechey Island. The first traces of the lost ones were discovered by Captain

Ommaney of the *Assistance* at Point Riley,[1] and the graves of three of those who had died during that winter (*vide* page 213) were subsequently found by Captain

GRAVES ON BEECHEY ISLAND.

Penny.   The neighbourhood was, as may well be imagined, thoroughly searched in the hope of finding a

[1] At Franklin's winter quarters were found several heaps consisting of preserved meat tins filled with gravel, raised to a height of two feet, and varying in breadth from three to four yards.

Dr. Sutherland computed the number of these tins to be about 700, while many more were also found scattered about during the search

record, or document, that would afford some clue as to
the direction it was intended that the *Erebus* and *Terror*
should take after breaking out of winter quarters, but
although diligent search was made nothing could be
found. From this point all traces of the missing expedition ceased, and the veil of darkness and obscurity
was again lowered, only to be lifted by Rae and M‘Clintock at a later date.

In the spring of 1851, under a careful and elaborate
system of sledging, organised by Captain Austin on the
lines originally laid down by Parry and James Ross,
travelling parties were despatched to search in various
directions. The only method by which the search could be
efficiently arranged was, of course, to follow the general
tenor of Sir John Franklin's instructions, in which both
Wellington Channel and a route to the southward and
westward of Cape Walker are mentioned ; but it was also
necessary for Captain Austin to provide for exhaustive
searches in other directions. With this object in view
Captain Penny undertook the examination of Wellington
Channel, while Austin despatched three extended sledge
expeditions to the westward—two were sent round Cape
Walker to the south-west, and one went due south into

for records. These tins were labelled "Goldner's patent," and had
been supplied, under directions from the Admiralty, to the expedition
as "preserved meat." From the fact that an enormous quantity of
these tins supplied to the navy, were subsequently found to contain
putrid meat, and from the fact that so large a quantity of meat as these
empty tins were calculated to hold, could not have been used by the
members of the expedition during their first winter, it is supposed
that the defective condition of the contents of the tins was discovered,
and a survey of them ordered. If this surmise be a correct one, the
loss of so large a proportion of what would be considered fresh,
in contradistinction to salt, provisions would be most serious, and
would so cripple their resources, as to lead in all probability to the
disastrous fate of the expedition.

the channel now called Peel Sound.   One of these, under
Lieutenant M'Clintock, explored to the westward as far
as Melville Island, while two parties, under Captain
Ommaney and Lieutenant Sherard Osborn respectively,
searched from Cape Walker to the south-west along the
north and west coasts of Prince of Wales' Land.   Lieutenant Mecham, travelling in the same direction, discovered Russell Island, and Lieutenant Browne explored
the western shore of Peel Strait as far south as latitude
72° 49'. The latter searching party, like that of Sir
James Ross in 1849, only on the other side of the same
channel, was actually directing its energies along **the**
same track taken by the *Erebus* and *Terror ;* they were,
however, at the time ignorant that they were following
in the footsteps of Franklin, for, unfortunately, no cairn,
no record, not even a trace had been left by the missing
ones, that could afford a clue to those who were in quest
of them as to the direction they had taken.   Lieutenant
Browne's travelling party actually reached within 150
miles **of the** position **where** the *Erebus* and *Terror*
were abandoned.   The different searching parties, despatched by Captain Austin, examined no less than
1500 miles of coast-line, 850 of **which were** hitherto
unknown.

Thus everything that human forethought and human
exertions could possibly devise or accomplish, appears
to have been done to facilitate the discovery of some
traces of the missing expedition ; but it was unhappily
without avail—the various searching parties returned
one after **the** other, **only to** report that their efforts
had not been crowned with **success,** and the fate of
Franklin remained **as** mysterious and as impenetrable
a secret as ever.

The total **absence of** cairns along the route pursued by Franklin is most unaccountable, for this well-known **form** of Arctic **beacon** is easily constructed from material always at hand ; they form conspicuous landmarks, and their **importance as** such was well known to Franklin **and his** officers.   **If** they had **been erected,** the direction for the search would have been indicated, and **an** enormous amount **of** labour would **have been saved,** while a successful issue of the search would possibly have been the result.   The only reason that can be advanced for this apparent neglect, of what has always been considered as one of the most important duties of an Arctic explorer, **is** the supposition that **the** channels were comparatively clear of ice when the *Erebus* and *Terror* passed through, and that it was in consequence deemed inexpedient **to** delay the progress of the vessels by stopping **to** build **cairns—a serious** omission, however, for their **absence** necessitated the expenditure of much **invaluable time, besides a** great waste of **money in** the prosecution of **a** long **and** fruitless search.

With the exception of the *Enterprise* and **Investi***gator,* the ships that sailed from England in **1850 in** search of Franklin, returned the following year ;—indeed **the** *Prince Albert* did **not even** remain **out a** winter, but came home **in the autumn of** 1850, bringing the earliest intelligence **to** England of the fact that Franklin **had passed** his **first winter at** Beechey Island.

We will now turn to the proceedings **of** the *Enterprise* and *Investigator.*   Sailing from England on the 20th January 1850, these vessels passed through the Straits **of** Magellan, and touching **at the** Sandwich Islands, proceeded at once to Bering's Strait ; shortly, however, after entering the Pacific the **two ships** accidentally sepa-

CAPTAIN SIR ROBERT MCCLURE.

(From a painting by Stephen Pearce in the possession of Col. John Barrow.)

rated, and they never joined company again during the remainder of the cruise.   Both these vessels made remarkable, and, so far as Polar navigation is concerned, wonderfully successful voyages.   The *Investigator*, under Captain M'Clure, sailed along the north coast of the American continent, and may be accredited with the discovery of the existence of *two* north-west passages, viz., one through Prince of Wales' Strait (where the ship wintered in 1850) into Melville Sound, and the other from the westward, round the north coast of Bank's Land to Melville Sound.   The last-named passage was actually accomplished by Captain M'Clure and his officers and crew; for after having passed two consecutive winters in the Bay of God's Mercy on the north coast of Bank's Land, where their ship was irrevocably frozen up, their position was luckily discovered by a sledge party from the *Resolute*, to which ship they retreated when they abandoned the *Investigator*.[1] They were subsequently, but not until after a fourth winter had been spent in the Arctic regions, transferred to the *Phœnix*, in which ship they were brought to England.   They thus had the supreme satisfaction and honour of being the first, and only, people who had crossed from the Pacific Ocean to the Atlantic to the northward of America.   In acknowledgment of this service the sum of £10,000 was awarded by the English Government to Captain M'Clure and the crew of the *Investigator*.

[1] Had the sledging parties from the *Resolute* not found the *Investigator* when they did, it was the intention of Captain M'Clure to abandon his ship and attempt a retreat on the Mackenzie or Coppermine Rivers.   The result would inevitably have been as fatal to his crew as was Franklin's unsuccessful attempt to reach Back's River.

In the words of the **Select Committee of the House of** Commons, appointed **to consider the amount of the** reward that should **be given to the** officers and **crew** of the *Investigator* **for the discovery of a north-west passage—**

"They performed deeds **of heroism which,** though not **accompanied by** the excitement **and glory of the** battle-field, **yet rival, in** bravery and **devotion to duty, the highest** and **most** successful achievements of war!"

The intelligence of M'Clure's success was first **brought to** England by Lieutenant Cresswell, one of **the** officers **of the *Investigator*.** At a public reception given to **this officer on his arrival** at his native place, **Lynn in Norfolk, Lord Stanley, in referring to** the discovery of the north-west passage, **thus** addressed **him—**

"It was a triumph that would not be valued the **less highly because it was not** stained **by bloodshed—a triumph** that was not embittered by any single painful **or** melancholy reminis- **cence—a triumph** not over man, **but over** nature—a triumph **which inflicts no** injury, **and which** humiliates no enemy—a **triumph not for** this age alone, **but for** posterity—not for **England only, but for** mankind."

The voyage of the *Enterprise*, under Captain Collinson, **was no less** remarkable. Like the *Investigator*, she also **sailed along the north coast of America,** and wintered **in** 1851 **at the south extreme of Prince of Wales' Strait. Thence she worked her way to** the eastward, spending **her next winter in Cambridge** Bay, **at the** east extreme of Dease **Strait, and not more than** 150 **miles from the posi- tion reached by the *Erebus*** and *Terror* when those ships **were abandoned. In** the spring of 1853, travelling parties from **the** *Enterprise* actually passed within **a very few**

miles—not more than twenty—from the spot where the
unfortunate vessels had been left, but unhappily without
discovering any remains of them, or traces of their crews.
It is most unfortunate that the western shore of King
William Island, which was only about forty-five miles
distant, should have been neglected; for had it been
visited, the traces that were afterwards discovered by
Rae and M'Clintock would assuredly have been found
by Collinson, although we cannot think that any survivors of the expedition could at that time have
been alive. The *Enterprise* returned to England on
the 6th May 1855, after one of the most adventurous
and remarkable voyages that has ever been made in
the Arctic Seas.

On the return of the ships from Lancaster Sound in
1851, much disappointment was not unnaturally felt at
the unsuccessful result of the search, more especially
when the hopes and expectations of the public had been
somewhat raised by the news taken home in 1850, by
the *Prince Albert*, relative to the traces found at Beechey
Island. Immediately on the return of that vessel she
was re-equipped for Arctic service by Lady Franklin,
and despatched in the summer of the following year,
under the command of Mr. Kennedy, for the purpose
of exploring Prince Regent Inlet.[1]

During this voyage Bellot Strait, a channel separating
North Somerset from Boothia Felix, was discovered.
Thence Mr. Kennedy prosecuted the search to the west

---

[1] The veteran John Hepburn, Franklin's faithful follower and companion in his adventurous land journey in 1819, served in the *Prince
Albert* on this expedition; also Lieutenant Bellot, a gallant officer of
the French navy, who had volunteered for the service, and who was
afterwards unfortunately drowned, while leading a sledge party in
Wellington Channel.

and north, as far as the north-east point of Prince of Wales' Land, which is only about thirty miles from Cape Walker. He regained his ship by making the complete circuit of North Somerset.

Here again the searching parties seem to have been actuated by the same unfortunate fatality as in former expeditions. Had Mr. Kennedy directed his steps to the *south-west* in accordance with his instructions, instead of exploring to the *north-west*, traces of those he was in search of would assuredly have been discovered. It seems almost incredible that so many of our searching parties should have examined, and thoroughly explored, the region in the immediate neighbourhood of the disastrous retreat of our fellow-countrymen, and yet just missed finding traces of them, or any evidence to show that they had visited the locality.

Lady Franklin, not satisfied with what had been accomplished, or rather with the want of success that had attended the various efforts to obtain tidings of her husband and his brave companions, fitted out the little screw steamer *Isabel*, and despatched her under the command of Commander Inglefield in the autumn of 1852. He returned after an absence of three months, having sailed to the head of Baffin's Bay, and having looked into Smith's Sound, but without adding or obtaining any information of importance, relative to the missing expedition.

In the early part of 1852 elaborate preparations were again made by the Government for a renewal of the search. The ships that had recently returned under Captain Austin, the *Assistance, Resolute, Intrepid,* and *Pioneer,* were brought forward, refitted and again made efficient for Arctic service. These vessels were placed under the command of Captain Sir Edward Belcher, who flew his pendant in the *Assistance*. The other three vessels were commanded respectively by Kellett, M'Clintock, and Sherard Osborn. The *North Star*, under Captain Pullen, was also attached to this squadron as a depôt or relief ship. They sailed from Woolwich in April 1852.

Sir Edward's instructions were, briefly, to despatch one of his vessels, accompanied by a steamer, up Wellington Channel, while the other ship and remaining steamer were to push westward in the direction of Melville Island. These orders were ostensibly based on the knowledge that Sir John Franklin had passed his first winter at the entrance to Wellington Channel, and it was therefore hoped that by searching that strait, traces of the missing expedition might be found. The object of sending a portion of the squadron to the westward, was with the view of meeting any of the travelling parties from the *Investigator* and *Enterprise*, which might possibly, it was supposed, have reached positions in the vicinity of Melville Island.

The directions given to Sir John Franklin for his guidance in the route he was to pursue were again ignored, and the searching vessels were particularly ordered to devote their attentions to the north and to the west, and not to the *south-west*, the course that Franklin had been expressly enjoined to take! As a matter of fact, Sir John had been specially warned to avoid attempting the passage to the westward by Melville Island, in consequence of the difficulties from ice experienced and reported by Sir Edward Parry, yet it was to Melville Island and its vicinity, that the attention of Sir Edward Belcher was especially directed. It must

not however be forgotten that these orders were, in all
probability, issued in view of the apprehensions then
being felt regarding the safety of M'Clure and Collinson, and the expedition was intended to succour and
relieve them equally with the prosecution of the search
for Franklin.

The western expedition, under Captain Kellett, was
ordered to establish depôts of provisions on Melville
Island, and they were likewise directed to send "travelling parties in a westerly direction for the purpose of
searching for traces of Sir John Franklin," and presumably also with the object of obtaining intelligence
of Collinson and M'Clure. Both parties, it will be
observed, were ordered to search localities to the north
of Barrow's Strait, for an expedition that had been
specially directed to proceed to the south-west of that
channel! These apparently extraordinary orders were
issued in accordance, it is stated, with the views of
experienced Arctic officers, and the existing popular
feeling at the time.

It will be unnecessary to enter into any detailed
account of these expeditions. Suffice it to say, that
Sir Edward, with the *Assistance* and *Pioneer*, wintered
in Northumberland Sound, having successfully taken
his ships up Wellington Channel to latitude 76° 52'.
Kellett, with the *Resolute* and *Intrepid*, wintered at
Dealy Island, on the south side of Melville Island, while
Captain Pullen, in the *North Star*, passed the winter
at Beechey Island. From these several stations both
sledge and boat expeditions were despatched to search
in every direction, and much good and useful geographical work was achieved. Commander M'Clintock,
with his usual energy, explored Melville and Prince Pat-

rick Islands to their northern extremities, while other officers examined, and accurately delineated, the coasts of Bathurst, Melville, and Cornwallis Islands. It was during one of these expeditions, in the autumn of 1852, that a record was found at Winter Harbour, in Melville Island, containing the important information that the *Investigator* was frozen up in the Bay of Mercy; she was discovered the following summer, and the officers and crew rescued and taken on board the *Resolute*, as has already been related. In the summer of 1853 Sir Edward Belcher ordered all the ships to rendezvous at Beechey Island; but before reaching that place his ship and the *Pioneer* were beset in the ice in Wellington Channel, where he was compelled to pass the second winter. A similar fate befell Captain Kellett, who also, with his two ships, was caught by the ice, and compelled to winter in the pack in Melville Sound.

In the following year, for some unaccountable reason best known to Sir Edward Belcher, the commander of the expedition issued directions for the abandonment of all four ships, and the officers and crews were conveyed to England in the *North Star*, *Talbot* and *Phœnix*. The last named steamer had been despatched from England under the command of Captain Inglefield in the summer of 1854, accompanied by a transport with stores and provisions for Sir Edward's ships.

The subsequent wonderful drift of the *Resolute* out of Barrow's Strait, Lancaster Sound, through Baffin's Bay, and into Davis Strait, where she was picked up by an American whaler, and afterwards presented by the United States Government to our Admiralty, furnishes a remarkable proof of the force and direction of the current in that region.

The wholesale abandonment of a fine squadron, without apparently **any** reason, was a **great blow not only to** the search for Franklin, **but** also to Arctic exploration generally. The Government, on the return of Sir Edward Belcher, regarded the fate of Franklin as conclusive; they decided that no further steps should be **taken** in the matter, and they allowed private enterprise to step in **and solve** the problem of that fate, **the solution** of which should undoubtedly have been **the** work **of** the nation. The apathy displayed **by** England at this **time,** in its bounden duty **to use every** effort to obtain reliable intelligence regarding its missing **sons, was in** striking **contrast to** the feeling that animated **the hearts of our American** kinsmen, who had **already done so much to assist us in our search for the** lost expedition.

In May 1853 the schooner *Advance*, fitted out by private subscription (the main burden of the expense being borne **by** Messrs. Henry Grinnell and George Peabody), and under the auspices **of the United States Government,** sailed from New York under the command of Dr. Elisha Kane, an accomplished and enterprising officer, who had served as surgeon under De **Haven in** the same vessel, the *Advance*, in 1850. Under the impression that Franklin had proceeded in a northerly direction, for reasons **that it is needless** to discuss here, except that the supposed existence of an open Polar sea was the principal **reason** for determining the direction of the search, Dr. Kane **sailed up** Baffin's Bay into Smith's Sound.

This expedition, so far **as the search for Franklin is** concerned, was, as might be anticipated from the direction in which it **was** ordered **to** proceed, a failure; but it led **to important** geographical **discoveries, the** principal being the exploration of the southern part of Smith's Sound. **The** little *Advance*, after many narrow escapes **from being destroyed by the** ice, was eventually secured in winter quarters in Rensseläer Bay, in latitude 78° 38′; this was, at the time, the highest northern latitude **in** which any ship had passed a winter.

Here two winters were spent when, as they **were** unable to extricate **her** from **the** ice, she was abandoned. After many perils **and privations, Dr. Kane and his** half-starving party **succeeded in reaching, by boats, the** Danish settlements on the **west coast of Greenland,** whence they eventually took passage to **New York,** arriving in that city on the 11th October 1855.

Meanwhile Dr. Rae was sent in 1853 by the Hudson's Bay Company **to connect his** discoveries round Committee Bay, with those of Sir James Ross on the western **coast of** Boothia Felix, in the neighbourhood of the Magnetic Pole. In the spring of 1854, having passed the winter in Repulse Bay, he started in prosecution of his orders. On the 20th of **April he met** some Eskimos in Pelly Bay, **from whom he received** much of the information detailed at page 231, *et seq*. **From these** people he also obtained various small **articles, such as** silver spoons, forks, &c., which had undoubtedly belonged to the officers and men of the ill-fated ships *Erebus* and *Terror;* the finding of these articles seemed **to** place the fate of our unfortunate countrymen beyond all doubt.

Having **collected** as much information as **could be** elicited from these nomadic tribes, and also having procured as many **relics** as could **be** obtained, Rae proceeded to **carry out the main object** of his expedition, in the prosecution of which he succeeded in establishing the insularity of what had hitherto **been called the King**

William Land of Ross. **He then** returned to England in order to report the important information he had obtained to the authorities.

The account brought home by Rae was considered by the Admiralty, already lukewarm regarding the desirability of further search, conclusive evidence as to the inutility of any further expenditure of money, in following up the traces thus revealed of **the** missing expedition. The discovery of the relics was considered by them, as final evidence of the fate of the **entire party**, and by paying Rae the reward offered to any person who should produce positive intelligence of the actual fate of Franklin and his followers, the Admiralty thought they would, finally and for ever, settle the matter of further search, and thus be relieved of further responsibility in the matter. It was therefore decided to pay Dr. Rae the sum of £10,000 as a reward for his discovery.

But although the Government appeared, or pretended, to be satisfied, popular feeling was still clamorous for a continuation of the quest, until, at **any** rate, more conclusive and satisfactory evidence regarding the actual existence, or otherwise, of some of our countrymen could be ascertained. With this object in view, and **in order** to allay public feeling on the matter, the Hudson's Bay Company, acting **under orders from the** Government, despatched Mr. James Anderson, a chief factor in their employ, down the Great **Fish River, for** the purpose of communicating with the Eskimos and thus obtaining reliable information relative to the report brought home by Rae. This expedition was undertaken in the summer of 1855. Anderson reached Point Ogle, at the mouth of the river, and examined the coast and island in its vicinity, and though undoubted traces of **the** missing expedition were apparent, he **failed** to discover the remains of any of **our** unfortunate country-**men,** nor did he succeed **in** finding the slightest scrap of paper, document, journal, or record that could throw any further light on the fate of those poor fellows, **who** had travelled thus far after abandoning their ships, in the hope—a vain **one as** it proved—of obtaining succour and relief.

Lady Franklin, **it** may **very** justly be surmised, was **far** from satisfied **at** the stand taken by the Government at this juncture, and at the apparent apathy with which the Admiralty received all suggestions relative **to** further endeavours to unravel the mysterious entanglement which surrounded the fate of the lost explorers. She **had** already fitted out **four** ships, **almost** entirely **at her** own expense, which had been despatched with the object of discovering traces of the missing expedition ; in spite of Rae's discoveries she still felt that the work was unaccomplished, and that further efforts should be made to dispel the mystery in which the fate of her beloved husband and his brave men **was** still wrapped. Her views were warmly supported by the leading men of science of the day, besides all those naval officers who had been engaged on Arctic service, and whose opinions were therefore of unquestionable value. On the 5th **of** June 1856, a memorial, signed by numerous scientific men and Arctic officers, was presented to Lord Palmerston, urging the necessity of further research—

" To satisfy the honour of our country and clear up a mystery which has excited **the** sympathy of the civilised world."

Detailed plans as to the locality to be searched and **the prospects of success,** were all clearly and succinctly expressed and submitted; but all to no purpose—the Government had fully made up its mind that no further search, at the public expense, should be undertaken, and they resolved to abide by their decision. This memorial was followed by a letter from Lady Franklin,[1] the noble-minded widow of the gallant commander of the lost expedition, dated December 2, 1856, and addressed, as the memorial, to Viscount Palmerston. In it she urged the necessity of continued search, pointing out that as the locality was now practically known, the area of exploration would necessarily be considerably limited, and she hoped, and expected, that a renewal of the search would, at any rate, result in obtaining satisfactory evidence of the actual fate of the lost expedition.

These touching appeals, affecting a country's honour as well as arousing its sympathy, were, however, of no avail; the Government turned a deaf ear to all entreaties for further research, and intimated that as the reward for ascertaining the fate of the missing expedition had already been paid to Dr. Rae, they were not prepared to reopen the question, by the further expenditure of a large outlay of money, and the probable sacrifice of many valuable lives, in vain and, what they supposed to be, quixotic endeavours to obtain more definite information regarding the fate of Sir John Franklin and his lost companions.

Under these discouraging circumstances, Lady Franklin resolved to endeavour to accomplish by private enterprise, that which the Government had declined to

---

[1] Lady Franklin had also written several letters to the Admiralty urging the necessity of continued search, and protesting against the reward of £10,000 being paid to Dr. Rae.

undertake the responsibility of attempting to carry out, although backed by the resources of a wealthy country.

Aided by private subscriptions, but principally at her own expense, she purchased and fitted out the little steam yacht *Fox*, of 177 tons burthen. The command of the vessel was given to that able and most energetic of Arctic navigators, Captain M'Clintock, than whom no better man could have been selected for the appointment. With him were associated Lieutenant Hobson, R. N., "already distinguished in Arctic service," and Captain Allen Young, an experienced captain in the mercantile marine, who not only offered his services gratuitously, but also contributed largely from his private fortune towards the expenses of the expedition. Dr. David Walker was the surgeon and naturalist. Provisions and stores for twenty-eight months were put on board, and the little vessel sailed from Aberdeen on the 1st of July 1857. The only instructions received by M'Clintock were to act according to his own judgment in endeavouring to rescue " any possible survivor of the *Erebus* and *Terror*," and to leave no stone unturned in his exertions to recover some of the documents or records of the lost expedition, and, as Lady Franklin enjoined, " the personal relics of my dear husband and his companions."

Everything went well with the little craft and her gallant crew until Melville Bay, a locality that has proved so fatal to many a well-found whaler, was reached, when, in attempting to cross to the north water, M'Clintock was stopped by the ice in the middle of August, and eventually the *Fox* was frozen firmly in the pack. For 242 days was she beset, drifting all that long cold winter helplessly to the southward, until released on the 25th April 1858, **after** having been carried in her icy fetters, from latitude 75° 30′ to 63° 30′ **N., a** distance of 1194 geographical miles ! It is impossible to imagine **the** suspense and anxiety passed by **all on** board during that fearful winter. As M'Clintock significantly writes, after one **more than** usually exciting day of danger—

" After yesterday's experience **I can** understand **how a man's** hair has turned grey in a few **hours."**

Immediately his ship was released, this energetic officer pushed northwards a second time, regretting the delay entailed by the besetment, but in no way daunted by the dangers **he had** encountered, and the hardships and anxieties he and his men had experienced.

More fortunate this time, the little *Fox* succeeded in passing through Melville **Bay, and,** without much difficulty, proceeded up Lancaster Sound to Beechey Island. Here they erected the marble tablet sent out **by Lady** Franklin to be set up **to** the memory of **the** lost **crews of** the *Erebus* **and** *Terror*, **in** the immediate neighbourhood **of** the place where they had **passed** their first winter. This tablet was left at **God-haven by the American** expedition, that **was** sent **in search of Dr. Kane in** 1855, **where it** was found and brought **on by M'Clintock.** It bears the following inscription :—

TO THE MEMORY OF

FRANKLIN,

CROZIER, FITZJAMES,

AND ALL THEIR
GALLANT BROTHER OFFICERS AND FAITHFUL
COMPANIONS WHO HAVE SUFFERED AND PERISHED
IN THE CAUSE OF SCIENCE AND
THE SERVICE OF THEIR COUNTRY.

THIS TABLET

IS ERECTED NEAR THE SPOT WHERE
THEY PASSED THEIR FIRST ARCTIC
WINTER, AND WHENCE **THEY** ISSUED
FORTH TO CONQUER DIFFICULTIES OR

TO DIE.

TO COMMEMORATE THE GRIEF OF THEIR
ADMIRING COUNTRYMEN AND FRIENDS,
AND THE ANGUISH, SUBDUED BY FAITH,
OF HER WHO HAS LOST, IN THE HEROIC
LEADER OF THE EXPEDITION, THE MOST
DEVOTED AND AFFECTIONATE OF
HUSBANDS.

———+←———

*" And so He bringeth them unto the
Haven where they would be."*

1855.

This stone has been entrusted to be affixed in its place by the officers and crew of the American expedition, commanded by Lieutenant H. J. Hartstein, in search of Dr. Kane and his companions.

This tablet having been left at **Disco by the** American expedition, which **was unable** to reach Beechey Island, **in** 1855, **was put** on board the Discovery yacht *Fox*, **and is now set** up here by Captain M'Clintock, **R.N.,** commanding the final expedition of search for ascertaining the fate of Sir John Franklin and his companions, 1858.

On the morning of the 16th of August the little *Fox* steamed away from Beechey Island, a locality fraught with many interesting associations, and pushed gallantly on with the object of passing through Peel Strait; but, in consequence of the great accumulation of unbroken ice in the channel, this intention was abandoned, and a course was steered up Prince Regent Inlet towards Bellot Strait. The adoption of this route appeared to M'Clintock to offer the best prospect of getting to the place which he was desirous of reaching, namely, the mouth of the Great Fish River and the western shore of King William Island, for this was the locality indicated by the Eskimos at Pelly Bay, from whom the relics and information had been obtained by Dr. Rae five years previously, where, it was hoped, further intelligence would be forthcoming.

On the 19th of August they were at Port Leopold, and on the following day were off Fury beach, with very little ice in sight; shortly afterwards, however, they encountered much loose ice coming out of Brentford Bay. Here they had a narrow escape from destruction, being beset by heavy pack ice, which carried the little *Fox*, at the rate of nearly six miles an hour, within 200 yards of the rocks. Fortunately this particular danger was averted, and they succeeded in extricating their vessel from the pack, leaving the huge masses of ice to be dashed violently against each other, and carried wildly hither and thither, by the various whirlpools caused by the rapidity of the tides and currents in Bellot Strait. Eventually, after numerous unsuccessful attempts to proceed, during which she passed three times through the strait, only to be stopped by heavy ice held fast by rocks and islets situated two miles beyond its western **outlet**, the *Fox* was secured **in** winter quarters **in Port** Kennedy, at the eastern end of **the** strait, **on** the 28th September 1858.

Sledging expeditions were at once undertaken for the purpose **of** exploring the country in the neighbourhood of their winter quarters, and also with the object of laying out depôts of provisions as far as possible on the routes **to** be followed **during** the spring, when the extended travelling parties would **be despatched to fulfil** the main object **of** the expedition, **viz.**, to ascertain the fate of Franklin and those under his command.

The **winter was** passed in making the **necessary pre**parations **for the** arduous work of the spring **and summer.** The plan for the preliminary spring journeys **was as follows**:—Captain M'Clintock, accompanied by **two men,** with a couple of dog-sledges dragged by fifteen **dogs, and** provisioned for an absence of twenty-four **days, was to** travel towards the Magnetic Pole with **the object of** communicating with the Eskimos, who, it **was expected, would be** found in **that** locality, while **Allen Young, with a dog-sledge and four men, was to ad**vance depôts of provisions in readiness for his main journey along **the coast of Prince of Wales' Land.** Hobson was left in charge of the *Fox*, with orders to send out in search of these two parties, should they remain absent beyond the period for which they were provisioned.

On the 17th February, the temperature at the time being about 40° below zero, M'Clintock and Young left **the little *Fox*** to carry out their allotted and self-imposed tasks. In spite of the intense cold, and the lameness of some of the dogs, and the repeated fits with which these animals **were frequently** attacked, they were able to accomplish **an** average daily distance of about fifteen or eighteen miles. For several days the weather was so severe that the mercury for their artificial horizons remained in a frozen state, and the rum had to be thawed before it could be used. On the 1st of March M'Clintock reached the position of the Magnetic Pole, where he was fortunate enough to meet the Eskimos he was in search of. One of these men was found to be in possession of a naval uniform button. When questioned regarding it, he said it had come to him from some white men, who had died from starvation on an island at the mouth of a river, and that they had obtained the iron, from which the knives in their possession were made, from the same source. Being joined by the remainder of the tribe, M'Clintock was able to obtain by barter more relics of the lost expedition, consisting principally of silver spoons and forks belonging to officers of the *Erebus* and *Terror*, a silver medal the property of Mr. A. M'Donald, assistant surgeon of the *Terror*, and other articles, thus setting at rest all doubts that might have been entertained regarding the fate of Franklin's unfortunate ships and their unhappy crews.

The Eskimos on being closely interrogated denied having personally seen any of the white men, although one man acknowledged to having seen their bones on the island where they died. Another said that a ship with three masts had been crushed by the ice to the west of King William Island, but that all the people had landed in safety; the vessel, however, sunk, so that nothing of value was obtained from her. The information thus obtained corroborated the statements made by the Eskimos to Dr. Rae; it also accounted for the disappearance of one of the ships, but gave no information regarding the ultimate fate of the other.

CAPTAIN SIR LEOPOLD McCLINTOCK.

(From a painting by Stephen Pearce in the possession of Col. John Barrow.)

Having obtained all the information, and collected all the relics that could be gathered from these people, M'Clintock returned to the *Fox*, in order to prepare for the more extended and important journeys that were in contemplation. During this journey, of twenty-five days' duration, he travelled a distance of 360 miles, and added to our charts no less than 120 miles of coast-line previously unknown. The mean temperature during the time the sledging parties were away, was 62° below freezing-point (Fahr.). Young had also successfully accomplished the work allotted to him, having advanced depôts of provisions, some seventy miles from the ship, on the coast of Prince of Wales' Land.

On the 2nd of April, the two principal sledging parties, under the command respectively of Captain M'Clintock and Lieutenant Hobson, left the *Fox*, provisioned for an absence of about eighty-four days. Each party consisted of a sledge dragged by four men, besides a dog-sledge and dog driver. Allen Young left the ship five days later in search of the ship supposed to have been wrecked on the coast of Prince of Wales' Land.

The two parties, those of M'Clintock and Hobson, travelled together until they reached Cape Victoria on the 28th, when they separated,[1] the latter to explore the western shore of King William Island from Cape Felix to the southward, and to make a diligent search for the ships and records; while M'Clintock proceeded to examine the east coast in a southerly direction,

---

[1] This arrangement was due to the generous resolve of M'Clintock, who, knowing from his spring journey that Franklin's crews had landed on the west coast of King William Island, magnanimously sent Lieutenant Hobson in that direction, feeling sure that the first traces of the lost expedition would be found there; he did this in order to ensure that officer's promotion.

towards the Great Fish River. Before separating, they ascertained from some Eskimos whom they met, that **two vessels had been seen** by the natives of **King** William Island ; **that one** had been crushed -by **the ice and sunk in deep water,** and that the other had been **forced on shore, and** was much injured. In the **latter ship was found the body of a** tall **man, who was reported to have had long teeth.**[1]

The Eskimos are unable to comprehend **or realise intervals of time, but** it was supposed that these vessels **had been seen by them** some years ago, and in the fall **of the year,** *i.e.,* **August or September.** M'Clintock was **further informed that a number of** white men from **these ships were seen** journeying with a boat, or boats, **in the direction of the Great** Fish River, at the mouth **of which their bones were,** it was said, found the following **winter. This was all** the information they were able **to** obtain **from** the natives, **but it** was **of** a most **important** nature, **for** it informed them that the existence **of the** missing ships was actually known to the Eskimos **; that** one had disappeared under the ice, and **that the** other had been stranded **;** it was therefore safe **to infer, with regard to** the latter **ship,** that it was **within the bounds of possibility to discover** the locality **in** which **she had been wrecked, in** which case they **might perhaps** find some **important** records or documents **relating to the** expedition.

On the 8th of May M'Clintock reached King William Island, and **visited a snow** village in which he found **some thirty or forty** inhabitants. From these people he

---

[1] This appearance of "long teeth " is supposed to be attributable to the disease of which the unfortunate man had probably died, *i.e.,* **scurvy.**

purchased several pieces of silver plate, **on** which the initials, or crests, of Sir John Franklin, Captain Crozier, Lieutenant Fairholme, and Dr. M'Donald were engraved, besides other articles that had undoubtedly been **obtained** from the missing expedition. The silver forks and spoons were readily exchanged for a few needles.

The natives informed M'Clintock that the wreck of one of the ships was about five days' journey from them, on the west **coast of King William Island, but that** little remained of it, **as everything of use had been** appropriated and carried **off by their** countrymen. **No** books, documents, **or** printed **matter had** been saved, they said, from **the** wreck, but **had all,** long ago, **been** destroyed by exposure to **the** weather. They further **said that—**

"The white men dropped **by the** way, as they **went to the** Great River ; that some were **buried,** and some were **not."** [1]

No satisfactory **approximation of** the numbers **of the white** men, **or** the interval of time that had elapsed since they died, could **be** ascertained.

Pushing onwards, Point Ogle was reached on the 12th of May, and the same **night** the party camped on **the** ice at the entrance **of** the Great Fish River. Montreal Island was subsequently carefully examined, but with barren results, for **there** was a total absence of all relics, and no vestige of a cairn could be found, or any indications that our missing countrymen had even visited **the** island. **It** must, however, be remembered that the country had not then emerged from its wintry garb **of** snow. On **the** 18th M'Clintock crossed over to the mainland in the neighbourhood of Point Duncan, and on

[1] **Voyage of the *Fox*,** by Sir Leopold M'Clintock.

the following day commenced his return journey. Re-crossing the strait to King William Island, the southern shore was examined, but **without** finding any traces of those whom they were seeking, neither did they find any signs of the **wreck** spoken of by the natives, until they reached the vicinity of Cape Herschel, when, shortly after midnight on the 25th of **May**, M'Clintock suddenly came upon a human skeleton lying face downwards, **on** the **crest of** a ridge, with its head towards the **Great Fish River**. The bones were bleached perfectly white. It was **supposed** to be the remains of a young man, and from the dress, was thought to be **a** steward, or officer's servant. M'Clintock was under the impression that the poor fellow had selected **the** bare ridge top as offering **the** easiest road **for walking, and to have** fallen on his face and died in **the** position **in which his** remains were found. Although diligent **search was made, no** records, or other relics, could **be found, until a spot** about twelve miles from Cape Herschel was reached, when a **small** cairn that had been constructed by Hobson was dis-**covered, in which** was found a note from that officer addressed to M'Clintock, containing the important and interesting revelation, **an** account of which has already been given in a previous chapter, namely, the discovery of the only known record left by the survivors of the *Erebus* and *Terror*, **that** tells us the sad mournful history of the missing expedition.

This touching but interesting document, a reduced fac-simile of which is here produced, was found by Lieutenant Hobson at Point Victory, on the north-west coast of King William Island. The important and exciting news it communicated was written round the **margin of** a printed form, usually supplied to ships with

H. M. S.hips Erebus and Terror
{ Wintered in the Ice in
28 of May 1847 { Lat. 70° 5' N. Long. 98° 23' W

Having wintered in 1846—7 at Beechey Island
in Lat 74° 43' 28" N. Long 91° 39' 15" W after having

ascended Wellington Channel to Lat 77° and returned
by the West side of Cornwallis Island

Sir John Franklin commanding the Expedition
All well

Commander.

WHOEVER finds this paper is requested to forward it to the Secretary of
the Admiralty, London, *with a note of the time* and place at which it was
found: or, if more convenient, to deliver it for that purpose to the British
Consul at the nearest Port.

QUICONQUE trouve ce papier est prié d'y marquer le tems et lieu ou
il l'aura trouvé, et de le faire parvenir au plûtot au Secretaire de l'Amirauté
Britannique à Londres.

CUALQUIERA que hallare este Papel, se le suplica de enviarlo al Secretario
del Almirantazgo, en Londrés, con una nota del tiempo y del lugar en
donde se halló.

EEN ieder die dit Papier mogt vinden, wordt hiermede verzogt, om het
zelve, ten spoedigste, te willen zenden aan den Heer Minister van de
Marine der Nederlanden in 's Gravenhage, of wel aan den Secretaris der
Britsche Admiraliteit, te London, en daar by te voegen eene Nota,
inhoudende de tyd en de plaats alwaar dit Papier is gevonden geworden

FINDEREN af dette Papiir ombedes, naar Leilighed gives, at sende
samme til Admiralitets Secretairen i London, eller nærmeste Embedsmand
i Danmark, Norge, eller Sverrig. Tiden og Stædit hvor dette er fundet
önskes venskabeligt paategnet.

WER diesen Zettel findet, wird hier-durch ersucht denselben an den
Secretair des Admiralitets in London einzusenden, mit gefälliger angabe
an welchen ort und zu welcher zeit er gefunden worden ist.

Party consisting of 2 Officers and 6 Men
left the Ships on Monday 24th May 1847

Gm. Gore, Lieut.
Chas. F. Des Voeux, Mate

the object of being enclosed in bottles and thrown over-board in various localities, for the purpose of ascertaining the set and general drift of oceanic currents. They are generally called "bottle-papers," and are printed in six different languages, each conveying a request that any person finding the paper will forward it to the Secretary of the Admiralty, noting the date and place at which it was picked up. The marginal notations that revealed the sad fate of the expedition, were written and signed by Captains Crozier and Fitzjames; the greater part of it being in the handwriting of the latter officer. This document had originally been deposited in the cairn by Lieutenant Graham Gore in the spring of 1847, when all was well with the expedition, and when they had every prospect of bringing their labours to a successful termination. One short year had altered all these bright and hopeful anticipations—twelve brief months from the time the first few lines were penned on this precious document, were sufficient to effect a change in their joyous aspirations, and to reduce the party from a band of eager and expectant explorers, buoyed up by a feeling, almost amounting to a certainty, of shortly accomplishing the great work they had set themselves to achieve, to a throng of struggling, half-famished men, fighting the great battle of life, with disease, starvation, and death staring them in the face.

Having made a careful and thorough, but unsuccessful, search in the neighbourhood for records, journals, or other relics of the lost expedition, M'Clintock pushed onwards, and on the 29th of May reached the west extreme of King William Island, which he named Cape Crozier, after the leader of that ill-fated band of men, to ascertain whose fate he was evincing such extraordinary exertions. From this point of land the coast-line trended somewhat abruptly to **the** north-eastward, and early on the following morning they pitched their tent alongside a large boat, another melancholy relic of the lost ships, **mounted on a** heavily constructed sledge. Deeply interesting as was this discovery, **it was rendered** still more so by **the fact that** the boat contained **the** portions of two human skeletons. **One was that of a slightly built** young **man;** the other was apparently **a large, powerfully** built person of middle age, and **was supposed to** be that of an officer. **In the** boat **was also** found a number of books, chiefly **of a scriptural or** devotional character, **five watches, a** couple **of** double-barrelled guns **(one barrel in each** being loaded and at full **cock), besides numerous** other articles of various descriptions, principally **clothing. A** little tea and chocolate were **all the** provisions that could be found, thus almost establishing the **fact that the poor** fellows had succumbed **to** starvation, and perhaps when in the very **act of** protecting themselves **from an** attack by polar bears, or other wild animals, for **their guns** were **by their** side and ready for instant use; indeed the appearances suggest that either for the supply **of food, or for** their own protection, **they had** been already **driven to** the necessity **of having recourse to their** firearms, as **one barrel from each gun had** been, apparently, discharged.

There is little more to relate regarding **the** last moments **of our** unfortunate countrymen. **The remark-** able absence **of** all records, journals, log-books, or other documentary evidence, **surrounds** their fate **with a myste-** rious halo **which it is** impossible to **clear** away, and **is** difficult **even to** penetrate. **All must therefore be left**

to conjecture, and we can only surmise that the unhappy members of the lost expedition, fell victims to sickness and starvation before they had succeeded in getting many miles from their ships; as a matter of fact, the boat, with the ghastly remains of its crew, was found only sixty-five miles from the position of the *Erebus* and *Terror* when they were abandoned, although seventy miles from the place where the first skeleton was discovered.

Having collected all the most interesting and portable relics[1] they could obtain, but having failed in finding traces of the two vessels, M'Clintock returned to the little *Fox*, which he reached on the 19th of June. Hobson had arrived five days before, and Allen Young returned some eight days later, having successfully determined the insularity of Prince of Wales' Land. Both these officers had made wonderful journeys, in the face of unparalleled hardships and difficulties.

The amount of new coast-line discovered during the spring journeys by M'Clintock and Hobson was nearly 420 miles, while that explored by Young was 380 miles, making a total, altogether, of 800 geographical miles of entirely new coast-line to be added to our charts. On the 10th of August the *Fox*, having been liberated from her icy bonds, steamed out of Brentford Bay, and without any further event worthy of particular notice, reached London on the 23rd of September, when the important and interesting nature of the discoveries was made generally known.

---

[1] Among the relics found and brought home was a sextant belonging to Frederick Hornby, who was a mate in the *Terror*. This was in after years presented by his brother, Admiral Wyndham Hornby, to Lieutenant Wyatt Rawson, R.N., who served as a lieutenant in the *Discovery* in the Arctic expedition of 1875-6. This gallant and promising officer was mortally wounded while leading the British army to the attack at the battle of Tel-el-Kebir.

Thus ended this last and most successful of all the numerous expeditions that had been despatched, with the object of ascertaining the fate of Sir John Franklin and his brave companions. Its success was due to the untiring energy, the ability, and skill displayed by M'Clintock and his officers and crew, and to the fact that he had decided to search in the right direction, and not proceed on a quest without any definite information to guide him, as was the case in the expeditions that had preceded him. A large share of the success is also due to the devotion and persistence of Lady Franklin, and the unselfish spirit that formed one of the chief characteristics of her heroic nature.

M'Clintock's discoveries revealed the fact, as an eminent author [1] has expressed it—

"That to Sir John Franklin is due the priority of discovery of the north-west passage—that last link, to forge which he sacrificed his life."

Valuable geographical information was also the result of this remarkable voyage. The existence of Bellot Strait was confirmed. The shores of King William Island were thoroughly explored, as well as the west coast of Boothia, whilst the insularity of Prince of Wales' Land was definitely established, besides the existence of a channel, a continuation of Peel Sound, leading down to Bellot Strait. Thus, it will be seen that much good and useful geographical work was accomplished by this expedition. This was fully recognised by the Government; £5000 was voted to Captain M'Clintock and his officers and men, while £2000 was

---

[1] John Brown, in his "North-west Passage and the Search for Sir John Franklin."

given for the erection of a monument in Waterloo Place
to the memory of Sir John Franklin.   Engraven on the
pedestal of this monument is the following inscription :—

FRANKLIN.

TO THE GREAT NAVIGATOR
AND HIS BRAVE COMPANIONS
WHO SACRIFICED THEIR LIVES IN
COMPLETING THE DISCOVERY OF
THE NORTH-WEST PASSAGE
A.D. 1847-48

———

ERECTED BY THE UNANIMOUS VOTE
OF PARLIAMENT

Her Majesty was also pleased to confer on Captain
M‘Clintock the honour of knighthood.   The freedom
of the City of London was likewise conferred on him,
whilst honorary degrees were bestowed upon him by
the different universities of England and Ireland.
The Patron's Gold Medal of the Royal Geographical
Society was subsequently awarded him—

"For his unflinching fortitude and skill, by which the
precious Record, unveiling the fate of Sir John Franklin
and the abandonment of the *Erebus* and *Terror*, was recovered,
and for his geographical discoveries."

while at the same time the Founder's Medal was
happily, and with exceptional favour, awarded by the
Royal Geographical Society to Lady Franklin—

"In token of their admiration of her devoted conduct in
persevering until the fate of her husband was finally ascertained."

The devoted and heroic widow, the fit consort of the

equally devoted and heroic Franklin, died in 1875, at the age of eighty-three years.   One of her last works, if not the very last, in connection with her husband's memory, was the erection of a marble monument of

STATUE OF FRANKLIN IN THE MARKET-PLACE, SPILSBY.

Sir John Franklin in Westminster Abbey.   It was unveiled only a fortnight after her death.   It was her great wish to write the epitaph herself, but dying before this was accomplished, it was written by Alfred

Tennyson, who was a nephew of Sir John by marriage. It is as follows :—

> "Not here ! the white North hath thy bones, and thou
>   Heroic Sailor Soul !
> Art passing on thy happier voyage now
>   Towards no earthly pole."

The late Dean Stanley added a note to this, to the effect that the monument was "erected by his widow, who, after long waiting and sending many in search of him, herself departed to seek and to find him in the realms of light, 18th July 1875, aged eighty-three years."

A statue of Sir John Franklin was also erected in the open market-place of his native town, Spilsby.

Sir John Franklin, it may be mentioned, was promoted to the rank of rear-admiral, in his regular place of seniority on the Navy List on the 26th October 1852, somewhat over five years after his death. His name was not removed from the Navy List until the exact date of his death had been ascertained by the discovery of the record by M'Clintock.

In the year 1846 he was elected a correspondent of the Paris Academy of Sciences.

CHAPTER XV.

*VOYAGES OF DR. HAYES—NORDENSKIÖLD—LEIGH
SMITH—THE GERMANS—CAPTAIN HALL—THE
AUSTRO-HUNGARIANS — SIR GEORGE NARES—
ALLEN YOUNG — SCHWATKA — THE " JEAN-
NETTE "—NORDENSKIÖLD ACCOMPLISHES THE
NORTH-EAST PASSAGE — LEIGH SMITH—GREE-
LEY—VALEDICTORY.*

1860-1884.

> "The bodies and the bones of those
> Who strove in other days to pass,
> Lie withered in the thorny close,
> Or blanched and blown about the grass."
> —*Sleeping Beauty.*

SINCE the **return** of Sir Leopold M'Clintock in 1859,
various expeditions, under different flags, sought to penetrate the icy solitudes of the north, in furtherance **of**
geographical discovery, and **in the elucidation of** inte-
resting questions appertaining to various branches of
science. These **were all more or less** successful, while
several penetrated far into the unknown area.

In 1860, Dr. Hayes, **who had won his spurs as an**
Arctic explorer under Dr. Kane, in the *Advance* in 1853
and two following years, sailed from Boston in a schooner
of 133 tons, named the *United States*, with the object of
continuing the line of exploration **up Smith** Sound followed by Dr. **Kane.** Without any event deserving of

special notice, he reached the entrance to Smith Sound, when his further progress in a northerly direction was stopped by ice. Being unable to push on, he secured his ship in winter quarters in latitude 78° 18′, just inside Cape Alexander, and about twenty miles south of the position in which Kane had passed his two winters. In the spring of the following year sledging parties were despatched to examine the west side of the channel in a northerly direction. The highest latitude stated to have been reached was 81° 35′. Animal life was abundant in the vicinity of their winter quarters, and no difficulty was experienced in procuring a constant supply of fresh animal food. The *United States* returned to Boston in October 1861.

The Swedes, under Professor Nordenskiöld, sent several expeditions to Spitzbergen between the years 1858 and 1872, for the purpose of scientific research, and more particularly with the object of making investigations with a view to future operations connected with the measurement of an arc of the meridian. In the course of these tentative voyages they succeeded in rounding Cape Platen, to the east of the Seven Islands, a point further to the eastward along the northern coast of Spitzbergen, than had ever before been reached. In September 1868 they attained in an iron steamer, named the *Sophie*, the latitude of 81° 42′, on the 18th meridian of east longitude.

Mr. Leigh Smith, an energetic and enthusiastic Arctic yachtsman, also on several occasions made very successful and interesting expeditions to Spitzbergen and adjacent seas; his observations and discoveries had the effect of considerably altering the hitherto assumed shape of North-East Land.

In 1869, the Germans, with praiseworthy zeal, fitted out an expedition, consisting of the *Germania*, a steamer of 140 tons, and a small brig called the *Hansa*, with the object of exploring the north-east coast of Greenland. As scientific investigation was to form a special feature of the work to be carried out, several scientific gentlemen formed part of the *personnel* of the expedition. The ships were under the command of Captain Karl Koldewey, who was in the *Germania*, Captain Hegemann being the commander of the *Hansa*. They sailed from Bremen in June, provisioned for a contemplated absence of two years.

Shortly after reaching the Greenland coast, in latitude 70° 46', the ships were unavoidably separated, and on the 22nd October the little *Hansa* was unfortunately crushed by the heavy ice floes by which she was encompassed. With materials saved from the wreck the crew succeeded in constructing a shelter for themselves on the floe, in which wretched abode the winter was passed, not, however, without considerable anxiety and excitement, for towards the end of the year the floe cracked right across, thus effectually causing the ruin of their somewhat fragile and insecure domicile; another one was however improvised from the remains of the materials saved. Finally, in June 1870, having drifted in a general southerly direction a distance of 1100 miles on their extremely precarious raft, the dimensions of which were, day by day, being gradually reduced by the melting of the ice, until it was only 300 feet in breadth, they succeeded in launching their boats, which had providentially been saved, and were thus able to reach the little Danish settlement of Friedrikshal, in the vicinity of Cape Farewell; here they were well taken care of by the hospitable Danes, and eventually sent home in the annual vessel trading between the Greenland ports and Denmark.

Meanwhile the *Germania*, by the aid of her steam-power, succeeded in reaching the latitude of 75° 30′, when her further progress in a northerly direction was checked by heavy ice, and she was compelled to retrace her steps to the southward until the Pendulum Islands were reached, **where the ship** was made **snug for the winter.** Sledging parties **were** despatched **during the** ensuing spring, which reached the 77th parallel, **the** highest latitude on the **east coast** of Greenland **that has ever been attained.** The most northern **point was** named **Cape** Bismarck. **On being released from their** winter quarters, exploration was carried out in a southerly direction along the coast, and the *Germania* eventually returned to Bremen in September 1870. The result **of** this expedition was to finally set at rest any hope that might have existed of attaining a high latitude along the east coast of Greenland, **for** the ice encountered was of such a heavy nature **as to** utterly preclude the possibility of navigating a ship **through it.**

In 1871, Captain C. F. Hall, **a native of** Cincinnati, sailed from New York **in an** old steam gunboat, which had been handed over to him by the Navy Department, and renamed the *Polaris*. His object was to **reach** the North **Pole** by way **of Smith Sound. Dr. Emil Bessels, a** German professor of great **ability and scientific** attainments, accompanied the expedition as chief of the scientific staff, while Moreton, who served with Kane in 1853, and Hans the **Eskimo, who was with** both Kane and Hayes, **were also on board.**

Captain Hall, it should **here** be observed, had always

been firmly impressed with the practicability of obtaining more complete and fuller **details relative** to the fate **of** Franklin's expedition than were brought home by M'Clintock. With the object of throwing more light on this interesting subject, he had voluntarily passed five years with the Eskimos on the north side of Hudson's Strait, for the express purpose of habituating himself to their mode of life, and acclimatising himself **to the** severity and hardships incidental to an Arctic winter, so that he might be the better fitted to prosecute his researches for the missing expedition. Having this in view, he was landed in 1864 from a whale ship near the south entrance of Sir Thomas Rowe's Welcome in **the** north part of Hudson's Bay, with only two Eskimo companions, and a boat laden with stores and provisions. For the succeeding five years this enthusiastic explorer lived entirely with the Eskimos, with whom he cultivated friendly relations. During this time he visited and explored Hecla and Fury Strait, and eventually reached the south-eastern shore of King William Island, where **he** obtained some relics of the Franklin expedition, but was unsuccessful, as others had been before him, in his efforts to find any of the documents or journals belonging to the missing ships. The evidence that he obtained from the natives, simply confirmed the statements brought **home by** Rae and M'Clintock, but **threw no** further light on the ultimate fate of the officers **and** men who had abandoned the *Erebus* and *Terror*. He returned to New York in 1869.

Proceeding **up** Smith Sound, the *Polaris* encountered but little obstruction from the ice, which was unusually loose and open, and **Hall** had the extreme satisfaction **of** carrying his ship to a higher northern latitude than

had ever been reached by any previous vessel, **viz., 82° 16'.**
Having attained this unprecedented success, **his** diffi-
culties commenced, for his ship was almost immediately
beset by heavy ice, in which he was carried some **distance** to the southward. She was, however, **in a few**
days extricated from her somewhat critical position in
the pack, and was eventually secured in winter quarters
on the east side of the channel, in a harbour protected at
its entrance by a grounded iceberg, which was appropri-
ately named Providence Berg, while the **harbour itself
was** called Thank God Bay. This was in latitude **81° 38'.**

In the month of October Captain Hall **started off
on** a reconnoitering expedition with a dog-sledge. **He**
was away **for a few** days only, and was taken ill almost
immediately after **his** return ; **he died on the 8th of
November. The loss** of Captain Hall was a death-blow
to the enterprise. The command devolved on the sailing-
master, an old whaling skipper, quite unfitted for the
conduct of such a service. Dissensions cropped up
amongst officers and **men,** and it was consequently
decided to return **to the United States** directly the
ship was released. But little exploring work, **as** may
be imagined, **was effected during** the spring, and
although the ship was liberated in June, it was not until
August that the homeward journey was commenced.
The conditions of the ice, however, in Robeson Channel
were vastly different **to what** they had experienced **the
preceding year,** for shortly after their departure from
Thank God Bay, the *Polaris* was beset in the pack, **in**
which she drifted helplessly down Smith Sound into
Baffin's Bay. On the 15th of October they encountered
a violent gale from the south-east, veering to south, and
finally settling down **at** south-west. After many and

severe buffetings, the already sorely-crippled ship was seriously squeezed between two heavy masses of ice, which, raising the vessel bodily, threw her over on her port side. Her timbers, from the violent pressure to which she was subjected, cracked with loud reports, and her sides seemed to be breaking in. In this critical situation, when, perhaps, the destruction of their ship was but the matter of a few moments, the necessary arrangements were made for her immediate abandonment. Provisions and stores were hastily thrown on the ice ; coal, provisions, clothing, and stores of every kind that were accessible, were hurriedly passed out of the ship, and placed as near as possible in the centre of the largest floe to which they were attached, while a couple of boats, fortunately, as it turned out, were also lowered and hauled up to a place of safety on the ice.

Suddenly, in the inky darkness of the night, the ship broke from the floe to which she had been secured, and driving before the raging gale, was, in a moment, in the wild commotion of the elements and the blinding snowstorm with which they were assailed, lost to sight to those of their companions who were receiving and stowing the stores and provisions on the ice. The party thus left in this unenviable situation consisted of Captain Tyson (the assistant navigator), and nine men belonging to the *Polaris*, besides nine Eskimos, including three women and a baby. Fortunately, in consequence of the prompt measures taken to pass the provisions out of the ship, they were in no immediate want of food, and their supply was subsequently supplemented by bears and seals that were occasionally shot by the Eskimo hunters. To the skill, energy, and success of the two Eskimos, Joe and Hans, the entire party owed their lives.

Without them they would all, undoubtedly, have perished from starvation. Seeing that there was but little hope of being rescued by the *Polaris*, of whose position, or even safety, they were ignorant, they proceeded to construct a house from materials that had been thrown out from the ship, in order to afford them some protection and shelter from the inclemency of the coming winter. Several snow-houses were also erected. The piece of ice on which they were encamped, and on which the entire party passed the winter, was about 100 yards in length, and 75 yards broad. On this they drifted down, all that long interminable winter, past Baffin's Bay and Davis' Strait, the floe gradually crumbling away and reducing in size as it drifted south, until on the 1st of April the party were compelled to take to their remaining boat, for the second one had long since been utilised for fuel. They were eventually picked up by the English sealer *Tigress*, off the coast of Labrador, in latitude 53° 35′, on the 30th of April 1873, having drifted on their precarious raft a distance of no less than 1500 miles during the 196 days since they were separated from their ship.

Let us now return to the *Polaris*, which we left being driven helplessly and rapidly, on the breaking up of the pack, in an easterly direction by the violence of the gale; those on board were quite unable to do anything to succour their companions who were so suddenly and so unexpectedly cast away on the ice, nor were they in a position to take any immediate steps to afford them relief, in consequence of steam not being ready, the murky darkness that prevailed, and the speed with which the ship was driven by the wind. Their boats also were with the party left on the floe.

On the following morning, the *Polaris*, being in a leaky

and shattered condition, was run on shore in Lifeboat Cove, Lyttleton Island, on the east side of the entrance to Smith Sound; and here, with the assistance of the Etah Eskimos, who provided them with fresh food in the shape of seals and reindeer, they passed a comparatively pleasant winter, in a house which was erected in the vicinity of the wreck. The winter months were occupied in constructing a couple of boats; in these the party embarked on the 3rd of June, with the intention of reaching one of the Danish settlements on the west coast of Greenland; they were, however, rescued on the 21st of the same month by the Dundee whaler *Ravenscraig* in Melville Bay. They were subsequently transferred to the whaler *Arctic*, Captain Adams, in which ship they were eventually taken to Dundee, and thence sent across to New York.

The success attending this expedition was very remarkable and quite unprecedented; it clearly demonstrated how very variable are the conditions of the ice in certain parts of the Arctic regions, and how much may, and can, be accomplished in what is termed a favourable ice year. In the short space of five days the *Polaris* succeeded in accomplishing a distance of five hundred miles through what had always been, and is still, considered an ice-choked sea, viz., from Cape Shackleton to the highest northern position she attained. But in twelve brief months everything was changed, for on her return to the southward the following year she was helplessly beset by heavy masses of ice, in those same channels that had the previous year been comparatively free and navigable, and she drifted down into Baffin's Bay at the average rate of about two knots an hour. The scientific results of this expedition were exceedingly valuable, although much important data, together with the greater part of the natural history **collections, were** unavoidably and unfortunately lost.

The **next** expedition of geographical importance was **the** Austro-Hungarian **one, under** the joint command **of** Captain Weyprecht of the Austrian navy, and Lieutenant Julius Payer, a military officer. The first-named officer was in command **of the ship, and was,** of course, solely responsible for its navigation and **for** all exploration by sea ; but to Payer was entrusted **the** organisation and the conduct **of** all sledging and **travelling parties on** shore. These officers had made **a preliminary** summer cruise in the waters it was intended **to explore, in a little** sloop called the *Isbjorn*, for the purpose **of ascertaining** the position and condition **of the ice. Payer had also** served **in the** German expedition under Koldewey.[1] **The** leaders were therefore not altogether unfamiliar with ice **navigation.** The main object of the enterprise was the achievement of the north-east passage, which they **hoped** to accomplish, by sailing round the northern extreme **of** Novaya Zemlya, **and** thence along the Siberian **coast to** Bering's Strait. **The** *Tegetthoff*, a steamer of **three hundred** tons burthen, was especially built for the purpose, and everything being ready, she sailed from Bremerhaven on the 13th June 1872. On the **29th of** the following month the *Tegetthoff* was beset by the ice off the west **coast of** Novaya Zemlya, from which besetment she was **with** some difficulty extricated ; but on the 23rd of August she **was** again beset off the **same coast,** and in spite of the powerful aid of steam, assisted by gunpowder, and the unremitting exertions of the officers and **men,** the unfortunate ship was held fast by the ice, never again to be

[1] **See p.** 280, *ante.*

released. In this helpless condition she drifted about at the mercy of the winds and currents of the Polar regions for two long years. **On the** 31st August 1873 a mysterious **unknown land was** suddenly observed, looming up in the far distance to the northward, to which they gave **the name of** Franz Josef Land, **thus** becoming the discoverers, although unwittingly, of **a new** and important tract of country **whose existence was hitherto unknown.** Payer thus alludes to the **discovery** :—

"About midday, as we were leaning on **the** bulwarks of the **ship** and scanning **the** gliding mists, through which the rays **of the** sun broke ever and anon, a wall of mist, lifting itself up **suddenly, revealed to** us afar off in **the** north-west, the outlines of bold rocks, which in a few minutes seemed to grow into a radiant alpine land ! At first **we all** stood transfixed and **hardly believing what we saw. Then** carried away by the reality of our good fortune, we burst forth into shouts of joy :—Land, land, land at last ! There was **not** a sick man on board the *Tegetthoff !* The news of the discovery spread in an instant. Every one rushed **on deck to convince** himself with his own **eyes,** that the expedition was **not after all** a failure—there before **us** lay the prize that could **not be** snatched from **us.** . . . For thousands **of** years this land had lain **buried from** the knowledge **of** men, and **now its** discovery had fallen into **the lap of a small band, themselves** almost lost **to** the world who, **far from** their home, remembered **the homage due to** their sovereign, and gave to the newly discovered **territory the name of Kaiser** Franz Josef's Land. With loud hurrahs we **drank to the** health **of our** Emperor in grog hastily made **on deck in** an iron coffee-pot, **and then** dressed the *Tegetthoff* with flags."

Strenuous efforts were made to extricate the ship from her **icy** thraldom during the summer and autumn of 1873, **but these** proving futile, a second winter, if possible **more cheerless** and wretched than the first, had to be endured. The general drift of the ship during the time of their besetment was governed, it was supposed, by the prevailing winds, and was not, it was thought, due so much to tide or current. This drift was in a general northerly direction. The position of the ship when she was first beset on the 21st August 1872 was latitude 76° 22', and longitude 62° 3' E. On the 1st of January 1873 she was in latitude 78° 37', and longitude 66° 56'. On the 1st February her position was 78° 45' N. latitude, and 73° 7' E. longitude, thus showing that she had been carried steadily during the period named in a north-easterly direction. From the last-mentioned date until the 1st of November, when the ship became station-ary in consequence of the attachment of the ice in which she was beset to the land, her drift was in a north and north-westerly direction. Her positions on the under-mentioned dates were as shown in the following table :

	Latitude.	Longitude.
April 1	79° 5' N.	66° 49' E.
May 1	79 15	64 58
June 1	79 2	62 43
July 1	79 15	59 14
August 1	78 56	60 40
September 1	79 40	60 33
October 1	79 58	60 41
November 1	79 51	58 56

The important and unexpected discovery of Franz Josef Land, very naturally instilled fresh hopes in the hearts of the explorers ; but, in spite of their apparent proximity to the land, they were, much to their chagrin and disappointment, unable to reach the shores of this newly found territory, in consequence of the fissures in the ice that lay between them and the coast, and the fact that the ship was still drifting at the mercy of the winds, in varying directions which they were unable accurately to determine; her position, therefore, would be uncertain, and perhaps difficult, or even impossible, to reach on the return of any exploring parties that might be rash enough to leave her for an extended trip. During the month of October, however, the *Tegetthoff* was carried to within three miles of an island, situated near to the mainland; this island was, as may readily be imagined, visited by nearly all the crew. Its position was in latitude 79° 54′. Payer writes of it:—

"An island more desolate than that which we had reached can hardly be imagined, for snow and ice covered its frozen débris-covered slopes."

From this date the ship remained immovable, firmly frozen into its icy bed, which was held stationary by grounded icebergs. Numerous bears visited the ship during the winter, and not unnaturally paid the penalty of their temerity and inquisitiveness, their flesh affording a welcome change to the diet which those on board had for so long been accustomed to. No less than sixty-seven of these animals were killed at various times by members of the expedition, producing about 12,000 lbs. of fresh meat. Several seals were also obtained.

Of course their prospects of release formed the subject of much anxious discussion during the winter. The apparently hopeless chance of extricating the ship being generally acknowledged, it was resolved to abandon her in the ensuing summer, and endeavour to return to Europe with the combined aid of boats and sledges. Before, however, the season was sufficiently advanced to make a start, it was decided to attempt, as far as possible, the exploration of the **unknown land to** which they had been so mysteriously carried.

With this object in view, Payer, with **half a dozen** men, left the ship for a preliminary sledge journey on the 10th of March, taking with him three dogs to assist in dragging the sledge.   Travelling in a north-westerly direction, they skirted the **coast of** Hall Island and ascended **Capes** Tegetthoff **and** M'Clintock, the latter being some 2500 **feet in height.   These** ascents were expressly made for the purpose of ascertaining the general trend of the land and its physical aspects, so **as** to facilitate the larger and more important work of exploration which, it **was designed,** should be undertaken at a later **period.   On** the journey they experienced great cold, **the** thermometer on one occasion falling **as low as** –58° Fahr.   They returned to the ship, on the 16th, fully satisfied with the result of their researches.

Eight days after his return Payer started on his extended journey to the northward, accompanied, **as** before, by six men **and** three dogs.   Passing up **Austria** Sound, between Zichy and Wilczek **Lands, the travellers** reached their highest latitude, in what was named Crown Prince Rudolff Land, in latitude 82° 5′, about 160 **miles** from the position in which they had left their ship.   The coast along which they travelled was intersected by numerous fiords, and fringed by numberless islands. **The geological features of** the land appeared to coincide with those of north-east Greenland, some of the hills rising to an altitude of **3000 feet.**   The valleys between the mountain **ranges were filled with large** glaciers.   **A** peculiar feature connected with this neighbourhood was that the low islands in Austria Sound were **covered**

with a glacial cap. Vegetation was poor and insignifi-
cant, but it must be remembered that the country was
wearing its wintry garb of snow at the time the explorers were travelling. Cape Fligely, the most northern
point, was reached on the 12th of April; even at this
early period of the year a large water space was seen, in
which the explorers could undoubtedly have gone some
miles further to the northward, had they been provided
with a boat. The furthest land seen to the north was
called Petermann Land, and this was estimated to be
beyond the 83rd parallel of north latitude. Having
planted the Austro-Hungarian flag at the highest point
reached, the homeward march was commenced, and on
the 24th of April they arrived alongside their ship, safe
and sound, after a toilsome and arduous journey. On
the 20th of the following month the colours were nailed
to the mast, the good ship that had been their home for
two years was then abandoned, and they started on their
long journey to Europe, carrying with them provisions
for three or four months packed in four boats which
were mounted on sledges. So heavy were the weights
to be dragged, and so rough was the ice and so deep
the snow over which they travelled, that after incessant
labour for a period of two months, they found that they
had only put a distance of eight miles between themselves and the ship! Fortune, however, favoured them
after this date, and on the 14th of August they succeeded
in reaching the edge of the pack ice, and were able to
launch their boats on the water, when good progress was
made. Favoured by fine weather, they crossed to Novaya
Zemlya, and skirting along that coast to the south, were
eventually picked up by a Russian schooner engaged in
the capture of walruses, which conveyed them to Vardo,

which they reached on the 3rd September 1874; thence home by mail steamer.

The next expedition that merits our attention is the one despatched by our own country in 1875 under the command of Captain Nares. This expedition is of such recent date, and is so well within the memory of the public, that only a brief reference to it is considered necessary. It was sent by the route followed by the American expedition under Hall, viz., by Smith Sound; for it was judged and very rightly, at the time, that in consequence of the report brought home by the officers of the *Polaris*, that particular route offered the best chances of success, if the attainment of a high northern latitude was to be the primary consideration. It may be mentioned that the direction to be followed had actually been determined before the news reached England of the safety and return of the Austro-Hungarian expedition.

The ships selected for the service were the *Alert* and *Discovery*, fairly powerful steamers of from 500 to 600 tons burthen. These vessels had been specially strengthened and equipped, and in every way adapted for ice navigation. They sailed from Portsmouth on the 29th May 1875. The orders received by Captain Nares were to the effect that he was to proceed up Smith Sound, and after establishing the *Discovery* in secure winter quarters in a high northern latitude, but to the southward of the 82nd parallel of latitude, as a relief or depôt ship, he was to push on in the *Alert* as far as navigation would admit. When further progress became impossible, the *Alert* was also to be placed in safe winter quarters, whence sledging parties were to be despatched with the object of attaining the highest northern latitude, and, if found practicable, to reach the **Pole** itself. Although Smith Sound was found choked with ice, rendering the progress of the ships slow and dangerous, Nares, with consummate skill and ability, succeeded in carrying his ships in safety to latitude 81° 44', where he left the *Discovery*, under the command of Captain Stephenson, to pass the winter in a snug harbour, which was called Discovery Bay, at the entrance of Lady Franklin Sound. Thence the *Alert* pushed onwards, encountering ice floes thickly packed and of a very massive description, but fairly good progress was made by adhering, especially when westerly winds prevailed, to the stream of water that invariably existed between the land ice and the main pack.

On the 1st September the *Alert* reached the latitude of 82° 24'; and this being a higher latitude than had ever been attained by a ship before, the colours were hoisted "amid general rejoicings" to celebrate the event. But on the same day her further progress was arrested by a solid pack of heavy ice which defied penetration, and the ship was hauled close into the shore, and secured behind some large grounded masses of ice, which afforded an effective protection from the pressure of the pack. In this somewhat precarious position the *Alert* was doomed to pass the succeeding eleven months; but an all-merciful Providence watched over the good little ship, and those on board spent under the circumstances an exceedingly happy and pleasant winter, more especially when it is considered that they were passing it in a higher northern latitude, viz., 82° 27', than any human beings had ever before been known to winter in.

During the autumn and early spring, sledging parties were despatched for the purpose of exploring in the immediate neighbourhood of their winter quarters, and also with the object of laying out depôts of provisions in advance, on the routes that it was intended should be taken by the extended sledge parties when they made their final start in the spring. It was whilst engaged on one of these preliminary sledging parties during the autumn, that they had the gratification of passing the highest latitude reached by Captain Parry in 1827 during his memorable attempt to reach the North Pole, and they thus had the satisfaction of knowing that they had reached a point nearer to the Pole, than it had ever before been approached. From this their highest position the land was found to trend away abruptly to the west; no land was visible to the north—nothing in that direction was to be seen but an illimitable sea of snow and ice piled up in large and confused masses.

On the 2nd of April, on a cold but bright morning, the main sledging parties started, the temperature at the time being minus 30°, which soon afterwards fell to 45° below zero. The disposition made by Captain Nares was for one party to proceed in a due north direction, travelling over the frozen sea, with the object of getting as far north as possible ; a second was to explore to the westward along what was known as the coast of Grinnell Land ; while a third sledging party, from the *Discovery*, was directed to examine the north-west coast of Greenland. Dogs were not used by any of these sledging parties, but the sledges were dragged entirely by men. These several parties were travelling for a period of about eighty days, during which time the north-west coast of Greenland was explored to latitude 82° 18' and 50° 50' W. longitude. The northern shore of Grinnell Land was thoroughly examined to the 85th meridian of longitude, while a position was attained on the frozen sea on the 63rd meridian of longitude, in latitude 83° 20′ 26″, being just within 400 miles of the North Pole. In consequence of the serious and severe **outbreak of scurvy** which attacked the travellers, and **the** exceedingly rough nature of the ice over which **they** were compelled to drag their sledges, **these several** parties endured great hardships and sufferings.

Chiefly owing to the outbreak of scurvy, and partly **also** from the knowledge that further extensive exploration from his base of operations was impracticable, Captain Nares wisely decided upon returning to England, which was reached by the two ships in November 1876.

In the same **year that** witnessed the departure of the English Polar expedition **under** Nares, Captain Allen Young, the companion **of** M‘Clintock in the *Fox*, an experienced **and enthusiastic Arctic** navigator, sailed from England **in the** *Pandora*, an old man-of-war of **430 tons** burthen, fitted **with** eighty horse-power engines, with the object, as he tells us, of visiting—

"The western coast of Greenland, thence to proceed through Baffin Bay, Lancaster Sound, and Barrow Strait towards the Magnetic Pole, and, if practicable, to navigate through the north-west passage to the Pacific Ocean in one season."

It was thought, and very rightly, that by following this **line of** exploration, the *Pandora* would most likely be **in the** vicinity of **King** William Island in **the summer,** when, as the land would be bare of snow, a fair prospect of finding some records, or perhaps the logs and journals of the *Erebus* and *Terror*, would be afforded them.

The scheme was undoubtedly a good one and was well thought out and planned, for no steamer, it must be remembered, had hitherto endeavoured **even to attempt the north-west** passage, and no search had been made for documents or papers of Franklin's expedition except in the early spring, when the country was covered with a thick layer of snow. The *Pandora* was provisioned for an absence of eighteen months, for although it was not intended to pass a winter, if possible, in the Arctic regions, the necessary precautions had to be taken in the event of the ship being unfortunately detained; it was intended and hoped that **the** programme would be carried out in one season. Passing through Baffin and Melville Bays without any hindrance from the ice, the *Pandora* entered Lancaster Sound and Barrow's Strait, and touching at Beechey Island on her way, pushed up Peel Strait, only to be stopped, when near the western entrance to Bellot Strait, by a solid and unbroken pack **of heavy ice,** which entirely arrested further progress to the south. In fact the *Pandora* was stopped by the same barrier of heavy ice, held stationary in the quiescent water caused by the meeting of the two tides, that arrested **the** advance of Franklin in 1847, and M'Clure and Collinson at later dates.

Every effort that was made to push through **was** futile, and after several attempts had been made, Captain Young was reluctantly bound to confess that the accomplishment of the north-west passage by the *Pandora*, for that year at least, was out of the question, and as the season was far advanced, for the 1st of September had already arrived, he retraced his steps through Peel Strait, though not without great difficulty on account of the severe weather experienced and the amount of ice that was met, and thence sailed for England. When they turned back they were within 140 miles of Point Victory, where the Franklin record had been discovered by Hobson. Thus ended this plucky attempt to achieve the north-west passage. Although **he failed in** his main object, Captain Allen Young can **lay claim to** having been the first to navigate a vessel in the icy waters of Peel Strait, unless, indeed, **as** has already been surmised, the ships **of Franklin had** previously sailed over the same route. The *Pandora* arrived at Spithead on the 16th of October, **thus bringing to** a conclusion this short but **most interesting** and adventurous voyage.

In 1878 a small party, under the leadership of **Lieutenant** Frederick Schwatka of the United States army, consisting of three white men and an Eskimo, left New York and were landed **by** a whaler near Chesterfield **Inlet,** in Hudson's Bay, **with the express** object of attempting to recover the logs and journals of Franklin's expedition, and, if possible, to clear up some of the mysteries connected with that sad **story. The winter** was passed in Chesterfield Inlet, at Camp Daly, **and on the 1st of April** 1879, the party being augmented **by a** band of fourteen Eskimos, consisting of men, women, **and children,** Schwatka started on his long journey to King William Island, the sledges being dragged by forty-four dogs.

On the 10th of June, after a **long and toilsome** journey, Cape **Herschel, on King William** Island, was reached, **and here a permanent camp was established.** From this base **the western and** southern **shores were** carefully examined until the **8th of November, when the party** started on their return to Camp Daly, **which** was not however reached **until** the 4th of March, after an excessively laborious journey, during which great hardships and privations were endured. This expedition revealed **no new** facts regarding **the fate of the missing** expedition, but it corroborated a great deal **of the infor-**

mation that had already been obtained by M'Clintock, and it brought home a few more relics. From the fact of Schwatka having travelled over a route already explored, the expedition was barren of any important geographical results.

The next expedition that sailed for the purpose of exploration in high northern latitudes was despatched by, and under the auspices of, Mr. Gordon Bennett, the proprietor of the *New York Herald*. The vessel selected for the service was Allen Young's old ship *Pandora*, which was renamed the *Jeannette*. She was equipped, provisioned, and stored for an absence of three years. Although the principal burden of the cost of this expedition was borne by Mr. Bennett, the officers and crew belonged to the American navy, and were subject to the United States Naval Discipline Act, as if the ship had been a regular man-of-war. Her complement was thirty-two officers and men, and she was commanded by Commander De Long, who, as an officer on board the *Tigress*, when she was engaged in the search for the *Polaris* people, had acquired some knowledge and experience of ice navigation. The *Jeannette* sailed from San Francisco on the 8th of July 1879, with the expressed object of reaching the North Pole, *viâ* Bering's Strait. She was last seen on the 3rd of September of the same year, steaming towards Wrangel Land. This was in accordance with De Long's instructions, for he had been directed to make his attempt as nearly as possible in the longitude of Wrangel Land.

Much anxiety was evinced when two years elapsed and no tidings of the ship had been obtained. Search expeditions were organised and despatched by the United States Government with special orders to seek diligently in the neighbourhood of Herald Island and along the Siberian coast, in search of the missing ship, but these efforts were unfortunately without success. In the latter end of the year 1882, telegraphic information was received from Russia that the unfortunate *Jeannette* had been crushed by the ice on the 12th of June of that year, in latitude 77° N., and longitude 155° E., having been beset in the ice and drifted about helplessly at the mercy of the winds and currents for twenty-two months ; the officers and crew, however, it was reported, had succeeded in making good their escape from the ship in three boats, which had to be dragged over the ice for some considerable distance before open water was reached. One of these boats was lost sight of in a gale of wind during the month of September, and was never afterwards heard of. The remainder of the party, having endured great hardships and sufferings from exposure and a scarcity of provisions, eventually succeeded, by the assistance of their boats, in reaching the mouth of the Lena, whence two of the seamen were despatched to the nearest Russian settlement to procure immediate relief, and also to telegraph the news of their safety, and the necessity of sending succour as speedily as possible. Unhappily, before assistance could reach these poor fellows, Commander De Long and the majority of the officers and crew succumbed to starvation. Mr. Melville and the few survivors, after undergoing incredible hardships, were eventually rescued and taken to New York.

The result of this expedition in a geographical point of view was unimportant, and hardly compensated for the great loss of life and terrible sufferings of those engaged in it, to say nothing of the large expenditure of money it entailed. The most important service **in-**directly connected with it, from the standpoint of geography, was the complete exploration of Wrangel **Land** by Lieutenant Berry, who was sent out in the *Rodgers* to search for the *Jeannette*.

The most signal geographical achievement of recent years has, undoubtedly, been the successful accomplishment of the north-east passage in the steamer *Vega* by Baron Nordenskiöld, ably seconded as he was by Lieutenant Palander, who was practically the captain of the ship.

This voyage proved that a well-found steamer, properly prepared and ably handled, could without great difficulty pass from the Atlantic to the Pacific, along the **northern** coast of Siberia. This was **a** matter of importance, bearing, as it did, on the practicability of opening up a great commercial sea route between Europe and the mouths of those large and important rivers, the Obi, the Yenisei, and the Lena.

The *Vega*, a steamer of 300 tons register, being provisioned for a couple of years, sailed from Gothenburg on the 4th of July 1878. Proceeding through the Norwegian fiords, *via* Tromso, she passed, without encountering much difficulty from ice, through the Jugor Strait to the southward of Waygat Island, and so into the Kara Sea. Stopping at various places along the coast of Siberia, for the purpose of collecting natural history specimens, and for general scientific observations, Cape Chelyuskin, the most northern promontory of the old world, was rounded on the 19th August ; a salute of guns was fired, and the ship gaily dressed with flags in commemoration of the important event. The position of this interesting headland was accurately determined by astronomical observations: its most northern **part was** found to be in latitude 77° 41' N., and longitude 104° 1' E.

Advancing to the eastward, they encountered much drift ice, which, though loose and open, consisted of heavier floes than had hitherto been met with since the Kara Sea was entered, while their progress was also somewhat impeded by fogs, which materially added to **the** difficulties of navigation. During the temporary detentions of the ship from these and other causes, valuable hauls were made with **the** dredge, resulting in the catch of many unexpected and interesting varieties of marine animal **types, all, however,** essentially peculiar to the Arctic regions.

On the evening of **the 27th** the *Vega* was off the mouth of the Lena, when, steering in a north-easterly direction, a course was shaped for the most southerly of the New Siberian Islands. This group of islands was passed on the 30th August, but landing was found to be impracticable in consequence of the rotten condition of the ice between the ship and the shore, which did not admit either of a boat being pushed through, or a man walking on its surface. Eastward from these islands was a clear open channel of water extending along the coast, which enabled the *Vega* to push **on at the rate** of 120 miles **a day for three days.** The Bear Islands were reached on the 3rd of September, when the channel became more **and more** narrow, being partially blocked by ice. Under these circumstances they were compelled to keep close in to the shore, where the water was unpleasantly shallow. Cape Schelagskoi was reached on the morning of the **6th, when their progress was** much impeded by loose ice. To add to their difficulties the hours of daylight were getting shorter, while their nights were getting, in a corresponding degree, disagreeably long.

On the 12th, North Cape (so named by Captain Cook) was passed, but here their further progress in an easterly direction was stopped by the impenetrability of the pack, and they experienced great difficulty in boring a passage through the ice towards the coast, where, eventually, **the** ship was anchored under **the** shelter afforded by **a** large mass of grounded ice. Here the *Vega* remained, unable to proceed, until the 18th, when, as the navigable season was far advanced, **it** was determined **at** all hazards to push on, and **endeavour** to complete the passage before winter finally overtook them.   Their progress was, however, slow and difficult; much ice was encountered, and the water was exceedingly shallow, thus necessitating the greatest caution on the part of Captain Palander and his officers. **On the** 28th they passed Koljutschin Bay, but were, almost immediately afterwards, stopped by ice; and although they kept the ship prepared for any eventuality at a moment's notice, hoping that a gale of wind or some other cause **might clear** the ice out of their way, they were doomed to disappointment, and on the **25th** November the necessary preparations were made for passing the winter.   This was terribly provoking, for only a few miles lay between them and the open water in Bering's Strait, the position of the *Vega* being about a mile from the coast at the north part of the strait. Here, however, they were destined to pass the winter, during **which** time much useful and valuable scientific work was performed by the different members of the expedition.   They were in constant, almost daily, communication with the natives of the country, the Tchuktches, who evinced a **very friendly** disposition towards them, and **kept them** plentifully supplied with bear and **rein**-deer meat.

At length, on the 18th of July 1879, the breaking up of the ice released the *Vega.* Two days afterwards she passed East Cape, and steaming into the waters of **the** Pacific, succeeded in accomplishing one of the greatest geographical feats of the age, and one that had baffled navigators for three hundred years, the achievement of the north-east passage. On the 2nd of September Yoko-hama was reached, at which port the successful explorers were received with every demonstration of joy by the Japanese, and by the representatives of the different **nations assembled there.** Thence, until Stockholm was reached on the 24th April 1880, their homeward progress was one long triumphal procession, in which nation rivalled nation, and port vied with port, in doing honour **to** the bold navigators, who had thus rendered them-selves famous by their dauntless courage, their skill, and their unbounded energy. Thus ended one of the most successful geographical expeditions **of** the present **cen**-tury: it was happily conceived, and gallantly carried **out. All honour to the brave Swedes who thus, for the first** time, carried to a successful **issue** an under-taking that had for three centuries defied the persistent efforts of the ablest, the most skilful, and the most courageous navigators of our own and other countries. All honour to the brave Palander, who so skilfully navi-gated the little *Vega* during her marvellous voyage round the north extreme of the old world; and all honour to that remarkable man, and eminent scientist, Professor, now Baron, Nordenskiöld, to whose subtle and **inquiring** mind is due the conception of the voyage, and to whose skill and energy its success was mainly due.

In the year 1880, Mr. Leigh Smith, who enjoyed, and very deservedly, the reputation of being a keen and successful Arctic navigator, and one who had assisted very materially in increasing our knowledge of the neighbourhood of Spitzbergen, sailed from England in his steam yacht *Eira*, with the object of reaching Franz Josef Land. The *Eira* was a vessel of 360 tons burthen, fitted with engines of 50 horse-power, and carried a crew, all told, of twenty-five men. But little difficulty was experienced in reaching the south coast of Franz Josef Land, the shores of which Leigh Smith explored to the westward for over one hundred miles, and in a northerly direction to latitude 80° 20′, on about the 40th meridian of east longitude. At this, his highest position, land was seen some forty miles distant in a north-westerly direction. In latitude 80° 5′ he discovered a snug, well-protected harbour, formed by two islands, with good anchorage in from five to seven fathoms, which he named Eira Harbour.

As it was not his intention to pass a winter in the Arctic Regions, Mr. Leigh Smith returned to England in October, having achieved a very successful amount of exploration in a very short time. From the size of the icebergs met with, besides other indications, it may be assumed that Franz Josef Land is of vast extent, and it is not at all improbable that the dimensions of this little known land will be found, when explored, to equal in size the large continent of Greenland. Many bears, walruses, and seals were seen, and a number of each were killed by the sportsmen.

On his return home, the Royal Geographical Society

presented Mr. Leigh Smith with their Patron's Gold
Medal, for the important discoveries he had made along
the south coast of Franz Josef Land, and for his previous
valuable geographical work along the north-east coast
of Spitzbergen. The Gold Medal of the Paris Geographical Society was also presented to him in recognition
of the eminent services he had rendered to the science of
geography.

With his appetite only whetted for renewed research
in Franz Josef Land by his late adventurous voyage
to its shores, Mr. Leigh Smith determined to prosecute
further exploration in the same direction. He accordingly set about refitting his little yacht immediately
after his return to England. In alluding to Mr. Leigh
Smith's intentions, in his annual address as President of
the Royal Geographical Society, delivered on the 23rd
May 1881, Lord Aberdare thus sums up his character—

"With the enthusiasm indispensable to an Arctic explorer,
he combines the attainments of a scientific observer, and the
skill of an experienced navigator. To these qualifications is
added that of indomitable perseverance."

The *Eira* being in all respects ready, Mr. Leigh Smith
started from Peterhead on his fifth Arctic voyage on
the 14th June 1881. The ship carried the same complement of officers and men as in the preceding year.
She was provisioned for fifteen months, and carried
with her materials for constructing a house on shore,
in the event of being forced to winter. Mr. Leigh
Smith's intention was to continue his previous exploration as far as possible in a northerly direction, and thus
extend the geographical knowledge of Franz Josef Land
acquired during the past year. After skirting along

the pack ice for some distance, and after making an
unsuccessful attempt to enter the Kara Sea, he succeeded in approaching the coast of Franz Josef Land;
but unfortunately at this juncture the little *Eira* was
so severely crushed by the ice on the 21st August, when
close to Cape Flora, in latitude 79° 56', that she sank,
two hours afterwards, in deep water. The loss of their
vessel was a terrible blow to their prospects. Luckily,
the short time that intervened prior to her disappearance, enabled them to save some of the stores and provisions from the wreck, and these were subsequently
eked out by walrus and bear meat, which they were
able to obtain in considerable quantities, and which,
happily, carried them safely through the winter. Everything else was lost. They passed, under the circumstances, a comparatively comfortable winter in a hut
built with stones and turf. The only fuel they possessed,
both for the purposes of cooking and keeping themselves
warm, was the blubber obtained from the animals killed.
During the spring they occupied themselves in fitting up
and equipping the boats, in which it was resolved to endeavour to escape to the southward in the summer; in
consequence of the necessity of employing everybody on
this important work it was impossible to undertake any
exploration with sledges on an extended scale, which
would otherwise have been done.

On the 21st of June they bade farewell to their
winter quarters, and, apportioning the party among
the four boats, started on their adventurous and perilous voyage to the southward, in much the same
manner as did that brave old Dutch navigator Willem
Barents three hundred years before, and from a locality
not very far distant from the scene of their retreat.

Eventually, after undergoing great hardships and fatigue, they succeeded in reaching the **coast of Novaya Zemlya on the 2nd of August, and** on the following day were fortunately rescued and brought home in the *Hope*, a vessel that had been specially sent out to search for them **under** the command of Sir Allen Young. Aberdeen was **reached on the 20th of** August, **when the news** of their **safety was** received with **universal** feelings **of relief,** allaying, **as it did, the** alarm and uneasiness that had **been** felt in England regarding their protracted absence.

The last expedition **to** which reference will be made was the one despatched by the United States Government in 1881, **under the command of** Lieutenant Greeley **of the United States army.** It had for its object the establishment **of a station in a** high latitude, at the head of Smith Sound, **where** synchronous meteorological, magnetical, **and** other observations **of** a like description, might be **taken in** accordance with a programme **that** had been drawn up by an International Polar Conference which was held at Hamburg in 1879. Lieutenant Greeley was also directed to carry out exploration in the direction of the North Pole, as far as **was** practicable.

The expedition consisted **of twenty-five** officers **and** men, nearly all **of whom** were soldiers serving in the **United States army.** The party was taken up Smith Sound **in the steamer** *Proteus,* **which,** without experiencing **much** difficulty from the ice, landed them in Discovery Bay, on the 11th of August. The *Proteus* returned to America **a week** after. Two winters were passed by the members of the expedition in Discovery Bay, during which time the interior of Grinnell Land was explored, as also the north-west coast of Greenland, when Lieutenant Beaumont's farthest point in 1876 was passed, and a position, reported to be in latitude 83° 24', was reached; they thus had the gratification of reaching a higher latitude than had ever before been attained, and of extending our knowledge of the coast of Greenland to a distance of forty miles in a northerly direction.

Two expeditions were sent out by the United States in 1882 and 1883, to effect the relief of Greeley's party, in accordance with previously arranged plans, but they unhappily failed in their endeavours to reach them, one of the vessels being crushed by the ice at the entrance to Smith Sound. These expeditions were both commanded by military men !

The second winter having passed without relief coming to their aid, Greeley decided to work his way south in search of that succour which was apparently unable to reach him, and without which, he was well aware, his party must inevitably perish. Up to this time the members of the expedition had enjoyed remarkably good health, and their numbers were still intact. On the 9th of August 1883 they quitted Discovery Bay, but failed to get further south than Cape Sabine, on the west side of Smith Sound, where they decided to encamp in the vicinity of the cape. Here a third winter was necessarily passed, but in a far different manner to the previous ones, for they had no other shelter from the severe inclemency of the weather than an imperfectly constructed snow-house, and no other provisions than the little that remained from the rations brought with them from Discovery Bay, and those found in the depôts that had been wisely established along the coast by Sir George Nares, for his travelling parties in 1876. It was not long before these scanty supplies were exhausted, but, for some time, they succeeded in keeping themselves alive, by subsisting on their sealskin clothing, and the lichens that were gathered from the rocks. Starvation and hardship, however, gradually reduced the original number of twenty-five, until by the middle of June only seven, including Greeley, remained alive. These few were happily rescued by the expedition that was despatched in 1884 to search for them, under the command of Captain Schley of the United States navy, who providentially found them, on the 21st of June, when the few wretched survivors were literally at death's door. A delay in their rescue of two or three days would have been fatal to the whole party—not one would then have been alive to relate the history of their proceedings and the appalling sufferings they had endured. With the exception of the exploration of the interior of Grinnell Land, and the continuation for some distance of Beaumont's exploration of the north-west coast of Greenland, but little was added to our geographical knowledge of the Polar regions. The terrible experiences of the survivors of this expedition fully bear out the necessity of scrupulously carrying out those useful and prudent measures that have been invariably adopted by English navigators when exploring in high latitudes, namely the practice of establishing depôts of provisions along what may possibly be a retreating route. It also illustrates the folly of employing inexperienced and ignorant men, in conducting an expedition that has for its object the succour of those whose lives are absolutely dependent on the arrival of relief.

Geographical exploration in the Arctic regions has now been brought down to date, and it shows us what a large share Sir John Franklin had in the development of our knowledge of those regions. The life of Sir John, as it has been the object of these pages to show, was essentially one of usefulness and activity. Joining the navy at an early age, and being passionately fond of the sea and everything appertaining to a seaman's life, he quickly acquired the rudiments of his profession, while his many manly qualities and earnest application to his studies soon attracted the notice, and earned the approbation, of his superiors. It is not therefore to be wondered at that, under these favourable auspices, he rapidly developed into an able, active, and accomplished young officer. Not content with the ordinary humdrum routine of the naval service, he invariably volunteered, whenever opportunities offered, for duties of a special and exceptional nature, and the more arduous and dangerous they were the more eagerly were they sought for by him.

Adventure and geography are so intimately associated the one with the other, that it is not surprising to find that a young officer of Franklin's energy and daring spirit should, in the course of a few years, blossom into an ardent and practical geographer. The love of exploration, especially in unknown regions and over untrodden paths, was inherent in him, and was in all probability intensified by his service under Flinders, and his long and intimate connection with that skilful and experienced surveyor. But although the southern hemisphere had its charms, it was the north, and the fascinating mysteries that surrounded the northern apex of our globe, that possessed the greatest attractions for John Franklin. To the exploration of these little known regions he devoted, as we have endeavoured to show, much valuable time and energy, and eventually, it may truly be said, he laid down his life in his endeavours to lift the veil that had **for** so long concealed one of the secrets of that mysterious portion of the world.

But it is as the discoverer of the north-west passage, that problem the solution of which had baffled so many able **and daring** navigators for the past three hundred years, and **which** he sacrificed his life to solve, that his name must, **and** always will be, intimately connected. Franklin and the north-west **passage being so closely** associated with each other have become almost synonymous terms, for he was, assuredly, the first actual discoverer of that long and diligently sought for channel of communication between the Atlantic and Pacific **Oceans;** he may also very fitly be regarded as having been, indirectly, the means of discovering other channels that may very correctly be termed north-west passages, for the discovery of them by Collinson and M'Clure was practically a corollary of the search that was instituted for him.

To Franklin, therefore, both directly and indirectly, is **due the discovery and exploration of a vast** hitherto unknown region, the result of which has been productive of much valuable scientific knowledge, more especially in its relation to geography.

The time **that** elapsed **between the year** 1845, **when** Arctic exploration, after **a long interval of** inactivity, was again **resumed, until the year** 1859, when the little *Fox* **returned** to England with the important announcement relative **to the sad** fate **of the** *Erebus* and *Terror*, may reasonably **be called the** Franklin era ; even before that time to as **far back as** 1818, there was but little accomplished, in **the way of exploring those** little known waters and territories, with **which he was not, in some** way or other, **connected or concerned.**

The failure of the *Erebus* and *Terror* to achieve the north-west passage was undoubtedly due to the vast accumulation of heavy pack ice, which was found to exist across the channel in which the ships were finally abandoned, and which was of such a nature as to defy penetration. This agglomeration of ice, which had originally, in all probability, been formed in that great unexplored area to the northward and westward of the Parry Islands, is drifted into Melville Sound along the north coast of Bank's Land, and is thence carried down through M'Clintock Channel until it impinges on the shores of King William Island, thus forming an impenetrable barrier across the channel. It was, we must infer, this insurmountable accumulation of ice that stopped Franklin's ships from proceeding to the south-west, and it was this same unyielding barrier that successfully defied the efforts of M'Clure and Collinson, when endeavouring to push forward from the opposite direction.

Professor Haughton, who is one of our highest authorities on tidal movements, and especially those in high latitudes, attributes the accumulation of ice at this particular spot to the meeting of the Bering's Strait tide with that of Davis' Strait, the effect of which is the formation of a "line of still water," in which the ice remains packed and immovable. The same physical features were observed in the neighbourhood of the Bay of Mercy, whence M'Clure made ineffectual attempts, during two successive years, to enter Melville Sound from the west, along the north coast of Bank's Land. All efforts to penetrate the ice in this locality, either from the east or from the west, have resulted in failure—navigation has invariably been stopped by impenetrable masses of ice, remaining practically im-

movable in a region of still water. This meeting of
two separate and distinct tides serves, in a great measure, to illustrate the principal physico-geographical
causes of the failure of Parry, Franklin, M'Clure, and
Collinson, and, at a more recent date, of Allen Young,
to successfully accomplish the north-west passage in a
ship. It is extremely improbable that these channels
are permanently blocked by ice. Indeed there is every
reason to believe that there are occasional, perhaps
periodical, seasons when a well-found steamship, under
the command of a skilful and energetic navigator, might
succeed in making the passage ; but, except for the honour
and glory of performing a geographical feat that has
hitherto defied all efforts that have been made to accomplish it, the results would be practically barren, for the
channels have already been thoroughly explored by travellers on foot, and therefore no further useful geographical information could be obtained, by the mere fact
of a vessel steaming from the Atlantic to the Pacific, or
vice versâ, by Bering's Strait and Baffin Bay.

But there is still useful work to be performed in
the Arctic regions, namely, to complete the exploration of that vast Polar area, comprising upwards of a
million and a half square miles, which is at present a
blank space on our charts. In order to carry this out
to a successful issue, our attention and our energies
should be directed towards the little known Franz
Josef Land, for it is in this direction that the greatest
prospect, almost amounting to a certainty, of success
will be obtained, and for the following reasons. It is
nearer to inhabited and civilised countries than other
parts of the Arctic regions, therefore a place to which
a start can be more easily made, and whence retreat

from it, in the event of a catastrophe, for the same reasons, is practically easy and assured. There is no reason to fear that any great difficulty will **be experienced** in reaching its shores; on the contrary, **we have** every reason to infer, from the comparative ease with which the little Dutch exploring schooner *Willem Barents* sighted its coast in 1879, and the absence of **any real** difficulty that attended Mr. Leigh Smith's efforts **to** visit its shores on the two following years, that a good steamer, specially designed for ice navigation, would easily succeed in reaching Eira Harbour, or even Austria Sound, every year. This being assumed, it is evident that Franz Josef Land **should** form the objective, and be the direction in which future Arctic exploration should be carried out.

But to ensure useful results it is essential **to** pass a winter in that little known land, so that exploration can be carried out by sledge parties during the spring and summer. In carrying out this service no danger need be apprehended from that terrible scourge scurvy, for animal food, **in the** shape of bears, walruses, and seals, is procurable in abundance, and such a measure of success would assuredly be secured during one travelling season, as would amply compensate for the expense incurred **in** the despatch of an expedition. Let us hope that we may soon **be in a** position to record the return of an English Arctic expedition crowned with laurels gained **in the exploration of** Franz Josef Land and beyond! **For such** a consummation **let** all **true** geographers devoutly pray. We shall then feel that the noble and gallant Sir John Franklin and his brave shipmates **did** not lay down their lives in vain.

INDEX.

32 FLEET STREET, LONDON.

The World's Great Explorers and Explorations.

EDITED BY

J. SCOTT KELTIE, Librarian, Royal Geographical Society ;

H. J. MACKINDER, M.A., Reader in Geography at the University of Oxford ;

And E. G. RAVENSTEIN, F.R.G.S.

UNDER this title Messrs. G. PHILIP & SON are issuing a series of volumes dealing with the life and work of those heroic adventurers through whose exertions the face of the earth has been made known to humanity.

Each volume will, so far as the ground covered admits, deal mainly with one prominent name associated with some particular region, and will tell the story of his life and adventures, and describe the work which he accomplished in the service of geographical discovery. The aim will be to do ample justice to geographical results, while the personality of the explorer is never lost sight of. In a few cases in which the work of discovery cannot be possibly associated with the name of any single explorer, some departure from this plan may be unavoidable, but it will be followed as far as practicable. In each case the exact relation of the work accomplished by each explorer to what went before and what followed after, will be pointed out; so that each volume will be virtually an account of the exploration of the region with which it deals. Though it will not be sought to make the various volumes dovetail exactly into each other, it is hoped that when the series is concluded, it will form a fairly complete Biographical History of Geographical Discovery.

Each volume will be written by a recognised authority on his subject, and will be amply furnished with specially prepared maps, portraits, and other original illustrations.

While the names of the writers whose co-operation has been secured are an indication of the high standard aimed at from a literary and scientific point of view, the series will be essentially a popular one, appealing to the great mass of general readers, young and old, who have always shewn a keen interest in the story of the world's exploration, when well told. It is, moreover, believed that not a few of the volumes will be found adapted for use as reading books, or even text-books in schools.

Each volume will consist of about 300 pp. crown 8vo, and will be published in cloth extra, price 4s. 6d., in cloth gilt cover, specially designed by Lewis F. Day, gilt edges, price 5s, or in half polished morocco, marbled edges, price 7s. 6d.

The following volumes are either ready or are in
an advanced state of preparation :—

JOHN DAVIS, Arctic Explorer and Early India Navigator.
By CLEMENTS R. MARKHAM, C.B., F.R.S.

[*Ready.*]

PALESTINE. By MAJOR **C. R.** CONDER, R.E., Leader
of the Palestine Exploring Expeditions.

[*Ready.*]

MUNGO PARK AND THE NIGER. By JOSEPH THOMSON,
author of "Through Masai Land," &c.

[*Ready.*]

MAGELLAN **AND THE** PACIFIC. By DR. H. H.
GUILLEMARD, author of "The Cruise of the Marchesa."

[*Ready.*]

JOHN FRANKLIN AND THE NORTH-WEST PASSAGE.
By CAPTAIN ALBERT MARKHAM, R.N.

[*Ready.*]

LIVINGSTONE AND THE EXPLORATION **OF** CEN-
TRAL AFRICA. By H. H. JOHNSTON, C.B., H.M. Commissioner and Consul-General.

[*June.*]

SAUSSURE **AND THE ALPS**. By DOUGLAS W. FRESH-
FIELD, Hon. Sec. Royal Geographical Society.

[*Shortly.*]

THE HIMALAYA. By LIEUT.-GENERAL R. STRACHEY,
R.E., C.S.I., late President of the R.G.S.

ROSS **AND THE ANTARCTIC**. By H. J. MACKINDER,
M.A., Reader in Geography at Oxford.

BRUCE AND THE NILE. By J. SCOTT KELTIE, Librarian
R.G.S.

VASCO DA GAMA AND THE **OCEAN HIGHWAY TO**
INDIA. By E. G. RAVENSTEIN, F.R.G.S.

Other volumes to follow will deal with—

HUMBOLDT AND SOUTH AMERICA.
BARENTS **AND THE N.E. PASSAGE.**
COLUMBUS **AND HIS SUCCESSORS.**
JACQUES **CARTIER AND CANADA.**
CAPTAIN COOK AND AUSTRALASIA.
MARCO POLO AND CENTRAL ASIA.
IBN BATUTA AND N. AFRICA.
LEIF ERIKSON **AND** GREENLAND.
DAMPIER AND THE BUCCANEERS.

&c.   &c.   &c.

GEORGE PHILIP & SON, LONDON & LIVERPOOL.

32 FLEET STREET, E.C.
MAY 1891.

GEORGE PHILIP & SON'S
List of New and Important Works

ON

Geography and Travel.

—◦—

Crown 8vo, Antique Cover, price 7s. **6d.**

HOME LIFE ON AN OSTRICH FARM.
BY ANNIE MARTIN.

WITH ELEVEN ILLUSTRATIONS.

OPINIONS OF THE PRESS.

"**Mrs.** Martin has furnished one of the most charming descriptions of African experience that have come under the notice of the reviewer, weary of book-making and padding. The work does not contain **a** dull page, and it is so short and so bright in tone that we should be doing an injustice to the author **if we quoted any** of the choicest bits. The account of 'Jacob,' the **secretary-bird, which** swallowed the kitten alive, **and,** hearing it still mewing in his capacious inside, went **about in** futile **quest** of another kitten to devour, is delightfully comic ; **so also are** the **experi-** ences of servants and household difficulties **on a** farm in the Karroo, near Port Elizabeth. . . . Before they agreed to 'combine forces,' **both** Mrs. Martin and her husband—alluded to **as** T.—had evidently travelled widely, wisely, and well ; **the** result being a sparkling little book of which it would **be** difficult to **speak too** highly. It contains eleven illustrations from photographs ; **and, while men** will enjoy it, ladies will appreciate it **even** more."—*Athenæum.*

"There **is** not an uninteresting page in this entertaining book, while there **are very** few pages indeed which do not contain something genuinely funny."—*St. James's Gazette.*

"Nothing has been published for a long time in the way of light litera- ture which can give more unmitigated satisfaction than this book."— *Manchester Examiner.*

"The book is a rarity altogether—rare in its pretty and tasteful bind- ing and its beautiful engravings, and especially in the amount of informa- tion it supplies **on** that very remarkable bird, the Ostrich."—*Newcastle Daily Chronicle.*

LONDON AND LIVERPOOL: GEORGE PHILIP & SON.

www.ingramcontent.com/pod-product-compliance
Lightning Source LLC
Chambersburg PA
CBHW021728110726
47902CB00005B/1388